BREAK MY FALL

BROKEN #1

CHLOE WALSH

Published by Chloe Walsh
Copyright 2014 by Chloe Walsh
All Rights Reserved. ©

Break my Fall
Broken #1,
First published, February 2014
Republished, February 2019
All rights reserved. ©
Edited by Aleesha Davis.
Proofread by Bianca Rushton.
Cover designed by Sarah Paige.

DISCLAIMER

This book is a work of fiction. All names, characters, places and incidents either are products of the author's imagination or are used fictitiously. Any resemblance to events, locales, or persons, living or dead, is coincidental.

The author acknowledges all songs titles, song lyrics, film titles, film characters, trademarked statuses, brands, mentioned in this book are the property of, and belong to, their respective owners. The publication/ use of these trademarks is not authorized/ associated with, or sponsored by the trademark owners.

Chloe Walsh is in no way affiliated with any of the brands, songs, musicians or artists mentioned in this book.

For my family.

AUTHOR'S NOTE

Break my Fall is the first installment of the *Broken* series, a
completed series. I hope you enjoy reading about these
characters as much as I enjoyed writing them.
Please note: this is a newly revised edition, 2019, with an extra
40,000 words.
Thank you for reading.
Chloe xox

ONE

THE HILL

LEE

I STOOD OUTSIDE THE RED-BRICKED, two-story house on Thirteenth Street, and with any hope, my new home. Several similarly styled detached houses sat side by side on either side of the road.

I was stalling.

I knew I was.

The record-breaking heat wave was causing me to sweat profusely – not an ideal look for an uninvited reunion, but it couldn't be helped. I had been sitting on a bus with no air conditioning for the past god knows how many hours in *one hundred-degree temperatures*. I was happy not to be dead. Sweat was the lesser evil.

With my desire to bathe overpowering my nervousness, I braced myself, stepped forward, and knocked.

Holding my breath, I watched as a light flicked on behind the small glass pane in the center of the door.

Breathe, Lee. You're okay now.

Muffled footsteps came from behind the white door, and I could see someone approaching from the tinted glass panel, but the distortion of the frosted glass rendered it impossible to see who exactly.

Please be her.

Please lord, let it be her.

The door swung open and my breath escaped my lungs in a heady rush. Relief flooded through me at the sight of my childhood friend. *My only friend.*

"Lee? Oh my god, what the hell are you doing here?"

"Hey, Cam," I croaked out, smiling shyly at the stunning blonde before me. Camryn Frey looked as gorgeous as the last time I saw her, though much taller now. I hadn't seen her since she moved away from Montgomery seven years ago, but we had stayed in touch. I was praying for her mercy now– *and her bathroom.* "I need to pee."

"Is that so?" A huge smile spread across her face. "Get in here, girl." She grabbed me before I had a chance to respond and tugged me inside, encasing me in a massive bear hug. "God, I've missed you, Lee Bennett."

I forced my body to relax, slowly accepting her embrace and the feel of another person's *touch* on my skin. I needed to calm the heck down. I wasn't in danger now.

It's over, Lee.

"I can't tell you how good it is to see you, Cam," I said, dragging myself from my thoughts, and meaning every word more than she could *ever* know. Releasing my hold on the two duffel bags I had taken with me, that was all I could carry when I left, I hugged her back. "But if I don't pee soon, my bladder's going to burst."

Chuckling softly, Cam released me and steered me down the hallway to a bathroom. Hurrying inside, I quickly relieved myself before washing up and re-joining her in the hallway. "Thank you," I breathed, feeling flushed and achy from being cramped inside a greyhound bus.

"So?" Cam mused, watching me with an amused expression. "You're here."

Nodding slowly, I blew out a shaky breath. "I'm here."

She arched her brow. "For long?"

I blushed. "I actually need a place to stay – temporarily of course," I hurried to explain. "I don't want to burden you." Rambling, I continued to pitch my plea. "It would only be for a few weeks, until I can get a job and get on my feet." Embarrassed, I clasped my hands together and shrugged. "Will you help me, Cam?"

"What kind of a dumbass question is that?" She smiled. "Of course, I'll help you."

Relief, more potent than I'd ever experienced, flooded my body. "Thank you." Smiling, I looked up at the girl who I had spent most of my childhood adoring and whispered, "So much."

Waving a dismissive hand in front of her, Cam grabbed my bags and gestured for me to follow her. "So, let me guess; you finally got sick of the sticks and decided to join me in the land of the living?"

I frowned at her. I loved our hometown of Montgomery, Louisiana. I was a small-town girl. Being here *wasn't* a choice. "Uh…no?"

"Okay, okay, that was low," she conceded with a sigh. "Just warn me if I'm going to have your crazy-ass daddy banging on my door, looking for his baby girl anytime soon."

"Don't worry," I replied, following Cam down a short hallway into what resembled a kitchen/dining room. "Daddy isn't going to come looking for me."

He'll have to find me first.

"Good," she replied breezily. "Because not even *I* am prepared to face Jimmy Bennett."

"This is a nice place, Cam," I offered, desperate to veer the topic of conversation to safer waters. "A *really* nice place." It was. The kitchen was modest in size, but the beautiful, hand-carved, oak cabinets on the left side of the room oozed expensive taste. A glass sliding door occupied the wall opposite the kitchen door, along with another row of oak cabinets that housed a stainless-steel sink and a glass top oven. Instead of ceiling high cabinets on that side, there was a window looking out onto a small patio garden.

"Yeah, it's pretty sweet," Cam mused.

"Yeah." *Understatement of the century.* The heavy kitchen table and chairs looked more expensive than everything in my father's house combined.

"You're actually in luck, Lee." Grabbing two bottles of water from the refrigerator, Cam beckoned for me to join her at the table. "We have a spare room."

"*We*?" I asked as I sat down on the plush chair beside hers.

"I live with my boyfriend and his best friend." Grinning, she passed me a bottle before opening hers and taking a swig. "Well, we share a house." She shrugged. "They're pretty cool guys."

"Oh." My heart sank into my butt. "You share with boys?"

Cam snickered loudly. "Relax, Lee-Bee, you'd swear I just told you the devil was camped out in the living room."

"It's not that," I began to mumble. "I just…I didn't…I wasn't –"

"Relax," she coaxed, tone gentle. "Derek and Kyle are cool. Besides, they're hardly boys and they're the same age as me. We all go to CU. That's where we met. They are seniors like me – or at least we will be next Fall."

The thought unsettled me further. "Maybe this isn't such a great idea," I muttered as I opened my water and swallowed deeply, trying to push down the hot ball of anxiety rising up in my throat.

"This is the *best* idea you've had in years, Lee." She smiled. "I can't count the number of times I've asked you to come here."

I could. "Thirty-four times." Cam had phoned me once a week since she moved away. We used to have to be careful to talk at certain times – usually late at night when my father had passed out. She started asking me to come stay with her when I turned eighteen last October – and every week since.

Coming here was the most reckless thing I'd ever done, and the knowledge that I would be living with college men… well, that scared the life out of me.

Reaching over, Cam gave my shoulder a reassuring squeeze. "I still can't believe you're here."

"This place is different from home," I croaked out. "I wasn't sure I had the right house until you answered the door." I glanced around, feeling nervous. "Are you sure they won't mind me being here?"

Cam swatted her hand at me like I had said something ridiculous. "It's not going to be a problem, Lee. I'm dating Derek, so he does what I tell him. And Kyle? He's always so busy with work and school that he's hardly here to begin with, so he won't care."

"Oh-okay?" I replied, uncertain. Not once in the numerous phone calls we'd shared had Cam mentioned she was seeing a man she lived with. I could only *imagine* the scandal that would cause back home. Although, to be fair, I tended to zone out when

Cam brought up the topic of boys. She'd had more boyfriends than I could count.

"Besides," she said excitedly. "You're gonna love it here. This place is the shit."

I seriously doubted it. Cam had regaled me with tales of her many adventures while living on *The Hill*–all of which made me a little queasy. "Um…okay?"

"So, you're gonna stay with us?"

My palms began to sweat. "If you're sure Derek and Kyle won't mind, then I would be very grateful for the room? I will pay of course. I plan on getting a job as soon as possible."

Cam grinned and clapped her hands. "Excellent, now let me show you our crib."

I stared blankly. "*Crib*?"

Cam sighed in exasperation. "Damn, Lee, you're sheltered. Haven't you ever watched MTV?"

I shrugged. I never watched television. The only television set we had at home was in daddy's room.

When Cam stood up and left the kitchen with my bags, I quickly climbed to my feet and shuffled after her. "Mine and Derek's rooms are down the hall, along with a bathroom you just used," she explained, giving me the grand tour.

"Great. Lovely. Thank you." I nodded and followed her up a wooden staircase to a narrow upstairs landing. It was simple in style, painted in a soft shade of green, with a few framed pictures of rock bands and one of the Rocky Mountains ordaining the walls. "This is your bathroom," Cam announced, opening the lone door on the left side of the hallway. "You'll share with Kyle – who, by the way, is pretty clean for a guy." My reluctance must have been obvious because Cam snorted. "Consider yourself lucky that your bedroom isn't downstairs. You only have to share with Kyle. I have to share the downstairs bathroom with Derek and anyone who comes to visit. And believe me, you don't want to know about half the shit I've had to clean up."

Horrified, I slapped on my most grateful smile. "I'm feeling lucky," I assured her. "And I'm grateful. Thank you."

"Stop saying thank you."

"Sorry."

"Don't say sorry."

"Right – sorry." I cringed. "I'm sorry."

"Oh, babe." Chuckling, Cam opened the bathroom door and gestured for me to take a look.

I blew out a breath when I stepped inside, and the first word that came to my mind was *swanky*. Good lord, it was like one of those bathrooms displayed in a home design catalog. I knew because I had browsed through enough of those catalogs at work when I'd been passing the time in between serving customers. Yeah, Moe's gas station in Montgomery wasn't exactly the liveliest of places to work, but it had suited me. *I missed it.*

Everything about this bathroom was modern; from the marble tiles, to the huge chrome shower. We only had a plain ole tub at my daddy's house, so I was excited to take a shower in this beast.

Following Cam back into the hallway, she pointed at two doors on the other side of the hallway. "The one on the right is Kyle's room. Expect *a lot* of traffic when he's home."

"Traffic?"

Cam smirked. "Yeah, Kyle's a popular boy. He gets a lot of *visitors*. They're always looking for a little something from him."

My brain went into overdrive as I pondered what Cam meant until I settled on drugs.

Oh my god, is that what she meant?

Oh lord, I hoped I wasn't moving into a room next to a pothead.

Dammit, knowing my luck that's *exactly* who I was moving next door to. One of those scruffy college boys who spent their time sleeping in class and selling dope to pay for the privilege.

"Cam – wait!" I grabbed her arm. "Do you mean what I think you mean?" I whispered, jerking my thumb towards his door.

"Would you *relax*?" she said, stifling a laugh. "He's not even home." Snickering, she opened the bedroom door next to Kyle's – *directly* next to Kyle's. "Are you planning on making any late-night visits to his room?"

"What?" I shook my head, disgusted. "Oh my god, no! I want *nothing* to do with that scene."

"Then you will be fine." Grinning, she wiggled her brows. "One look at that innocent face of yours and Kyle won't try anything."

Try anything?

What could he try to do; drag me into his room and force-feed me *drugs*?

Oh, holy crap.

"Will you stop worrying and come see your new room?" she commanded, dragging me inside. "This room is rarely used. It's the smallest of the four bedrooms, but it's decent."

My eyes took in the soft cream carpeting and matching, cream-colored curtains that draped to the floor. A large window occupied the majority of the yellow painted wall opposite the door.

"Whoa." This room looked too nice to belong to a house full of college kids. A double bed with a white timber frame took up a large portion of the room, along with a matching wardrobe, nightstand, and..."I get my own TV?" I blurted out the question when I noticed the huge flat-screen television mounted on the wall opposite the bed.

"Uh huh," Cam replied, sounding amused. "But don't get too excited. It's just one of Kyle's old ones, and it doesn't have cable. But it *does* have a built-in DVD player that works, so that's a bonus."

"Oh, Cam." Swinging around, I grabbed her for a hug. "Thank you so much."

"Get some sleep, Lee." She hugged me back. "I'll see you in the morning."

"Do you mind if I take a shower?" I called after her when she moved for the door.

"Go for it, babe," was all she replied before closing out the door.

I stood for a moment breathing in the silence and allowed a small smile to creep across my face.

I could relax.

Finally.

TWO

LEE

"GOOD MORNING," I said when I walked into the kitchen the following day.

The shaved-headed man sitting at the table raised his brow in surprise. "Good morning to you, too." His razor-sharp green eyes studied me and I began to fidget nervously. "I take it you're the infamous Lee?"

"Yes," I replied, hating how meek my voice sounded. "And you're Kyle?"

He threw back his head and laughed.

What's so funny?

"Nope, you have the wrong man, sweetheart. I'm Derek."

Blushing, I muttered a half-hearted sorry.

"It's all good." He grinned broadly. "Although when you meet Kyle, you'll wonder how you ever confused us." He waggled his brows. "I'm way sexier."

I wasn't sure what to say to that, so I just nodded and mumbled, "I'll take your word for it."

"So, Lee," Leaning back on his chair, Derek scratched his chest before asking, "are you in town for business or pleasure?"

"Oh, I'm…business.," I answered, fumbling with my words. "I need to find a job."

"What kind of job?"

"Any job," I confirmed honestly. "I'm not in the position to be picky."

"Well, yesterday's paper is on the table if you want to take a look through it." Derek stood up from the table then, and I automatically took a step backwards.

Breathe. Just breathe…

"Cam's already gone out and I'd offer to give you a tour," he continued to speak as he rinsed his cup and placed it in the sink. "But I'm late for my job."

"Oh-okay. Thank you." I tucked my tangled curls behind my ears. "I will check that out."

He walked right up to me and I automatically backed away. "I'm not a rapist, you know," he said slowly. "I need to get into the fridge." Brows furrowed, he regarded me with a hurt expression. "You're blocking my way."

"Oh." I jerked away from where I was standing. "I'm so sorry. I don't think you're a…that."

Derek didn't say anything for a moment as he pulled out a container of food. "If you see Cam, tell her I had to go into work early."

"Of course." I nodded. "No problem."

He regarded me once more before blowing out a breath and muttering something about a *nodding dog*.

I waited for the front door to slam shut behind him before I released my breath. God, I needed to get a handle on this.

I made it.

I was safe.

I was *free*.

Pushing open the heavy glass door, I stepped into the foyer of The Henderson Hotel. The paper Derek had left in the kitchen advertised a job opening in the housekeeping department, so here I was.

I had been all over downtown Boulder looking for work, but to no avail. The sheer size of the city made me want to crawl into that cozy bed I'd crawled out of this morning and *rock*. It was a miracle I had managed to stay calm during my job-search. Crowds made me nervous.

Slapping on my bravest smile, I approached the impressive, oval-shaped desk at the other side of the spacious lobby. A middle-aged, blonde woman dressed in a sharp, navy shirt looked up from behind the desk as I approached. She stared at me for a moment, her eyebrows raised. "Can I help you, honey?" Her voice was raspy, like she smoked twenty cigarettes a day for a few years too many.

I sucked in a deep breath. "Yes, my name is Lee Bennett and I would like to apply for the housekeeping job advertised in the paper."

The woman's gaze held a smidgen of sympathy. "Sorry, Doll. We don't hire high school kids. Too unreliable. Besides, there's an application procedure you need to go through to secure an interview."

I blanched as my heart sank in my chest. "I'm not in high school, ma'am." I stood a little taller, trying my best to look more grown up. "I can promise you that I'm a hard worker – and reliable. I'm very reliable."

She nodded her head in what looked like consideration. "Are you starting college soon? Because the boss isn't interested in college kids, either. He needs staff who are serious about their job."

Her straight-laced attitude put me at ease. Straight talking, I understood. It was insinuations and code talk that I didn't. I smiled at her. "I'm not going to college and have no plans to, ma'am. I just moved to Boulder and need a job. I can promise you that I *am* serious."

She leaned forward a little, her gaze drifting over me. "Where are you from, honey?"

"Louisiana, ma'am," I confirmed.

"Louisiana." A soft smile ghosted her lips. "You're a long way from home."

Thank god. Deciding to remain silent, I continued to smile at her.

"Do you have any experience in housekeeping?" she finally asked.

"I have experience in serving, till work, and I keep a clean house," I hurried to tell her. "And I'm a real fast learner."

After a pause her face broke out into a wide grin. "Alright. You're hired."

"I am?" A shiver of relief ran down my spine. "Just like that?"

"Just like that," she confirmed with a smile. "I've got a good feeling about you, southern girl. You could be good for this place."

I beamed at her. "Thank you so much, ma'am."

"Come on back here, Doll, and let's get you set up. The name's Linda, by the way."

I followed Linda through the door behind the counter, amazed at how easy this had been.

KYLE

"Aren't you going to consider my offer? It's what's best for the company, Kyle."

I stared at the man sitting in front of me. He looked exactly like me – thirty years into the future. "Nope," I replied, shifting my legs onto my desk.

That irritated him.

Good.

Let the bastard squirm.

I folded my arms across my chest just to make a further point.

I'm the boss here, asshole.

"Why do you have to be so fucking awkward?" he snarled. "I'm trying to help you out, son."

"Son?" I had to clench my fists to keep myself from knocking him out on his ass. "It's a little late to be calling me that, don't you think? Why don't you go and focus your attention on that shit-stain of a son of yours, and let me take care of myself?"

His face reddened and I could tell he was losing his cool facade.

Three, two, one…

"You stupid, little shit," he hissed. "You know what your problem is? You're too goddamn proud to ask for help."

I smirked, relishing in the fact that I was annoying the crap out of him. He was showing his true colors now like the serpent he was. "Let's just cut the crap here, David," I deadpanned. "You're pissed that your dear old dad entrusted me with his empire and *not* you." That was *exactly* what this little intervention was about.

"You're going to destroy everything he built." David slammed his chair back and leaned over my desk. That's right. It was *my* desk. Not his. "You're a fucking kid. You haven't even graduated from college. You don't know the first thing about running this place, nor will you have the time once you go back to school in the Fall. He was *my father*. This company should have been *mine*."

Ah finally; a little truth.

I was wondering when he would admit it.

Slipping my legs off the desk, I leaned towards him. "It sucks when your father lets you down, doesn't it?" I smirked. "*Dad*?"

THREE

HOUSE PARTIES

LEE

I KNEW COMING HERE WAS a bad idea from the get-go. Parties were *not* my thing. This was my first one, actually. Leaving home and moving across the country was most definitely coming back to bite me in the butt. The Hill was a million light years away from the world I had left behind. I was shy. I kept myself to myself. Cam was my polar opposite – vivacious and wildly spontaneous. This party had her name stamped all over it, and I knew I didn't have a hope of escaping.

As I walked into the bedroom Cam had allocated to me, I discovered a drunk couple were already occupying it. Dammit, I should have locked my door. I would in the future.

"Heads up, Lee –" I turned just in time to receive a beach ball in the face.

I glared at the perpetrator whose face was newly familiar to me.

Derek Porter.

From the brief amount of time we had spoken this morning, I'd gathered he was a joker. "Excuse me, Derek," I muttered, as I moved past him. I needed some space.

Outside in the back garden wasn't much better, but at least I wasn't in danger of flying beach balls – or worse, flying food. Were these people really over twenty-one? I felt forty beside them.

"Will you lighten up and have some fun?" I heard Cam say from behind me.

Turning around, I watched as she approached me in all her partial naked glory. I took in the skimpy, beige stretch dress she wore, the one that barely covered her girly parts, and cringed for her. The color of her dress complimented her sun-kissed skin and long blonde hair, but it was short. *Very short.* Lord, she was stunning to the eye. I could never wear anything so revealing with such confidence. I hadn't worn a dress since the *second grade.*

Tonight, I looked frumpy beside Cam –still in the white shirt and black pants I'd worked in. Discreetly, I pulled my long, dark hair from its ponytail. My curls, now a tangled mess, flowed down the middle of my back. My black sneakers were worn but clean and were staying firmly on my feet. God knows what could be on the ground at a party like this.

"Smile," Cam continued to say. "And relax. Have *fun*."

"I can't help it," I strangled out. "I'm not used to this, Cam. I'm exhausted and I have to get some sleep."

I was supposed to start my next shift at 7am sharp tomorrow morning. The hotel was uppity on a large scale, with two bars and two restaurants on the ground floor. Thankfully, I was tucked safely out of the way, cleaning the rooms. There were sixty-one bedrooms, twelve on each floor, and the honeymoon suite on the eighth and top floor. Linda said the hotel was just one in a chain of twenty or so across the United States, and the pay was great at eleven dollars an hour. I knew I had been damn lucky to get the job. My only previous experience in the work-force had been as a cashier at Moe's Gas Station in Montgomery. However, my abrupt departure two months ago meant I couldn't exactly call on Moe for a reference. I hadn't seen my old boss, or stepped foot inside the building, since my father's *decision* to have me quit.

I worked my first ten-hour shift at the hotel today and it was *great*. The other staff seemed friendly, especially one of the bartenders I had met on my break. I think his name was Mike.

The only downside to my new job was the uniform. Linda had called me into her office at the end of my shift tonight and handed me a bundle of clothing covered in plastic wrapping, and a name tag. I had taken it out of the packaging and gaped at the indecent length. For the first time in my life, I had thanked Jesus for being short. A fitted, black maid's dress was to be my uniform from tomorrow onwards. I predicted my pinafore would fall just above my knees.

Hopefully...

Because I was definitely *not* the type of girl who could afford to dress skimpily. Feeling self-conscious, I smoothed down my t-shirt. The thought of showing too much skin made me nervous.

"Lee, I know you're not used to parties and crowds, but could you please try to enjoy yourself? This *is* for you." Cam batted her big, baby blues at me and I wanted to strangle her. This was so *not* for me. "Oh, come on, dry balls, let's have a shot," she said when I made no attempt to answer her.

Grabbing my shoulders, she steered me back to the kitchen and poured some black liquor into a pair of glasses. "To your fresh start." Smirking, she clinked her glass against mine. "Cheers."

"Cheers," I muttered begrudgingly, and tipped the foreign substance to my lips. I wasn't a drinker, either. My only experience with alcohol occurred when I was twelve. Cam swiped a bottle of daddy's whiskey off the shelf and we'd snuck out back to drink it. I had been so sick afterwards, and when daddy caught us I was punished so badly that I hadn't touched a drop since.

However, the appeal of fitting in for once in my life swayed me, and I swallowed it down. The taste burned my throat and my eyes watered. "Oh, Jesus!" I spluttered, holding my hand across my mouth. "That's nasty."

She filled another shot of the black stuff and this time I swallowed it without choking.

"Yeah! that's it, girl – chug it back," Cam cheered.

KYLE

This was *not* the early night I had planned. There were people all over the house and I felt unusually unsociable. Most of the time I enjoyed a good party, but after the last few days of bullshit I'd put down, I just wanted to crash. I'd been in New York all week and had stopped by the office on my way home tonight. It was just as well I had because my nosy fuck of a father was snooping around again.

Christ, he was like a dog with a bone. It had been over eighteen months. He needed to accept my grandfather's decision. Hell, *I* needed to accept my grandfather's decision.

My roommate, Cam, had phoned me at the office earlier with some sob story about a friend of hers needing a dig out. I had a spare room at the house, so I gave her the go-ahead.

To be honest, I hadn't paid much attention to the conversation. I'd been too busy dealing with dear old dad. Cam and her crazy-ass drama had been the furthest thing from my mind.

I was, however, curious as to who this Lee dude was. Cam seemed really excited about the guy moving in, but with Cam, you never knew what to expect. She knew her fair share of creepy bastards.

She'd promised on the phone that Lee would pay rent – like it was a deal breaker for me. I couldn't give two shits about the money. It wasn't an issue for me. I owned the house outright, had – without knowing – since freshman year of college. My grandfather had led me to believe I was leasing the place. *Character building* had been his intention, I guessed. I hadn't discovered the place was mine until his will-reading. The sneaky fucker had bought it when I started at C.U.

Cam and Derek lived here because they were friends, not because I needed extra cash. The old man had left me well cushioned. They'd been my roommates from day one, and their being here gave my life some semblance of *normality*. I could act my age around them and just be a normal twenty-two-year-old guy, and *not* the owner and CEO of a fucking multi-million-dollar corporation. I kept the house minimalistic in its appearance because of this fact. I wanted a normal damn life. The life I had before my grandfather went and died on me, leaving me in the driving seat of his empire.

Scanning the room, my eyes zoomed in on the tiny brunette standing next to Cam.

Holy shit, she was something else.

Her small, heart-shaped face was partially concealed by a dark head of curls. I focused on those curls and the way they hung over her tits.

Fuck, what a pair she had.

Even in the boring white shirt she wore, it was easy to tell the girl had been blessed in the breast department. Her narrow waist cinched in the middle, curving out to form the sexiest pair of hips I had ever seen. Her pants were snug on her soft curves. Christ, I could only imagine what her body looked like under the shitty clothes. Now *those* were the curves of a real woman. She wasn't a matchstick like most of the girls I knew.

She radiated healthiness.

My gaze drifted to her waist again. Fuck, I could think of nothing else but burying myself between those goddamn hips. I took a second look at her and my cock twitched. Jesus Christ, I had a fucking semi from just looking at her. *What the hell was wrong with me?*

Derek, who was standing beside me, noticed who I was staring at and chuckled. "That's her, man. Isn't she something else?"

"That's who?" Tearing my attention off the smoking hot brunette, I narrowed my eyes at my best friend, feeling suddenly and oddly possessive. Shit, looking back at her, I was ready to beat my fists against my chest and stake a claim on this girl. "Who *is* she?"

"Our new roommate." He pointed to where Cam and *little miss titties* were standing. "Cam's latest rescue baby."

"The fuck?" I gaped at Derek and he burst into a fit of laughter. "Tell me you're joking."

"I'm not joking."

"Shit." *Damn, she was beautiful.* "Lee is a she," I pointed out.

"Yep." Derek grinned. "And what a *she*, she is."

I knew right then that Rachel was going to flip out. I was under strict orders as to what I could and *who* I couldn't do, and hell, this girl was going to cause a few problems for me.

FOUR

WANNA TAKE A SHOT WITH ME, SWEETHEART?

LEE

THIS WAS *NOT* A GOOD IDEA.

Five shots in, and I was feeling a little worse for wear.

At least the party wasn't bothering me anymore.

Nothing was bothering me now.

I felt a presence behind us. "Oh, baby, you softened the Ice Queen."

"I resent that," I managed to slur, as I turned to glare at Derek. He had nicknamed me ice-queen after our first meeting this morning. Derek obviously didn't care for my standoffishness. I had offended him, but he didn't know a thing about me, or why I was the way I was. I wasn't a naturally cold person, but life had dealt me some crappy cards, and experience had taught me to guard myself. *Especially* around men. After all, my father was the perfect role model for the type of man I needed to stay away from.

When Derek wrapped his arms around Cam, she began to giggle and coo… and then they began to suck face.*Again.*

I flamed in embarrassment. Another thing I was *not* used to seeing. *Ever.* "Get a room," I grumbled, leaning over the kitchen counter for support.

This was all so new to me. I had never been allowed to date a boy, let alone live with *two*. My father had been strict in the extreme. The only place I was allowed to go to, besides school, was my job. I had no friends and people tended to avoid me. Well, everyone except Cam. She had lived next door to me until I was twelve, and even though she was three years older than me, we had been inseparable as children. Our parents had been friends until my mama died and my daddy got mean. Cam knew my situation and remained friends with me anyway. She was my lifeline in a world of isolation. That meant a lot to me – more than she would ever realize.

I felt someone press against me then and I tensed. Pushing closer to the counter to make room for them to pass, I urged my body to relax and I inhaled slowly. I was a nervous wreck after what happened and I tried so carefully each day to stay in the background. I *never* wanted to be called a tease again.

Hot breath on the side of my neck caused me to jump. "You gonna share that?" A deep, husky voice asked, as a male arm swooped around me and grabbed the bottle of whatever the hell it was off the countertop.

"It's all yours," I turned to move out of his way, only to stop dead in my tracks. Whoa, maybe it was the alcohol, or maybe I was turning into a PG version of Cam, but lord, the guy in front of me was incredible. I took in his gray suit pants and half-buttoned white shirt. My god, he was well built. Arching my neck to see his face, I exhaled a shaky breath.

A head of dark, unruly hair framed his face. His eyes were a striking shade of deep ocean blue, seductive and entrancing, with long dark eyelashes and perfect eyebrows. His eyes danced with humor and his full lips turned up into a half smile, exposing the cutest dimple in his cheek. It was more than cute. It was...*hot*. I was drunk, but not drunk enough *not* to notice him. Good Lord, he was beautiful. Did boys like him really exist? I thought I might be imagining him.

He smiled crookedly and raised the bottle. "Do you wanna take a shot with me, sweetheart?" The huskiness of his voice made him sound dangerous, yet he was soft spoken...an enigma. His voice was spine tingling and very sexual – not that I knew much about that, but, hey, a girl could guess.

"Uh," was all I said – all I could say. "Uh..." No guy had ever asked me to do anything with him, except for Perry Franklin who had asked me to senior prom. Sneaking out to go to prom was a decision I would regret for the rest of my life. What surprised me now, was the fact that I *wasn't* afraid of the boy in front of me. Well, *boy* was the wrong choice of word to describe him. He was all *man. One hundred percent.*

He tilted his head to the side, studying me with a curiously amused expression. Frowning, he asked, "Do you speak?"

Oh fantastic, he thought I was slow. "Yes," I forced the word out, but it sounded little more than a whisper.

He smiled down at me and leaned closer. Heart racing, I arched my back until I was flush against the counter behind me. Heat burned inside of me, drifting low in my belly. Good grief, I was on *fire.* What was happening to me?

Smiling, he asked, "Yes to a drink with me, or yes, you can speak?" He was flirting with me. I knew enough to at least know that.

However, this guy was *way* out of my league. He could eat me up for breakfast. I was not going to encourage him. I couldn't handle him.

"Both." Wait, I shouldn't have said that. I slapped my hand over my mouth in surprise and he chuckled, eyes twinkling, exposing that damn dimple again.

Kings of Leon's *Closer* was pumping from the stereo, but I swear I could hear my heart hammering above it. I wondered if he could, too.

Pressing close enough to my body that I could feel the muscles beneath his shirt, he reached over my head and pulled two glasses from the cabinet. As he poured our drinks, I concentrated on keeping my breathing even. This was the closest a man had been to me in a while, and my body seemed to be awakening from eighteen years of hibernation.

Handing me a glass, he clinked it with his. "Cheers," he drawled and tipped his glass back. My legs weakened as I watched his throat move when he swallowed.

He looked at me expectantly and I quickly cleared my throat before tipping my drink back, gulping it down sloppily.

He took my glass from me and I reached around to hold the counter for support.

A drop of liquor trickled from my chin to my throat.

I watched him watch me.

His gaze flickered from my eyes to my neck.

He smiled darkly.

A low growl escaped his throat.

Oh, sweet Jesus…

He dipped his head to my neck and I felt something hot and wet sweep across my throat. "Hmm." Lifting his head, his piercing blue eyes locked on mine. "Sweetest fucking shot I've ever had."

Helpless, I just stood there, staring up at him with my mouth hanging open.

Did he just lick me?

I could vaguely make out the sound of wolf whistles in the background, but my focus was completely on him. He poured me another shot and pressed the glass into my hand. "Drink," he ordered, tone husky, eyes darkening with every breath he drew in.

Trembling, I brought the glass to my lips. He was pressed so close to me, I could barely breathe. I felt something hard nudge my belly and I reddened with realization.

He smirked unashamedly, daring me with his eyes to do something. What, I had no clue, but I *wanted* to…

I tossed my drink back quickly, ignoring the burning in my throat. I couldn't focus on that when there was a far hotter fire burning deep in my belly.

He moved quickly then. One of his hands swept around to clasp the back of my neck, while the other clenched my hip. I opened my mouth in surprise and he lowered his head, crushing his lips against mine.

Holy Mary, mother of god…

He growled against my lips and I swear I nearly melted.

I should be afraid of this–of him–but the only emotion bubbling to the surface was desire.

My body betrayed my sensible nature, and my arms wrapped around his neck, dragging his body closer to mine.

Feeling wild and reckless, I strained my head up towards him, lips moving against his, chest rising and falling rapidly, as his hands moved over my flesh. Scorching me. *Branding me*. He was so much taller than me that it was a struggle to reach him. His lips were soft but demanding, and when his tongue invaded my mouth, I forgot where I was. I forgot *who* I was.

With slow, tentative strokes, I moved my tongue against his, unsure if I was doing it right. I guessed it was because he growled in approval and dug his fingers into my hip, gripping me tightly, encouraging me to come closer to the *danger zone*. My hands gripped his hair, pulling him any which way, I didn't know. Clinging to him, I felt my knees weaken, as I sagged in his arms, allowing him to take my weight for me.

He sucked on my lip, running his tongue across my lip before probing deep inside my mouth. When he stroked the roof of my mouth, a deliberate, skilled move, I moaned loudly.

His hand moved from my neck to clutch my throat. That move should have scared me, but instead it was *thrilling*. My body was responding to his touch, my nipples tightening, as I slammed my body to his.

Somewhere in the back of my mind, I knew this was bad. Wrong. Inappropriate. *Dangerous*. This was everything I wanted to leave behind, but my body was in control, and my body wanted him – *more of him.*

His hands moved to my waist and he hoisted me onto the counter, his lips never parting from mine.

Mmm, this was so much better.

Clamping his hands on my thighs, he pushed my legs apart and stepped between them. One of his hands curled under my shirt, and I felt myself dampening in my core as he knotted his free hand in my hair and dragged me roughly towards him.

One moment, we were devouring each other and the next he was wrenched away from me.

Whimpering from the sudden lack of contact, I gasped for air, scrambling to clear my frantic thoughts.

"What the hell do you think you're doing?" A shrill, female voice demanded.

Blinking my eyes open, I saw an angry looking redhead standing between us. She looked at blue eyes with disgust and then turned her furious glare on me, giving me a look of pure poison.

He merely shrugged as he stared at me, wiping the corner of his mouth with his fingers. Reaching past me, he grabbed a bottle of beer and then leaned towards my ear. "Best fucking shot ever," he whispered before pressing a lingering kiss to my cheek.

I just sat there, mouth open, staring at his back as he left the kitchen, with the redhead hot on his heels.

"I said *enjoy yourself*, but Kyle? Aside from the fact that he's your roommate – and that's all shades of messed up – the guy is beyond complicated. What were you thinking, Lee?" Cam asked in a slurred tone of voice as she slouched beside me.

I had no answer for her.

I had no answer for *myself*.

My mind was frozen on the fact that Cam had said the sex god was *Kyle*.

Oh my god, I just made out with my roommate.

Cam stared at me for a while longer and then shook her head. "Stay away from him, Lee. He has some weird thing going on with that nasty bitch. Girls like you aren't cut out for guys like him." With that, she turned and headed back outside.

Girls like me?

What was that supposed to mean?

Was I so plain that a guy like Kyle couldn't be interested in me? Yeah, sure, I wasn't as tall, or as skinny as Cam and the redhead, but I wasn't ugly, dammit.

God, I needed to get out of here.

Hopping down from my perch of desire and shame, I made my way through the crowded hallway. On shaky legs, I climbed the staircase, silently praying my bedroom was now vacant. If not, I was grabbing a pillow and sleeping in the damn bathtub. The guests could pee in the street for all I cared.

When I reached the top step, voices in the upstairs landing halted me in my tracks.

"Don't '*Rachel*' me, Kyle Carter. Who the fuck is she?" that familiar female voice all but screamed.

Freezing at the mention of his name, I held my breath and strained to hear more.

"She just moved in... a friend of Camryn's from down south. Fuck, why am I explaining myself to you? Her being here has *nothing* to do with me," I heard him say, voice hard now.

Oh my god, was this Rachel person his *girlfriend*?

Did I just make out with another girl's *boyfriend*?

"Because you promised me, Kyle," she snarled. "You *swore* to me after everything that happened. You *owe me*."

What happened last time?

What did he owe her?

"And I'll keep that promise. Rachel," he growled right back at her. "She's nothing to me, but don't pretend that you own me, sweetheart, because until that day comes, I'm a free man."

I didn't want to hear anymore.

With my head down, I climbed the rest of the steps. Kyle and the redhead were standing outside of his bedroom, blocking the path to *my* room.

"Excuse me," I choked out, as I brushed past them and half-ran, half-stumbled to my bedroom door. Shoving the door open, I was relieved to find it dark and empty. I dared one last peek at the pair, who were now entering the bedroom next to mine.

I guess that was what Cam meant by *traffic*.

He wasn't a pothead.

He was a *bed-hopper.*

"Keep walking, little girl," Rachel huffed, as she stormed into his bedroom with her nose cocked in the air.

Mortified, I looked up and my eyes met Kyle's. He was standing in his bedroom doorway, looking at me intently. Blushing, I tore my eyes away from his and darted inside my room. Locking my door, I climbed fully clothed into my bed.

But sleep never came that night.

Not with the loud moans coming from the room next door.

KYLE

"You better mean it, Kyle." Storming into my room, Rachel stripped off her scrap of a dress and my stomach churned. It always happened when I saw that scar on her stomach.

Cringing, I hung my head in shame. "I mean it." The words tore from my lips. They were painful to speak, even more painful to follow through on.

"I'm not messing around here," she added, dragging my thoughts from the past.

Of course I fucking meant what I said. I wasn't the type of man who broke promises. Rachel Grayson had my balls nailed to the wall. I was trapped and she knew it, but I'd be damned if I'd regret kissing my new roomie.

Jesus, I was rock hard still thinking about her.

"You know the rules," Rachel bit out, tearing me from my lust-filled thoughts.

Yeah, I knew the rules and so did she. I fucked who I wanted, when I wanted, and so did she. It wasn't an exclusive arrangement, so why did it bother her when I kissed Lee?

Jesus, the taste of her was still in my mouth. Even the sound of her name in my head made me hard. But the hurt look in her eyes back in the hallway made my stomach flip.

Fuck.

Why did that even concern me? I was like a robot. I didn't *feel* things for girls – well, nothing other than wanting to get them naked. I'd closed off those emotions years ago when I experienced first-hand the way women really worked. But her sad eyes… Christ, I was getting soft.

She was beautiful.

But young.

Too young for the likes of me.

Why did she look so sad?

Did someone hurt her?

Had *I* hurt her?

She didn't know me, and if she did, she wouldn't want to.

I was a waster, a fucking genius with numbers and figures, but I hurt anyone who got too close to me. It was a supreme talent of mine. *Just look at the girl standing in front of me now.* I shuddered when I thought of all the ways I had hurt the girl in front of me.

In ways I could never repair.

"I'm here with you, aren't I?" I told her, feeling more depressed than usual.

"Are you?" Rachel walked over to me and rested her hands on my hips. "Are you really here with *me*, Kyle?"

Resigned, I pulled my shirt over my head. "Yeah." I shrugged. "I am."

FIVE

A PRINCESS IS BORN

LEE

I WAS *NEVER* DRINKING AGAIN.

An out of tune marching band was banging around in my head all day long and I honestly didn't know how I wasn't fired at work, because I had vomited–profusely –in two of the bathrooms I was supposed to be cleaning.

Worse than nursing the hangover from hell was donning this god awful work uniform. I had been close to a panic attack when I got dressed this morning. My pinafore was so tight around my chest that I was in fear of bursting the seams. The length wasn't much better; falling a good two inches above my knees. However, I was covered in the important areas, so I focused on that slightly positive piece of information.

Vomiting and skimpy uniform aside, I trudged on, making it through my work day in one piece. It was after ten before I got home from the hotel that night. Exhausted, I went straight to my room and changed into my pajamas before heading downstairs to the kitchen in search of caffeine.

When I reached the bottom step of the stairs, the sound of voices floating from the living room caused my heart to flutter. Anxious, I rushed past the closed door in my bid to get coffee.

The kitchen was spotless when I stepped inside. Cam must have cleaned up most of the post-party mess and I was grateful. I didn't think I could deal with the smell of stale beer. My stomach still felt raw. Quiet as a mouse, something I was good at being, I switched on the kettle, leaning against the counter while I waited for it to boil. Instant coffee was going to have to do. I didn't have the energy to prepare anything more lavish – not that I was used to lavish.

A door clicked open and the voices grew louder for a brief moment before it clicked shut once more.

Palms sweating, I stifled a groan, hoping and praying that they weren't going to have another party. Cam's voice called from the hallway. "You back, Lee-Bee?"

I debated whether or not to answer before deciding against it. I slipped up to my room quickly after the whole *'kissing my new roommate' incident* last night, and when I left for work this morning, she was still asleep. I couldn't answer the questions I *knew* Cam would have any more than I could answer my own.

I was appalled at my behavior.

Cam had been right about one thing, though; I needed to stay *away* from Kyle.

He had a very weird thing going on with Rachel, and I didn't want to get in the middle of it. They were so strange. They didn't behave like boyfriend and girlfriend –

The sound of someone clearing their throat startled me and I all but jumped clean out of my skin.

Dammit, Cam…

Keeping my back to her, I focused on preparing my coffee.

So, she was waiting for *me* to bring it up.

Great.

I took a deep breath and, with my coffee cup in hand, I turned to face her.

My heart jackknifed in my chest when I realized it wasn't Cam who had walked into the kitchen.

It was *Kyle.*

He was leaning against the doorframe, with his arms folded across his chest, and his face set in a deep frown.

Startled at the sight of him, my cup slipped from my fingers, shattering against the kitchen tiles.

"Jesus," he muttered before unfolding his arms and striding

towards me, moving with an air of confidence to him. Clamping his hands on my hips, he literally *lifted* me off my feet, moving me away from the broken glass, and depositing me a good three feet from the damage. His touch burned me and I shuddered. "Did you burn yourself?" he asked as he stepped back from me, hands leaving my body.

I shook my head. "N-no. I'm okay."

Nodding, he let out a heavy sigh. "Thank fuck for that." Walking across the kitchen, Kyle grabbed a broom and dustpan from beside the back door.

"Wh-what are you doing here?" I managed to squeeze out as I watched Kyle sweep up the broken shards of glass. He was dressed much more casually tonight. His black t-shirt rode up his back while he bent over, and the small strip of tanned skin peeking out from his shirt made my body *burn*.

Kyle did dangerous things to a pair of jeans.

I didn't know if I was turned on or embarrassed. I guessed both. To be honest, he kind of blew me away.

"I live here." He tossed the glass in the trash and turned to face me. "Besides, I never miss Thursday night poker with Cam." He smiled fondly when he said Cam's name.

They must be friends.

Close friends.

Jealousy swirled inside me.

Had they done stuff together – other than poker? Cam had a reputation, and so did Kyle by the sounds of it.

I frowned at the thought.

Maybe he was more Derek's friend?

Cam had said he and Derek were best friends…

Ugh, I didn't care.

I *shouldn't* care.

Kyle smiled and leaned against the counter–the same counter as last night.

Don't think about it, Lee.

"I was away for a few days," he continued, tone breezy. "Do you know Cam well? I'm Kyle, by the way." His smile was friendly, but his eyes were guarded.

I eyed him warily. He was behaving as if he hadn't kissed me last night. Maybe he didn't remember? He could have been drunk. Like me. *Ugh.* "Uh, yeah. I just moved here from

Louisiana. I've known Cam my whole life. We used to live next door to each other. She moved away when I was twelve, but we kept in touch. I'm Lee." I held out my hand but he made no move to shake it. Instead, he studied my outstretched hand with an arrogant smirk before bursting out laughing.

He was laughing *at me*.

My cheeks reddened in embarrassment.

"It's a little late for formalities, princess, considering I was closely acquainted with your mouth last night."

Princess?

What a *jerk*.

"My *name* is Lee," I bit out, trying and failing not to grind my teeth. I couldn't help it. I was extremely aggravated by his nonchalant cockiness. "I would *appreciate* it if you addressed me by my Christian name."

My anger only made Kyle laugh more. "Princess it is then." Chuckling, he ran a hand through his dark hair. It looked amazing, tousled in such a sexy way. Good grief, what was happening to me? I was drooling over a man who obviously seemed to enjoy tormenting me.

"How well do you know Cam?" I asked, partially because I wanted to change the subject, but mostly because I was desperate to know if he had been one of Cam's flings.

Kyle's mood changed from mischievous to cool in a heartbeat. "Careful, Princess," he said, tone cold. "Keep talking like that and I'm gonna think you're jealous." Shrugging, he added, "And there's nothing worse than desperation in a woman."

"*Desperation*?" I could think of worse things. *Like my foot up his butt*. "You're the one who kissed me last night and then took a completely different girl into your bed with you."

Kyle grinned. "I did." The dimple in his cheek deepened as he prowled towards me, not stopping until he was directly in front of me, taking up my personal space, and dwarfing me with his tall frame. "And you enjoyed every second of me kissing you. Didn't you, Princess?

What a dog!

"You suck," I decided to come right out and tell him. Stunned by my forwardness, I held his gaze and repeated my earlier sentiment, voice trembling, right along with the rest of me. "You *really* suck, Kyle."

He arched a brow, smirk firmly etched on his face. "Do you?"

My eyes widened in horror. "Oh my god!"

"Are you upset that I didn't take *you* to into my bed?" Reaching out, he stroked the space between my breasts with his finger, blue eyes dark and locked on mine. "Hmm? Is that it? Because we can change that tonight. Right now, if you want?"

Shaking my head, I backed up a few steps until my back hit the kitchen table. "My God, you *are* in love with yourself." I laughed humorlessly. "Believe me, Kyle, not every girl in the world wants to fall into bed with you." Folding my arms across my chest, I leveled him with a look of distaste. At least, I hoped that was what I was displaying. "I happen to have more respect for myself than to crawl into a bed that was occupied a few hours ago by another *woman*." I couldn't believe I was saying all of this, but his cockiness irritated me, and if I was honest, turned me on. "So, no," I confirmed. "We won't be changing anything."

"Are you sure about that, Princess?" Stepping further into my personal space, Kyle snaked out a hand and brushed a loose tendril of hair behind my ear. Heart racing wildly from the minimal contact, I leaned against the table for support. He trailed his finger from my temple to my chin, his touch featherlight, and it caused my skin to erupt in goose pimples. "Because your body seems to disagree." He tipped my chin upwards, forcing me to look at him. It was a bad idea. He was too freaking *sexy*. "Are you *really* sure?" he asked, this time his voice barely more than a whisper as he leaned close. His blue eyes pierced through me, his hot breath fanned my cheek, and my eyes fluttered closed, my lips parting recklessly.

I felt his lips brush against mine, soft, plush and tempting, but he wasn't kissing me. No, he was *challenging* me. *Daring* me to do it. To make the first move. To take what I *wanted.* My heart rate spiked and my breath quickened. When I felt his tongue trail across my lower lip, I caved and crushed my lips against his, wanting him to feel as disturbed by me as I was by him.

A deep growl of appreciation tore from Kyle's chest seconds before his tongue slid into my mouth. Moaning in unfamiliar pleasure, my hands snaked around his neck as he hoisted me onto the table. Spreading my legs apart, he grabbed my hips and stepped between my thighs. His lips moved to my neck and I was lost in the moment, as he pulled me roughly against his hard chest, while he ground his even harder erection against my core.

Feeling frantic, I gave myself up to sensation, ignoring the voice in the back of mind, the voice that sounded awfully like my daddy, when it hissed the word *whore* over and over again.

The sensation of vibration against my lips as Kyle's soft chuckle reverberated through my ears brought me back down to earth with a bang.

Humiliated, I tore my mouth from his before pushing him away, disgusted with myself for my weakness.

What the heck was wrong with me?

"You keep telling yourself that you don't want me, Princess." Stepping back, he rubbed his lower lip with his thumb and smirked at me. "See how long that lasts."

Flustered, I tried to form the words I needed as I watched him stroll towards the kitchen door, shit-eating grin firmly etched on his face. "I wouldn't sleep with you… if you… if you… I just wouldn't, okay!" was all I managed to come up with.

My words only made him laugh harder, and I felt like throwing something. *At his head*. "I always change my bedsheets, Princess." Pausing at the door, Kyle spun back around and winked at me. "I just thought you should know that." He shrugged innocently. "You know, for when you *crawl* into my bed."

KYLE

"Dude, do you want me to deal you in?" Derek asked when I walked back into the living room. Derek, Cam, Mo, and Dixon were sitting in a circle around our coffee table playing poker. I usually played, but tonight I couldn't focus, and a man needed to be on form when playing Cam. That little shark could fleece the best of them.

Shaking my head, I sank down on the couch and began flicking through channels on the TV, but my head wasn't in it. No, it was upstairs in Lee's room, imagining her undressing...

Christ, Lee Bennett was a curvy ball of temptation. I nearly lost it when I saw her barefoot in my kitchen earlier. Her peachy ass looked damn fine in those jeans.

I couldn't fucking wait for her to give in. It would only be a matter of time. I could feel her neediness when I had my tongue down her throat – I could feel her hardened nipples straining against me, while she moaned and whimpered into my mouth...

Holy fuck, I had to have her.

I shifted sideways, discreetly re-arranging myself, while mentally willing my semi to simmer the fuck down.

Jesus, she was going to be bad for my health.

Cam looked up from her cards and eyed me suspiciously. "Well, well, well, aren't you grinning like the cat that got the cream?"

Shit, I hadn't realized I was grinning. I shrugged in response. I *was* pleased with myself. I had felt guilty over the way I treated Lee last night, and strangely off-kilter, but after her little princess-tantrum in the kitchen, I was more amused than anything. *The nickname was staying.*

"Was that Lee I heard in the kitchen with you?" Derek asked, as he tossed a card down on the table.

Cam's eyes narrowed and she glared at me. "What did you do?"

"Oh, man, is that your new roommate's name?" Mo asked longingly. "Because, hot damn, she's fine."

"Cat that got the cream," Dixon snickered. "More like the pussy got creamed."

"Dude," Derek groaned. "That's nasty."

"Have you seen those hips?" Dixon pressed, eyes dancing with amusement. "I would *bury* myself between them. She wouldn't know what to do with –"

I was on my feet and had the bastard by the throat before he could finish. "Watch your fucking mouth," I warned, eyes locked on his. "You don't talk about her like that. Ever. You got that?"

He blinked in surprise. "*I…don't?*"

"No," I barked, forcing myself to release him. "You fucking don't."

"Why not?"

That was a very good question. One I didn't have a rational answer to. She was just a girl. Just another girl. What did it matter what they said? Why the fuck did I care?

"A word, Kyle." Narrowing her eyes, Cam climbed gracefully to her feet. "In private." Inclining her head towards the door, she added, "*now,*" before stalking out of the room.

"In future, keep your perverted thoughts to yourself," I warned Dixon as I trailed after Cam. "In fact, keep that girl out of your thoughts altogether."

"You've got it, dude," he shot back, smirking.

Swallowing down another swell of unwelcome anger, I hissed, "she's not for you," before walking out of the living room in search of Cam.

Jesus, that creep made my skin crawl.

Mo was all right, but his twin brother, Dixon, was just another example of Cam's poor choice in friends. Speaking of Cam, she was standing in the kitchen, glaring at me like I'd stolen her last condom.

What the hell?

"Stay away from her, douchebag," Cam hissed when I stepped through the doorway. "She's vulnerable."

I studied her hardened expression for a minute before blowing out a defeated sigh. Shit, she was serious. "Cam, you're looking at me like I'm the spawn of *Austin Powers*," I replied. "Christ, I'm not a serial womanizer."

"You aren't?" She arched a finely-plucked brow. "Could've fooled me – and half the female population in Boulder."

"Fair point," I conceded. My past was pretty colored, but then so was hers. "But don't act like you're whiter than the driven snow."

"I never claimed to be." Exhaling heavily, Cam looked me straight in the eyes before saying, "Lee's sheltered and new to the city. She's not used to our lifestyle, and doesn't need the drama that comes from being with you."

Well, that was a warning if ever there was one.

No girl deserved the drama that came from being with me.

I didn't like it, but she was right. "I know," I bit out.

"Lee's a good girl and she has had a really shitty life," she continued, not missing a beat. "I don't know why she chose to come to me, but I'm sure as hell glad that she did. That girl needs my help, Kyle, and I don't want her running again."

"*Running*?"

"Running," Cam confirmed grimly.

"Are you going to evaluate?"

"Nope," Cam replied tersely. "Are you going to leave her alone?"

"What's she running from?" I tried again. "Is she okay?"

"I'll tell you who *will* be running soon," Cam countered. "You, Kyle. *You* will be running if I catch you taking advantage of that girl. You will be running like the hounds of hell are nipping at your heels. She's *not* for you. She's not a toy. She's not a fucking game. She's my best friend, and you are not screwing this up for her. So, stay away from her."

"Okay," I muttered. *Jesus.* "Point taken."

I'd never heard Cam talk so passionately about anyone before – not even Derek. Lee was important to her.

What was she running from?

Something bad?

Someone bad?

A weird possessive feeling came over me.

Shit…

"Are you sure you get it?" Cam pushed, hands on her hips. "Because this is me warning you nicely. Next time I catch you with your tongue down her throat, I'll cut your balls off."

"Jesus," I muttered, stomping down on my disappointment. "So, in other words, don't touch her?"

"Exactly." Cam smiled sweetly. "Well, you can be friends with her, but be a doll and try to keep it in your pants. That girl is nothing like us, and I'd really hate to castrate you before you have a chance to reproduce all that handsomeness." Cam patted my cheek.

"Yeah, that will *never* happen," I shot back, tone laced with disgust.

"Ha," Cam laughed. "Famous last words, Carter. I envision you having seven – no, six kids. Let's keep it to a nice, even half-dozen baby Carters to drive you batshit crazy."

"The fuck?" I paled. "Why would you even *think* that? You're supposed to be my friend. You don't wish shit like that on friends, Cam!"

"You can name the most willful one after me," she continued to taunt, laughing her ass off at my expense. "Cam Carter." Her eyes danced with excitement when she added, "I'll have a baby Porter the same age as Cam and they can be best friends."

"You're fucking crazy," I growled, gaping at her.

"You never know, I might have a boy." She wiggled her brows. "We could be in-laws."

My mouth fell open. "You better keep your son away from my daughter, you freak."

"Look at you getting all protective over your imaginary baby," she cackled. "Ah, you crack me up, Kyle. It's like shooting fish in a barrel."

"This conversation is over," I grumbled, feeling truly disturbed.

"Fine – back to Lee," she said, switching gears faster than I could keep up. "She really needs this place, Kyle – more than you know. So just be gentle with her."

Be her friend.

Keep it in my pants.

"I can do that," I promised, and I hoped that I could.

SIX

WHITE FLAGS AND NAKED ABS

LEE

AS THE DAYS PASSED BY, I found myself reminiscing about our kiss at any given opportunity, and then touching my fingertips to my lips every time I thought about his lips on mine. I thought about him all the time... I tried to block it out – *block him out* – and forget it ever happened, but it was an impossible feat. *Twice. He kissed you twice*, my brain hissed. *And you loved every second of it.*

The sound of footsteps approaching pulled me from my lust filled reverie. Grabbing my half-eaten bowl of oatmeal off the kitchen table, I hurried to the sink to clean up after my breakfast of champions. I felt guilty enough for barging in on my roommates without eating their food as well. I didn't usually eat at the house. My meals were free at work, but I was starving when I woke up this morning. Thinking about the thirty dollars' worth of tips I had stashed in my purse, I decided I would go grocery shopping after my shift this evening.

Rinsing off my bowl, I quickly dried it off, only to freeze on the mortal spot. My breath hitched in my throat when my eyes landed on Kyle's half-naked body. I hadn't seen him in three days and I suddenly realized that my memory sucked. It didn't do the man nearly enough justice. Unable to stop myself, I let my gaze trail over his chest, his pecs, those ripped abs, and that dusting of dark hair from his navel, trailing under his pants...

"I think we might have gotten off to a bad start," Kyle said, grinning sheepishly, as he waved a white shirt around in his hand. "How would you feel about a truce?"

"A t-truce?" I forced the words out of my mouth – and my eyes *away* from his bare stomach. Focusing on his face, I tried again. "You want a truce with me?"

"Yeah, Lee Bennett." He nodded slowly, eyes dancing with mischief. "I think I do."

All of a sudden, I felt very exposed to this man, and found myself tugging at the hem of my nightdress. Even though I was covered to the knees, it wasn't enough around him. "I hadn't realized we'd waged war," I replied, trying to sound nonchalant, desperate to keep the nervousness I was feeling *out* of my voice.

He grinned even wider, and the move caused the dimple in his cheek to deepen. His boyish smile made the sharp angles of his handsome face soften.

Good god...

Well, maybe not full on *war*," he conceded with a low chuckle as he strolled into the kitchen, moving straight for me. "But we definitely had a little wrangling going on." Not stopping until he was standing in front of me, towering over me, he rested a hip against the counter and smiled. "So, let's call a truce on any unforeseen battles that may develop into full blown war."

Confused and frazzled, I shook my head and stared up at him. "Huh?"

Not bothering to respond, Kyle just winked at me before taking the bowl I was holding from my hands and pouring cereal into it. My stomach clenched when he poured some milk in my bowl and grabbed *my* unwashed spoon off the draining board. Leaning against the counter, he scooped some up some cereal.

"You're weird," I noted, eyeing him with wary curiosity. "You're a very strange man."

"Your honesty wounds me," he snickered before shoveling a spoonful of cereal into his mouth. "Prin...cess," he mumbled between bites, as he waggled his brows playfully.

My heart rate spiked when he called me that. "I'm sorry," I hurried to apologize. He was trying to be nice and I insulted him.

"Don't be," he said between bites. "You were being honest." Pushing off the counter, he tossed the bowl in the sink after only a few mouthfuls, and strolled over to the fridge.

I stared down at the bowl in dismay.

What a waste of good food.

"I *was* being weird," Kyle continued, rummaging in the fridge. "And I *was* an asshole to you."

Huh.

I wasn't sure what to say to that. He *was* an asshole and it had taken him three days to admit it, but his honesty threw me. I didn't know what to make of this man.

Shaking my head to clear my thoughts, I locked eyes on Kyle's butt as he hunched down, rummaging inside the fridge. Oh, boy could he fill those suit pants.

With a bottle of water in one hand, he stood up and turned around, catching me gawking.

Busted.

He smirked and every ounce of blood in my body rushed to my cheeks. With his blue eyes trained on mine, he opened the cap of the bottle and swallowed deeply. Tilting his head to one side, eyes still locked on mine, he lowered the bottle from his lips and frowned. "You look young."

I did? "I do?"

He nodded slowly. "How old are you?"

I was stumped by the seriousness in his tone of voice, and instantly wary. "What does my age matter?"

"It *matters*, Lee, because I don't want to get arrested for harboring a minor in my house." He eyed me warily. "That's why it matters."

"Your house?" I gaped at him. Kyle owned the house? I thought he was just renting a room like the rest of us. "I'm eighteen," I hurried to say. "I'm an adult."

He grimaced. "Barely."

"Legally," I confirmed shakily.

"Eighteen." He exhaled and the look of relief on his face was as clear as day. "Legally." He nodded once and turned to leave.

"Wait?" I called out. Hurrying after him, I caught a hold of his forearm and pulled him to a stop. "You said this was your house?"

"Yeah." Now he was the one to look wary. He nodded slowly, attention focused on the hand I had on his. "Why?"

"You d-don't mind?" I stepped away quickly, removing my hand. "I mean, are you okay with me being here?" I prayed to god that he wouldn't mind. "I've found a job, so I won't be here for too long, I swear."

Please don't let him mind.

"You got a job already?" He scrunched his brow, tone laced with surprise. Doing what?"

"Cleaning," I replied. "I can start paying you rent as soon as I get my first paycheck."

Kyle had a look of contemplation etched on his face for a long moment before masking it with his signatory shrug of indifference. "I'm cool with you staying here." He shrugged again. "The room is yours for as long as you want it, but you won't be paying me for it."

What was he talking about? *Of course* I was going to pay him for it. "Kyle, I can't stay here rent free. Why would you even say that?"

"Because you're just a kid and it looks like you need someone to give you a break." He shrugged and moved away from the counter. Stopping in front of me, he smiled. "Well, I'm giving you one."

His blue eyes were so penetrating, I felt like he could see inside my head. I stepped closer – an action I wasn't entirely in control of. He seemed to have this amazing ability to *lure* my body to his. "I'm eighteen, Kyle." I whispered, heart fluttering around like a caged bird in my chest. "I'm not a child."

"No, Lee –" he stroked his thumb over my chin, fingers grazing my cheek almost tenderly, "you're definitely not a child."

Shivering, I repressed the urge to lean into his touch.

Something in my eyes caused him to jerk his hand away from my cheek. "Keep the room," he said, tone gruff, as he retreated to the doorway. "It's yours."

"I'm paying you," I croaked out, wrapping my hands around myself, feeling a sudden chill sweep through my bones. "I can't stay here otherwise."

"Fine. You can pay eighty bucks a month." he replied, tone breezy. "All inclusive. No more. No less. Take it or leave it." Not waiting for a response, he turned around and walked out.

———

As promised, I picked up some food at the grocery store after my shift. All through work, and my long walk home, the conversation I had with Kyle ran through my mind. I went over every detail and word with a fine-toothed comb until I was blue in the face, not to mention, more confused than ever. I was disturbed at why he would offer to let me stay rent-free just like that. He disturbed me, period.

"Wait," Cam mumbled in confusion when I filled her in on my latest roommate drama later that night. "Kyle said you can stay here for *free*." Her eyes widened as she spoke. "No conditions?"

I nodded.

"I don't understand that guy," she sighed. *Well neither did I.* "You must've made quite an impression on him."

"I obviously said no, Cam," I quickly added. "I told him that I couldn't stay here if he didn't accept my rent money. He told me he charges eighty dollars per month. Is that what you and Derek pay?"

Cam's eyes widened and she practically choked on the cookie she was nibbling.

Oh great.

Of course it wasn't.

Kyle felt *sorry* for me.

"…Because you're just a kid and it looks like you need someone to give you a break. Well, I'm giving you one…"

Cam patted my arm. "Look, Lee, the guy's obviously trying to make up for being such a douche, and I say let him. It's not like you can afford much more right now. And trust me, Kyle can."

Whether that was true or not, I didn't want any of my new roommates to think of me as a charity case. "You should have warned me that he owns this place, Cam," I muttered, rubbing my temples. "I would've liked to have known that."

Cam shrugged. "Kyle's private about things. He doesn't like people knowing about how much he has."

Sighing heavily, I whispered, "You still should have told me."

SEVEN

KEEP YOUR DISTANCE

KYLE

KEEPING my distance from that girl was going to be harder than I thought.

I had avoided coming home for three days after Cam had warned me off. I thought three days would be more than enough time to forget about her. It never took me longer than a couple of hours to forget about girls – usually less.

Not this girl, though…

I had a business trip in Kansas this week, shit, I was *still* supposed to be in Kansas, but by ten-thirty last night, I couldn't stay in that hotel room another damn minute.

I was *not* a coward, dammit. I didn't run from anyone or anything, and one little girl wasn't going to make me start now. *No woman*, no matter how sexy she was, or how good she tasted, was going to chase me out of my own damn house. So, I caught a last-minute red-eye flight home, and jumped into a cold shower the minute I walked through the front door. I knew I had to call a truce with her, and put an end to this intense thing we had going on. Problem was, I didn't know how to work this.

She was in my head, which was completely fucked up on a whole new level. I didn't care. I *never* cared. She was doing something to my thought process, and I didn't fucking like it. Not one goddamn bit.

When I finished showering and heard her rambling around in her bedroom this morning, I knew I needed to either call that truce or keep my distance. Instead of being sensible and staying the hell away from the girl who reminded me of Eve from the garden of pure goddamn *temptation*, I'd given it a few minutes and then followed her down to the kitchen. All of my best intentions had fallen clean out of my head when I saw her standing in my kitchen in that scrap of a nightdress.

Fuck Adam. In this instance, I was Eve and Lee Bennett was the most irresistible apple I'd ever seen in *my* life – ever tasted, too.

I couldn't remember half of the bullshit that had spilled from my lips. My entire focus had been on Lee and those curves she hid beneath that goddamn nightdress. I was actually sort of proud of myself for *not* bending her over my kitchen table and taking her then and there. The look in her eyes assured me that she would have let me, but dammit, she looked so young. So vulnerable. So fucking lost.

Just like me…

She said she was eighteen, which meant I had four years on her.

Too old.

I was too goddamn old to even contemplate it.

I was going to have to make sure she stayed away from me. She was a fucking temptation and the girl made me weak. I didn't do *weakness*.

My phone buzzed on my desk, dragging me from my thoughts, and alerting me to an incoming call from Rachel. "Hey," I said flatly, holding my phone almost half-heartedly to my ear.

"I need three hundred."

Christ, that girl went through money like it was going out of fashion. "I'll have it transferred into your account by lunchtime." I hoped that cash was all she wanted. I needed a *Rachel-free* day.

"No need. I'm in the lobby. You can give it to me now."

Fuck.

My.

Life.

"I'm on my way." Hanging up, I stood and walked over to the

bar in the corner of my office. Days like today were the reason Jack and I were such good pals. Pouring myself a large glass of whiskey, I chugged it back before quickly pouring another.

If I needed a reminder of how devious women really were, then I needed to look no further than the redhead waiting on me downstairs.

It would serve me well to remember that.

Women were only after one thing.

And it sure as hell wasn't *love*.

LEE

I loved pizza. Seriously, it was freaking amazing. Tucking into my third slice of margarita, I chewed in contentment while I listened to Derek and Cam banter back and forth with each other. Derek had looked at me like I was crazy when I told him it was my first time having pizza. Cam had knowingly changed the subject. They were actually quite comical together. I guessed Derek had more to do with it than Cam. He was a funny guy.

"So, how's the job going, Lee?"

Smiling, I swallowed a mouthful of pizza before responding with, "It's going great, Derek. I really like it."

Returning my smile, he nodded and took another sip of his beer. "Where'd you say it was again?"

"The Henderson Hotel?" I swallowed another piece of cheesy crust before adding, "Just off 11th street. Do you know the place? It's pretty swanky."

"Yeah, I sure do know where it's at," Derek choked out, eyes bulging. "Jesus."

"Don't you dare," Cam hissed, nudging him in the ribs. "I mean it."

"Don't what?" I asked warily.

"Nothing, nothing," Derek replied, a little too eagerly for my liking. "I'm just surprised to hear that you're working there. I heard that the owner has some issue with hiring young girls." He directed the last bit towards Cam, who was shooting dagger-eyed glares back at him. "That's all."

"Okay, what's going on, guys?" They were freaking me out with all their eye-balling. First Linda, now Cam *and*Derek. Was there something weird about the owner? "Am I in trouble or something?" I heard myself ask. "Oh my god." My eyes widened. "Is the owner dangerous?"

"Nothing's going on, babe," Cam said smiling. "And you are not in any form of danger. *Derek* just doesn't know when to keep his mouth *shut*. Do you, Der?"

"That's right." A nervous chuckle escaped him. "I need to learn to shut up more often."

I narrowed my eyes. "Keep his mouth shut about what?"

Neither one answered, and I got the distinct feeling that I was missing something.

EIGHT

KYLE

"DO you want to do something today? I hear there's a good band playing in The Avenue later?"

Shaking my head, I pulled my boxers up my hips before reaching for my black slacks. I had a killer headache and that skin crawling morning-after itch to get her the fuck out of my house as fast as humanly possible. "I can't, Lacey." Buckling my belt, I bent down and picked her dress up off my bedroom floor. "I have plans," I added, tossing her dress onto my bed – to where she was still sprawled, tits out, pussy bare.

"It's Casey," she huffed, pouting, as she sat up on my bed and began to twist her black hair around her fingers.

"Good for you," I muttered, entirely uninterested in making small talk, as I grabbed my prescription off the window sill and popped one out. How the fuck was I supposed to remember her name? We'd both been wasted last night and *she'd* been more interested in sucking my cock than having a conversation, which was fine by me. She was more than willing, and I needed the release. That might make me an asshole, but it was either fuck her or burst into the room next to mine and take my frustrations out on the tiny brunette who put them there.

"What's that for?" she asked, watching me. "Are you sick?"

"No," I muttered, swallowing down my pill. "I'm hyper."

"ADHD?"

I nodded stiffly.

"Well, you were definitely *hyper* last night." Her eyes lit up. "God, I can only imagine what you'd be like in bed without the meds slowing you down."

Fuck you. Pulling a shirt on, I bent down to tie my shoelaces. "Yeah, so I'm going to need you to take off, Casey. I have a lot on today." I noticed her lace thong under my bed and cringed.

"What the fuck, Kyle?" she growled, jumping off the bed. Standing in front of me, butt-naked, with her hands on her hips, she narrowed her eyes. "You're dismissing me? Just like that?"

In the cool light of day, she looked older than she had last night at the bar last night – when I was shit-faced on whiskey. Good looking girl, I noted, eyes roaming over her face. Definitely in her dirty thirties, though, which would explain the kinky ass-play shit. The older ones were fucking insane in bed. I let my gaze trail over her and stifled a groan. Jesus Christ, why did every woman think it was sexy to see hipbones and ribs? It was about as sexy as fucking a skeleton. No man wanted to fuck one of those.

"I thought last night meant more than sex?" She reached over and stroked my arm. "Hmm?"

Where the hell did she get that from? It *never* meant more than sex. I was a fucking douche to sleep with her. I should have been able to spot the clingy ones by now. How had I missed the signs?

"It was great sex," I lied, walking to the door. Truth was, I couldn't remember fucking her, but she smiled, appeased, so I continued. "But that's all it was."

"I thought –"

"I'll let you get dressed," I called out before closing the door behind me.

Cam, Derek, and Lee were all in the kitchen when I walked in. Muttering a half-hearted "morning," I moved straight to the cabinet where I kept the painkillers, in search of relief.

"Good morning, stud," Derek replied with a stupid grin on his face.

"It's good?" I replied as I popped two Advil from the packet and poured a glass of water "Could've fooled me."

"Rough night last night?" Cam asked, tone a little cattier than normal.

"Yeah." Shrugging, I popped the pills into my mouth and quickly washed them down with water. "You could say that."

Gripping the countertop, I closed my eyes and breathed deeply, listening to Cam and Derek as they continued whatever conversation they were having before I came in.

Don't look at her, dipshit, I mentally chanted over and over again when the urge to turn around and look at Lee Bennett threatened to overpower me. *She's not for you, so just keep your head down and your eyes off her.*

My willpower lasted a grand total of twenty-two seconds before I caved and turned to study her. And Jesus Christ, my chest ached at the sight. She was a perfect breed of woman. *Soft curves, big, lonesome eyes, gentle nature...Stop it!*

"Sleep well?" I asked her, more to distract myself from my wayward thoughts than anything else.

Lee's gaze shifted to me, and those gray eyes caused a shiver to roll down my spine. "No, not really," she replied in a soft, southern drawl of hers.

Fuck, even her voice was perfect.

I moved towards her, unable to stop myself. Easing myself onto the chair opposite her, I leaned back and gave myself full permission to study her face. On closer inspection, I could see dark shadows under her eyes. "Oh, yeah? Why's that?"

"I can't sleep at night," Lee replied, cheeks tinged with pink.

"You can't?" I felt a strange swell of concern build up inside of me. "Why not? Are you okay?" Was she finding it hard to settle in? Maybe she was homesick? Shit, was she going to leave? The words *don't leave* were on the tip of my tongue, but I swallowed them down, feeling unnerved that they had worked their way into my mind in the first place. All these niggling doubts and worries started to build in my head – all about *her.* Fuck, what was that about?

Lee blushed and ducked her head so I couldn't see those big gray eyes of hers. It was just as well because her plump, rosy lips were calling out to me. "No, no, I'm fine," she hurried to assure me. "It's just..." Pausing, he dragged her lower lip into her mouth and whispered, "You're kind of loud."

Loud?

The fuck was she talking about?

"I'm loud?" I asked, keeping my tone soft and coaxing, as I rested my elbows on the table and leaned towards her.

Lee nodded slowly. "Um, yeah."

"Yeah?" I reached a hand towards her but quickly checked myself. *Don't touch her, asshole.* "What am I doing that's so loud?"

"I'm going to take off, Kyle," a familiar female voice called out. Reluctantly, I tore my eyes off Lee and turned around just as Lacey, or Casey, or whatever the hell her name was welded her mouth to mine.

Tensing, I quickly understood what Lee meant when she said that I was loud.

Fuck.

She'd been awake all night, listening to the sound of me fucking a random girl.

How many nights had that happened?

Too many to count.

I'd brought three girls back this week alone. I'd *had* to. I loved to fuck. Sex was a release for me. I wanted to fuck *her*. Repeatedly. Exclusively. Constantly. But I couldn't. Because she was off limits to me. Cam had made that pretty damn clear. Still didn't stop me from wanting her, though…

Lacey / Casey stuck her tongue down my throat and I felt like gagging as I tried to pry her fingers off my face. I didn't want her kissing me. I didn't want any of this. The sound of a chair scraping off tiles filled my ears as I managed to free myself from her hold – and her mouth.

I caught a glimpse of Lee just before she disappeared from the kitchen. Jerking to my feet, I moved to go after her, but reluctantly stopped short in the doorway.

What are you doing, dumbass?

Don't chase her.

You don't fucking run *after any woman.*

Especially not that one.

Forcing my feet to remain rooted to the floor, I watched Lee as she hurried up the staircase.

This was the way it had to be.

It was better in the long run.

She needed to hate me.

NINE

LEE

I SETTLED into a comfortable living routine on The Hill. On weekdays, I went to work, came home, and went to bed. On weekends, I did pretty much the same thing, except I replaced work with hanging out with Cam and, more often than not, Derek.

We invented a chores schedule for housework and meal prep, with Derek usually taking over the kitchen and smothering out whichever one of us whose turn it was to cook. He worked full-time in a kitchen when school was out, and on the weekends when he didn't have classes. Because of his slight superiority to the rest of us when it came to cooking, he had branded himself the house's version of *Gordon Ramsey*. He was, by far, the best chef out of the four of us, though, so I didn't tease him about it. The man made a mean lasagna and I was even beginning to enjoy his witty retorts and banter.

Cam was fun to live with, too – lively and a general wise-ass – and we had fallen back into our friendship with ease.

But Kyle?

He was a *jerk*.

The man flaunted himself around the place like he was *king of* the hill – pun intended; prancing around the kitchen in just his jeans, or worse, his *boxer shorts*. I dutifully ignored him every time he was around – or at least, I pretended to.

Cam told me that Kyle's job required him to travel a lot, which explained the sporadic hours of the day and night that he sauntered in and out of the place. But when he *was* here, he was distracting, a smart-mouth, and had zero modesty. He also had no filter on his tongue. Seriously, the man had a real bad potty mouth.

I decided Kyle was tormenting me on purpose. He *had* to be doing it on purpose. If he wasn't banging on our bathroom door when I was showering, hollering at me to hurry up, he was blocking my way to the coffee pot, giving me one of his 'you want it, come and get it' looks.

I had gone without coffee most mornings this week because avoiding Kyle's half-naked body was much safer than pressing up against him. He would love that; to know that he was getting to me.

The sad fact of the matter was that he *was* getting to me, in a big way, and I had to pull my thoughts out of the gutter whenever I saw him dressed in one of those sexy designer suits he wore. *Or worse, his boxers.*

Never in a million years would I have guessed that Kyle had a job that required a suit and tie. It just didn't seem like the usual attire a college boy wore for a summer job. He looked *beautiful* in a suit, but there was an element of a caged animal about him when he wore one. I knew this didn't make any sense, but sometimes, when I dared a peek at him in one of those suits, I got the distinct impression that he was *trapped*.

I had thought up a dozen different potential jobs that he might do, all of which involved physical work. He didn't have the body of a man stuck in an office all day. He had the hard, toned build of an athlete. He was all broad shoulders, ribbed muscles and narrow hips. Not the standard office-boy, that was for sure.

Another thing I realized about Kyle was that he was guarded. He chatted openly about mundane things like college and football, and I'd learned he was finishing his degree in business management in the fall, but he closed himself off the *second* anything personal was brought up. Anything *deeper*. I didn't understand why he behaved this way, and I was far too intimi-dated by him to ask. Besides, I had made a promise to myself that I wouldn't care. Kyle could do *Kyle* and I would do *me*. We were poles apart, and it made zero sense for me to want to get to know a man like him.

The strangest part of it all, though, was the fact that he had started showing up at the hotel. There was a restaurant on the ground floor of the Henderson Hotel, and in the past three weeks, I had seen Kyle there on no less than *five* occasions. Thankfully, he hadn't noticed me – I always managed to hide behind a pillar in the lobby before he saw me – but it was unset-tling. On all five occasions, he had been having lunch with a different woman – his catch of the day, I presumed.

I had started to skip eating in the restaurant, choosing to eat out back on the picnic tables rather than risk the chance of bumping into the obnoxious jerk. It drove me crazy that he ate at the hotel. There were dozens of other places he could go to eat, but no, he had to choose the one building *I* worked in.

On a positive note, I had actually made a couple of friends at work – Linda, being one. I also liked talking with Mike. He was one of the bartenders, and only a few years older than me. We had met briefly on my first day and I had bumped into him again at the picnic tables last week. He'd invited me to sit with him, and I'd figured it would be rude to say no. He had been witty, and down to earth, and I had actually found him *easy* to talk to. The following day, when I went out back for lunch, Mike was there with an extra sandwich for me. After that, we had fallen into a comfortable lunch pattern. He always seemed to get his break at the same time as I did, so we ate together. I had to admit that it was really nice to be friends with a man and not have to worry about him blowing hot and cold on me. That was the way it felt with Mike. *Real. Easy. Light.* He didn't flirt with me, or make me feel uncomfortable. He was just plain *nice*. He was attractive in that all-American, wholesome kind of way. The boy was all blond hair, brown eyes, and sun-kissed golden skin. But he didn't have an ounce of the raw sexual magnetism that Kyle had. Where Mike was sweet, attentive, and cute, Kyle was rough, edgy, and mind-blowingly *sexy*.

I decided that Kyle's appeal had something to do with the way he moved. He didn't just walk, he *prowled* like a wild animal;

cool and confident, but full of raw strength and vibrating intensity. There was also this element of *danger* to him. He was rude, obnoxious, and breathtakingly *beautiful,* and he seemed to get a real thrill out of baiting me.

I hated that I was so damn attracted to him. I hated that I found him attractive, *period*. It was purely a physical attraction, I reminded myself. It couldn't be any more than that – not when he was so mean to me. The fluttering in my chest when he was near was just biology. He was beautiful, and any girl would feel the same when he spoke, or smiled, or laughed…

After many sleepless nights thinking about him, I had decided to put my attraction to my roommate down to two things.

First, he was my first consensual kiss.

Second, I was not the only woman to feel like this.

Kyle had plenty of admirers. Women *swooned* over him. I'd seen enough of his admirers coming out of his bedroom in the mornings – Rachel being the most frequent visitor.

While it was clear they were not an exclusive couple, there was definitely something strange going on with them. I watched them when they were together and it was *odd*. Apart from the fact that Kyle didn't seem to like her very much, when Rachel said jump, he said how high. He did *everything* she told him to and it really irked me. He was a jerk to me, but that didn't stop me hating the way she spoke to him. It was as if she enjoyed degrading him.

And no matter what she said or did, he *always* took it.

KYLE

"Close your mouth, dude, you're drooling."

I tore my gaze from Lee's ass to find Derek grinning at me from across the kitchen table. "Screw you," I muttered, keeping my voice low and my eyes off *her*. I tried so hard not to be that creepy guy; the one who stared at his teenage roommate like she was dinner, but sometimes, I lost the run of myself. She was *something else.*

Derek smirked. "I'd say screw Lee, but you're not allowed."

"What was that, guys?" Lee asked, as she stood up from where she had been hunched over, rummaging around in the refrigerator, and looked at us.

"Oh, Kyle here was just enjoying the view," Derek said, grinning.

He was loving this.

Bastard.

Aggravated, I kicked him under the table and smiled when his face contorted in a pained grimace.

Lee frowned. "The view?"

"It's a beautiful day after all," Derek explained, pointing to the kitchen window.

"Smooth, asshole," I muttered, kicking his shin again.

"Dude, quit it," he whined. "I'm gonna bruise."

"Good," I hissed between clenched teeth.

"Yeah, it's a beautiful morning," Lee agreed, completely oblivious to the true meaning of Derek's words.

Thank god.

"So, what are your plans for the day?" Derek asked, focusing his attention on her. Waggling his brows, he teased, "Any hot date lined up tonight?"

God, he was a sadist.

Fucking torture me some more, why don't you…

"Hardly," Lee said, and I breathed easily again. I hadn't realized I'd been holding my breath, waiting for her answer.

"Really?" Derek frowned. "Why not? It's Friday. You should be going out and having some fun. I don't believe for one second that you haven't been asked on a date by one of the guys at your work."

I was going to *beat* him, and I was going to enjoy doing it.

Lee blushed and poured some milk into a glass. "Well you should," she said quietly. "No one has."

"I could hook you up with one of my friends," he offered. "They all think you're hot. Especially Dixon."

"Uh –" Lee spluttered her coffee. "Um…" She looked at me briefly before focusing on Derek once more. "I'm not sure," she finally replied.

"I think you should," Derek pushed. "Live a little."

He was baiting me.

And it was *working.*

"Ouch, dude, what the *hell*?" Derek cried, staggering to his feet.

"Oh sorry, man. Did I step on your foot?" I asked, smiling almost manically at him. Shoving my chair back, I stood and walked over to where Lee was standing, purposefully leaning too close to her to get a cup from the cabinet. She shivered when my chest rubbed against hers and my ego swelled. Yeah, fuck Dixon Jones. She was aware of *me.*

"Do you want to go out with Dixon, Princess?" I stared straight at her, and she shook her head eagerly.

"Uh, no." Swallowing deeply, she tucked a stray curl behind her ear. "Not at all."

Relief, more potent than was safe, flooded my body as I watched her watch me. "Hear that, Der?" I called out to my best friend, keeping my eyes trained on Lee's. "She doesn't want to date any of your asshole friends."

"They're not all assholes," Derek began to protest, but I cut him off.

"Leave it alone, Der," I bit out. "Leave *her* alone."

I had to leave then.

Getting too close to her was dangerous.

TEN

LEE

I MADE my way down the stairwell at the back of the hotel – the one that led to the staff doorway outside. It was a much longer route than taking the elevator and cutting through the restaurant, but it was much safer than potentially facing Rachel in the restaurant – or Kyle.

"Hey, you made it." Mike smiled at me from the picnic bench when I stepped outside.

"Hey," I said, making a beeline for our bench. "Sorry I'm late." Sinking down opposite him, I exhaled a heavy sigh. "Work is hectic today."

Mike smiled. "I know the feeling." He then proceeded to hand me a plastic covered sandwich, and a can of soda. "It's just cold cuts of beef today, I'm afraid. We're fresh out of tuna."

I smiled, grateful. "Thanks Mike. Beef is great."

He grinned back at me. "I wasn't sure if you were one of those vegetarian girls. You always have fish in your sandwiches."

"You're the one who *makes* my sandwiches, remember?" Smiling, I shrugged. "I'm not fussy about my food, but, truth be told, I'm a red meat kind of girl."

We slipped into easy conversation after that, and I actually snorted soda from my nose when Mike told me about the last big drama at the hotel.

"No way?" I asked, as I patted my napkin to my face. "Are you for real?"

"True story," he chuckled. "Mindy was in housekeeping, and I guess you could say that she got a little too up close and personal cleaning his *family jewels*."

I gasped. "Isn't he the guy in Washington? A senator or something?"

Mike chuckled. "Not anymore. Their affair was leaked to the media. You wouldn't believe the number of journalists and paparazzi around here at the time. It was *huge* news. A public figure getting off with an underage housekeeper. The boss was *furious* –" he paused and frowned. "I'm actually surprised he hired you. After the drama with Mindy, he doesn't hire young girls. There was too much of a backlash for the hotel chain from the media, not to mention Mindy's parents."

I took another swig of my soda while I thought about what Mike had said. I guessed that's what Derek had been suggesting a few weeks back when he had asked me where I worked. "What's he like?" I asked, feeling curious. "Our boss, I mean. Have you met him?" I hadn't. Everything went through Linda around here – at least, that was my experience since starting here.

A vein twitched in Mike's neck. "Yeah, I've met him," he said flatly. When he noticed my worried look, he offered me a smile. "When he's here, which is rare, he's a good boss. But he's usually jetting off around the country, handling issues with the other hotels in the chain. Most of the staff seem to like him, though. But Linda is the one who really runs this place. "

I could hear the undertone in his words. "*Most* of the staff?"

"You don't miss much, do you?" He scrubbed his face with his hand and sighed. "Let's just say, he and I have some personal issues and leave it at that."

"Personal issues?"

Mike nodded stiffly.

"Okay, so are you doing much for the weekend?" I asked, trying to change the subject, and steer the look in his eyes away from murderous.

Mike smiled, his features softened, and then he delved into telling me all about his plans for the coming weekend. I tried to appear interested, but my mind kept drifting back to what he had said about our boss.

"He and I have some personal issues."

I wondered what they were.

ELEVEN

SKIPPING TRACKS AND HEARTBEATS

KYLE

LEE WAS ON HER OWN.

Her bedroom door was cracked open, and she was lying on her bed, reading. I knew I shouldn't go inside. Cam would have my balls for it, but I'd never had much willpower and she zapped it to shit. Besides, I was exhausted from the sheer effort it took to keep my distance from her.

Tonight, I was weak.

Tonight, I wasn't staying away.

"What are you reading?" I asked, tapping softly on the doorframe.

Clearly startled, Lee scrambled into a sitting position, pulling the set of earplugs she was using from her ears. Her cheeks were glowing red, her curls a loose tangled mess, as she looked up at me, wide-eyed. "I'm sorry, Kyle. Did you call me for something?"

Jesus, she was fucking stunning.

Not bothering to try and talk myself down from the ledge I was hell bent on throwing myself over, I stepped inside. "I asked what you were reading." Not stopping until I was sitting on her bed, I reached over and retrieved the book that had slipped from her fingers when I startled her.

"Oh, it's just a book," she replied, cheeks flaming. "I like to read."

"Yeah?" I mused. "Me, too." I skimmed the page and holy fuck... "You're reading *porn*?"

No fucking way.

Innocent little Lee had a stash of girl-porn.

"It's not porn." Blushing, Lee snatched the book out of my hands. "It's a romance novel."

"If you say so," I chuckled.

"It's really not porn, I swear," she defended. "It's a love story."

I arched a brow, mildly curious. "Tell me about it."

Her eyes widened. "About the book?"

"About the love story."

"Uh, well, it's about a man and a woman," she said, voice sweet like honey. "And they're conflicted."

"Yeah?"

She nodded slowly and turned her attention to the cover of the book. "They're both harboring deep feelings for each other, but they're afraid to take their relationship to the next level."

"What are they afraid of?"

"Life."

"Life?"

"Repercussions," she clarified quietly. "Getting hurt. Being…broken."

My brows furrowed. "Broken?"

"They're both a little fractured already," she whispered. "I guess they're scared of being broken any further? Or worse, breaking each other."

"Hmm."

"Yep."

"How does it end?" I asked, sprawling back to rest on my elbows.

A ghost of a smile teased her lips. "With a happy ever after."

"You know that's not real life, right?" I asked gruffly. "There is no happy ever after in this world."

"Maybe not," Lee agreed softly. "Which is why I like to read about them instead."

"Hmm." Feeling thrown off kilter, I stared at the paperback in her hands before casting a quick glance around her tidy room. "You're neat, Lee Bennett."

"I should hope so," she replied.

"You like things to be tidy?"

She nodded. "I like to clean. It calms me. It, uh, distracts me."

"From what?" Twisting onto my side, I turned to face her. "What do you need to be distracted from?"

"My not-so happy ever after?" she offered with a humorless laugh.

I frowned. "You're not happy?"

"Sometimes," she whispered. "Some places."

"What about now?" I leaned closer. "What about here?"

"Sure," she breathed. "Sometimes."

"And me?" I held my breath, unsure if she got my meaning – and feeling even more unsure if I was ready for her answer.

"You?" She nodded slowly. "Sometimes."

Well shit…

"Let's see what kind of music you're into," I blurted out, desperately trying to distract myself from those lips of hers, and the raw, aching thud in my chest. I reached for the iPod on her lap, only to accidentally brush the bare skin of her thigh with my fingertips. Lee whimpered and my cock twitched.

Shit.

"It's Cam's iPod," she muttered, recovering quickly, as he held out one ear plug for me to take. "This one's my favorite," she added as she took the iPod and tapped on the screen. "I feel like I can relate to the words."

Flopping onto my back, I popped it in my ear and listened carefully as a slow, melancholic guitar riff filled my ear. I was expecting some cheesy boy band to fill my ears, so when Kings of Leon's song *Closer* filled my ears, I was thrown.

The girl had good taste in music.

This song always made me shiver. There was something so incredibly haunting about the intro. It just sucked you right in.

Lee mirrored my actions, laying on her back beside me, with the other ear plug in her ear.

Closing my eyes, I folded my hands on my stomach and allowed the lyrics to sweep through my mind.

How the fuck was Lee relating to those lyrics? *I* was relating to the lyrics. Shit, I was *reacting* to the lyrics. This song was the epitome of sex songs and I had an embarrassing bulge in my jeans, harder than die-cast fucking metal, as she lay beside me.

Keeping my eyes clenched shut to block the view of her tits rising and falling when she breathed, I willed myself to get a handle on this fucking obsession. She was just a girl. Just *one girl. You're overthinking everything, Carter. Don't touch…*

"Do you ever wish," Lee began to say, capturing my attention instantly, "that when someone listens to a song, they're thinking the lyrics about you?" She turned her face to mine, chewing on her lip, as she gauged my reaction.

"What do you mean?" I asked, eyes locked on hers, chest constricting with every breath I forced my lungs to take.

She shrugged almost helplessly, big, gray eyes honed on mine. "I wonder what it would feel like to have a man want me the way these singers want the women who inspire their songs."

Goddammit.

"Men want you, Lee," I told her, tone gruff and thick. "You don't need a song to know that."

"They do?"

Nodding slowly, I moved my hand from my stomach to rest beside hers. Brushing the back of my hand against hers, I exhaled a heavy sigh. "They do."

"Do you?"

"Do I what?"

"Ever think the words of a song about a woman."

"What do you mean? A song like this? Or –"

"It doesn't matter," she mumbled, cheeks turning bright pink. "That was a weird thing for me to ask you."

Fuck, I didn't want her to get skittish again.

"Sometimes," I offered. *Like right now. Right now, I'm imagining you.* "Do you?" I asked her.

"Yeah, Kyle." Lee exhaled heavily and looked up at the ceiling, "All the time."

There was a long stretch of silence then, while the song continued to play, and I mulled over her words. If it wasn't for the fact that she was so fucking naïve, I would think she was hitting on me. Shit, *was* she hitting on me? I couldn't tell. I tried to gauge her expression, but her eyes were closed, blocking me out. "Who do you think of when you listen to this song, Princess?" I asked, needing her to say my name more than I needed my next breath. Call it selfish, pointless, or reckless, fuck, call it whatever you want, I *needed* to be that person for her. I wanted to be the one she thought all of her songs about. *Jesus, I was so fucked...*

Lee sighed deeply before turning her lonesome, gray-eyed gaze back on me. "I don't think you want to know the answer to that."

"Is it Dixon?" The name burst into my brain, and like a bad scene from a horror movie, I couldn't get it out of my head. "Do you like him?"

Lee giggled softly and that only irritated me further.

"Is there something funny about what I said?" I asked, pulling the earplug out and standing up. "Are you already with him or something?"

Lee laughed harder. Great, I was going out of my mind with jealousy and *she* thought it was a big, fucking joke. "You really don't get it, do you, Kyle?" she asked, her voice suddenly serious.

No, I *didn't* get it, and I didn't want to hear anymore. "Fuck this," I growled before walking out of her room. "And fuck feelings," I muttered under my breath as I stalked into my room.

TWELVE

RACHEL GRAYSON

LEE

I PLANNED on having a lie-in on Saturday morning. Having worked a whole bunch of double shifts this week, I figured I deserved the rest. However, my body seemed to have invented its own internal clock, and, just like *clockwork*, I rose at 7am. Deciding on having breakfast before showering, I stumbled out of bed and trudged down to the kitchen. Making a beeline for the coffee pot, I filled a mug and sank down at the kitchen table, feeling sleep-deprived and slightly off-kilter.

Like always, my thoughts went straight to Kyle and that moment we shared in my bedroom the other night, but the sound of a doorbell cutting through the air, followed seconds later by Rachel's high-pitched, shrill of a voice, prevented me from mulling over my predicament too deeply.

I guess Kyle's back from his latest excursion. He'd been gone since last Tuesday. Four days should have been more than enough time for me to get a handle on my emotions. *It wasn't.*

"Why the hell didn't you come over last night when I told you to?" she demanded, as she stalked into the kitchen. "When I ask you to do something, Kyle, you better fucking do it." She tossed her designer purse down on the table, narrowly missing my coffee cup, before delving back into the momentous ear-chewing she was giving my roommate. She was so wrapped up in her rant that she didn't seem to notice me sitting right there. Either that, or she just didn't care.

I hated to admit it but Rachel was truly gorgeous. Today, she had on a pair of beige skinny jeans, skyscraper heels, and a pink cashmere sweater. Her flaming red mane was scraped back in a severe bun, and her makeup was flawless, enhancing her green eyes and high cheekbones. The only thing about Rachel that was less than perfect was her ultra-thin lips. However, she looked like the type of person who could afford to have that corrected if desired.

Feeling self-conscious, I lowered my pajama-assed self further down in my chair, praying for the ground to open up and swallow me whole.

Kyle strolled into the kitchen a few moments later, moving straight for the refrigerator. I thanked god he was fully clothed this morning in black slacks and a light-blue, fitted shirt. "Can you *not* do this first thing in the morning," he grumbled, head stuck in the fridge. He pulled out a bottle of water and walked over to the sink. He didn't acknowledge me either. *Lord, I was completely invisible to these people.* "Goddamn, Rach."

"Fine," she snapped, folding her arms across her chest. "I'll stop when *you* explain where the hell you were last night."

"I didn't get around to coming over," he replied flatly. "I got home late. You know I'm busy." He sounded tired, and almost instantly, a swell of concern rose up inside of me. He worked too hard, took on too many hours, did too much traveling... Stopping myself short, I tucked the worry building up inside of me away. He wasn't mine to worry about.

Keeping my head down, I dutifully ignored the both of them, but the way she spoke to him got to me and I couldn't help but cast a sneaky peek at Kyle. He wasn't looking at Rachel. He wasn't even facing her. He was standing poker straight with his back to the both of us, looking out the kitchen window.

"Well, if you kept it in your pants a little more, then maybe you wouldn't be so *busy*," she spat back at him. "You can be such a bastard sometimes."

Kyle shrugged off what Rachel said as if he heard it every

day, and it made my blood boil. What was her problem? She didn't *own* him.

"Well?" Rachel pushed. "I'm talking to you."

"Don't make a big deal out of this, Rach," he replied, tone weary. "I have to *work*. You have no complaints when you're spending my money."

Why was she spending his money?

Did she not have her own job?

I wished Kyle would make a big deal out of it. I wished he would make a *huge* deal out of it and kick her sorry butt to the curb.

"Don't make a *big deal* of it?" she hissed, looking furious. "I don't ask you for much, Kyle. Just a little of your time. It's the least you can do considering what you did. You *owe* me."

"Leave him alone," I blurted out, unable to listen to another word. "So what if he doesn't call you? Big deal. He doesn't *owe* you for that."

Kyle swung around and gaped at me, brows furrowed in surprise. He looked genuinely stunned to see me sitting there. I guess he hadn't been ignoring me; I was just plain invisible to him.

"Morning, Princess." A small smile crept across his face, causing me to blush.

I shrugged and returned his smile. "Morning, Kyle."

"Princess?" The look Rachel gave me was actually quite terri-fying. "Did you just call her *princess*?"

"Relax," Kyle grumbled, tearing his eyes off me to glare at Rachel. "It's a pet name."

"Then call her *mutt*," Rachel hissed through clenched teeth. "Like the dog she is."

"Don't do that," he growled. "Don't be a bitch to her."

"*I'm* a bitch?" Rachel laughed humorlessly. "That's rich coming from the asshole who moved his fuck-buddy in with him."

"You're delusional," Kyle shot back, bristling.

"No, I don't think I am," Rachel countered. "She's your little friend from Cam's party. The same little whore camped out in the bedroom next to yours. And now she's defending you as well as warming your bed. That makes her a desperate little *bitch* to me!"

"You need to stop," he warned, jaw ticking. "You're not doing this in my house."

"I'll do whatever I want in this house," Rachel snarled. "Do you hear me, Kyle? I'll do whatever the fuck I *want*!" Turning her attention to me, Rachel didn't stop until she was towering over me. "Keep your nose out of my business, little girl, and keep your eyes off my man. He doesn't need you to defend him. He doesn't need you to do shit for him. He's *mine*."

I was proud of myself for not shrinking away from her, even though every instinct in my body demanded I do just that. She was a mean ole bully. I *hated* bullies. I couldn't stop the blood from rushing to my cheeks, though. Embarrassment was searing me and my face was on *fire.*

Resting her hands on the table, she leaned close and hissed, "You got that, *princess*?"

I did get it – or at least I should have, but my legs were moving. Against my better judgment, I pushed my chair back and climbed unsteadily to my feet. Trembling my head to toe, I kept my eyes on hers, refusing to show her just how badly she intimidated me. That was what she wanted, and I refused to give her that kind of power over me. The night I left Louisiana was the night I decided to *never* allow anyone to have that kind of power over me again. "*Your* man?" I forced myself to say, standing firm. "I didn't realize you owned him. Maybe you should have brought his slave papers with you," I added before stepping around her and moving for the door.

Kyle snickered, and that only seemed to make Rachel angrier. "Don't you dare laugh," she warned him. "Hey – wait! I'm not done talking to you."

I rolled my eyes to the heavens. "Well, I'm done talking to you."

KYLE

I hated being here.

In her apartment.

In her bed.

I wasn't a fucking prostitute – although, since I was the one handing out all the cash, that remark was futile. If I didn't come over tonight, Rachel would go bat shit crazy – *again,* and that crazy would more than likely be directed at Lee. In my own sick way, I was trying to protect her.

"I want you to stay away from that girl." Straddling my lap, Rachel trailed her long fingernails down my chest, and I wanted to peel my skin off. I wanted to throw her off me, get the fuck out of her bed, and as far away from her as humanly possible.

But I didn't because I *couldn't.* So instead, I leaned back on my elbows and resigned myself to my fucked-up reality. "What girl?" I asked, forcing myself not to recoil from her touch. I didn't want to breathe the same air as this girl, let alone have her hands on my skin. Jesus. I was a poor excuse for a man.

"Don't act stupid, Kyle." Narrowing her eyes, she continued to pop open the buttons of my shirt. "You know exactly who I'm talking about."

"She's my roommate," I decided to offer up. "Just like Cam. Nothing more."

Rachel scowled at the mention of Cam's name, and I had to smother a huge *ha-fucking-ha* laugh. Cam gave her a hard time at any given opportunity and I loved her for it. I sure as hell couldn't do it. "You have shitty taste in friends," Rachel huffed.

No, I had shitty taste in *women* – her being the shittiest.

"I see the way you look at little miss *southern belle* –" she finished with removing my shirt and then moved to hers. Pulling her shirt over her head, her bra-less, plastic tits fell into my face. I didn't even stir. Not even one goddamn twitch. "I'm not blind," she continued, moving for my belt buckle. "You're different when you're with her." Unsnapping my belt, she tore at my fly. "Why is that?"

I was treading dangerous waters here and I needed to be careful. Rachel was testing me. "I don't look at her any differently to how I look at Cam," I lied. Thrusting my hips upwards, I pushed my jeans down my thighs, despising myself as I worked to rid myself of my clothes. The only fucking reason I was currently sporting a reluctant semi was because she had brought up *Lee*.

"Liar," she hissed, glaring down at me, as she continued to test my loyalty. I didn't have any. Not to her, at least.

"She's too much of a mouse to look twice at," I forced the words out, disgusted with myself for saying what I needed to say to keep Lee *safe*. "I don't fuck hillbillies, Rachel."

Rachel grabbed a condom off the nightstand and I wanted to die. "Just as long as you remember that," she mused, tearing the foil wrapper open. "You made me a deal two years ago –" she sheathed my cock and lowered herself onto me. "and I plan to make you keep it."

After that, I closed my eyes and thought of *Lee*.

THIRTEEN

AT THE MOVIES

LEE

"I STILL CAN'T BELIEVE you spoke up to Rachel like that," Cam laughed as we stood in line at the movie theater the following Wednesday night, making the most of the two-for-one couples deal the theater was offering. "I love it, and I love *you* for doing it!"

Yeah, well, neither could I. "I don't know what came over me, Cam," I replied, still feeling rattled about our showdown last weekend. "I've never spoken to anybody like that in my whole life. I don't even *like* Kyle, but she's just so *mean* to him – and what's worse is he *takes* it. It's disgusting."

"The two-for-on offer is for couples only, ladies," the man behind the counter said when Cam asked for our tickets.

"And?" Cam replied sharply.

"And that's the rule," the man replied, withering a little under Cam's narrow-eyed glare. "You'll have to pay separately."

I moved for my purse, but Cam held a hand out, stopping me. "Are you being serious right now?" she demanded, resting her elbows on the counter and leaning close. "Or are you just a narrow-minded, homophobic asshole? Because I'm a paying customer, standing in your establishment, holding up a fifty-dollar bill, and wondering if I've been transported to the past"

"Cam, it's okay –"

"No, Lee, it's not okay," Cam shot back. "It's not okay at all. If I'm gay, straight, or asexual, what the fuck does it matter to him?" She glowered across the counter at the man. "I'm with *her*, we're a *couple*, tonight is a couple's *night*, and I want my goddamn tickets."

"It doesn't matter," the man choked out. "I was just making a point."

"Would you have made the same *point* if I was standing here with a man?" Cam challenged.

The man blushed. "I-I-I…"

"No, of course you wouldn't," she sneered. "Well, here's a tip; this is the twenty-first century. Join us in it or fuck off back to the nineteen-fifties."

"I didn't mean to offend you –"

"Just give me my damn tickets," she growled. "I'm done talking to you."

"Okay. Okay."

"And the next time a same sex couple comes to you for tickets, stem the bigotry, hold the discriminatory comments, and hand them the fucking *tickets*."

"Whoa," I breathed, when Cam passed me a ticket. "That was pretty bad-ass."

"He needed a reality check." Cam shrugged nonchalantly. "I gave him one." Grinning, she added, "Kind of like the reality check you gave Rachel the devil Grayson."

"Ugh," I groaned.

"Well, I, for one, am damn glad you put that bitch in her place. I'm usually the one who chews out that gold-digger. Der and I cannot *stand* the girl, but Kyle's his best friend, so Der doesn't get involved. We all hate her, though. Like, our entire group of friends *loathe* her." She cast a meaningful glare at the man who was dutifully preparing our sodas. "Don't worry; we loathe you, too, fucker."

"Cam," I chuckled, shaking my head. "You're so bad."

"It's true," she laughed. "Everyone hates Rachel."

"Really?" I smiled at that. At least everyone else could see what I was seeing. It made me feel a little better about my outburst.

"She'll probably want revenge," Cam warned. "Especially since you took her down a peg or ten in front of Kyle."

"Oh god." Rachel didn't like me as it stood. "Perfect."

"And you committed the mortal sin when you kissed him at the party," she added.

I cringed in shame. Did she have to bring that back up? I tried not to think about the kiss – both kisses – at least not until I was tucked up in bed at night. "He kissed me first," I offered lamely.

"You kissed him, he kissed you," Cam laughed as she paid for her popcorn, giving the man behind the counter the evils. "Does it really matter who kissed who when the end result was your tongues sliding around in each other's mouths?"

Did it? No, no, it didn't matter. "He doesn't like me, Cam," I whispered, paying for my goodies. "Rachel has nothing to worry about." I grimaced before adding, "It's the other women he's with that she should be angry with." *Not me.*

"Hmm." Cam stared at me for a long moment before her gaze slipped to something over my shoulder. "I wouldn't be so sure about that, if I were you, Lee-Bee," she mused, arching a brow.

"Sure about what?" My eyes widened. "Kyle liking me? Because he doesn't, Cam. He absolutely does not."

Smirking, Cam raised a hand and waved. "Hey, *Kyle.*"

Wait – *what?*

"What a *surprise* to see you boys here," Cam said, tone laced with sarcasm, as she walked straight past me. "You're not checking up on us, are you?"

I spun around and quickly turned back, heart racing wildly in my chest.

Why, Jesus, why?

"Of course not," I heard Derek purr. "Now, come here and give me a kiss."

That was a big fat *lie.* From what I'd seen, Derek was *always* checking up on Cam. There was a truckload of trust missing from their relationship. It wasn't my business, though, so I didn't ask questions.

"I'll meet you inside Lee-Bee," Cam called out.

Keeping my back to them, I didn't bother answering. My night had just taken a major nosedive. Not because Derek had shown up. No, it had more to do with Mr. Tall, dark, and sarcastic, and the way my heart wouldn't calm the heck *down*.

Heart racing, I paid for my soda and popcorn, all the while plotting how I could get out of seeing this movie. Cam had driven us here, and it was a twenty-minute car ride back to The Hill, with lots of different turn offs. *Dammit*, I would never be able to find my way home.

Falling on empty, I reluctantly turned around and made my way over to the doorway with the sign 'screen one' over it, moving at a snail's pace. With any luck, the boys had chosen to see a different movie. I didn't believe that for one second, though. Derek hadn't shown up for any other reason than to keep an eye on Cam.

Maybe I could just wait outside in the lobby until it was over? Dammit, I had been looking forward to seeing the movie. How was I supposed to relax with *him* in close proximity?

"Hey, Princess."

Jumping at the sound of his voice, not to mention the feel of his warm breath on my neck, I jerked sideways and ended up spilling my entire tub of popcorn on the floor.

"Whoa, there's no need to be so jumpy," Kyle chuckled from behind me. "It's just me."

Yeah, it was just him; the walking, talking. bane of my hormones.

I turned around to scold him for sneaking up on me, but the words just wouldn't come out. Why did he have to look so good? It wasn't fair. God must have been in a real good mood the day he made this man.

My eyes took in the dark jeans and tight gray t-shirt he was wearing, and I sighed. Couldn't he wear clothes that made him less...*edible*? It wouldn't matter much what he wore, I thought dejectedly. Kyle smiling that perfect smile of his was enough to turn me into a puddle of mush on the floor. *That dimple did strange things to my heartstrings.* "Why did you sneak up on me?" I asked, when speaking was manageable again. "You really scared me just there."

He threw his head back and laughed, a deep virile sound. My heart-rate accelerated instantly. I couldn't turn my eyes away from his throat and the way his Adams apple vibrated. "I was just waiting for you," he mused, smirk still firmly in place. "Cam said that it was your first time at the movies." He shrugged sheepishly. "It's a big place. I didn't want you to get lost."

Gee, thanks for that, Cam.

As if I needed any more help to look *country*.

Kyle took a step towards me then and I exhaled a ragged breath. Lord, I needed to get a grip on these feelings. I backed up and managed to snag the heel of my shoe on an upturned piece of carpet. My coke flew out of my hand as I flayed my arms out.

Oh great, I was going down.

Before I could holler for help, two arms snaked around my waist, pulling me flush against a chest of hard, ripped muscle. I knew he was *ripped* because I had to endure looking at said toned stomach every day. "You're a little clumsy tonight, aren't you, Princess?" Kyle chuckled, as he held me flush against him.

"Uh…" I couldn't think of one thing to say. An involuntary shiver rolled through me. "I guess I am," I finally whispered. "A little off-balance, that is."

"Yeah," he replied gruffly, blue eyes burning holes in mine. "Me, too." He straightened then, putting some space between our bodies, but he kept his hands on my hips and the move *thrilled* me.

When he realized what he was doing, Kyle jerked his hands away and roughly cleared his throat. "We should probably go in."

"Yeah," I breathed, still staring up at me. "We probably should."

"I, uh…" Shaking his head, he took a step towards me before quickly spinning on his heels and stalking off in the direction of screen one.

I trailed after him, desperately trying to get a handle on myself.

It was my nerves that were causing the butterflies in my belly.

Nothing else.

KYLE

This movie was the biggest croc of shit I'd been forced to endure in a long-ass time. It was your typical chick flick; girl meets boy, girl falls in love, boy screws up and girl runs off. Then the boy fixes the shit pile he's gotten himself into and gets nailed. Kiss kiss, bang bang, happy ever after. *Bla-fucking-bla.* It was *painful* to sit through and I had paid ten bucks for the privilege.

Derek owed me big time for this. His paranoia over Cam cheating was the reason I was currently sitting in a movie theater, packed with women weeping and crying. I was surrounded by hormones and it was freaking me the fuck out. Fair enough, Cam had a past, but Derek needed to trust her. He couldn't leave the girl alone for a damn minute. Sometimes, my best friend acted like a vagina.

"That's it, Cam. Oh, yeah, baby, suck it just like that."

Those two had no fucking shame. Even *I* drew the line at getting a blowjob in public. Well, at least not while sitting next to my *friends*.

Not taking any chances, I shifted as far in my seat from them as I physically could, all the while praying that Cam was one of those rare, trooper type girls that swallowed. I prayed the girl was going to take one for the team. If not, this was going to get messy. And if that fucker came on me, if his jizz came anywhere near *my* body, then I was going to end him. Buddy or not.

A soft groan from my other side alerted me to the fact that I was now squashing *Lee*. Goddammit, I couldn't cut a break. We were squashed into one of those *love seats*; the double seats used for making out. It was ironic considering I couldn't touch the girl who was pressed up against me. The one girl I wanted to touch more than I wanted my next breath. "Uh, sorry," I whispered, easing back a little so that she could breathe again, but not far enough to put myself within aiming distance of Derek's dick.

"It's okay." She looked up at me and smiled shyly. Her eyes were like saucers and I could practically see the innocence pouring out of them. "I guess I'd be moving closer to you, too, if I had to sit on your side," she whispered, pointing at Cam and Derek, who were now gone *way* fucking past the point of no return.

"They're animals," I noted, disgusted.

Lee blushed and turned back to face the screen, dutifully ignoring our friends who were...Jesus, I didn't want to *think* about what they were doing.

Lee focused all of her attention on the movie and I focused all of my attention on *her*. She looked so damn hot in a pair worn, denim cut-0ffs, and a plain yellow tee. My attention was riveted to her, all of her, from her wild mane of curls, to her little button nose, to her huge fucking rack straining against the cotton fabric of her shirt. I wasn't used to being around girls who dressed like that. So casual. So...simple. The women I knew wore tight little dresses and low-slung tops. They had make-up plastered on their faces, orange skin from too much fake tan, and hair wrangled into all types of weird styles. Even Cam was guilty of the make-up and short skirts.

Lee wore none of that shit.

She didn't need to.

Her sun-kissed skin was naked, and she had her curly hair bunched up in a messy ponytail, with the odd rogue curl escaping to frame her pretty face. I itched to reach out and tuck those silky curls behind her ear, but that would be *bad*. That would be edging closer to a line I wasn't supposed to cross – a line that was blurring with every passing day.

I thought about the look on her face the morning she had defended me to Rachel. The way she stuck up for me? It wasn't something I was used to. I expected to feel annoyed with her for interfering in my business. Instead, I felt *pleased.*

That shy little smile Lee had given me in the kitchen that

morning…it had *changed* something in me. It made me *feel,* and I hadn't felt anything in forever. The girl was fucking amazing and she didn't even know it. That made me even more determined to stay away from her. Lee didn't need to be marred with my bullshit. I had to remember that. She was too good for me.

"Now, Cam, it's gonna be now, baby."

Screw lines, I practically sat on Lee's fucking lap. "Dude, you're in a movie theater," I hissed, stomach churning. Unable to stifle a gag, I added, "show a little restraint."

"Are you really this squeamish?" Lee whisper-laughed, eyes dancing with humor, as she smiled up at me.

I smirked. "Oh, you think it's funny, do you?"

Grinning, she nodded. "You're supposed to be this big, tough man," she snickered. "And you're gagging. Like a little *baby.*"

Huh.

Well shit.

"Oh, you're going to tease me? Fine, two can play that game, Princess." Feeling playful, I reached out and tickled her, making her laugh harder. It was a pleasant sound and I liked it – probably more than I should.

"Stop, Kyle – stop! I'm ticklish," she strangled out as she tried to wrestle my hands away from her sides, but the move only drew her body closer to mine. Writhing on the seat, she smothered a laugh, chest heaving, and I couldn't tear my eyes off her chest and the way her tits strained against her shirt as she breathed hard and fast. "Oh, Kyle, please… I can't take it anymore."

Fuck, I was turned on and it had nothing to do with the sex noises coming from the love seat next to me, and *everything* to do with Lee and the way I felt when her body rubbed against mine. Without thinking about what I was doing, I pulled her onto my lap so that she was straddling me.

"What are you doing, Kyle?" she asked breathlessly.

Fuck if I knew anymore.

Unable to stop myself, I slid my hands down her sides and gripped her hips, pulling her down on my lap as I thrust upwards, hips moving instinctively against hers, dick straining to get between those thighs, minus any clothes.

I rolled my hips again and she moaned softly, eyes darkening.

Christ, she wanted this, too. It was written all over her face. She *wanted* me.

Dammit.

Reckless, I rocked my hips against her, pulling her down hard on my lap as I moved. A small whimper tore from her lips and her eyelids fluttered. "Do you feel that?" I asked gruffly, keeping my eyes trained on her face, basking in the sexy expressions she was making. "Can you feel what you do to me, Princess?"

Lee nodded, dragging her plump lower lip into her mouth.

And all at once it was too much.

"Fuck the line –" Grabbing the back of her neck, I pulled her face down to mine and sealed my lips to hers. Lee moaned – a real, genuine, honest to god moan of pleasure – and I thought I might lose it.

Starving for this girl and all that she was, I plunged my tongue inside her mouth, kissing her deeply. She tasted unbelievable. Her hands were in my hair, tugging me closer, demanding more from me than I was sure I could give. "You taste like fucking heaven," I breathed against her lips, unable to stop myself from pushing the limits. I couldn't help myself. Nothing made sense when it came to this girl. "I need more," I growled, shifting us both until I had her on her back. Never taking my lips from hers, I pressed her curvy body into the seat, reveling the feel of my hips thrusting against her. Her breathless little moans and cries were driving me fucking insane. I honestly couldn't think of anything except the driving urge I had to be inside her.

Deciding I was already thoroughly fucked, I slipped my hands under her shirt, desperate to feel her everywhere.

"God, Kyle, yes…"Lee cried out softly as she bucked her hips against me, driving me forward with her moans of encouragement. "Please…god, yes…"

Fuck.

Call it insanity, but I *had* to taste her. Losing all self-restraint, I tore my lips from hers and slipped my head under her shirt, too aroused to care when I heard the sound of her breath hitch in her throat. She wanted me and I wanted her. That was the only thing I knew at that moment. Drunk off desire, I pulled at the lace cups of her bra, groaning when her full breasts stroked against my face. Harder than I'd ever been in my life, I latched my mouth around her pebbled nipple, suckling deeply, as I slipped my free hand between her legs. Stroking her over her jeans, I flicked my tongue over her nipple, rocking my body against hers, and drowning in her moans.

"Kyle, yes…"

"Mmm, Kyle…"

"Uh, Kyle…"

"Kyle, get the fuck up, man!"

Wait… *what?*

Freezing at the sound of Derek's voice, I blinked rapidly, suddenly realizing that it was a lot brighter under this shirt than what it had been when I first ducked under. With great effort, I pulled my head out from under Lee's shirt and looked up to see the lights had come on.

"Dude, you're in a movie theater," Derek said in a mocking tone as he grinned down at me. "Show some restraint."

LEE

I couldn't look Cam in the eye.

She was *furious*.

I couldn't look Derek in the eye.

He was *laughing* at me.

I couldn't look Kyle in the eye…because he ran off.

"What the hell was that?" Cam demanded when she eventually calmed down enough to talk to me. "Lee?"

"I don't know," I strangled out, and I honestly didn't. One minute Kyle and I were getting along, and the next I was on my back, with his tongue in my mouth and his hands on my body.

When the lights came on, Kyle had quite literally *jumped* off me, muttered something about being sorry, and then bolted without so much as a backwards glance.

Cringing in shame, I leaned further into the passenger seat of Cam's Ford Focus, wishing there was a secret button I could press that ejected me from this car and, with any luck, this life.

"Well, you sounded as if you sure as hell knew," she huffed as she indicated onto a street I was finally familiar with; thirteenth street.

Thank God!

I needed to get away from Cam and spend some time working on these feelings. I needed to figure out what the hell happened back there.

What were you thinking Lee…?

"What were you thinking, Lee?" Cam asked, voicing my thoughts aloud. "Haven't I told you – no, haven't I *warned* you not to go there with him? You are *not* cut out to be with a guy like Kyle Carter."

"Don't you think I know that, Cam?" My voice was barely a whisper. Her words hurt because I knew she was telling the truth. "Don't you think I know that I'm not good enough for him?"

Cam frowned as she pulled into the driveway and killed the engine. "Wait, Lee – no! I didn't mean that *you weren't –*"

"I know what you meant, Camryn, and I know that I can't compete with girls like Rachel Grayson. I'm plain-looking and have too much hips and thighs. I have little education and even less money. I'm a small-town girl with no mama and a two-bit drunk for a daddy. I know I don't have the pedigree and I don't care about that. What I do care about is the fact that my *best friend*–my *only* friend in the whole world – would count all that against me."

Inhaling sharply, Cam swung around to face me. "Firstly, I do not think – nor have I ever *thought* – any of those things about you, and if you ever suggest so again, I'm going to be really pissed." She grabbed my hand and squeezed it gently. "You are a good person, Lee. That's what I meant when I said you weren't cut out for Kyle. You are *too good* for him. I love Kyle like he's my own brother, but babe, he is *never* going to be good enough to have your heart. And that's where this is going, Lee-Bee. I can see it. It's written all over that pretty face of yours."

What was she saying?

Did she think?

How could she know?

"Kyle has issues," Cam continued. "I'm not sure what they are exactly, but I know they have something to do with Rachel Grayson." I already guessed that. "He doesn't talk about it, but I know the girl has something on him, something big. There is no other possible reason why he would tolerate her."

"What do you think is going on with them?" I couldn't help but ask.

"Who knows?" Cam shifted in her seat. "He was different when we were younger – he was fun and easy-going, and he didn't have that nasty temper. He was seeing Rachel back then, too, but it wasn't anything serious for either of them." She paused and fiddled nervously with the hem of her sweater. "Anyway, during winter break of our sophomore year, Kyle's grandfather died. He was visiting him in Denver when it happened. He called Derek to let us know, but he never came back to The Hill over the holidays. He was gone for *weeks*, Lee. It was like he had vanished into thin air." She frowned deeply before adding, "And when he finally did come back, he was…*different*."

"Different?"

She nodded. "He wasn't the same Kyle."

I didn't get it. "So, you're saying Kyle changed when his grandpa died?"

Cam released a pained sigh. "I really don't know what I'm trying to say here, Lee. One minute he was the same old Kyle we knew and loved, and then the next he was…empty. Void. Numb. Gone. Something happened to him – something more than just the grief of his grandfather dying." She let out a long breath. "And he's been Rachel's lapdog ever since."

"Lapdog?"

"Uh-huh." She nodded. "He does everything she says. Rachel snaps her fingers, tells Kyle to jump, and the boy jumps. He doesn't even ask how high. He just fucking jumps. I don't understand it, and I don't want you getting dragged into their drama. "

I tried to piece the puzzle together in my own head, but all the information Cam had given me was swirling around and not making much sense. "I'm so confused," I finally admitted.

"It's okay to be confused," Cam offered kindly. "We all are. But you need to stay away from him, Lee," she said softly. "He'll hurt you. He won't mean to, but if you don't steer clear, he'll end up hurting you real bad, babe. "

Inhaling a steadying breath, I forced the words, "Cam, you have nothing to worry about," out of my mouth. Forcing a fake smile, I added, "From the look of horror on his face back there, he won't be touching me again." Having said that, I pulled my hand free from hers and climbed out of the car.

"Where are you going, Lee?" Cam called after me as I hurried into the house. "We need to finish talking about this–"

Ignoring her, I kept walking, moving for the staircase at top speed.

I couldn't talk about it.

I couldn't think about it.
I needed the world to stop and let me off.

FOURTEEN

BITCH SLAPS AND BAD VIBES

KYLE

MY PHONE WAS RINGING on my nightstand. I didn't need to look at the screen to know who was calling me.

She knows.

Pulling the covers over my head, I prayed for sleep to take me, even though I knew it wouldn't. I hadn't slept a wink last night. My conscience kept me tossing and turning all damn night. Every time I closed my eyes, the image of Lee's hurt face filled my mind. Running out on her last night was one of the shittiest things I'd ever done. It was my piss poor attempt at protecting her. The hurt look on her face... Jesus, I didn't think my opinion of myself could get any lower. I was *wrong*.

My phone rang again, just as loudly and as obnoxiously as before.

It won't be long now...

The loud hammering on the front door – not to mention the familiar female voice screaming my name – signaled that time was up.

She's here.

"Goddammit." Throwing the covers off my body, I trudged

downstairs, in no hurry to deal with her crazy ass, but knowing that if I didn't, she'd only get louder.

Inhaling a calming breath, I pulled open the door, stepping aside as she stalked inside, hissing, "You fucking bastard," as she went.

I rolled my eyes and muttered, "hello to you, too, Rachel," before closing the door behind her and leaning against it.

"I heard about your little date night at the movies," Rachel hissed as she glared up at me.

"Yeah." I nodded and her eyes darkened. Christ, what did she want me to do, lie to her? There was no fucking point.

"Did you have fun?"

I shrugged. "I had a great time."

Her face reddened. "You no good sack of shit. The one girl I tell you not to touch and you maul her!" She slammed her index finger against my chest. "In public, no less."

"What do you want me to say, Rachel? That I don't want any other girl but you?" I asked, moving away from the door – and the crazy redhead. I couldn't stand still anymore. I needed to move, to run, to breathe, dammit!

"Yes," she snapped, moving into my personal space once more. "That's exactly what I want you to say."

"You'll never hear those words from my mouth," I replied flatly. "Not in a million years."

"Kyle!"

"I'm serious," I shot back. "If it wasn't for the accident, I wouldn't have you inside my fucking door, and you know it."

"What are you trying to say?" Rachel demanded.

"Do you want me to spell it out?" I countered. "I'm saying that you *trapped* me."

I knew the slap was coming long before her hand connected with my cheek. It was a usual occurrence. "Do you think you deserve to be happy?" she demanded, pushing and shoving at my chest. Again, nothing new there. The girl loved her fists. "You know what that accident cost me."

Yeah, I knew and that's why I was standing here, putting up with this *shit* from her.

"You're a fucking waste of fresh air, Kyle Carter," she continued, pushing at me. "You should have died that night."

I couldn't have agreed more with her. It would have been a helluva easier to have died in that car crash than deal with the consequences of my actions, and live this fucking empty life.

LEE

Trembling from head to toe, I remained motionless in the living room until I heard the front door slam shut. I took that as a sign Rachel had left and released a breath I felt like I had been holding in for an eternity.

I'd been in here cleaning when Rachel barged in earlier, screaming and shouting at Kyle. They had a massive fight – *over me*. She knew about last night. About us hooking up at the movies. Someone obviously told her and she was *furious.*

I cringed thinking of the horrible things she said to Kyle, however my urge to run out to the hall and protect him had disintegrated the instant I heard the sharp crack of flesh hitting against flesh.

I knew that sound well.

I had felt it often enough.

Panicking, I sat on the couch, focusing on my breathing, while trying to ignore the survival instinct inside of my gut that was screaming at me to *run.*

Go, Lee.

What are you waiting for?

Get out of here!

It's not safe…

The door flew open and Kyle appeared in the doorway, causing my racing thoughts to fly right out of my head at the sight of him.

"Lee?" His eyes widened in surprise when he noticed me sitting on the couch. "Were you listening to that?"

His red and puffy cheek was proof as to who had received the slap I had heard being bestowed. A moment of relief surged through me, followed swiftly by an even greater feeling of anguish. I was on my feet and in front of Kyle within seconds. "Are you okay?" Trembling, I reached up and stroked his cheek, wincing when I felt the heat emanate from his skin. She got him good. "Did she hurt you?" I demanded, voice shaking. "Are you sore?" I could feel the tears trickling down my cheeks, and I couldn't stop them. "You're not any of those names she called you," I hurried to add. "Don't listen to her, okay?" The dark side of me was relieved – relieved that it hadn't been Kyle. That he didn't hit…*women*. Thinking this wasn't the reason I was crying. It was the reason I couldn't *stop*. I was a terrible person.

"Why are you crying?" Kyle asked, looking confused.

"Because she hurt you," I choked out, sniffling. "And said all those terrible things to you."

"So, you're… *crying*?" He looked genuinely perplexed. "For me?"

Sniffling, I nodded up at him. "Of course I'm crying for you."

"Hell, Lee, don't do that." Sighing heavily, Kyle clasped my face in his hands and looked down at me. "It's fine." His face was etched with concern. "I'm good. See? It's all good."

"You're bruised."

"I'm big enough to take it," he chuckled softly, stroking my cheeks with his thumbs, wiping my tears away. "Relax, okay?" He pulled me against his chest and wrapped his arms around me, hugging me tightly. "Everything's fine."

Slowly, I felt my body relax against the warmth of his chest. Concentrating on the feel of the rapid beat of his heart against my ear, I managed to compose myself. "I'm fine," he continued to reassure me. "Please don't cry for me, Princess. I can't take it."

Shivering, I pulled away from him and walked over to the couch. Sinking down slowly, I dropped my head in my hands as a shudder rolled through me.

Don't think about it, Lee.

Don't think about him.

"What was that?" Kyle finally asked when the silence grew thick around us.

"I don't like violence," was all I could say as I leaned forward and rested my elbows on my jean clad knees. I could hardly tell Kyle about the turbulent emotions whizzing through me, all of which were directed towards him. I couldn't tell him about...

"Are you sure that's all it was?" he asked, blue eyes watching me carefully. "Because I'm gonna be honest with you here, Lee; your reaction was scary."

Oh great. I freaked him out. "I'm sorry." I faked a smile. "I didn't mean to scare you. I just...I really do *not* like violence." I shrugged, feeling helpless. "And I don't like knowing that she hits you because of *me*."

Kyle let out a pained sigh. "That wasn't your fault. Rachel doesn't need much of an excuse to fly off the handle. I'm just glad you haven't been around to witness her other outbursts." He smirked. "You would have flooded the damn house with those raindrop tears."

I knew he was trying to crack a joke, but it wasn't funny. "You mean she does that a lot to you?" I could hear the disgust dripping from my tone.

"She has a bad temper and when she loses it, she lashes out." Kyle shrugged as if it wasn't the huge deal it absolutely *was*. "I don't like it, but I understand it."

"What?" I could feel my body shaking as I jerked to my feet. "Why would you let her do that to you?"

Kyle laughed, but I could tell it was forced. "Have you looked at me lately, Princess? I can take a few bitch-slaps here and there."

How could he make jokes about this? "It's not a joke, Kyle," I choked out, wiping my cheeks with the back of my hand. "She shouldn't be hitting you – she shouldn't be hitting *anyone*. God, she treats you so badly, and I can't stand it. That girl needs to see someone – a therapist, or a shrink. What if she does this to someone other than you? What about when she has children –"

"Back up, Lee," Kyle barked, cutting me off. "Just back the fuck up!"

Oh, I backed up – all the way to the opposite side of the room. I could feel the anger vibrating from him and it had me on high-alert.

"Whatever psychobabble analysis you've constructed in your head about Rachel is bullshit and you can forget it," he spat, looking suddenly furious. " You don't know shit about her, and you definitely don't know shit about *me*. So keep your self-help tips and your goddamn opinions to yourself. I'm not interested in hearing anything you have to say right now." With that, Kyle stormed out of the room, slamming the door behind him.

Numb, I lowered myself to the floor and clenched my eyes shut, refusing to shed another tear over that man.

KYLE

I was a bastard. That much was obvious. Jesus, I shouldn't have gone off like that on Lee earlier. I was pissed with Rachel for slapping me again and took my frustration out on the girl who was trying to comfort me. Yeah, I was a special sort of stupid.

Hours later, and I was still cringing at the memory of Lee's terrified expression when I shouted at her.

The fuck was I thinking?

Dammit!

It was obvious Lee was nervous, but what she had said touched on something that Rachel would never have to deal with – and that, like Lee's tears, was entirely my fault. Rachel had every right to hit me. Christ, *I* would hit me if I were her.

That didn't excuse the way I treated Lee, though. She had tried to comfort me when she thought I was hurt. She'd given me one of the best nights of my life yesterday – until I went and screwed it up.

The girl was nothing but *goodness*.

I owed her an apology, and I would give her one, just as soon as I could look her in the eye again.

FIFTEEN

SHARP HEELS AND SHARPER TONGUES

LEE

I WASN'T sure whether I should go downstairs or not. I didn't know if Kyle wanted me to come down. This was his house, and I knew he was still here. I could hear him rustling around in his bedroom all afternoon after our argument, slamming closet doors, and muttering cuss words.

He joined the others downstairs a little over thirty minutes ago when the pizza guy came to the door, but I was still shuffling around my room, worrying myself into an early grave, and debating whether or not I could face Kyle Carter – and his wrath.

"Lee, come on down, girl," Cam called for the fiftieth time. "The pizza's getting cold."

There was nothing else to it; I was just going to have to face him. He would have to deal with it.

Nervous, I walked downstairs and poked my head around the living room door before entering. Cam and Derek were cuddled up on the love chair, eating each other's faces, which left only the couch to sit on. That option wasn't looking very good either, not with Kyle sitting in the center, with Rachel sprawled across his lap.

Dixon and Mo were sitting on the floor near the coffee table, so I focused on them. "Lee, you're here," Dixon smiled broadly when I stepped inside and made a beeline for the twins. "I thought I wasn't gonna be able to stop myself from eating your slice."

Ignoring the two pairs of eyes boring into me, I lowered myself onto the floor and smiled brightly. "Well, I'm here now, Dixon, so hands off." Out of the corner of my eye, I could see Kyle shift out from beneath Rachel on the couch.

"Do you want to sit?" his deep voice asked, but I didn't dare look up.

Instead, I quickly shook my head and grabbed a slice of pizza from the box. Hoping like hell that Rachel wouldn't put a beating on me, I focused on the two boys next to me. The Jones twins.

They were very much alike, but not identical. Both boys were lanky and thin. They both had brown hair, but Mo had green eyes and Dixon's were brown. Dixon had his eyebrow pierced, which distinguished them from one another even more.

Dixon nodded his head in my direction. "You're looking good, Lee. You got your eye on any man here in Boulder?"

I heard a choking noise from behind me. "You okay, bro? Do you need a drink?" Derek asked.

"No, I'm good, Derek," Kyle replied.

Oh god…

Realizing that everyone had gone quiet, waiting on my response, I prattled off something vague about concentrating on work right now.

"How's Olivia doing in Ireland?" Cam asked then, taking the heat off me, much to my relief.

"Good, I think," Moe answered quietly.

"Olivia?" I asked, curious.

"Our douche of a sister," Dixon replied with a sigh. "She ran off with an Irish dude."

My brows shot up. "Really? To Ireland?"

"Oh yeah," Dixon replied. "She's a real genius, that one. She thinks she's in *love*."

"Which is ironic considering the only thing Patrick Connolly loves is the bottle," Moe offered. "I can't believe she married the guy."

"Stop talking trash about your sister," Cam laughed. "Liv is a fun girl."

"Yeah, well now she's a *married* girl."

"Stubborn fucking girl," Dixon muttered before turning back to face me. "Our brother, Max, hit the roof when he found out."

My eyes widened. "Really?"

He nodded. "He's convinced she's going to get herself killed over there."

"Shit, Kyle," Derek chuckled. "Didn't you hook up with her during Freshman year?"

A loud sputtering noise tore from Kyle's throat. "Uh, no, I don't think so."

"Yeah, dude, I'm pretty sure you did."

"No, I'm pretty sure I didn't, Der."

Derek grinned. "I'm pretty sure you've hooked up with everyone."

"And I'm pretty sure you should drop this before I stick my foot up your ass," Kyle shot back hotly. "*Now.*"

Derek snickered. "So sensitive."

Feeling uncomfortable, I turned back to Dixon and made some small talk, desperate to distract myself from the awkward situation I had found myself in. Happy to talk about himself, Dixon continued to prattle on while I ate my slice of margarita, making it perfectly clear that he was the outgoing twin. I was also fairly certain that he was the bad twin – if such things existed. Moe was sweet and shy and *nothing* like his brother.

"I'm heading out," I heard Rachel announce. Moments later, I felt a burning pain shoot through my fingers, so searing that I visibly flinched. Hunting for the source of my pain, I glanced down at my hand to find the sharp heel of a stiletto pressing into my skin.

Stunned, I gaped up at her and paled when I found her smirking down at me. She was doing this on purpose, I quickly realized. Trying to tug my hand free was pointless. She wasn't giving an inch.

"Good night everyone," Rachel said sweetly, as she glared down at me. The look of malice in her eyes had rendered my body paralyzed. "Goodnight, princess," she mouthed before digging her heel deeper into my flesh.

I held in the scream that was bubbling in my throat, refusing to give her the satisfaction of knowing that she was hurting me.

"Bye, bitch," Cam said. "Don't let the door hit you in the ass on the way out – oh wait, never mind." She waved enthusiastically at Rachel. "Oh, and if you have some free time on your hands, maybe you could go play with traffic? Just saying…"

"Bitch," Rachel huffed. She moved her foot and I yanked my hand away. Cradling it to my stomach, I covered it with my free hand, desperate to soothe the ache. "Kyle, walk me out," Rachel snapped. "Now."

Wordlessly, Kyle rose from the couch and followed Rachel out of the living room.

"She should buy him a collar and lead," Cam growled. "And a dog tag with his name on it."

"Babe, don't," Derek chastised.

"Why? It's the truth," Cam shot back huffily. "He's her bitch and you all know it."

"You okay there, Lee?" Mo asked, eyeing me with concern.

"Me? Uh, yeah, I'm good…I'm uh –" Pausing, I quickly climbed to my feet. "I'm just really thirsty." Hurrying out of the room, I moved to the kitchen, not stopping until I was in front of the sink with the cold water running from the faucet.

Grimacing, I held my throbbing hand under the running water and sighed. Thank god Rachel was skinny; otherwise my hand could have been in a lot worse condition. I reckoned it was just bruising. My fingers stung something fierce, but I could move them, and I'd had a lot worse.

"I'm really sorry about today."

Stunned to hear him, I spun around and found Kyle standing in the kitchen doorway.

He was sorry?

He *looked* guilty.

"Me too." I turned off the faucet and wrapped my hand in a tea towel. "I interfered in your business." Concentrating on my fingers, I added, "I won't do it again."

"Did you hurt your hand or something?"

"Hmm?"

"Your hand," Kyle repeated in a sterner tone, causing me to look up at him. "Are you hurt?"

"No," I lied.

He arched a disbelieving brow and moved for me. "Then what are you doing?"

"Oh…" I glanced down at my hand and then back at him. "I'm not sure?"

Before I could say anything else, Kyle closed the space between us. Taking my hand in his, he slowly unwrapped the towel with gentle fingers. "Holy shit, Lee!" He traced my swollen flesh with his thumb. "How'd you do that?"

"I caught my hand in the door," I blurted, not daring to say a word against his precious Rachel.

"Damn." Kyle blew out a breath. He believed me. *Of course* he did. I was good at covering things up. "You need to be more careful." He trailed the pad of his thumb over my fingers, his touch featherlight and entirely welcome. "You could have snapped these."

I grimaced. Kyle didn't realize how careful I needed to be. "Thanks," I replied flatly. "I'll be sure to remember that."

He frowned and I blew out another breath. "I need to go," I croaked out, stepping around him.

"You know I'm sorry, right?" he offered, blocking my path. "Lee?" He was close. Too close. "I didn't mean to hurt you."

"You already said that," I replied, taking a step away from him and closer to the door. I needed to put some serious distance between us. Cam was right; I didn't want to get in the middle of his drama with Rachel. She was dangerous and I wasn't nearly strong enough to handle a girl like her.

"Lee – wait."

"For what?"

"Don't go."

"Why not?"

Kyle stared at me, brows furrowed deeply, and I felt naked. It was disturbing how my body reacted to something as trivial as one look from Kyle, but I was on fire, burning up.

"We're all gonna hit the club," I heard Derek call out. "Are you two in?"

"Yeah, sure," I blurted out, relieved to have a temporary escape from Kyle and his penetrating stare.

SIXTEEN

THE CLUB

KYLE

THIS WAS ALL I NEEDED; Lee in a fucking dress and Dixon chasing after her like some lovesick puppy. Granted it was one of those long dresses that girls wore during the summer, but I wanted to strangle Derek for his stupid fucking idea. I needed to go clubbing like I needed a hole in the head. Why was she even here? Lee didn't *do* clubbing. Ever. Hell, she didn't even do house parties. Her being here was messing with my head and I couldn't take my eyes off the way she moved her body around the dance floor. The girl had hips for days.

"You *need* to get a handle on this, dude."

Pissed off, I gave Derek my best death glare. "You don't know what you're talking about, Derek." Besides, this was all his fucking fault. Clubbing was his genius idea. *Goddammit!*

"We both know exactly what I'm talking about," he countered calmly. "Your infatuation with little Lee over there – " he pointed over to where she was being accosted by Dixon. "Dude, either walk away from her or do something about it. But stop sitting on the fence like a fucking girl."

"I'm not sitting on the fence," I bit out.

"Kyle, you're sitting on the fence so hard, I'm shocked you don't have splinters in your ass."

"Screw you, Der."

"I'm screwing Cam," Derek shot back with a smirk. "Who are you screwing? Rachel? Or *Lee*?"

"I'm not screwing her. I wouldn't do that to her –" Breaking off, I ran a hand through my hair and tossed another shot back my throat. "Just drop it."

"Shit," Derek chuckled. "You've caught yourself some feelings, haven't you, buddy?"

"Nope," I denied.

"Yeah," Derek laughed. "And denial is a river in Egypt, bro." Slapping my shoulder, he added, "Do whatever you want, Kyle – you always do. But bear this in mind; that girl's a keeper, and if you don't do something about it, someone else will. Is that what you want? Dixon Jones to snare her?" With that, Derek sauntered off in the direction of his girlfriend,

Feeling a steady flow of murderous venom in my veins at the thought of Dixon Jones putting his hands-on Lee, I stood up and made my way through the crowd until I was standing right behind her. Making a point of glaring at Dixon, I settled my hands on Lee's hips and tugged her against me, daring the fucker to make a move on her now.

Try it, I mentally chanted. *I fucking dare you.*

Lee staggered backwards against my chest and leaned sideways to see who had touched her. "Kyle," she whispered and I felt her body relax against mine. Her gray eyes were wide, her swollen lips tempting.

Fuck it…

Placing a possessive arm around her middle, I leaned in close and pressed my lips to her bare neck. Shivering, Lee moved to turn around to face me, but I stopped her, keeping her ass pressed to my ever-growing hard-on. "What are you doing?" she asked, voice trembling.

Fuck if I knew. I had no idea what I was doing anymore. Hell, I thought I was just warning Dixon off, but now I couldn't move away. I wanted to *keep her* and that was a terrifying thought.

Allowing myself to lose my mind in her, even if it was just for tonight, I pressed my hand to her stomach, and used my free hand to tilt her chin up. Those gray eyes locked on mine and I knew I was ruined. Repressing a shiver, I leaned in and kissed her, softly at first, but she moaned into my mouth and I lost control.

Fisting the fabric of her dress in my hand, I roughly cupped her chin in my hand and kissed her deeply, wildly, giving her everything I could in the moment.

Her small curled around my forearm, touch gentle, and I knew I was fucked.

LEE

I knew I needed to run for the hills – or, quite literally, back home to The Hill – but I couldn't move a muscle. No inner strength or resolve was strong enough to fight the pull Kyle Carter seemed to have over my body. I knew it ran deeper than physical attraction, for me, at least, but I dare not admit that tonight – not even to myself. Feelings were dangerous – especially now that his body was pressed close to mine. The lighting on the dance floor was practically nonexistent, and with the exception of the strobe lighting flashing wildly overhead, we were cloaked in darkness. I could barely see him, but I could smell him, feel him, and, oh god, I could *taste* him. *Whiskey, mint, and man...*

Losing all touch with reality, I allowed this man to continue this reckless game of cat and mouse as he kissed me deeply. Keeping my back pressed to his chest, his touch was possessive, his fingers splayed across my lower belly, as he took his fill in the form of torturous, heart-bruising kisses. It was a dominant move, letting me know who was in charge, and I couldn't find it in myself to care.

Turning in his arms, I reached up on my tip-toes and hooked an arm around his neck. Unable to stop myself, I tugged hard on his hair and Kyle growled into my mouth, his movements quickening as he ground his body against mine. And I was pliant. God forgive me, I was completely pliant for this man.

I could feel his throbbing erection digging into my belly, and right or wrong, I wanted him badly. I needed him to take this further because I wasn't sure how to. I had no freaking clue what I was doing. I was running purely on raw, primal, feminine instinct. Running my hand down his hard chest, I gripped his belt buckle with trembling fingers, praying he would get the hint. *Please hear me. See me. Please care…*

He did.

Sinking his teeth into my lower lip, Kyle growled against my mouth and it was a deep, guttural sound. His actions should have hurt, but I was too aroused to feel anything but excitement. When he released my lip, he ran his tongue over it soothingly, and I sagged against him.

"You're so fucking perfect," he whispered against my lips, eyes glazed over. "Jesus Christ, Princess."

"Do you want me?" I asked, trembling from head to toe, as I peered up at him through hooded lashes. *Please say yes. Please say you want me as badly as I want you. Please say you care…*

His pupils darkened. "I shouldn't," he confessed, as he cupped my cheeks between his hands. He looked crazed with hungered desire. "I'm not a good bet for you."

"You should," I countered bravely, taking one of his hands and placing it on the skin covering my racing heart. "And I think you are."

Shuddering, Kyle muttered a string of curse words and clenched his eyes shut. I could feel his hand tremble against my flesh. "This isn't. I'm not…You're too –" His eyes blinked open and he jerked his hands away. "Fuck," he hissed, before stalking off, leaving me standing on the dance floor. Feeling rejected, I watched him walk away from me, taking my heart with him.

Again.

SEVENTEEN

LEE

KYLE WAS AVOIDING ME. That much was obvious. It wasn't the typical *storming-out-of-a-room-whenever-he-saw-me* kind of avoidance. No, he was far too smooth for that. Instead, he chose to live life like an ostrich by putting his head in the sand. In Kyle's world, if he didn't see me, or at least if he pretended he didn't see me, then I didn't exist.

Sure, he was polite to me on the rare occasion Cam wrangled him into eating dinner with us, and he always held the door open if we were passing one another in the house, and he made a huge effort to put the toilet seat down in our shared bathroom. But that's where it ended. He never touched me or stood too close. He avoided sitting next to me like you would avoid a victim of swine flu, and he *always* excused himself from the room when we were left on our own. But the tension between Kyle and I was still there, simmering away beneath the surface. I pretended not to notice the looks he gave me when he thought I wasn't looking, or the way his eyes followed me around the room, but I'd be a liar if I said I wasn't affected.

Cam, Derek, and Kyle were all returning to college soon, which would help some with keeping out of his way. No matter how hard I tried, though, I couldn't shake the swell of jealousy that filled my heart every time I thought about it. Their opportunities were limitless, mine less so. I had some brains, but little opportunity to use them – other than reading. Even more frustrating was the thought of the worldly girls he would meet on campus. Girls like*Rachel*.

I tried not to let Kyle's standoffishness hurt me too deeply. I was busy with work and rarely at home during the day anymore. Distraction was a must nowadays, and I had Linda pile so many extra shifts on me that I shouldn't have had time to think about Kyle. I still did, though. *Constantly. Depressingly.*

I thought back to an evening two weeks ago when Kyle had come home early from one of his business trips…

It was a Thursday night and I had decided to join in a poker game. I was sitting on the floor next to Dixon Jones, listening to him attempt to teach me the rules, when Kyle strolled into the room. The moment his eyes scoped the room and landed on me, I felt a switch in his body language. Rigid and silent, he took the armchair opposite to where I was on the floor, observing the game with a look of pure thunder on his face. Scowling furiously, he declined all offers of joining us when Derek offered to deal him in. Whenever Dixon leaned too close to me, or let his hand hover on top of mine for too long, Kyle either shifted in his chair or cleared his throat. It didn't make sense, but his bad moods were stifling, so I didn't dare make eye-contact with him.

Kyle's boiling point was a little while later, when, after I won my first and only hand, Dixon leaned in and kissed my cheek. I hadn't wanted Dixon to touch me, much less kiss me, but he did, and I was too stunned to move a muscle.

Kyle wasn't.

Jerking out of his seat, he stormed out of the room, slamming the door violently behind him.

I went after him, unsure as to why I was chasing certain rejection, but I did. "Is everything okay, Kyle?" I asked when I found him in the backyard. Closing the back door behind me, I wrapped my arms around my middle and stepped into the night air.

Kyle was facing the garden wall, resting his forehead against the cool stone. The minute he heard my voice, he swung around to face me. "Is everything okay?" His eyes darkened as his frown deepened. "How

*can anything be okay with you here?" His tone was laced with disgust.
"Hmm?"*

*Stunned, I remained silent, watching him watch me with a look at
frustrated fury etched on his face.*

A beat passed.

My heart hammered harder.

*"You need to –" Breaking off before he finished, Kyle kicked over a
flowerpot and muttered something about "how I was just like the rest of
them," under his breath before stalking back inside...*

After that, life was miserable in the house. Kyle made rude,
suggestive comments whenever he had the opportunity, and I
stayed in my room more often than not. I wasn't sure why he was
so angry with me for playing poker. I could only presume that he
didn't want me mixing with his friends. For that reason, and my
fear of upsetting the man who had the potential to make me
homeless at the snap of his fingers, I didn't join in any more
poker games or go downstairs when they were throwing a party.
Instead, I kept a wide berth of Kyle Carter and his tumultuous
mood swings.

KYLE

The girl was driving me fucking insane. Seriously, it was getting out of hand. I couldn't get Lee Bennett out of my head. By day, I was plagued by inappropriate thoughts of her at the worst, and I meant *worst*, most inconvenient of times. During business meetings. During college lectures. When I was trying to eat lunch. When I was trying to handle Rachel. It was ridiculous. By night, when I was alone, I gave into my depravity and rubbed myself raw to the memory of those perfect tits, and the way she felt when she was pressed up against me.

Jesus Christ, I wanted her so bad, I could think of little else. I had lost count of the number of women I had slept with in my pathetic bid to get Lee Bennett out of my head. It didn't work. Nothing ever *worked*. No matter how beautiful, or glamorous, or horny these women were, every time I came it was to the mental visual of *her* face – which completely fucking defeated the purpose.

She was doing this on purpose, I decided, deliberately taunting me by flaunting herself around the house and flirting with my friends. A few weeks ago, at the club, Lee asked me if I wanted her. Was she insane? *Of course* I fucking wanted her. That was the goddamn problem. That was why I walked away from her that night. That was why I continued to stay away. I was doing this *for* her. I was trying to protect the girl, dammit! For the first time in my life, I was trying to do right by a female – *before* I ruined her beyond repair. I wished Lee would stop making it so fucking hard for me.

"Dude, where are you going?" Derek called from across the campus quad, jerking me out of my dark thoughts. "We have class in like ten minutes?"

I shook my head, feeling flustered and off kilter. I was supposed to be prepping for class and instead I was lost on Lee again. "I have work to sort out," I called over my shoulder. Lies. My schedule was cleared for school. I *always made* school a priority. *Not today, apparently.* "I'll catch up with you later." I needed to breathe. To find somewhere or something that could give me a reprieve from my thoughts. *From my roommate.*

This semester was going to be harder than normal. Last year, I'd managed work and school, kept my grades up and the business thriving without too many glitches along the way, but Lee was throwing a spanner in the works, and my thought process was all over the place. Knowing the weight of responsibility that I now had resting on my shoulders, and the countless employees depending on me to cut them a check every week, should have given me the grounding I needed to get my head out of my ass and concentrate on finishing school, but knowing she was at home made it fucking impossible.

I was so goddamn screwed.

EIGHTEEN

LEE

DESPERATE TO GET out from under my roommates' feet, not to mention Cam and Derek's overly zealous PDAs, I left home extra early today, deciding on getting a head start on my work chores at the hotel. Two months had passed since Linda first hired me and I found myself settling into a comfortable work routine.

Every day I clocked in, checked the room Rota, grabbed my cleaning cart, and set off in the staff elevator. I liked to start on the top floor and work my way down the list. I was scrubbing the skirting boards in the third-floor corridor when Linda's voice sounded from behind me.

"There you are," she said, sounding slightly breathless, as she rushed towards me.

Startled, I looked up from my hands and knees position on the floor. "Uh, hey?"

"The boss wants you in his office ASAP." She pulled me up and started loading my clothes and spray onto my trolley. "I'll get this cleared away, but you better get downstairs. He's in a foul mood today."

Anxious, I stood and straightened my pinafore. "Is there

something wrong?" Linda never asked me to do anything besides work my cleaning route. "Am I in… some sort of trouble?"

"Yes and no." Guilt flashed in her eyes. "I went over the boss man's head when I hired you." She grimaced. "He usually does the hiring and the firing."

"Firing?" I swallowed down a gulp of air as my hands fluttered to my chest. "Oh god –"

"Oh, don't worry, Hun," Linda coaxed, offering me a smile that didn't quite reach her eyes. "He's not the worst of them. He just… Well, he didn't realize I hired someone so young."

"Because of the trouble?" I blurted out, remembering what Mike had told me once. "I wouldn't do that, Linda," I hurried to add. "Not ever!"

"I know," she agreed, patting my arm. "And once he meets you, he'll see what a responsible, steady-headed and capable young lady you are." She forced a smile. "Now, go on and don't keep him waiting." She gave me a little shove towards the elevator. "We'll talk later."

"Yeah," I blew out a trembling breath and ambled towards the awaiting elevator. "I hope."

KYLE

KYLE

I was bristling with tension. Goddamn Linda and her need to save all the strays. I'd told the woman time and again that I wasn't hiring any more kids, and what did she do? Hire a teenager. The deadliest type of teenager; a fucking teenage *girl*.

Reaching across my desk, I grabbed the envelope that contained the more-than-generous check I had written out, and waited impatiently. It would soften the blow of being let go. Either way, I didn't care. I had a hotel chain to protect and Linda really should have known by now that young girls didn't work out here. I thought of the last disaster we had that involved a minor member of the staff and cringed. Jesus, I had to call in some major PR companies to cover up that shit heap of drama.

There was a small knock on the door and I inhaled a steadying breath. "Come in," I called out, keeping my back to the door as I stared blindly out the floor to ceiling window that looked out onto the city. Jesus, I hated firing people. It wasn't something I enjoyed or relished doing but it had to be done. After Mindy Simmons and her scandalous affair with a certain guest and politician, I wasn't going to have another young girl drag my grandfather's name through the gutter. Hell no, I was never going to be incriminated in that type of farce again.

Fucking women.

I heard the door creak open and then quickly close again, but

I didn't turn around. I didn't want to look at this girl Linda was so obviously fond of in the eyes. Linda had spoken up for this Delia kid. Apparently, the girl was doing a fantastic job in house-keeping and had yet to make a mistake, but I couldn't risk it.

"I'm sorry to call you in here like this, Delia," I began, keeping my tone neutral. "But I'm afraid I have some unfortunate news." I rolled my eyes at the shit that was pouring from my mouth. "Your services will no longer be required. Your employment with the Henderson Hotel chain is over." Clearing my throat, I muttered, "Effective immediately."

Her breath hitched in her throat and then I heard the distinct sound of a female sniffling.

Girl tears.

Fuck, I needed a drink.

"I have enclosed a severance check for your inconvenience," I added, wincing. Making young girls cry was *not something* I was proud of. "You'll find that I have been more than generous." *Blah, blah, fucking blah.* "I hope it will tide you over until you gain employment elsewhere."

More sniffling.

More silence.

Agitated, I spun around with the intention of mollifying this girl, only to have my breath catch in my throat when my eyes landed on *her?*

"*Lee?*" I choked out, completely taken aback.

"*Kyle?*" she strangled out, looking as stunned as I felt.

"What are you –" My words broke off and I shook my head. "I don't –"

"I'm getting fired?" Tears rolled down her cheeks as she leaned against my closed office door. "Did I do something wrong?"

Fuck.

"Lee," I repeated, totally confused by her being here – and totally turned on by the way she looked in that uniform. Unable to stop myself, I walked right up to her. "I thought your name was *Lee?*"

"It is." Craning her neck, she looked up at me, her pale gray eyes wild with fear. "I mean, it's what people call me. My full name is Delia." She twisted her hands together nervously. "Lee is a nickname that stuck." She shrugged limply. "I prefer it to Delia."

Well shit. Wasn't irony a cruel, fickle bitch?

"Christ." Releasing a harsh breath, I pulled at my tie, desperate to loosen it and find air. It seemed to be in short supply whenever she was around. How the fuck was this happening to me? Why did bad things *always* happen to me? It was torture enough to stay away from her at the house, but now she was in my goddamn office, dressed like *that*.

"Wait –" My eyes narrowed as a sudden bolt of realization dawned on me. "Did you know I owned this place?" I stiffened. "Did Cam tell you? Is that it? Huh? Did you think you'd get a job here just because you live with the boss?" Feeling furious and worse, oddly disarmed, I shook her shoulder to make her look at me. "What the fuck kind of game are you playing with me?" I demanded. "Did some little bird tell you that I was a good cash cow? Was that your plan? Move in with me, get your feet well and truly under my goddamn table, and then fuck with my head?"

"What are you *talking* about?" Lee strangled out, flinching away from my touch.

"Answer the goddamn question," I growled, respectfully dropping my hands to my sides. "Did you do this on purpose?" A weird sinking feeling settled inside of me. something that felt an awful lot like hurt. "Are you trying to use me, Lee?"

"I'm not playing any game with you, I swear," she cried hoarsely. "I literally didn't even know you worked here until I walked into this office."

"I don't work here, Lee, I own here!" I shot back, voice equally as hoarse. "And I don't believe you."

I wasn't naïve enough to believe her.

I knew women. They trapped men with money – or they tried to. Was that it? Was that why she was here? Had she watched Rachel do it and thought she'd jump on the bandwagon? How convenient it was that she appeared at my house out of nowhere and now she was in my hotel as well. I stared hard at her, trying to read the lies in her expression, but only saw the truth in her eyes.

Fuck!

"Are you accusing me of something, Kyle?" she asked, hurt filling her eyes.

"I don't know, Lee," I shot back, flustered. "Are you admitting to something?"

"I don't play games." Sniffling, she placed her small hand on my forearm. "Not ever."

I watched her warily, feeling uncertain. My gaze flicked from her eyes to her hand on my skin and I held my breath.

"Whatever kind of women you are used to dealing with –" her voice was barely more than a soft whisper, "They're not me."

No, they were definitely nothing like Lee Bennett.

My shoulders loosened, tension slowly seeping out of me. "Lee, I just –"

"I'm not sure why you hate me so much," she continued in that sweet southern drawl. "But I'm not trying to trick you. I would never do that to anyone. And I don't want your money, either." She looked me right in the eyes, gray on blue, and whispered, "I'm not that girl."

"You think I hate you?" I asked gruffly.

She shrugged her small shoulders and looked away.

Was she serious?

She thought I *hated* her?

"You're wrong," I heard myself say, stepping closer. "You couldn't be more wrong, Lee." I was obsessed with her. Yeah, I was an asshole to her, but that was because it was the only way to keep her away from me. *To keep her out of harm's way.* I promised Cam I'd keep my distance and I took my promises seriously. Yeah, I had caved a few times, but I never crossed the point of no return.

"I am?" she asked, tipping her chin up to look at me.

I nodded slowly. "How did I not know this was where you worked, Princess?" Losing all self-control, I reached a hand between us and playfully fingered the collar of her dress. "How have I never seen you in *this*?"

"I got changed here at the hotel," she breathed, chest rising and falling quickly. "Please don't be mad."

Mad? I was close to losing my fucking sanity from all the watching and *not* touching. She had something over me. Something that made me lose my head. The look of desire in her eyes made me move closer until our bodies were flush together.

I knew she wanted me back. I had no doubt about it. It was obvious from the way her gaze kept flickering from my eyes to my mouth and the way her small hands knotted in the front of my shirt.

I leaned in close, my lips millimeters from hers. "You, looking at me like that –" I traced my thumb across her bottom lips and she sagged against me. This was so wrong. My balls would be nailed if Cam found out, let alone Rachel, but Lee pressed her curvy little body against me and all thought and reason flew out the window. I grabbed her ass, hoisting her into my arms. "You're gonna cause me some big problems, Princess," I added, and resigning myself to the fact that I couldn't fight this pull a second longer, I crushed my lips to hers.

My first mistake was touching her, my second was *tasting* her. I knew I was deep shit, I knew I was drowning, but when I heard Lee's sexy little moan as she wrapped her arms around my neck and kissed me back, I lost all control.

I should stop this.

I need to stop this.

She wrapped her legs around my waist as I pressed her up against the door, feeling every soft curve and angle of her beautiful body. My lips moved to her neck, my hands to the back of her dress, as a frenzied concoction of lust spiraled inside of me. Mentally thanking Linda for her ridiculous choice in employee uniforms, I lowered the zipper on Lee's pinafore.

Screw Cam. Screw Rachel. In fact, screw the whole damn world. I *needed* this. I needed to get this girl out of my system. Maybe, once I fucked her, I could get on with my life and not be so goddamn obsessed with her.

Liar.

Setting Lee down on her feet, I busied myself with getting her out of that goddamn uniform. I ripped and tugged at the front of her dress until her bare breasts were exposed to me. I sucked in a sharp breath at the sight. Jesus, she had the perfect tits. "Damn, baby, you don't wear a bra at work?"

"I can't," she whimpered, pebbled nipples straining as she breathed hard. "My uniform is so tight that it, uh, doesn't tie properly when I wear one." She bit her lip and I lost my fucking head. *Again.*

Lowering my head, I pulled one of her rosy tips into my mouth, nuzzling and lapping at her for all I was worth. She shook violently as I pinned her to the door, keeping her caged in with my hips, while I took my fill. "You like that, Princess?" I asked, tone husky. "Hmm? You like when I suck on your gorgeous tits?"

"Yes…god…" Writhing against me, Lee shivered. "Don't stop."

Harder than I'd ever been, I tore at the hem of her dress, hitching the fabric up to her waist so I could access her sweet pussy – because I just *knew* this girl would be sweet *everywhere*. Pressing my cock against her, I continued to lap and suckle her nipples, reveling in the taste of her.

Lee's hands were in my hair, encouraging me with wild, reckless tugs. I needed no further encouragement. Freeing my erection, I pushed her panties aside and rubbed the hard crown of my cock against her pussy lips. Fuck, she was so wet. "You want this?" I purred, driving myself crazy. "You want my cock inside you, Princess?"

"Kyle, I'm –" Whimpering, she nodded and crushed her lips to mine. "Please just make me –"

"Shh, baby, I've got you." Hitching her thigh around my waist, I angled our bodies and kissed her deeply. "You're gonna come so hard for me, Princess." I reared back, ready to slam myself into her, only to still when a loud knock reverberated through my ears.

I froze and gaped at Lee. The look of horror in her eyes brought me crashing down to earth with a bang.

"Shit!" I hissed, practically dropping her on the floor, as I jerked away from her. "Hold on," I barked, tone thick and gruff, as I tucked my raging hard-on away. "Goddammit to hell!"

Swinging back around, I looked at Lee and had to bite back a groan. I swear to god, she was the sexiest thing I had laid eyes on, leaning against the door of my office, with her little dress bunched around her waist, exposing her bare breasts and pink lace panties. "Kyle." She pressed her hand to her mouth, breathing hard and fast. "What do we –"

"Mr. Carter, the O Donnell party have arrived and are requesting your presence," one of my staff called out from beyond my office door. "Mr. Carter?"

Yelping, Lee jerked away from the door like it had scalded her.

"I heard you before, dammit!" I ran my hands through my hair in frustration. "Tell them I'll be with them in five." My voice sounded strained, even to my own ears. "Now, stop fucking knocking and *leave*."

The sound of footsteps retreating filled my ears and I quickly turned my back, unable to look at Lee. Every time I did, a flurry of emotions ran through me. Stalking over to my desk, I grabbed my suit jacket and shrugged it on, all the while I mentally warned myself to *get a fucking grip*. My head was swimming. What the hell did I almost do? She was my *employee*.

Unable to stop myself, I looked over my shoulder and stifled a groan when my eyes landed on Lee as she struggled with the zipper on her uniform. I let out a harsh breath and stalked over to her. "Here." Clamping one hand down on her waist, I zipped her back into a pinafore that genuinely was too small for her tits. Desperately trying to ignore the way my heart wouldn't calm the fuck down, I took a safe step back.

"Thanks," she mumbled, blushing.

"Yeah." Jaw ticking, I nodded sharply and shoved my hands into my pockets. "You should probably go back to work."

"I'm not fired?" she asked, turning to look at me. Surprise flickered in her eyes and her pink stained cheeks were fucking adorable. She looked so fragile that I wanted to wrap her in my arms and hold her.

Jesus, that was a reckless notion.

"For now," was all I replied before bolting from the room.

I had to get away from this girl.

She was *lethal* to my self-control.

LEE

Kyle was Mr. Carter.

Mr. Carter was my *boss*.

The same boss who had just ravaged me in his office.

Lord, I couldn't wrap my brain around it.

After escaping from Kyle's office, I hid in a toilet cubicle in the staff bathroom until it became blatantly clear that the person outside knocking wasn't going to go away. With a heavy sigh, I stood up, tightened my hair band to secure my ponytail, and splashed some water on my face to cool my burning cheeks. It didn't help. My face, and every inch of my body, was on fire. Bracing myself, I pushed my thoughts aside and opened the bathroom door.

"I thought it was you in here." Linda stood in front of me, worrying her lip. "Well?" She looked anxious. "How did it go?"

"Okay, I think," I whispered, slipping past her into the corridor. "Maybe?"

"You think?" She fell into step beside me as we walked towards the staff locker room. "Maybe?" she asked, confused. "What does that mean?"

"Well –" I racked my brain, trying to think of something formidable to say. "It means I'm not fired."

Her brows shot up. "He didn't fire you?"

I shook my head. "He said that my job was safe for now."

Her brows rose even higher. "Really?"

Blushing, I nodded. "He had to meet a party of guests, so we only spoke briefly." Very briefly. *Most of our conversation was carried out with our tongues.* "He was nice." *You're a terrible liar, Lee Bennett.* "Kind," I forced myself to add.

We were walking back to the staff locker area, but Linda stopped me short in the middle of the hallway and grabbed my shoulders. "Oh, Doll." She had a look of sheer amazement on her face. "How did you do it?"

"Uh." I shook my head, confused. "How did I do what?" I wanted this conversation to be over with. All I wanted to do was get my work done and see Kyle again. I needed to know where his head was at. Was it possible that he liked me the way I liked him? I thought about the way he had kissed me and couldn't help but get my hopes up.

"I think you may have cracked the stone," she murmured.

"The stone?" I raised my brow at her, but she just smiled happily and walked on.

NINETEEN

DAMAGE CONTROL

KYLE

I SAT in my truck and waited – impatiently – for Lee to finish her shift and come out of the hotel. I'd checked her schedule and knew she finished at eight. It was a quarter after. She was late. Drumming my fingers, I flicked through the channels on the radio, but I didn't hear a single song. I was too fucking nervous. Jesus, I hadn't been nervous about anything since I was a kid. What was Lee Bennett doing to me?

Making you weak, that's what!

We had to talk and I wasn't looking forward to it. Hell, I was downright dreading it. What the fuck was I supposed to say? *'Hey Lee, thanks for letting me suck your tits earlier, but I'm not interested in more?'* What a croc of shit.

Of course I was interested in more. I was interested in every single detail of her life. That's why I'd spent the last three hours in my office, snooping around in her personal life. I told myself it was for employer purposes, but that was a bullshit lie. I didn't need the piece of paper in my hands telling me every detail about her to know that I was crossing lines.

I wasn't sure what I was looking for when I checked up on her, but I was relieved to discover she had no criminal record, no record of drug or alcohol abuse, either. She didn't smoke and had ticked single on her employment sheet. I'd made a few calls to her high school in Montgomery and discovered that Lee had perfect school attendance for the first three and half years of high school, until she dropped out back in April, two months before senior graduation. What confused me was why a girl, with a 4.0 GPA, would drop out with two months to go. I was so engrossed in my findings that I almost didn't notice her coming out of the building.

Almost.

When her eyes landed on my truck, she halted in her tracks for several moments before slowly walking towards me. Shoving the paperwork into the glove box, I pressed a button on my console and the passenger window rolled down. Lee looked straight in the window at me and smiled shyly.

"Get in," I said, not returning her smile. "We need to talk."

Her smile faltered and my pulse sped up.

Jesus, this was going to sting like a bitch.

LEE

My heart flipped inside my chest when I saw Kyle parked outside when I came out of work. I was so prepared for my usual walk home that when I saw him there, clearly waiting on me, my stomach did a little somersault.

"Get in," he said grimly. "We need to talk."

The smile I was wearing quickly evaporated. My heart stopped flipping and sank in my rolling stomach. This was *bad*.

I opened the passenger door and climbed in. Well, I *attempted* to climb in, but to no avail. After the third attempt at trying to hoist myself into his freakishly high truck, Kyle climbed out, rounded his truck, muttered a string of curses under his breath, and then literally picked me up before depositing into the passenger seat. I couldn't fasten the complicated seat belt either, so he ended up strapping me in, much to his dismay.

"So, how was your day?" I asked, when the silence in the car became unbearable.

Kyle shifted in his seat and turned down the volume on the radio. I hadn't realized it was on. My head was in the clouds around this man. He had rolled his sleeves up to his elbows, and I was having a hard time concentrating on anything other than the light dusting of hair on his muscled forearms. *Arm porn,* Cam would call it. I didn't know a whole bunch about porn, but everything about him was beyond beautiful.

"It was –" His words broke off and he cleared his throat before trying again. "Lee, we need to talk about what's happening here." He gestured between us. "With us."

"Yeah." I agreed with that. I nodded for him to continue. "I'm listening."

Kyle sighed, but said nothing. Drumming his fingers against the steering wheel, he opened and then closed his mouth several times before blowing out a sharp breath and running his hand through his hair. "Fuck," he muttered, and I could see the turmoil in his eyes. He looked like he was at war with himself.

Deciding to keep quiet, I watched him carefully and waited for him to speak.

After what felt like an age, he finally did. "Lee, what happened back there in my office can't happen again." He looked me dead in the eyes. "It can't happen again *anywhere*."

And there it was.

He regretted it.

He regretted *me*.

I sank back in my seat, heart shriveling up in my chest.

Kyle took my silence as a means to continue torturing me. "I shouldn't have touched you," he continued. "It wasn't…right." Shaking his head, he plucked at an invisible threat on his thigh. "And I'm not good for – I *can't* let it happen again, Lee." He looked at me again, blue eyes burning holes straight through me. "Do you understand why?"

No, I didn't understand, but I didn't want to hear all of the reasons why he didn't want me, so I nodded and forced a pained smile.

"I'm not good for you, Lee," he added hoarsely. "I can't give you *more*."

"More?"

"More," he confirmed grimly. "And you're the type of girl who deserves *more*."

"I didn't ask for more," I offered weakly.

"Yeah, well, we live in the same house and now you're working for me," he snapped, sounding frustrated. "I'm sorry if I led you on, or made you think this was more than it is, but it can't happen again."

I couldn't listen anymore. I couldn't bear it. "It's okay, Kyle," I whispered, desperate to get home so I could crawl into my bed and die of the humiliation. "I understand."

Several minutes passed in tense silence before Kyle released another heavy sigh. "I'm sorry, Lee." He turned the key in the ignition and his truck roared to life. "I really am."

I merely nodded in response.

Me too.

———

The moment Kyle pulled into the driveway on Thirteenth Street, I fell out of the passenger seat, desperate to get away from him. Landing on my hands and knees, I quickly righted myself and hurried for the front door, ignoring his voice as he called my name. Just as I slid my key in the hole, the front door swung inwards.

"Lee? You're crying." Cam stood before me, clearly bewildered. "What happened?"

Barging past her, I made a beeline for my room, not stopping until I was up the staircase and safely inside. I couldn't talk to her right now. I couldn't talk to anyone. Slamming my bedroom door shut, I flung myself face down on my bed, only to jerk when it flew open again.

"Lee, what the hell is wrong with you?"

"Go away, Cam," I sobbed, covering my face with my pillow. This was humiliating enough without an audience.

I felt the mattress dip beside me. "Not until you tell me what happened?"

Sniffling, I pushed myself up on my forearms and looked over my shoulder. Cam was sitting on my bed with worry etched on her face. "Why didn't you tell me Kyle owned the hotel?" My voice cracked and I sucked in a trembling breath. "Why didn't you tell me he was my *boss*?"

Cam paled. "Who told you?"

"No one," I snapped. "I discovered that little piece of information all by myself when he called me into his office today to fire me!"

"And did he?" she demanded, tone hard. "Fire you?"

"No," I mumbled, sniffling.

"Good," she said, sounding somewhat relieved. "Because I would have killed the big douche."

"How could you not tell me?" Twisting around to face her, I

wrapped my arms around my knees and hiccupped. "How could you not tell *him*?"

"He's the boss." Cam scrunched her nose up. "It's up to Kyle to know who's working for him."

"Fine, then me, Cam!" I choked out. "Why didn't you tell *me*? That was so humiliating. You have no idea. He thought I was trying to take his freaking *money*. He practically accused me of being a gold-digger."

"That's exactly why I didn't say anything!" she shot back. "He doesn't like people knowing how much he's worth. The boy has some serious trust issues, and it wasn't my place to say anything." With a reluctant sigh, she added, "And I didn't tell douchebag because he doesn't hire anyone under 21. He had a lot of drama with some teenage employees a while back, so it's like a cardinal rule of his to never hire teens. When you told me that you got the job, I partly guessed he didn't know." She shrugged and tossed her blonde ponytail over her shoulder. "I was just trying to have your back."

That was a solid explanation.

"Oh," I mumbled, feeling bad for my overreaction. Cam always had my back. "I'm sorry for being a bitch."

She smirked. "Don't worry about it, babe. I'd be furious if my roommate pulled me into his office to fire me, too." She stood up and stretched her back out, groaning in relief when it audibly clicked back into place. "Der is an animal," she said by way of explanation. "I can't even begin to tell you how good that boy has been for my flexibility. Last night, we found this kama-sutra article online with different posit –"

"La, la, la," I blurted. "I don't want to know about your sex life with Derek."

"Well, I want to know about yours," she countered with a mischievous glint in her eyes. "Did something happen?"

"H-happen?" I croaked out. "Happen to who?"

Cam arched her brow. "With Kyle, and don't bullshit me."

"Nope." I swallowed deeply. "Nothing happened." He just gave me the time of my life in his office before ripping my heart to shreds in his car.

Her eyes narrowed. "Are you sure?"

"Yep," I squeezed out, lying through my teeth. "Quite sure."

TWENTY

PRICE TAGS

KYLE

I DIDN'T SEE Lee around much after our talk. Well, *my* talk. She hadn't said more than a few words. It was safe to say that I had fucked up monumentally. I'd hurt her badly enough that she was avoiding me. The girl, who was sweeter than honey, couldn't bear to be in the same room as me and I had no one to blame but myself for the whole goddamn mess.

At home, she was noticeably absent. I did see her at work, but I respected her enough to keep my distance. I didn't want her to feel uncomfortable – something I clearly made her. I knew from Derek that Lee had been out with him and Cam. It just put proof to the pudding that I was the one she was avoiding. I should feel relief that she was steering clear of me, but instead, I just felt... *empty*.

Lately, Linda had her working extra shifts, waitressing in the main-floor restaurant. I wanted to tell Linda to fuck off and keep Lee upstairs out of harm's way – and out of view of all the bastards who ogled her. If I was being really honest, I also wanted to rip the tight, little black server skirt and white blouse off her curvy body and do the worst kinds of things to her, but I couldn't do a damn thing. My balls were nailed to a Rachel owned wall.

Linda was already suspicious as to why I kept Lee on instead of firing her as I originally planned – as everyone expected me to. I couldn't be pissed with Linda for being suspicious. The woman had razor sharp intuition and she knew my ass better than anyone. She was on to me and this time, she was dead on the money.

I never could hide much from Linda, not even when she showed up at the McMullen Center with my grandfather to take me away from my millionth and final foster home. I'd been a lonely twelve-year-old kid with a dirty mouth and an even worse attitude, furious with the world and everyone in it. I'd never told anyone – because, frankly, it made me sound like a pussy–but I honestly thought Linda was an angel that day. An angel sent down from heaven to take me away from the hellhole I'd been thrown into. She helped my grandfather raise me…well, truth be told, the woman had practically raised me herself, and I hadn't made it easy. I was pretty fucked up back then. The poster boy for kids with chips on their shoulders. Mistrustful, wary, angry, bitter, unruly, vengeful… I was all of those things and a lot more with it. I'd given both Linda and Frank hell for the first couple of years.

Frank Henderson was all right for an old guy; smart and shrewd, but he never had the slightest clue of what to do with a pissed off teenage boy who was angry at the world. I still wondered what the hell he'd been thinking when he came to claim me. Don't get me wrong, I was grateful, *really* fucking grateful to get out of the system, but I could never understand his reasons for doing it. I mean, why bother? The old man uprooted his whole life–and his hotel manager's life –to play mommies and daddies with me. I understood even less the day I walked into his lawyer's office and was handed the deeds to his business.

Twenty hotels and countless more properties, investments, shares, not to mention money. A shit ton of dirty, old money all thrust into the pockets of his bastard grandson who'd barely made it out of the system in one piece.

Everything Frank Henderson had worked his whole life for, he had entrusted to me. He'd been a proud man and yeah, we got along when he was alive, but sometimes I wondered if I ever really knew the man. Linda said that was exactly how Frank had felt about me. That he never really knew the boy beneath the stone wall I kept up around me.

Since Frank's passing, Linda was all I had left in the world that I could call family. Sure, I had blood relatives in the form of my father, his wife, and their son, but I'd rather chew my own fucking arm off than associate with them. I could barely tolerate those pretentious pricks and felt no remorse for feeling that way. My *father* didn't deserve my remorse. He didn't deserve a damn thing from me. And the only feelings I had for him were of pure hatred. Hatred for knocking up a sixteen-year-old girl with a fondness for white powder, and for walking away without care for the repercussions.

I was one big beating heart of a repercussion.

It was no wonder that I was such a prick. Having a cold-hearted whore for a father didn't exactly bring out warmth and fuzziness in a guy. I was an asshole for pushing Lee away, though – for being the reason she locked herself away in her room as soon as she came home from work every night.

I guess the apple never falls too far from the tree.

It's better this way, I thought dejectedly, *this way, she can't get hurt*. Because as much of a heartless prick as I was, I never wanted to hurt the girl. I didn't want to be the one responsible for the pain in those gray eyes. Or worse, *disappointment*.

My phone rang and I answered it without checking the screen.

"Hey, handsome," she said in her usual fake, sultry tone. It sounded like someone was scraping their nails down a chalkboard when she spoke. "Miss me much?"

Depressed, I leaned back in my chair, shifting my feet to rest on my desk and reminded myself to check my fucking caller ID in the future. "What do you want, Rachel?"

"I'm in the foyer. I thought we could have lunch?"

Yeah right. Having lunch with Rachel meant she was looking for something. And that something usually came with a big fat price tag.

"Grab a seat in the restaurant," I muttered, dejected. "I'll be there soon."

TWENTY-ONE

DESPERATE GIRLS AND DISAPPOINTING BOYS

LEE

"WHAT CAN I get for y'all today?" I stood with my notepad and pen in hand, braced to take their orders.

She was sneering at me.

He was staring wide-eyed and fumbling with his car keys.

Every inch of my body shook as I watched Rachel watch me. Not daring to steal another glance at Kyle, I trained my attention on the notebook in my hand and reeled off today's specials, stumbling over my words as I went. This wasn't the first time I'd endured serving Rachel. She often came here with an older, well-dressed, dark-haired man, who I presumed was in his late-forties, with razor sharp blue eyes and an even sharper tongue than his companion. This was, however, the first time that I had to serve her and Kyle together. *As a couple.*

"How's your hand, little girl?" Rachel asked once I was finished listing off the specials.

"I, uh…" I let my words trail off, too taken aback by the situation I found myself in to form a coherent sentence. "Would y'all like some drinks?" I didn't dare make eye contact with the evil redhead. She really didn't like me. It didn't take a genius to figure that much out.

When she didn't respond, I reluctantly turned my attention to Kyle. It was the first time I'd faced him since the office incident and I was shaking in my second-hand pumps. "Can I get you something, Mr. Carter?"

He at least had the decency to look embarrassed. "I'll have a milkshake, Lee."

"What flavor?"

"Strawberry, please."

I nodded and scribbled his order down, desperate to get away before I burst into flames of shame.

"*Lee*? That's her name?"

Rachel clicked her fingers against the table and I forced myself to look at her with as much of a smile that I could muster. "That's right. Now, would you like anything before I take this order in?"

"What kind of a name is that for a girl?" she continued, arching a brow.

"It's short for Delia." I cringed, my face glowing with embarrassment. "It was my mama's name." I forced another smile. "I was named after her."

She smirked cruelly. "Well then, your *mama's* name is disgusting."

The pen fell from my hands as I struggled to reign in my temper. That bitch crossed the line bringing up my mother. "Excuse me?" I spluttered.

"You heard me," she replied sweetly.

"Back off, Rach," I heard Kyle say quietly, which only made my eyes fill with tears. Why did he have to be involved with such evil? "Just leave her alone, okay?"

Dumbfounded, I just stared at her, wondering how so much evil could be contained in such beautiful packaging.

"My boyfriend gave you an order," she continued, clicking her nails on the table. "I know you're a little slow on the uptake, hick, but when a customer asks you to get them something, *you get it.*"

"Goddammit, I told you to leave it," Kyle growled, looking mortified. "Lee, I'm so –"

"Don't talk to her," Rachel snapped.

"Are you okay, Lee?" Mike asked as he bent down and handed me my pen. I shook my head and he placed his hand on my shoulder. "Why don't you go take your break?" He offered me a warm smile. "I'll serve these two."

I nodded, grateful for the escape.

Thrusting my notepad at Mike, I spun on my heels and rushed for the door.

"Lee, wait up!"

I could hear Kyle calling my name, but I was too embarrassed to stop.

I needed out.

KYLE

"Keep your bitch on a leash, Carter," Mike snarled as he glowered at us. "Lee doesn't need your skanky girlfriend in her face."

I was up and in his face in seconds. "And what would you know about her?"

"A lot more than you think." Mike sneered at me and I wanted to stick my fist down his throat. "We're friends."

"*Friends*?" I hadn't realized Lee and Mike were *friendly*. The thought alone made my blood run cold. "Since when?"

"Like I said before, keep your bitch on a leash," he replied, not answering my question, knowing full well his response would rile me up.

"Don't even think about going there," I warned, barely restraining myself from rearranging his smug as fuck face.

"Or what?" he taunted, not backing down.

"Oh boys, are you fighting over me again?" Rachel laughed. "I thought we did that already?"

"Don't start," I warned, glaring down at her. She was *enjoying* this.

"Don't tell me what to do," she shot back with a glower.

"Why don't you get back in your coffin, Rachel," Mike snapped.

"Fuck you, Mike," she hissed back, jerking to her feet, and I could feel her anger wafting off her in waves. "I wouldn't talk to me like that if I were you."

"I've already done that, sweetheart, and it wasn't that memorable," he drawled. "And I'll talk to whores any goddamn way I please."

Looking furious, Rachel stormed past the both of us.

"Stay away from her," I warned, turning my attention back to him.

"Who – Rachel?" Mike smiled darkly. "You can keep her."

He turned and headed back to the kitchen.

"That's not who I meant," I shouted after him.

He turned around and grinned at me, his brown eyes full of malice. "I know."

TWENTY-TWO

I'LL THINK ABOUT IT

LEE

I WAS an emotional wreck by the end of my shift, Exhausted and drained. I finished stacking the chairs on top of the tables with a heavy heart and a serious lack of hope. Thank god I was on morning shifts for the rest of the week. These late-night shifts had me beat. Picking up the mop bucket, I headed out back to empty it down the drain, only to pause outside Linda's well-lit office.

Huh, I thought everyone had left?

Tapping lightly on the frame, I poked my head around the door to check she hadn't accidentally left her light on, only to find Linda sitting at her desk. She looked as exhausted as I felt. Mike was sitting on a chair opposite her, with his foot propped on the desk. They had been speaking in low, hushed voices but both stopped when they noticed me in the doorway.

"I'm going to head home now," I told her. "If that's okay?"

"Of course." Standing up, she broke into a fit of wheezing before clearing her throat and smiling. "Thanks again for covering all these extra shifts, Doll."

"Anytime." I smiled and turned to leave but Linda called me back.

"I heard about what happened earlier."

"You did?" I shot Mike a look.

He shrugged apologetically.

"I'm sorry that happened to you," Linda continued. "That Rachel is a piece of work. I'll put you back on housekeeping for the rest of the week."

"I'm still scheduled for the morning shift tomorrow though, right?" I asked, worried at the thought of loss of earnings. I needed money because I needed to get out of The Hill as fast as possible.

"Yes, Doll," Linda said with a smile.

"Great. Thank you." I breathed a sigh of relief. "I'll see you both in the morning."

I was exiting the hotel from the staff entrance when Mike stopped me. "Is somebody collecting you tonight?" he asked, blocking my path. "Or can I give you a ride?"

"Um…" We ate lunch together every day, but I didn't know Mike well enough to take a ride from him. "My friend Cam is waiting on me," I lied.

His face fell. "Oh, that's too bad," he said, recovering quickly. "I thought we could have dinner." Smiling, he stepped closer. "Maybe grab a movie?"

"A movie?" Wait, was Mike asking me out? "You barely know me?"

Smooth, Lee.

Mike grinned that big, white smile of his. "Maybe I *want* to know you."

"Um…" Mike had a great smile, but I didn't feel anything when he smiled at me – nothing compared to what I felt when Kyle did. *Not that Kyle smiled at me very often.* "I'll think about it." Offering him a weak smile, I waved him off and hurried away. "Goodnight, Mike."

Yeah, that was not going to happen anytime soon.

I didn't need any more complications in my life.

KYLE

"Come on, Kyle. It'll be fun," Cam groaned as she pulled on her coat, covering up the barely-there scrap of a dress she was wearing. It was Friday night and that usually meant hitting up a few bars and a club in town. I wasn't feeling it tonight. *I was too full of shame.* "You do remember the meaning of fun, don't you, old man?"

"Ha-ha," I deadpanned.

She clapped her hands mockingly. "Very good," she praised in a sarcastic tone of voice. "Fun starts with laughter."

Jesus, she was a wise ass.

"Go on without me," I told her. "I'm just gonna crash early."

Cam frowned. "I swear you are sounding more like Lee by the minute."

I forced a laugh, but my chest was aching. I fucked up big time today. I sat back and let Rachel talk to Lee as if she was a piece of shit off the street. I should have done something. Instead, I did nothing. I owed the girl a super-sized apology, with a side order of groveling. And I would give that to her – if I could get her to talk to me again.

TWENTY-THREE

LEE

AFTER ESCAPING MIKE, I picked up a large cheese pizza from a 24-hour deli, holding it close to my chest on my thirty-minute walk home to Thirteenth Street. It was past 11pm when I finally reached our front door, bone tired and famished.

Letting myself inside, I tossed my purse in the hall and kicked off my sneakers. Friday night was the biggest party night in my roommates' lives, so I knew the house would be empty. No one was ever here on a Friday night – except for me. Grateful for some alone time, I grabbed a bottle of water from the fridge and trudged into the living room with every intention of eating myself into a pizza-coma in front of the television.

Finding Kyle sprawled out on the couch was *not* something I had anticipated, or was thrilled about. I was still really upset about what happened earlier. For several moments, I debated turning around and running upstairs, but I forced my feet to move forward. I was going to have to get used to being around him. He was my roommate after all. *And my boss.*I could be cordial.

"Hey," he croaked out, pulling himself up to make room for

me to sit down, when I stepped inside. "You're late tonight." His eyelids were heavy. I had woken him up. "Are you okay?"

"Yeah, I know." I took a tentative seat on the couch, as far away as I could from him, still clutching my pizza and water. "I just finished my shift," I heard myself explain. "Linda had me cover Theresa's shift."

"Again?" he asked, stretching.

I nodded.

He frowned. "That's the third time this week."

Again, I nodded, surprised that he would know that.

"Linda needs to get her shit together," Kyle growled, sounding frustrated. "I'll have a word with her."

"Please don't," I begged, grabbing ahold of his arm in alarm. "I like Linda and she's good to me. I don't want her to be upset with me."

"She's working you too hard," he replied, unyielding.

"I asked her to," I countered.

"Hmm."

"Please?"

"Fine." Exhaling a sigh, he moved to pat my thigh but I jerked away. Cringing, he cleared his throat. "Just make sure that you say no if you're too tired, Lee." He cleared his throat again. "I don't want you getting worn out."

"Thank you." I plopped the pizza box in between us, needing a little space. "I appreciate that."

"So…" He turned the volume down on the television and ran a hand through his dark hair. "Did you walk home?"

"Huh?" I wasn't sure why he was even speaking to me. He usually ignored me. Pathetic as it sounded, I craved his company. "I always walk home."

His eyes darkened and he nodded stiffly. "Right."

"What's wrong?"

"Nothing," was his mumbled response.

"Are you…hungry?" I asked, offering him a slice of pizza — more like a peace offering.

"Are you… *sharing*?" he asked, blue eyes locked on mine.

"I'll share with you," I whispered.

He smiled and reached for a slice.

———

For the next couple of hours, Kyle and I sat side by side, gorging on pizza, and watching crummy sitcom reruns. It was strangely *nice*. It felt *right*. "So, how come you're not out tonight?" I asked between bites of reheated pizza. Licking the sauce from my fingers, I turned to look at him.

"I'm just sick of drama," he confessed, balancing a bottle of beer between his knees, as he tore into his own slice. "Honestly, I'm in dire need of a chick-free/drama-free night," he added between bites. "It's exhausting."

"Um, hello? In case it slipped your attention, I happen to have a vagina," I said as we both went for the last slice. I immediately blushed from my words.

Did I just say vagina to Kyle?

Good Lord, never in a million years would I have spoken like this back home. I could feel the heat burning my cheeks as embarrassment flooded me.

A choked noise tore from Kyle's throat as he ripped the last slice of pizza in half and handed me the bigger half. My stomach grumbled in appreciation. "I'm well aware that you have a vagina, Lee." He looked over at me, smirking, and then poked me in the ribs. "But you're different." He sighed heavily. "You're not like…you're just very different."

"Is that a *bad* thing?" I asked.

"It's a *confusing* thing," Kyle admitted quietly. He stretched his hand towards me and rubbed his thumb across my chin. "You have a little tomato sauce," he explained. "Just… here."

"Oh." I could have sworn he stuck his thumb in his mouth. I immediately looked away. "Thanks."

"No problem," he replied gruffly. "Listen, I need to apologize to you about what happened at the hotel."

I was wondering if he would bring up the restaurant incident. I hadn't because I was too afraid he would leave. God, I really was pathetic. Tucking my legs beneath me, I turned to face him and smiled. "Kyle, we're having a nice evening. We don't need to –"

"Rachel was a bitch," he blurted out. "And I was a tool. She shouldn't have spoken to you like that, and I shouldn't have let her."

Stunned, I could do nothing but nod. "O-okay?"

He frowned. "No, Lee. It's not okay. She made you cry and I

did *nothing*." He released a frustrated growl. "I should have done *something*."

Yes, he should have, but he never did. For the millionth time, I wondered why he wasted his time with Rachel. She was just plain nasty. Surely whatever was between them couldn't be worth the hassle of staying with her. Kyle could do so much better than her.

"It's okay," I finally said with a shrug. "It's not like you talk to me anymore anyway. I'm used to being ignored by you."

He flinched and I felt bad immediately. "Is that how you feel, Lee?" he asked, looking wounded. "Like I ignore you?"

Of course that's how I felt. That's what he did every time he saw me.

I nodded slowly.

"I'm sorry, Princess," he said. "I don't mean to... I don't want you to feel like that."

My heart skipped a beat when he called me *princess*. It had been a long time. "Kyle, it's okay. Honestly, I overreacted by crying," I decided to soothe him by saying. "Rachel just touched a raw nerve by bringing up my mama."

"I've never heard you talk about your mother." He leaned closer. "Why is that?"

"Um, maybe that's because I never knew her enough to talk about her." I shifted uncomfortably. "She died during childbirth." I turned back to the television. "Having me."

I heard Kyle's sharp inhale, but I kept my eyes focused on the television. "Shit," he said. "I didn't know that, Lee."

I turned to face him and smiled. "How could you?"

He shrugged, looking helpless. "I'm sorry."

"Yeah." I nodded. "Me, too." Feeling a little shaky at the mention of my mother, I jerked to my feet. "I'm thirsty. Would you like anything from the kitchen?"

"You don't serve me here, Lee," he mumbled, rubbing his jaw.

Shrugging, I went and grabbed myself another bottle of water and then took a moment to steel my nerves before returning.

"My mom's dead, too," Kyle announced when I sat back down on the couch.

My heart sank in my chest. "Wh-what?"

"My mom," he confirmed quietly. "She's dead, too."

"Oh my god, I'm sorry." Without thinking about it, I reached over and clasped his big hand in mine. Losing a mother was the worst feeling in the world for a child. To be missing that crucial element, a mother's love. "How old were you when she passed?"

"Three," he replied. "I don't remember her."

"Three is young," I offered, giving his hand a little squeeze. "I bet that was hard, huh?"

"It's weird," he mused. "I haven't spoken about her in years." He laughed humorlessly and shook his head. "I don't even remember the last time her name came up in conversation."

"What was her name?" I asked gently.

"Sarah," he mumbled. "Sarah Carter."

"That's a real nice name," I whispered.

"I guess." With another shake of his head, he muttered, "Well, I just wanted you to know that you weren't alone in the whole dead mom club."

"Um…okay?" His face looked like the subject was closed and I briefly wondered why he had brought it up if he wasn't going to discuss it further. I was desperate to change the subject, though, and keep him from leaving. "What about the dad club?" I offered, smiling. "Are you in the dead, or the deadbeat, or the –"

"Try the non-existent," he snorted.

"Oh."

"Yeah," he confirmed grimly. "Oh."

"So, are we going to try to be friends now?" I blurted out, desperate to both change the subject and find out the answer. I held out a hand for him to shake. "Are we friends, Kyle Carter?"

Kyle shook his head and smiled softly. "Yeah, Princess, we can try." He took my hand and shook it before pulling me closer, so close that I could feel his breath on my face. "But if this goes wrong, just remember that I warned you." He looked me deep in the eyes. "Remember that I tried to protect you from me."

When he released my hand and leaned back, my head was swimming. What did that mean? He tried to protect me from him?

"I'm confused," I admitted, pressing my fingers to my temples.

Kyle smirked. "I'm a confusing guy."

That he was. "You said earlier that I was different from other girls?" I shifted closer. "How am I different?" I needed to know. It really bugged me that he didn't think I was a normal girl.

Kyle sighed and turned to face me. Pulling one leg up on the couch, he let the other hang on the floor. Smiling, he drained the last of his beer before setting the bottle down. "Do we really need to have this conversation?" His smile was infectious and I felt myself mirroring his body language, relieved that we were off the topic of parents.

"We most definitely do," I replied. "My female pride is wounded." Grinning, I added, "Don't try and dodge the question, sir."

"Sir?" Laughing, he sat up straighter, resting one arm over his bent knee. His eyes were a tranquil blue. "Are you shitting me?"

"That's what everyone at work calls you." The girls at work called Kyle Carter worse names than sir – filthy, sexual names that were too vulgar to contemplate saying out loud. "And since we're on the subject of work," I said. "What's with ordering strawberry milkshakes?" He did this regularly. "Are you nine years old?"

Kyle gaped at me and I snickered. "Twenty-two," he replied. "And I'll have you know that milkshakes are a great source of calcium." He looked me up and down and winked. "Maybe you should try one sometime, little miss *I-can't-get-into-a-truck-without-a-boost.*"

"Hey –" I leaned over and playfully tugged on his shirt. "I think we both know by now that I'm vertically challenged, so quit dodging and answer my question."

Kyle reached up and pulled my hand onto his lap and played with my fingers. I didn't think he even realized he was doing it, but it felt right when he touched me. "When I say you're different, it's because you are, Lee," he said, voice soft. "Plain and simple."

"Gee, thanks, Kyle," I replied, wounded. "So I'm plain, simple, *and* a short-ass." I pulled my hand back, but he was too quick for me.

"Don't get pissy." He looked down at our joined hands and then back at me. "I meant that as a compliment." He was smiling. "You're not like any other woman I've ever met." He entwined his fingers with mine. "You're honest and kind. Shit, you're probably the only girl in the whole damn world I can say that about." Sighing, he furrowed his brows. "Lee, what you represent is the exact *opposite* of everything I hate in women."

I blew out a shaky breath. "Really?"

"Really," he confirmed. "Being around you is as easy as *breathing*. It's addictive." He exhaled deeply and smiled his half-moon smile. "Satisfied now?"

Was I satisfied with that?

I wasn't sure, but I *was* confused. He never stayed around me long enough to test his theory. Finally, I nodded, accepting his answer as the best explanation I was going to get. If I was the exact opposite of what he hated, then did that mean he... No, I wasn't going to get my hopes up. I knew enough about Kyle Carter to know that he had an incredible talent for pulling the rug out from under my feet.

Kyle gently squeezed my fingers and I lifted my gaze to his. "What?"

He smiled. "You looked lost in thought."

"I guess I'm trying to figure you out." I frowned. "You are a mystery, Kyle Carter. Every time I think I've figured you out, you reveal another layer."

He snorted and laced our fingers together once again. "Well, when you figure me out, can you tell me, because I'd love to know?"

I thought he was joking, but his expression was serious, and oddly vulnerable. I just smiled in response. I had no reply for that.

"Since we're on the topic of sharing, do you wanna tell me why you're not in college?" he asked then. "You're eighteen, Lee. You should be starting your freshman year, not bussing tables and cleaning toilets for minimum wage."

Whoa, where did that come from?

"There is no law against not going to college, Kyle." I did *not* want to go into this. I felt inferior enough as it stood, especially since I learned he was my boss as well as my landlord. I was so far down the food chain from him, I was practically scraping the barrel.

Sensing my mood, Kyle swiftly changed the subject. "When's your birthday?"

"October second." I looked at his smiling face and felt my heart speed up. "When's yours?"

"March eleventh." He grinned, the sexy dimple causing havoc to my insides. "Yours is closer. We should celebrate." He waggled his eyebrows suggestively when he said, "Maybe we could do a few *shots*?"

I stared at him open-mouthed and he laughed. I wasn't used to this version of Kyle, nor was I prepared for how much I liked this version. A lot. *Maybe even more than a lot.* "I thought we were doing the friend's thing."

"We are," he purred.

"Then no flirting," I shot back breathily.

He smirked. "Are you sure?"

No! "Friends don't flirt," I replied lamely.

"Noted," Kyle mused. "But on a serious note, you should be in college, Princess."

I clammed up inside, my body tensing at the mention of college – *again* – and pulled away from him.

"What's wrong?" he asked when I stood up. "Lee?"

"I'm just tired," I replied, offering him a small smile. "I'm going to go to bed."

"Really?"

I nodded. "Night, Kyle."

I thought I heard Kyle groan as I closed the door behind me.

KYLE

Lee rushed out of the room so fast after I mentioned the college thing that I knew I touched a nerve. The wounded puppy look on her face made me want to kick myself in the balls. Christ, I hated being the one to put that look in her eyes. *And I'd been doing so well.*

But I wanted to know why she didn't finish school. There was more to her story than met the eye and I was beyond curious.

The whole mother thing had thrown me through a loop, though. I still couldn't believe I opened up to her about my mom. I didn't talk about Mom. *Ever.* It was too fucking painful.

Frustrated, I stood up and walked upstairs. I couldn't believe I had agreed to this friendship thing. The thoughts I had of her were far from *friendly.*

I shook my head, annoyed with myself for stopping outside her bedroom door, and forced my legs to take me safely into my own damn bedroom.

Fuck it, I was going to do this whole friend deal.

I *could* be her friend.

I hoped.

———

"Mama, I'm scared." I could feel the wetness in my pants trickling down my legs, making me sore. Mama was going to be mad. I was

wearing my big boy pants. I was supposed to go pee in the potty.
"Mama, slow down."

"Everything is going to be okay, Kyle," Mama told me. She was
crying, though, and it made me sad.

Mama was driving too fast. Everyone was honking their horns at
us. I didn't like this. Nope, this was bad.

"I promise you," she added, "Where we're going, you'll never be
hungry again, my baby boy."

My belly grumbled when she talked about food. "Where we going,
Mama?" I asked, clutching the fabric of the car seat.

"I love you, Kyle, do you know that?"

"I wanna go home, Mama." My belly hurt and my pants were wet. I
continued to chew on a piece of paper, pretending it was candy. I liked
candy. It tasted so nice, and made me feel so happy. I wanted to be
happy now, but I wasn't. I was so scared and everything was moving
too fast.

It was racing…

"This is the best thing for both of us," Mama added with a sob
before increasing the speed.

The car I was sitting in lunged forward.

"Mama," I screamed, covering my eyes with my hands.

I knew what was coming next.

Pain.

Darkness

And the stench of death…

"Christ!" Gasping for air, I threw the bed covers off my body and
jerked to my feet. I took a quick glimpse at the clock on my nightstand and saw that it was a minute after four in the morning.

Fuck, that dream wrecked me.

Always did.

Breathing hard and fast, I flicked on my light and paced my
bedroom floor, shaking my wrists out, as I tried to get a handle
on myself. What the hell was wrong with me? Why was subcon-
scious fucking with me again? Slapping the heel of my hand
against my forehead, I tried to force my earliest childhood
memories out of my head and reason with myself.

A quiet knock on my bedroom door had me swinging around
and when a small head of curls poked through the crack, I gaped.
"Lee?"

"Are you okay?" she whispered, wide-eyed.

"Uh…" I scratched my bare chest. "Yeah? Why wouldn't I be?"

"Oh." She sagged in visible relief. "I heard you calling out. I thought you might be in trouble. I thought there might have been an intruder or something."

I arched my brow. "And you came to save me?"

"Well, we are friends now." Pushing the door open, she waved the hairbrush she was holding in her hand and shrugged sheepishly. "So, I was going to give it my best shot."

I smirked. "Thanks, *Lara Croft*, but I'm good."

"Who?"

"*Tomb Raider*," I filled in, waiting for the penny to drop.

Lee blinked. "Is that a book?"

Jesus. "Have you ever played video games?"

"No," she replied simply.

"Well, shit," I mused, rubbing my jaw.

She blushed. "Oh -okay. I guess I'll let you get back to, uh, pacing."

"Wait!" I called out, feeling a sudden burst of panic when she turned to leave. "Don't go."

"Why?"

Because I'm scared of being in my own head right now – I'm scared of remembering. "I'm bored," was all I could come up with. "Wanna hang out?"

Her brows shot up. "But it's bedtime?"

I snorted. "I'm pretty sure you're not on a curfew, Princess."

Her cheeks flushed a perfect shade of pink. "Right."

"So…do you want to hang out with me?"

She considered me for a long moment before smiling shyly. "Alright."

Thank Jesus.

TWENTY-FOUR

BOY FRIEND NOT BOYFRIEND

LEE

SINCE STRIKING up our friendship deal, and because Cam and Derek were a couple, I found myself spending a lot of time with Kyle when we were at home. Cam and Derek were sickeningly obsessed with one another and in a weird way, Kyle and I usually ended up pairing up together for pretty much everything. When our friends were making out, Kyle and I hung out. When they had their tongues down each other's throats at the movies, he shared popcorn and whispered back and forth. When they were screaming at one another, we cracked private jokes behind their backs. When we went out to dinner, and they slipped off to do god knows what in the bathrooms, we talked.

I think I secretly used the Cam and Derek couple card as an excuse to allow myself to be around Kyle so much. He made me feel alive and, once he lowered his guard enough to enjoy himself, he was a great guy to spend time with. I had even gotten used to being around him without drooling – well, almost. He was still the most beautiful man I had ever seen in real life. I didn't think that could ever be changed or altered.

We had even started hanging out outside the house without Cam and Derek – purely platonically, of course. He gave me a ride home from work most nights, and I tagged along with him to the library where he was a member. It was *heaven* in that library. I loved reading and hadn't had the opportunity to join a library since I arrived. I had always loved reading. It was my jam. Besides, I had never been in a library so well stocked. The library in my old high school was outdated by about thirty years.

To be fair to him, Kyle never pushed me on the subject of college since our pizza night, and had bravely faced the tufting of the elderly librarian on several occasions to check romance novels out for me until I finally got my own membership. *Girl porn*, he called them.

He was amazing and we had become friends – *close* friends. I spent most of my free time with him, and with every day that passed, I became more and more enthralled with the man behind the suit. I lived for our private talks, when he sought me out at work, or when he touched me without realizing he was doing it.

The one thing I struggled to deal with was Kyle's *women*. Every time I had a shift waitressing, he was there with a different woman and it drove me freaking crazy. I tried to be rational about the situation; Kyle owned the hotel and many of his lady friends were business clients, but that didn't stop my skin from crawling, or stop the acid in my stomach from burning my throat every damn time he was with one. I had already snapped four pencils taking their orders. Because we were friends now, Kyle always sat in my section. We even talked some during work, and there were days when he actually sought me out to tell me some ridiculous tale or other, but it wasn't easy for me to see him with other women. Some days, I wished he could read my mind and see how much him being with other women hurt me. The worst days were the ones when he brought Rachel to the hotel. Yeah, those were dark days. When Rachel was with him, Kyle sat in a different section and ignored me. On those days, I cried in the bathroom, because being ignored by Kyle Carter was about the worst feeling in my world.

"You with me, Princess?" Startling at the sound of Kyle's voice in my ear, I turned to look at him and smiled. We were sitting in his truck in the parking lot of the library and I had clearly zoned out for half the drive here.

Kyle was looking at me curiously as he unbuckled his belt. "You okay?"

"Yeah, I'm sorry. I was daydreaming."

He grinned. "About all the girly porn you're about to read?"

No, about you. Always you, Kyle.

"Funny, but no." I fiddled with the buckle on my belt, but it didn't budge. You would think from the number of times I had been in this truck, I would have mastered the art of unbuckling myself, but sadly no. The clasp was as stiff as always, and, like usual, I got muddled up with the other harness thingy attached to the seat.

"What were you thinking about?" he pressed. "Hmm?"

"Who – me?" I pulled some more at my buckle, flustered and embarrassed.

"Yeah, you." His eyes twinkled and his dimple deepened as he grinned. His closeness thrilled me and I had to tell my body to calm down.

"Oh, nothing much." I was so *not* telling Kyle that he was all I ever thought about. "Except that maybe you should get a truck with normal seat belts, and not these baby harnesses."

Kyle burst out laughing. "Baby harnesses?" He leaned over and swiftly unbuckled me. "It's called an off-road harness, baby."

I snorted to mask my pleasure at being called *baby*. "Off-road? It's a pretty jeep and all, but why don't you have a nice little car." I smiled sweetly at him. "Something girl-friendly?"

"Truck." Kyle leaned over and clasped my chin in his hand. "It's a truck, Princess. And besides –" he paused to press a kiss to the tip of my nose, "You're the only girl who rides in my baby." Releasing my chin, he slapped my thigh playfully and climbed out of the truck.

Shivering, I strived to compose as I watched Kyle round the front of his truck and move for my door. Yanking it open, he said, "And please don't call my truck *pretty*. You'll hurt her feelings."

"I'm sorry, Mr. Carter," I laughed, heat swelling inside at his close proximity. "It's the prettiest, manliest truck I've ever seen."

Kyle growled in feigned frustration and then clamped his hands around my waist. "Your sarcasm wounds me, Princess."

My breath hitched in my throat, and I had to work really hard not to give my feelings away, as he lifted me out of the passenger seat and set me on the sidewalk in one swift movement. I held in the gasp that was trying to force its way up my throat. Kyle always helped me in and out of his truck when we rode together, but every time was like the first time and having his hands on my body did strange things to my heart.

"Ready to give the old librarian a heart-attack with your taste in reading material?" he teased, taking my hand in his.

Startled, I looked down at our joined hands and bit back a smile. "I sure am."

Chuckling softly, he entwined our fingers and led me up the steps to the entrance of the library.

'Be calm, you idiot, this means nothing,' I chanted to myself as I hurried after him. I couldn't contain my excitement when we got inside.

God, I loved this place.

I loved that Kyle was the one who brought me here.

I think, when you broke it down to the bare bones of what I was feeling, I just loved my friend.

KYLE

"Oh, I love this place," Lee squealed the minute we stepped foot inside the library in Boulder. "Kyle," she breathed, squeezed my hand tightly. "I love it."

Goddammit, I was jealous of the library now.

I wanted to get that kind of reaction from her. It was a major blow to my ego when she reacted with indifference to me, but squealed with pleasure at the prospect of checking out some books.

Quickly on, I realized that Lee was a bookworm. She was quiet in crowds, was absent for parties, but the girl loved to read. I silently thanked baby Jesus for asking her to check out the library last month. At the time, I was supposed to be picking her up from work, but had to run into the office to sign some paperwork, and had asked Lee if she wanted to check out the library down the street from the hotel, rather than wait around the hotel for me.

When I pulled out my library card and handed it to her, I honestly thought I was witnessing the first orgasm from a plastic card that *didn't* hold any monetary value. It was as if I had handed the girl my credit card and told her to go wild. She *freaked* with excitement.

Stunned, I had watched her as she literally skipped down the sidewalk towards the library, holding my card like it was the crown fucking jewels.

I'd brought her back here dozens of times since, and every single time she was as excited as the first.

"Hey –" I pulled on Lee's hand, drawing her back to me, struggling with the concept of letting her go. "Calm down, geek." Brushing my thumb over her knuckles, I whispered, "You'll get your word-food soon enough."

Lee smiled up at me, her plump lips stretching to reveal that perfect, straight, white smile of hers. God bless the girl, she was the poster girl for orthodontists worldwide. Her gray eyes sparkled as she beamed up at me. My breath caught in my throat. It happened sometimes when I stared at her for too long. She was *stunning*. "Well, let's hurry," she pleaded, tugging on my hand. "I need to be filled right now."

My cock twitched the minute those words came out of her mouth.

Jesus.

Lee, innocent as the day is long, let go of my hand and darted to the closest aisle, with her ass swaying in those damn jeans as she went, completely oblivious to my raging hard on. "Kyle?" she called after me. "Are you gonna come?"

Well shit.

"Yeah." I shook my head and trailed after her. "I think I am."

TWENTY-FIVE

LEE

I ALWAYS DREADED Saturday mornings in Montgomery. After four months of living in Boulder, I could safely say that I still did– for less painful but far more embarrassing reasons. We were in *Deacon*, Cam's favorite department store at the mall. The very store she dragged me to on my first day off work *every* weekend. I hated shopping, but Cam coveted her customary Saturday splurges and always dragged me along with her.

The guys had come with us today, but had skulked off in the direction of the liquor store.

Lucky.

There was a party tonight at Dixon's and Derek and Kyle had both decided that the case of beer they planned to bring with them wasn't enough. Apparently, they were low on supplies – even though our refrigerator was crammed with beer.

Those damn traitors.

I wished I was as smooth at evading my best-friend's shopping hauls, but I wasn't much of a liar.

I was rewarded for my honesty by becoming Cam's human shopping basket and was currently holding more bras and panties than I'd owned in my whole life.

I hoped the other shoppers didn't think they were for me because I could *never* be as provocative as Miss *Victoria's Secret* in front of me. "Cam, I think there's a hole in the fabric of these panties." I held up the panties for closer inspection and blushed when recognition eventually dawned on me. "*Crotchless* panties? Really, Cam?"

"Don't knock it until you try it, Lee-Bee." She smirked as her eyes glided over the rails of dresses. "And besides, my man likes to snack."

"Ugh!" I thought I might vomit. "Please." I made a gagging noise. "Don't say another word."

"He gives *amazing* oral," she continued. "Seriously. The boy can go for *hours*."

I gaped at her. "What?"

"It's true," she replied with a shrug. "I timed him on my phone once and he was still going strong after three orgasms and a –"

"Oh my god, stop!" I hissed, mortified. "I don't want to know about you and Der's messed-up sex life."

"Fine," she conceded. "But one of these days you're going to come to me with a zillion sex-related questions and I'm going to – oh my god! Look at this dress." Yanking a tiny red dress off the rack, she held it out in front of me and whistled. "You would look fierce in this." Batting her baby blues at me, she smiled. "Try it on for me?"

"No way," I spluttered, stumbling away. "Put it back." Calling that scrap of material a dress was pushing it. It looked more like underwear. It was a short sparkly little number, red in color, with a deep plunge line. Come to think about it, we were in the lingerie section of the store so it *had* to be underwear.

"Oh, come on, Lee," she pressed, unperturbed. "It's fabulous and you'll look smoking hot wearing it tonight."

That was *never* going to happen. "If my daddy thought I was wearing clothes like that, he'd whoop me from here back to Louisiana, Camryn Frey."

Cam grinned wickedly. "It's a good thing your daddy isn't here then, isn't it?" Winking, she turned on her heels and walked towards the counter. "My treat."

"I won't wear it, Cam. I swear it. Please put it back," I choked out, practically tackling her. "Besides, I'm not even going to the party, so buying me something to wear is pointless." I tried to grab the dress from her hands, but the damn giant held it out of my reach. "Don't do this to me."

"Would you calm down," Cam laughed as she handed the dress to the girl behind the counter. "Oh, and FYI, *Princess*, you *are* going to the party tonight."

"But I –"

"No buts. I am tired of watching you hide away from your life. It's high time you got off the side-lines and jumped into the game."

That was not going to happen. "I like the sidelines."

"You'll like the game more," she assured me, pulling out her credit card. "And who knows? You might even *score*."

Dammit, she was impossible. "Hell will freeze over before I wear that, Camryn," I huffed, dumping her bras and panties on the counter. "Put it back. *Please*."

"Easy, Princess." Kyle's voice came from behind me and I automatically jumped. "You good?"

"No," I groaned, eyeing the cashier who was currently sliding my new underwear dress into a pretty pink bag.

"Did you two have a fight?" Derek teased, glancing from me to Cam with an amused expression.

Great, the guys arrived to witness my shame.

"Oh guys, maybe you can get Lee to loosen up." Cam handed her card over to the cashier, who swiped it through the machine. "She's having a coronary over a little dress shopping for the party tonight."

I glared at Cam. "*Little* being the operative word. And I told you that I'm not going."

Kyle raised his brow in surprise.

"Whatcha buy?" I could hear the humor in Derek's voice.

"Oh, baby, you're in for a treat," Cam purred back at him.

"What about you?" Kyle asked, watching me carefully.

"Nothing," I strangled out. "I didn't buy anything and I won't be wearing anything."

"Whoa, Lee, it's not that kind of party," Derek teased, covering his eyes with one hand and pretending to beat me away with the other. "We're not *nudists*."

"Ugh!" Snatching the bag from Cam before she could embarrass me any further by showing them, I clutched it to my chest protectively.

"I can't believe you actually got the Ice-Queen to buy something *other* than jeans, " Derek laughed. Scooping up half a dozen pink bags containing his girlfriend's new underwear, he slung an arm around Cam's shoulder. "I'm shocked. "

They both laughed at my expense.

"Are you guys done?" I snapped, storming off in the direction of the exit.

"Awh, come on, Ice-Queen, we were joking," I heard Derek call after me, but I was too upset to stop. I walked out straight out of the store and made my way to the entrance of the shopping mall.

"Hold up." An arm swooped around my waist, halting me in my tracks, and my heartbeat soared from his familiar touch. "Calm down." Kyle pulled me closer, keeping his chest pressed to my back as he whispered in my ear. "They're only trying to get a reaction out of you, baby."

Baby.

My heartbeat jumped clean off the Richter scale. "I'm not like that." Shivering, I turned in his arms and looked up at him. "I can't wear things like that, Kyle."

"Like what?"

"Like what Cam wears," I squeezed out.

He stared hard at me for the longest moment before exhaling a sigh. "Come on." He clutched my hand and led me outside. "I'm getting you out of here."

"What about Cam and Derek?" We all drove here together in Kyle's truck. We couldn't leave them behind.

Kyle pulled his phone out and fiddled with it for a few seconds before putting it back in his pocket. "They can get a bus, or walk. I really don't give a shit." He slung an arm around my shoulder and led me to his truck. I'm taking you for food."

When we got to his truck, Kyle opened the passenger door and pulled me closer. "I texted Derek –" he lifted me up without a second thought and I sank into the passenger seat, my heart continuing to somersault around in my chest, "So don't worry about them."

"Oh…okay?"

Rounding the hood of the truck, Kyle climbed into the driver's seat beside me. "You good now?" he asked as he buckled me in. It was routine for us now.

"Yeah," I breathed, completely mortified at my reaction in the store. "I'm sorry for being dramatic. I don't know why I reacted like that." I clasped my hands together. "I just hate when Derek calls me that."

"Ice-Queen?"

I nodded. "I know he's only joking, but it hurts..." I ducked my head and let my hair cover my burning cheeks. Tears filled my eyes and I quickly batted them away, feeling like a fool for getting so emotional over something so silly. It wasn't the dress that bothered me so much as it was the mental image of what would have happened to me back home if I had worn said dress. A shiver of fear rolled through me at the thought.

"Look at me." Kyle tipped my chin up with his knuckles. "Der was an asshole to you." He trailed his thumb over my chin. "He won't be again." Releasing my face, he leaned back, but kept his eyes on mine. "You're not used to being on display like that." Running a hand through his hair, he sighed. "Cam should've known better."

"I'm being ridiculous," I croaked out. "She was trying to be nice by getting me a dress and I behaved like a lunatic –" my words broke off as my emotions threatened to get the better of me. As my *memories* threatened to swallow me whole.

"You're gonna be sorry, you little bitch!"

Block it out, Lee.

"You should've been drowned in a barrel at birth!"

Block him out.

"Spreading your legs like the whore you are!"

"Lee, don't cry," Kyle commanded hoarsely, dragging me out of my reverie. "I can't cope with it."

"I'm not," I blubbered. "I s-swear."

"Goddamn." Unbuckling my seatbelt and yanking me into his arms. "Shh," he coaxed, settling me down on his lap. "Please don't cry." He smelled so good. I felt secure in his arms. "I could kill them both if you stop?"

"Cam and Der?"

He shrugged. "I can make it happen."

Sniffling, I choked out a laugh. "You're proposing murder?"

"In exchange for no girl tears?" He nodded. "Abso-fucking-lutely."

"No." Wiping my cheeks with my sleeve, I forced myself to

get a handle on my emotions. "I think we should keep them alive."

"You're sure?"

I laughed harder and climbed back onto my seat. "Yeah, Kyle. I'm pretty sure."

"Okay." He sighed dramatically. Leaning over the console, he buckled my belt once again "But only because that's what you want."

"Thanks." I smiled at him. "I appreciate that."

He winked. "Anytime."

KYLE

"Penny for your thoughts?" I asked, watching Lee like a hawk from across the table. She'd barely taken a bite of her burger and had been exceptionally quiet since we arrived at the restaurant. I knew something was bothering her – something a lot deeper than Cam's slutty dress, but I couldn't get in. I couldn't break down the barrier that separated me from her secrets.

Lee jerked her head up at the sound of my voice, expression alarmed, before her lips curved into that killer smile of hers. "I'm sorry," she hurried to say. "I'm not great company for you, am I?" Whether she was loud or quiet, drunk or sober, asleep or awake, *her* company was the only kind I wanted.

"Is the burger bad?" I figured that was a safer thing to ask instead of freaking her out by admitting how badly I wanted to burst down her walls and demand she tell me every single detail of her life.

Jesus, I had some major issues.

I held my tongue and resisted making demands because I didn't want to screw up the friendship thing we had going. I was enjoying it – I was fucking tortured by it, but still, I enjoyed every minute I got to spend with Lee.

Besides Cam, Lee was the first female I was actually friends with. In my life, women were divided into two categories. Girls I fucked, and girls like Cam, who I had no desire to fuck whatso-ever. That might make me an asshole, but I had good reasons to build barriers.

But with Lee, it was different. I didn't just want to fuck her. I wanted to be around her. I wanted to do things with her, go places with her, and make plans with her. I wanted to tell her all the dumb shit that happened throughout my day, and spend my nights curled up on the couch, listening to her laugh her way through reruns of *The Golden Girls* or *Married With Children*.

If someone had told me four months ago that Lee and I could be in a room together without arguing or trying to rip each other's clothes off, I would have laughed in their face. Well, I still wanted to rip her clothes off, but I was refraining. *Barely.* Suddenly, I was hit with the very depressing reality that my best friend was the sexiest girl I'd ever laid eyes on and worse, I was in the fucking friend zone.

Jesus, I wanted to kick myself in the nuts.

It was unsettling how much I liked being around her. She was innocent, and fresh, and so goddamn honest, different from any other girl I had ever met. Best of all, she was *nothing* like Rachel. Thinking about Rachel was what kept my ass firmly in my chair instead of leaning over the table and showing Lee just how much I wanted her. Thinking of Rachel chilled me to the bone.

I often thought about how different my life would be if I was free to make my own choices. In a perfect world, it would be Lee every time. But this wasn't a perfect world. Knowing we could only be friends didn't stop me imagining different scenarios in my head – all of which ended with a naked Lee writhing beneath me.

I had come close to having an apocalyptic fit when I found out that Mike still had his eye on her. Linda had mentioned how taken Mike was with my new BFF, and how she hung out with him every day on her lunch break.

I wanted to *kill* him.

I wanted to *keep* her.

I wanted to lock her up and have the only key, but shit, I didn't own the girl, and I never would. I couldn't tell her what to do and I definitely didn't want to get into why I hated that prick so much. I'd fire his ass if I thought it wouldn't give him so much satisfaction. Fuck it, I would fire him anyway except it would go against my grandfather's wishes. Lee didn't say much about him to me, but I saw the way he looked at her in the restaurant. He was eye-fucking her every time her back was turned.

It made me sick that she continued to eat her lunch with him every damn day, even when I'd offered to have lunch with her on more than one occasion. I knew that creep, and there was only a matter of time before he put the moves on her. She was too good for that dipshit.

Too good for everyone.

"Kyle?" Lee's hand brushed against my cheek, startling me. "You're gone pale."

"Shit, I am?"

She nodded, concern flashing in her eyes. "Are you feeling okay?" she asked, stroking my cheek, pressing her palm against my forehead. "Hmm?"

For a brief moment, I debated faking an illness to have her touch and pet me some more, but the concerned look on her face kept me honest. "I'm okay, Princess," I replied. "I was just thinking."

She moved her hand from my face to the hand I had resting on the table. Squeezing it gently, she whispered, "Can I ask what about? You looked pretty angry."

I smiled at her to ease her worry. "Just work stuff." I didn't trust myself to say any more.

TWENTY-SIX

LITTLE RED DRESS

LEE

HELL HAD FROZEN OVER. Yep, it had turned to ice, frozen over, and I had lost my mind in the process.

Standing in front of Cam's full-length mirror, I pulled at the red fabric clinging to my body and grimaced. "Fabulous," Cam exclaimed, clapping her hands. She looked stunning tonight in a short, canary-yellow, boob tube dress. It clung to her narrow frame perfectly. Her hair was curled to the side and her make-up was seamless.

Self-conscious, I tugged the hem of my dress down to cover my thighs, but that only caused my boobs to spill over the low plunging neckline. "Jesus." I pulled the material over my chest, causing the dress to rise up my thighs again. "Camryn Frey, I am going to kill you and it's going to be painful."

Cam snickered as she pulled at my dress, straightening it so that everything was covered. "You look gorgeous, Lee. Panty tearing, jeans bulging, erection approved, orgasm ready sexy."

My mouth fell open. "You did not just say that."

"I did." She dropped a pair of black stilettos into my hands. "Now, put these on. We need to get over to Dixon's place soon.

It's past ten and Kyle is getting pissed waiting. He needs to drop some contract or other off at the hotel."

My heart sank. "I thought you said Kyle was coming with us?"

Cam shrugged and ignored my question. She never answered my questions about Kyle since the whole movie theater make-out fiasco. "Just put on your shoes and let's go already," she ordered as she skipped out of the bathroom.

Oh god, I had turned into Cam's real-life personal Barbie doll. I looked at myself once more and groaned. Cam had painted my lips blood red, and straightened my hair so that it now fell to my elbows. My eyes were smoky...well, that's what Cam had called the dark, sooty coloring framing my pupils. My cheeks were flushed, but that had nothing to do with make-up and everything to do with people seeing me dressed like this. I was practically naked. The dress covered me in important places, but only just.

I checked and rechecked the length of it, making sure my scars were covered before inhaling a steadying breath and forcing myself to face the music.

KYLE

"Dude, do you have to work? Couldn't you call Lucinda or whatever her name is to go instead?" Derek scowled at me for the tenth time. "You are the boss, remember?"

"Her name is Linda," I bit out. "And no, Derek, I'm not going to call the poor woman on a Saturday night just so I can go get smashed. Besides, she can't sign shit for me, and I need to get this contract handled asap. I can give you a ride to the party, but that's it, man."

Cracking open another beer, Derek huffed loudly. "You suck, dude."

I rolled my eyes, choosing to ignore him. There was no point talking to *drunk Derek*. I honestly didn't know how Cam handled him when he was like this. Then again, I didn't know how Derek handled *sober Cam*, so I guess they balanced each other out.

I didn't mind not going to the party. I wasn't a fan of Dixon Jones, and I much preferred the idea of burying myself in paperwork at my desk than listening to that jackass all night.

I offered to give Cam and Derek a lift on my way to the office to smooth Der over. Besides, I was half-hoping that they planned on staying over at Dixon's place. If they did, then I had Lee to myself.

Bristling with tension, I checked my watch again and sighed. Goddamn Cam. She took forever to get ready. I figured the quicker I got to the hotel, the sooner I would be back to Lee, therefore I needed Miss Frey to hurry her skinny ass up. Maybe I could get some take out on my way home and Lee and I could watch a movie? Some Mexican food, or pizza. Yeah, Lee liked pizza. She didn't eat much at dinner earlier –

"Surprise," Cam cackled from the hallway, jerking me from my thoughts.

"Ahhhhh," Derek screamed back in a high-pitched, feigned scream as he jumped off the couch and wobbled to the door.

Shaking my head, I kept my back to the door and continued to tap an email out on my cell.

"That was some surprise, baby," he continued to slur. Jesus, he had too much to drink already. I could hardly hold back my laughter when I thought about the condition he would be in tomorrow morning. Fucking idiot. "I'm shocked!"

"Oh, shut up," Cam laughed. "I meant surprise because of *this*."

"Holy shit," Derek strangled out.

"I know," Cam squealed in delight. "I'm a miracle worker."

"Kyle…uh, come here, man," Derek called out, sounding a little shell-shocked.

Sliding my phone back into my jeans pocket, I stood up and went over to join him in the doorway. "You better not be naked, Cam –" My body froze to the spot, my words sticking on my tongue, when I took in Lee's half-naked body.

Holy shit.

What the fuck was she wearing?

I couldn't talk. I couldn't breathe. All I could do was just *stare* at her gorgeous tits spilling over the fabric of her tiny red dress. Staring harder, I swore I could see her nipples. I *could*. I fucking could see her nipples. Thighs and nipples were all that was going on inside my perverted head. *Thighs and nipples. Tits and ass. My cock in her pussy.*

"Hey," Lee said shyly as she clasped her hands behind her back. Yep, I could definitely see her nipples when she did that.

"Come on, guys," Cam called as she and Derek headed out the front door, making a beeline for my truck.

"Are you okay?" Lee asked quietly, as she swayed towards me. "Kyle?"

I shook my head, trying to pull my thoughts from the gutter. "What is *that*?"

"Huh?"

"*That*," I repeated, my voice thick with desire. Stunned, I reached out to touch her, to make sure I wasn't making this up in my head. *Big mistake.* Lee yelped and I looked down confused. I thought I was holding her arm, but no, I was cupping tit - full, perky, nipple-d tit. "Oh, shit." I jerked my hand away and held my palms up. "I'm so sorry."

"It's okay," she hurried to say, cheeks stained pink. "It was Cam's idea." Grimacing, she pointed to her body. "The dress, I mean."

I didn't answer her. What could I say?

'Thank you, Cam, for flaunting this beautiful girl in front of my nose?'

"It's awful, right?" She chewed on her bottom lip. "Oh Kyle, I look foolish."

I gaped at her. *Foolish?* No. *Edible?* Hell fucking yeah.

"Uh –" I cleared my throat and tried again. "You don't look foolish, Lee. I'm just, uh, surprised to see you dressed like that." I let my gaze trail over her once more, a dangerous move, but I couldn't help myself. "You're beautiful."

"I am?"

Jesus, she was killing me. "Yeah, Lee." I nodded. "You are."

"Are you sure you can't come to the party with us?" She smiled shyly at me. "I want you to."

Aw, shit...

I pulled my phone from my jeans pocket and dialed, knowing that I was a lost cause. The voice on the other side answered and I exhaled heavily. "Linda? Yeah, it's Kyle. I'm gonna need a favor."

TWENTY-SEVEN

STOLEN GLANCES AND SEX NOISES

LEE

I HOBBLED along in my stilettos with Kyle as he spoke quietly into his phone. Excitement bubbled inside of me when I heard him say that he couldn't make it into the office. He hung up as we reached his truck and opened the passenger door for me. Cam and Derek were already waiting in the back seat. No, scratch that, Cam and Derek were already steaming up the windows in the backseat.

"Thank you," I told him.

"For what?"

"For not leaving me alone with those two."

Kyle smirked. "Anytime." When he reached for my hips, I was so much more aware of his touch. My lack of clothing did little to soothe my frazzled nerves that only seemed to spike out when he touched me. Lifting me onto the seat, his hands lingered on my hips for an achingly long moment before he cleared his throat and stepped away. His fingertips brushed my bare thigh as he moved, causing a shiver to roll through me.

When he helped with my seatbelt, his fingertips lingered on my waist that little bit longer than usual. I knew something was different between us tonight. I could *feel* it.

Clearing his throat for the millionth time, Kyle turned the key in the ignition and pulled out of the driveway. His usual arm porn was on full display and a delight to look at. God, he had the most beautiful forearms. I wondered if that was a weird thing for a girl to admire, but decided I didn't care.

Ignoring the loud breathless cries and groaning coming from the backseat, I sat beside Kyle in what felt like a crackling silence, eyes trained on those damn forearms. The more my roommates moaned in the backseat, the tighter I pressed my thighs together, mortified at feeling aroused.

"Yeah, baby, suck it. Just like that…"

Kyle cleared his throat loudly, but Derek didn't seem to notice.

"Fuck, you taste so damn good…"

I folded my arms across my chest, my pathetic attempt to hide my rigid nipples. The vivid memory of Kyle touching my breast earlier did not help matters. I was so turned on that it was taking everything in me to stay in my seat and not straddle Kyle and beg him to take me.

"Are you cold?" Kyle asked, breaking through my filthy thoughts.

"Me?"

"You," he confirmed with a small smile.

"Uh, a little." I lied, hoping that the crisp night air could disguise my truth.

Stretching over the console, Kyle reached under my legs and grabbed a jacket off the floor of the truck just as Cam screamed, "Oh yes! There, Der, I'm close. Oh fuck, baby, you're so good at that."

"Jesus Christ," Kyle muttered, running a hand through his dark hair.

Shivering, I quickly slipped the jacket on. "Thanks." Kyle's scent lingered on the collar and I couldn't stop myself from breathing in deeply. He cleared his throat again and I jerked my nose away from the collar. "So…" I said, turning to look at his strained face. "Are you excited about the party?"

I watched as his brows furrowed and he flicked his gaze to me. "Not really, Princess."

"Why not?"

He turned his attention back to the road and his knuckles

turned white from the force of his grip on the wheel. "I don't like to share."

I was about to ask what he meant by sharing when Derek screamed, "Oh fuck, yeah, baby. You're gonna swallow me up."

Kyle slammed on the brakes, causing us both to jolt forward. His hand shot out in front of my chest, stopping me from slamming my face against the dashboard.

There was a loud bang from the backseat followed by a "What the fuck, dude!" and a "Oh my god, Kyle!"

"We're here," Kyle announced as he jumped out and slammed his door so hard the vibration shook through me. He swung my door open a heartbeat later and moved for my seatbelt. Lowering me to the ground, Kyle pressed me up against the side of the truck. He caged me in with his big body and I held my breath in anticipation when he lowered his face to within an inch of mine.

"Kyle?" I slid my hands up his chest, needing to touch him. "Are you okay?"

Kiss me, I mentally implored him. *Please just kiss me.*

Closing the distance between us, he pressed his lips to the curve of my jaw as he trailed his fingertips up and down my hip. "Be careful tonight, Princess," he whispered in my ear. Pressing another kiss to my cheek, he stepped back, turned his back to me, and walked away.

KYLE

I had to get out of that truck. *I had to get away from her.* Listening to the 69er occurring in the backseat, fueled with the gorgeous brunette sitting beside me, was too goddamn much for one morally challenged guy.

I was at my breaking point and well aware of it. Never in my life had I wanted anything as desperately as I wanted Lee. Just her. On her own. With no other girls. For keeps.

Sweet Jesus Christ, what was happening to me?

Skulking into the wooded area at the back of Dixon's yard, I swallowed down a mouthful of beer from a Dixie cup and forced myself to get a fucking grip. My heart was hammering in my chest, my palms were sweating, and I needed to make it *stop*. Closing my eyes didn't make a blind bit of difference; the image of her tits and that sliver of black lace between her legs as she sat in my truck were burned into my memory.

She was all I could see.

She was all I could think of.

And I left her.

Alone at a party full of dudes.

And Dixon Jones.

Fuck. My. Life.

TWENTY-EIGHT

ABSENT FRIENDS AND FLYING FISTS

LEE

KYLE LEFT the party without an explanation or a goodbye. I had been looking around for him for the past hour and he was nowhere to be found.

Shoving the stabbing feeling of rejection in my heart aside, I forced myself to focus on my surroundings. Dixon's home was a glorified pig-sty. There were empty beer bottles and Dixie cups scattered over every available surface – including the floor. Countless sweaty bodies filled the downstairs, pushed together from the sheer lack of room, and I was feeling claustrophobic. I had lost Cam and Derek in the swarm of people after ten minutes of arriving and, without any sign of Kyle, I felt very out of place – and very alone.

Shuffling along, I scoped out a perch on the staircase and stayed there, sipping my bottle of beer, and trying to keep out of everyone's way.

I was on my third beer when Dixon stopped short in front of me. "Lee, baby, you came."

"Hey, Dixon." I forced a smile, uncomfortable. "Thanks for inviting me." I gave him an enthusiastic thumbs up. "Great party."

He leaned against the bannister and folded his arms. "You don't look like you're having a great time."

"Oh, I am," I lied, blushing. "I just...I really need to use the restroom." *God, I was hopeless.* "I don't know where it is."

"It's upstairs." Grinning, he reached for my hand and hauled me up. "Here, let me show you."

Without giving me a chance to respond, Dixon dragged me up the staircase, stopping outside a door at the end of the landing. Smirking, he winked at me. "It's in there."

I stared blankly. "Uh... thanks?"

"Do you need a hand with anything?" He stepped closer. "Or two hands?"

"Uh, no?" I pushed past him quickly and slipped inside. "I think I can manage." Slamming the bathroom shut behind me, I flicked the lock and sagged against the doorframe. Lord, I was so out of my comfort zone.

KYLE

Where the hell was she? I had been through this house with a fine-tooth comb and there was no sign of Lee. Irritatingly, there was also no sign of Dixon.

My blood turned to lava and I slammed my fist against the wall in sheer fucking frustration.

"Dude, what the fuck?" Derek pulled at my arm. "What did we say about hitting walls?" he continued, his voice laced with amusement. "It's a big no-no, bro—"

"Where is she?" I demanded, cutting him off.

"Cam?" His brows rose in confusion. "She went on a beer-run —"

"Not Cam, you dickhead," I snarled. "Lee! Where is *Lee*? Did she go with Cam?"

Derek slapped his forehead with the heel of his hand. "Ah, shit, man. I totally forgot about Ice. I haven't seen her since we got here."

"Are you fucking insane?" I grabbed his shirt and dragged him towards me. "You left her alone in this fucking meat factory?" I scanned the room again, more anxious than before.

"I'm sure she's fine," he tried to placate. "Just chill out and cool your beans —"

"Derek, she is *not* used to this," I bit out. "She is not *like* us. You should have been watching out for her."

"I have a girlfriend to watch out for," he snapped, shoving me away. "Ice is not my priority or my goddamn responsibility, Kyle."

"She's your roommate," I spat.

"And she's yours too," he shot back heatedly. "You think because you lie to yourself that the rest of us can't see what's happening between you two?" He shook his head. "Wake the fuck up, dude. If that girl is anyone's responsibility then she's *yours.* Not mine. Not Cam's. *Yours.*"

With that, Derek stalked off while I stood there frozen, watching him leave.

My responsibility?

No.

No goddamn way.

I had enough of those to last a lifetime.

"Hey, Carter," Dixon slurred, coming to stand beside me.

"You." I blinked twice at the sight of him. Relief flooded through me. "Thank Jesus."

"Did you see Lee tonight?" he asked, swaying on his feet. "Holy shit, man. I'm still hard thinking about those tits."

Jealousy swiftly replaced my relief. "Did you touch her?" I demanded, getting up in his face.

"What?" Dixon's eyes widened in surprise. "No, Christ, I didn't lay a finger on her, I swear."

I released the breath I didn't know I was holding and nodded stiffly.

"She ran out of here before I had a chance," he added. "Before that, she locked herself in the bathroom." Frowning, he shook his head and wandered off. "That chick is weird, dude – hot as fuck, but weird."

"So, she's gone?" I called after him.

"Yep."

"Where?"

"Fuck knows."

Jesus. Shaking my head, I moved for the door only to stop in my tracks when a familiar face stepped in front me. "You can't have them both, brother," Mike taunted. "Consider what I'm saying."

My fist shot out of its own accord, connecting with his jaw with a satisfying crack. "Consider that, brother," I sneered, stepping over him as he groaned and writhed around on the floor.

TWENTY-NINE

SHARING SHAMPOO

LEE

I HAD a pain in my ass. My butt, quite literally, was throbbing. Twisting around under the covers, I winced when I thought about the long walk home from Dixon's party last night. I had slipped on a damn banana skin halfway home. I thought those types of accidents only happened in cartoons, but nope, it happened to me in real life. Six-inch heels and banana skins were a lethal combination.

After butt-planting the sidewalk, I had taken off my heels and walked the remaining four blocks barefoot –which brought me to my second ailment. My feet were *killing* me. I'd cut them on the gravel along the way.

By the time I'd made it back to Thirteenth Street, barefoot and bleeding, I'd literally thrown myself down on my bed fully clothed, too exhausted to shower and change into my jammies. Sleep had found me quickly, but not before my bedroom door had opened just before I dozed off.

At first, I had thought I was dreaming, but then the mattress dipped beside me, I felt his fingertips gently graze my cheek, and I quickly realized that I was awake. Feigning sleep, I had suppressed a shiver when his lips gently brushed against my forehead before he whispered the words, "Night, Princess," in my ear and left my room.

Confused was an understatement for how I was feeling. I couldn't figure Kyle out. I knew even less about where I stood with him. It was such a mess.

Feeling icky, I climbed out of bed and headed straight to the bathroom, deciding that I was in dire need of a shower. Switching on the shower, I adjusted the temperature of the jets and then headed back to my room to grab my toiletry bag. I spent an ornate amount of time deciding which fresh pair of jammies I wanted to dress in before grabbing my dressing gown off the back of my door and crossing the hall to the bathroom.

This time, when I slipped inside and closed the bathroom door behind me, I could barely see in front of me from all the steam. Making a mental note to not leave the shower running for so long again, I stripped out of my clothes and stepped inside.

"Princess?" Kyle's familiar voice came from behind me and I screamed at the top of my lungs.

Oh my god!

Oh my freaking god!

"The fuck are you doing in here?" he chuckled, slapping a hand over my mouth to muffle my screaming. "And please don't scream. I'm dying of a hangover here."

"Kyle?" I strangled out, yanking his sudsy hand away from my mouth. "What the hell are you doing in here?"

"Uh… showering?"

"Excuse me?" I spluttered, keeping my back to him.

"I'm showering," he repeated, sounding amused. "I needed a shower, I walked in and it was running, so I'm showering."

Oh, hell no, he did not steal my hot water.

"No," I bit out. "*I'm* showering. Get the hell out of here."

"No can do," he shot back, sounding amused.

"Why not?"

"Because I was here first."

My mouth fell open. "No, you weren't!"

"I think I was, Lee," he chuckled and the move caused his wet torso to press against my back.

"You're a liar." Shivering, I cupped my breasts to protect my modesty and hissed, "This is my water."

"I'm not selfish," he teased, lips brushing my earlobe. "I can share."

He was joking but I didn't find it funny. This was all so much easier for him because he only saw us as friends. *Friends that shower together?* "Kyle, Get out. Now," I growled.

He fully laughed at me.

"Kyle!"

"No."

"Yes."

"Shh, I'm washing my hair."

With my back to him, I tried to shove him out with my butt, but he snaked an arm around my stomach and pulled me close. "Play nice, baby," he purred in my ear, fingers splaying across my bare midriff. "You don't wanna slip on some soap and land on my cock now, do you?"

So, it was going to be like that?

Fine.

If he was comfortable in his nudity then dammit, I could be, too, or at least pretend to be.

Two could play this game.

"Fine. I can see that neither of us are backing down," I replied. "So, you just cover your eyes and I'll cover mine."

"Yes, ma'am," Kyle chuckled.

"And no peeking."

"No peeking. Gotcha."

"I mean it, Carter."

"Relax and wash your hair, Bennett."

"You're impossibly annoying."

"And you're impossibly amusing."

Ugh. Covering my eyes with my hand, I drew on all my courage, turned to face him, and held my palm up. "Pass the shampoo, please."

I heard his sharp intake of breath and I stiffened. "Don't you dare peek, Kyle Carter."

He didn't answer me.

No shampoo appeared, either.

Curious, I peeked through a gap in my fingers and my breath hitched

His eyes were glued to my body.

He wasn't smiling anymore.

"You said you wouldn't peek," I breathed, covering my breasts with my hands. This was too much. My skin tingled. "You lied."

Kyle backed up, standing directly under the shower head now. Water cascaded down on his naked body as he tilted his head to one side. "I know." There was a hungry glint in his eyes as he raked them over every inch of my body. The blue of his eyes was barely visible now, smothered by the blackness of his dilated pupils. "Fuck." His jaw strained. "Fuck, Lee."

Heat pooled between my legs as I watched him watch me. Every intimate moment we had shared, every longing, every urge I felt for him, all boiled down to this moment. *It was now or never.* Exhaling a ragged breath, I dropped my hands to my sides, exposing myself entirely to him.

His eyes darted to my chest and I could feel the heat of his stare on my body. It was burning me up. "Shit," he croaked out gruffly. "You're so beautiful."

"Really?" Trembling from head to toe, I kept my hands at my sides, and waited to see what he would do.

He dragged his bottom lip between his teeth and bit down hard. The move made me wet. His eyes locked on mine once more and I could see the conflict mixed with hunger.

Decision made, Kyle stepped closer and took my hands in his. Placing my arms around his neck, he hooked an arm around my waist and pulled my naked body flush to his.

Our eyes locked.

My heart thundered wildly in my chest.

This was it; the moment I had been praying for since the last time he'd kissed me.

"I'm a bad bet for you," he said, chest rising and falling quickly.

"I'm aware," I breathed, sagging against his muscular frame.

"You should have climbed out," he told me, stroking my cheek with his free hand. I could feel his strong heartbeat thundering against my chest.

"I couldn't do that," I whispered back.

He lowered his lips to within an inch of mine. "No?"

"No." I knotted my fingers in his hair. "It was my shower first."

A trace of a smile ghosted his lips before he pressed them to mine. There was a tenderness in his kiss that I never thought him capable of. This kiss held none of the raging intensity of our other kisses. It felt *deeper*.

Months of feeling nothing but intense desire for this man, fueled by the feel of his lips finally on mine, caused me to lose my freaking mind. Breathless and frantic, I flung myself into his arms, slip-sliding against him as I moved. Our wet bodies collided with an audible smack. Kyle's back hit the shower wall behind him and I was on him, willing him to touch me all over. I pressed myself against him, urging him on, and his hands dropped to my hips, steadying me.

"Lee, wait –" the moment Kyle opened his mouth, I thrust my tongue inside, desperate to taste him. I could feel his erection slapping against my belly and my body trembled with anticipation He *wanted* me and I was on cloud nine, but I wanted more than this tenderness.

I wanted it all.

He was trembling, but his hands stayed on my waist, unmoving, as I kissed and nipped at his lips, seeking a reaction from him.

It didn't come.

Rejection coursed through me and I tore my mouth away, breathing hard.

He didn't want me.

"Lee."

Gasping for air, I practically threw myself out of the shower.

"Lee, wait –"

I didn't wait.

Wrapping a towel around my body, I fled the bathroom like my life depended on it.

.

KYLE

I let her leave.

Lee was here, she was naked, she was kissing me, offering her body up to me, and I *let her leave*.

What the *hell* was wrong with me?

Filled with self-loathing, I stood under the now-freezing water, hard as rock, and completely reeling. Lee had handed herself to me on a soapy, naked platter and I'd frozen like some virgin teenager.

"Fuck." I smacked my palm on the tiles. "Goddammit to hell!"

It took another solid seven minutes to get my dick under control and by then, I was truly depressed. Flicking off the water, I stepped out and wrapped a towel around my waist, all while trying to rid my mind of the mental image of naked Lee.

Im-fucking-possible.

That look on her face, those gray eyes full of trust, would be branded in my mind for the rest of my life.

That face was the reason I kissed her.

Those eyes were the reason I stopped.

I didn't deserve her trust. I couldn't give her what she deserved and Lee deserved a hell of a lot better than me. Knowing I didn't deserve her didn't stop my body wanting her, though, and the images of her full breasts dripping with water – those perky, rosebud nipples were *haunting* me. When I thought of her smooth stomach, those curved hips, and that small triangle of curls, I wanted to fucking weep.

Goddamn, I needed a drink.

LEE

Derek was standing in front of the stove, stirring some concoction of his, when I skulked into the kitchen later that afternoon.

He took one look at me, stopped stirring, and narrowed his eyes. "What did you do?"

"What are you talking about?" I asked as I fluttered around the room like a caged bird.

He waved his spatula at me. "You're all fidgety and you look as guilty as sin."

He could read me too well. I wondered what Derek would say if I told him I'd tried to seduce Kyle in the shower this morning?

Probably laugh his ass off because it was so stupid.

"Nothing." I stopped fidgeting and went and sat in a chair. "I'm just bored."

He studied me for a long beat before shaking his head and returning to stirring. "You're a strange one, Ice."

I sagged, relieved that he was going to let this one go.

Cam barreled into the room seconds later. "Hey guys," she squealed.

Derek's attention went straight to Cam. "Hey, you." His eyes softened, his mouth curled into a gooey intimate smile. "You good?"

A stab of jealousy spiked through me. I wanted a man to

smile at me like that. Correction, I wanted *Kyle* to smile at me like that.

"Why are you so happy?" I asked her, a little too catty for my liking. I felt bad instantly. It wasn't Cam's fault that she had a man whose eyes lit up when she walked into the room, and who looked at her like she was the only girl in the world.

"Whose glass is half empty today?" she teased, ruffling my curls.

"Sorry," I mumbled, cringing.

"Don't worry about it," she replied, still grinning at her boyfriend. "So, I just organized a bash for Saturday." Clapping her hands together, she practically floated into Derek's arms and smacked a loud, mushy kiss to his lips.

I groaned internally.

"Another party, Cam?" Kyle said from behind me and I almost fell off my chair.

Great.

Full of shame, I tensed and lowered my head, debating on the quickest exit. I couldn't exactly run out, though, could I? Cam and Derek would think I'd lost my mind. To be fair, I sort of had.

Kyle walked over to the sink and I tried to keep my eyes off his naked back, *I really did*, but I was a lost cause. Why did he have to walk around half-naked? It was almost October and it was cold. Going around shirtless was hardly sensible. More importantly, why did he have to look so damn good?

"Yes, another party, old man," Cam said in a sarcastic voice. "Jesus, can you do us all a favor and bring the old Kyle back? As in, freshman year Kyle? Wherever you left him, it's time he came home. This uptight version of you sucks ass."

"Nice," Derek snickered.

"I'll keep that in mind," Kyle mumbled, clearly off his game. Normally, he always had a comeback for, well, pretty much anything. Today, he was distracted. The chair next to mine scraped against the tiles and he sat down, his shoulder brushing against mine. His scent engulfed my senses. *Fresh soap, expensive cologne and man.*

I felt his hand on my leg under the table and I snapped my head up, eyes locked on his. "Are you okay?" he mouthed, eyes laced with guilt.

I nodded weakly.

He squeezed my thigh and I couldn't take it anymore. Jerking out of my chair like a scalded cat, I backed all the way up to the door.

"Lee?" Cam stared after me. "What are you doing?"

"I, uh, I need to go, ah, do something," I blurted before bolting from the kitchen.

THIRTY

NIGHTMARES AND SEX DREAMS

KYLE

DRAINING the contents of my beer bottle, I tossed it in the trash and repressed the urge to roar. Fucking Cam. She was ridiculous. Once again, she had turned my house into a glorified nightclub and it was only Friday. Her 'party of the year' bash wasn't supposed to be until tomorrow night. Apparently, tonight was the warm-up. Bodies were everywhere. Some were dancing. Most were drinking. And a few of the wild ones were fucking.

Folding my arms across my chest, I leaned against my kitchen counter and observed the carnage, feeling a helluva lot older than my twenty-two years. A part of me wished I could just switch off and enjoy myself like my friends so obviously did, but I couldn't do it tonight. It didn't seem to matter how much alcohol I poured down my throat or how many girls propositioned me, my head was stuck where my body wanted to be; with the girl upstairs.

Lee never came downstairs when Cam was throwing a party and I was usually grateful for that, figuring that it saved me from getting into fights I had no right to pick. Tonight, though, I missed my friend. We hadn't spoken since the shower incident earlier in the week and I was depressingly lonely. She was avoiding me again and it hurt like a bitch.

On a bright note, I'd managed to escape Rachel tonight. She attached herself to some poor bastard earlier and the last I had seen she'd dragged him into Derek's room. Fine by me. It was his fucking funeral.

Feeling out of sorts, I wandered through my house, not consciously knowing where I was going until I found myself standing outside her bedroom door. I knew I needed to turn around and leave, fuck off into my room and work out my frustrations with some lube, but I didn't do that.

Instead, I knocked.

The moment I rapped my knuckles against the timber frame, I regretted my actions. What was I going to say to her – give me attention because I don't seem to function without you? Yeah, that would go down about as well as a lead balloon. Maybe she was asleep? I hoped she was.

For both our sakes...

The door opened inwards and Lee stood in the doorway, sleepy-eyed and drop-dead gorgeous in nothing but a white t-shirt. "Kyle?" she asked in that soft voice of hers, stifling a yawn. "What's wrong?" Concern flickered in her big gray eyes. "Are you okay?"

Stifling a groan, I resisted ramming my fist in my mouth as I took in the sight of her adorable deer-in-the-headlights expression. Her curls were tousled and flowing freely down her back. And her tits? Yeah, they were straining against the fabric of –

"Is that my shirt?" I asked, studying her closely. It was the only censored thing I could think of to say. The uncensored version went something along the lines of *'Hey, Princess, I can't stop thinking of you. Dick move, huh? Speaking of dick, I have a raging fucking hard-on and all I can think of is burying myself inside your tight, little pussy, but I'd settle for holding your hand'*.

Christ, I was sick in the head.

"Oh, yeah – I'm sorry." Blushing, she bit down on that pouty bottom lip, knotting her fingers in the hem of the shirt. Her nipples strained against the material and I had to look away. Yep, no bra for the win again. "My jammies are in the laundry. I didn't think you'd mind me borrowing it. I can take it off if you want?"

Sweet Jesus, she was *killing* me.

"No, keep it," I croaked out. It nearly killed me to tell her to leave it on, it went against my nature, but what could I do?

Lee stepped aside and gestured me in. "Would you like to come in?"

Halle-fucking-lujah.

I guessed we were avoiding the whole shower incident talk – which was fine by me. I had enough regrets about that morning to last a lifetime.

I followed her into her room, closing the door behind us.

"Can you lock it?" she called over her shoulder. "I don't want any strays from the party coming in here."

Smart girl. "What – like me?" I joked, flicking the lock.

"No, you're always welcome," was her sweet reply as she strolled over to her bed, hips swaying as she moved.

I could see ass cheek.

Bare ass cheek.

Oh. sweet fuck she was going commando.

No bra, no panties…

"So, what's up?" Lee asked, dragging my thoughts from the gutter, as she climbed back into bed. "Why aren't you downstairs with your friends?"

Because I want to be upstairs with my best friend?

Think, Kyle, think… "I got bored." *Stupid, Kyle, stupid…*

"Okay." She looked confused. I didn't blame her. I was confused myself.

"And my room is, uh, occupied," I added. Well, that made me sound a little less creepy, but it was a bullshit excuse. No one would dare use my room.

"Really?" She gave me a sympathetic smile. "Well, you can sleep in here if you want? I was just about to watch a movie if you want to join me?"

Oh, fuck yeah. "What movie are you watching, Princess?" I asked, pulling my shirt over my head and shoving my jeans down.

Her eyes widened but she didn't protest when I climbed into bed beside her. Blowing out a shaky breath, she flicked off the lamp on the nightstand, reached for the remote and pressed play. "*Twilight,*" she mumbled as she pulled the covers up to her chin. With a little hesitation, she reached over and draped her duvet over my waist. I bit back a smirk. "It's Cam's. It was the only

DVD I could find, but we can watch something else if you'd prefer?"

The only light in the room was coming from the television screen, but I swear I could see her blush again. "No, that's cool." I hooked an arm behind my head and settled down. "I can cope with a little vampire action." Our legs brushed and she shivered. "So long as you don't go all *team Edward* on me."

She frowned in confusion. "*Team Edward*?"

"You're eighteen, right?" I arched my brow. "Girls your age usually go batshit crazy for the vampire in this movie."

"Oh," she replied, nestling down on her pillow. "Well, I've never seen this before."

I gaped at her. "Lee, every teenage girl has seen this film."

She shrugged and turned her attention back to the movie. "I guess it's like you said; I'm not like other girls."

No, Princess, you're definitely not…

———

When I jerked awake several hours later, my body was rigid, my cock painfully hard, and I knew there wasn't a hope of me falling back to sleep.

Blinking the sleep from my eyes, I glanced at the alarm clock on her nightstand. It read 3:48 in blood red digits. The party was still going strong downstairs. I could hear the faint sound of music and voices drifting up here. Jesus, the place was going to be a shitbomb in the morning.

"No…please…"

Concerned, I glanced down at Lee, who had somehow become the little spoon to my big spoon. In sleep, my arms had somehow found their way around her body and she was nestled into my chest, her cheek resting on my arm, her small hand clutching my forearm to her chest. Her body was shaking, her lip quivering, as she whimpered and jerked in her sleep. Instantly, I realized this was what had woken me up.

"Don't," she continued to mumble, body twitching. "Please."

Tears trickled down her cheeks and my heart wrenched, horrified. Kissing her hair, I gently rocked our bodies, desperate to comfort her. "It's okay," I coaxed, my voice barely more than a gruff whisper as I held her to me. "I'm here."

"No, no, no," she continued to whimper, distressed in her sleep.

I never realized Lee had nightmares, but judging from the way her body shook – and the gut-wrenching cries that had woken me up – they were violent ones.

"Shh, baby," I whispered, pressing another kiss to her curls. "I've got you."

Trembling, she snuggled closer to my body, seeking some sort of comfort from me in her sleep. On instinct, I tightened my arms around her and buried my face in her neck, relieved when her body relaxed against mine. "It's just a dream," I continued to whisper, nuzzling her damp neck with my nose. "You're safe." She was close now – too fucking close – but the closer she was to me, the more her body relaxed. Her t-shirt had ridden during the night and now her naked ass was pressed against my junk.

I knew I was a saint because I doubted there was another guy on the planet who could sleep with this girl and *not* touch. Well, that wasn't technically true considering I was touching her, just not in any of the ways I wanted to.

Fuck.

My.

Life.

Several minutes passed by before her body relaxed against mine and her distressed whimpers morphed into contented sighs. When she finally stopped crying in her sleep, I heaved a sigh of relief.

Jesus Christ, that had scared the shit out of me.

What the hell had she been dreaming about that terrified her so much? The movie? Vampires? Fucking werewolves? Shit, I didn't know. I wasn't sure I *wanted* to know. I'd never heard any sound so gut wrenching.

A soft moan escaped her lips and I froze, locking my body into place. A few seconds later, it happened again; another audible moan, and then another and another after that.

Fuck, she was clearly dreaming of something else entirely now.

With her head nestled in the crook of my arm, she released a contented moan and rocked her hips, grinding her ass against my raging hard-on.

This feel of her was heaven. The need for her was hell. I could think of nothing other than how easy it would be to push inside her right now. Goddammit, I should have taken off my boxers last night. They were wet now – from her and from me.

Lee moaned again, mumbling something incoherent, and I couldn't resist anymore. I lowered my head and pressed a kiss to her neck.

"Kyle."

I pulled back and froze, eyes locked on her sleeping face. Was she awake? I didn't think so. Was she dreaming about me?

"Hmm, Kyle."

She *was* dreaming about me. My male pride soared. Eyes locked on her face, I watched as she wet her lips with her tongue and rocked her peachy ass against me.

"Lee? Are you awake?" I whispered when her small nails dug into my arm like a little kitten's claws before retracting and moaning loudly again.

Fuck…

The hand she had been using to grip my forearm slipped under the covers – covers that I quickly kicked away just in time to see her hand slip between her legs.

Fuck, this was the hottest thing I'd ever seen.

Like some sick perv, I watched her work herself over. Lee's lips parted while she touched herself and I swear to god I was jealous of her hand. I didn't think about what I was doing when I reached down and covered her hand with mine, feeling how she fingered her little clit with her slick fingers. Making mistakes came naturally to me and this was a colossal one, but I couldn't find it in me to care as I rocked my hips against her and felt her fingers quicken.

Losing all resolve – and all sanity – I pushed her hand aside and replaced it with mine, wanting this more than my next breath. She was dreaming of me, dammit, so if she was coming tonight, it was going to be from my hand.

Biting down hard on my lip when I felt how wet she was, I pinched her clit between my thumb and forefinger. Her legs fell open, giving me access to all of her. Releasing an appreciative growl, I continued to rub her clit as I thrust against her ass, feeling my pre-cum wet my boxers.

All of a sudden, Lee jerked and her breathing changed.

She was awake.

Trailing my finger over her slit, I slowly pushed a finger inside her, growling when I felt her walls clench around me. Jesus, she was so fucking tight. Suckling her neck, I continued to slide my finger in and out her, keeping rhythm with my thumb as I circled her clit.

"Mmm," Lee moaned, bucking into my touch. "Kyle..."

Oh yeah, she was definitely awake.

"Tell me to stop, Lee," I told her, pushing a second finger inside her slick heat. Crooking my fingers, I arched my wrist, finding that spot that made most girls lose their fucking minds.

"I don't want you to stop, Kyle," she cried out, writhing against me. "Not ever."

"Fuck." I upped my pace, thrusting my fingers in and out of her, slamming my poor, neglected cock against her ass. Her moans turned to cries and then screams as she bucked wildly against me, begging me for more.

Happy to oblige, I slid my fingers out of her tight pussy and rolled her onto her back before sealing her mouth with mine.

Like an addict chasing his next hit, I plunged my tongue into her mouth, dueling with hers, desperate for my Lee-fix. This girl had some weird sort of hold over me and right now, with my heart hammering in my chest like it was, I knew there was a strong chance I'd give her anything she wanted.

"Please," Lee moaned against my lips, breathing hard, as she clutched my face in her small hands. "I just –" I rocked my hips against her and her eyes rolled back. "More," she finally strangled out, nodding eagerly as she pressed her lips to mine. "Definitely more."

Settling between her spread legs, I devoured every inch of her perfect skin, starting by kissing a trail from her lips to her neck, and her collarbone to her breasts. Shoving the fabric of her shirt – my damn shirt – out of my way, I latched onto one of her straining nipples and sucked, loving every cry and whimper that tore from her throat. Flicking my tongue over her nipple, I trailed a line of kisses across her breastbone before taking her other nipple in my mouth, determined to be fair in my affections to each of her fucking beautiful tits.

"Kyle," Lee cried out when I moved lower, tracing my tongue over her navel and then nipping on her hipbone. Pulling herself up on her elbows, she looked at me in confusion, her face flushed with a cocktail of embarrassment and desire. "Wh-where are you going?"

Smirking, I dragged her hips towards me, angling her body in the perfect position, and lowered my face. "Shh, baby," I whispered, pressing a soft kiss to her pubic bone. "I've got you."

"Wh-what – omigod!" I pulled her clit into my mouth and she cried out, body arching upwards. "Sweet Jesus…" Pushing at my face, she tried to squirm away. "No, Kyle. You don't have to… you're not supposed to –"

"Eat your pussy?" I purred, running my tongue up her slit before pushing inside. Curling one arm around her thigh, I used my free hand to press her stomach to the mattress, keeping her still as I nuzzled her. "Tell me it doesn't feel good and I'll stop."

"But this is…isn't this dirty –"

"Bullshit," I growled, kissing and suckling her. "Your pussy tastes perfect."

"But it's – oh god please! It's so…*wrong*!"

"I'm gonna tongue fuck you until come on my face," I growled, lapping at her. "And then, when you're a shaking mess on this bed –" I paused to bite her thigh. "I'm gonna start all over again." Sucking her clit into my mouth, I sucked hard before releasing her and kissing her softly. "Because this is the sweetest pussy in the world and I'm gonna make you feel good –" I stroked her thigh, "So, lie back and enjoy this."

With an audible moan, Lee flopped onto her back, covered her face with her hands, and let her legs fall all the way open. Smirking at her modesty, I made a mental note to show her how little modesty I possessed as I fucking ravaged her with my tongue. I took it all; every scream, every plea for more, every tug of my hair, every drop of her sweet juices on my tongue as I pushed her body to the point of no return. "Kyle," she screamed out, fingers knotting in my hair. "I feel…omigod, something's happening to me!"

I smiled to myself as I flicked her clit with my tongue, my rhythm merciless. Yeah, something was happening all right; she was coming on my face.

THIRTY-ONE

BAD BOYS AND BIRTHDAY BLUES

LEE

HE MADE ME COME.

My very first orgasm at the hands – and tongue – of Kyle Carter.

Confused didn't begin to explain the complicated ball of emotions twisting around in my gut. Last night was amazing… right up until I fell asleep in his arms and woke up alone. He crept out of my bedroom in the early hours of this morning and there had been silence on the western front ever since. If I didn't feel so fricking stretched and sated, I would've thought I dreamt the whole thing up. But finding his shirt from last night on my bedroom floor, along with several love bites on my inner thighs, I knew that what had happened between us was very much real.

After spending most of Saturday holed up in my room, wallowing in self-pity and dying of shame, I ventured out of my room with my stomach growling loudly. Starving, I forced all thoughts of Kyle from my mind and forced my feet to trudge downstairs.

When I stepped off the bottom step, the smell of smoke and alcohol immediately assaulted my senses. God, I hated cigarette smoke. It always reminded me of my father. Music was blasting from the living room and I was familiar enough with Derek's taste in music to recognize the song as Eminem's *Shake That*. As per usual, the house was jam-packed with bodies and if I wasn't so hungry, I would have high-tailed it back upstairs to the sanctuary of my bedroom. My plummeting blood-sugars trumped my anxiety and I pushed past the crowds in my search of carbs. I knew I had a candy bar tucked away in the back of the fridge and I prayed that it was still there. I needed comfort food.

I could have wept when, having stepped around a couple making out, I put myself in Rachel's path. My heart sank in my chest when I watched her stalk towards me in a pair of denim cut-offs that barely covered her butt and a white tank. She wasn't wearing a bra and her perky nipples were visible through the flimsy fabric.

"Cute outfit." she sneered when she reached me. "I guess you couldn't afford an actual shirt of your own?"

I mentally cursed myself for coming downstairs in my thread-worn sweatpants and Kyle's white shirt that was about ten sizes too big for me. Choosing to ignore Rachel and her nasty comments, I side-stepped her and kept moving for my candy bar. Girls like her made my skin crawl. I had suffered for years at the hands of girls just like her at my high school back home and I was a firm believer in smothering a fire, not fueling one – hence my silence.

"Are you deaf, ignorant, or just plain slow like Kyle said you were?" she called after me in an obnoxiously loud voice. Several people turned to look at me and I flamed in embarrassment. "Do you want to know what else he says about you? What we laugh about in bed?"

Inhaling a deep breath, I urged myself to calm down and *not* retaliate.

She wants to hurt you.

Don't give her the satisfaction.

With my head down, I kept walking, disgusted with Kyle for ever going there with such a nasty human being. What the hell did he see in Rachel Grayson? She was such a bitch. Sure, physically she was beautiful, but that girl was pure poison inside. I had yet to witness one redeemable quality. In truth, I didn't think she had any…

"He says you're a small-town dummy with no education," she

hissed, catching a hold of my arm and dragging me back to face her. "Good enough to clean his bed but never in a million years good enough to be *in* it." Her green eyes narrowed with malice. "He pities you," she continued to taunt. "You fed him that poor little lost girl line and he ate it right up, but don't get too comfortable under my kitchen table, hick, because I call the shots around here. If I say you're out, then you'll be back to the trailer park you crawled out of quicker than that." She snapped her fingers in my face for emphasis. "Because when it comes down to it, Kyle Carter will choose me." Leaning close to my ear, she whispered, "He will *always* choose me."

Blinking rapidly, I tried to make sense of everything she just said, but my mind was reeling. Did he say those things about me? Did he laugh with her behind my back? Would he do that? *Why*? I could handle Rachel saying bad things about me, but not *Kyle*. We were supposed to be... ugh, I didn't know what we were supposed to be, but I never thought he saw me as a *small-town dummy*! *A hick*.

My hunger abandoned me and I turned to go back to my room, both depressed and disappointed.

"What are you saying to her?" Cam demanded, appearing out of thin air to stand beside me.

"The truth," Rachel replied, turning her glare on Cam.

"Oh please." Cam rolled her eyes. "You wouldn't know the truth if it smacked you in the face."

"You're really starting to grate on my nerves, Frey," Rachel countered, livid. "Keep it up and I'll get rid of you, too."

"Oh, you will?" Cam shot back mockingly. "You and what army, bitch?"

"I have Kyle –"

"You have *leverage*," Cam sneered, cutting her off. "That's not the same thing."

Rachel's nostrils flared. "And what would you know about it?"

"I might not know what you're holding over his head, but I know more than you think," Cam taunted. "Like how you skulk off once a month for dinner dates with his daddy." Rachel's brows shot up and Cam's smile darkened. "Didn't think anyone knew about that, huh? I wonder what Kyle would think about you breaking bread with his old man?"

To be fair to Rachel, she recovered quickly. "He'll be my father-in-law soon enough," she replied, smirking cruelly. "It's only a matter of time, sweetie."

"Over my dead body," Cam growled, pressing her forehead to hers.

"That can be arranged," Rachel spat back.

"I'm shaking in my *Louboutin's*," Cam replied. "Which, FYI, I paid for myself – unlike your worthless, gold-digging ass."

"You're going to be so damn sorry you messed with me," Rachel hissed before stalking off.

"Off you fuck, *Dirty Diana*," Cam called after her. "*Dirty Diana*," she chuckled, nudging me. "Get it?"

Yeah, I got it. Michael Jackson's classic was blasting from the stereo and Cam looked thoroughly amused by her dig. Meanwhile, I stood, frozen in the hallway, and watched as Rachel stalked away with her flaming red ponytail swaying as she went.

"Don't even think about it," Cam growled when I moved for the staircase. "We are having birthday shots. It's not every day a girl turns nineteen."

Don't remind me. "I don't feel like it," I mumbled, stomach twisting up in knots.

"I don't care," Cam countered. I debated whether or not to run, but Cam took the option away from me. Grabbing my hand, she pushed through the crowd and dragged me into the kitchen. Filling two glasses to the brim with vodka, she pressed one into my hand and grinned. "Cheers," she said, clinking my glass with hers. "Here's to not letting skanks like Rachel Grayson get you down."

Screw it; she was right. I wasn't going to let Kyle, Rachel, or anyone else bring me down. Numb, I tossed it back, draining the contents in three gulps. "Cheers," I gasped, wiping my chin with the back of my hand. Reaching for the bottle, I poured myself another drink, downed it, and then poured myself another after that for good measure.

———

Several hours – and several hours – later and I was slumped at the kitchen table, observing a game of suck and blow with my new *friends* when Kyle finally decided to show up to the party.

He strolled into the kitchen in a plain black t-shirt and faded blue jeans. He looked very hot and *very* occupied with his arm draped casually over the shoulder of a willowy blonde who had been blessed with legs like a staircase.

Pain hit me square in the gut and if I wasn't already sitting down, I would've collapsed. I hated this. How he could be. How he sabotaged every little bit of hope I had.

Don't cry, Lee.

Just let it go.

I watched as lowered his head to her ear, whispering sweet-nothings no doubt, and I had to look away. It was either look away or throw up. Besides, there was no point in torturing myself. I needed to just *quit* him.

"Wah-hey, new girl," the blond drunk guy to my left cheered. "You're up!"

Trembling, I forced myself to suck the card that the blond drunk guy was blowing against my mouth. *It's okay*, I continued to chant in my mind. *This is normal. This doesn't make you a whore.*

We were setting a record around the table for keeping our card up when I felt a hand clamp down my shoulder and roughly drag me out of my chair. "What the fuck are you doing?" Kyle was standing in front of me, chest heaving. He looked *furious*. He also reeked of whiskey. As drunk as I was, I could tell he was in a far worse state. His eyes were bloodshot, his body swaying.

Electricity jolted through me at the sight of him; that familiar pull tugging me towards him, but I needed to be wary. I couldn't trust myself to control myself and I couldn't trust *him* not to hurt me again.

With great effort, I forced myself to turn away. Choosing to ignore him seemed to be the safest option for my poor, barely-hanging-in-there heart.

I moved to sit back down, but Kyle wrapped a muscular arm around my waist and dragged me back to him. "Kyle," I growled, pushing at his arm. "Let go."

"Party's over," Kyle snarled, glaring at a blond drunk guy as he kept my back pressed firmly to his chest. "Get the fuck out."

"Kyle, man." Blond drunk guy shifted awkwardly in his chair. "I didn't know she was yours." He held his hands up. "Sorry, bro. No harm done."

"Don't worry, I'm not," I hissed, breaking free from his hold. "I'm not his anything."

"Lee!'

"No!"

"Lee – get back here!"

"I said no!" Swaying on my feet, I made a beeline for the counter and grabbed a bottle of beer. Kyle yanked it out of my hands before I could put it to my lips. "What's your *problem*?" I screamed, finally losing my cool. The alcohol flushing through my veins gave me the courage I needed and I shoved him away when he tried to wrap his arms around me. "Get away from me!"

"Were you with him?" Kyle demanded, swaying on his feet as he reached for my hand again.

"Were you with her?" I snarled right back, yanking my hand away.

His brows knitted in confusion. "Who?"

"The fucking girl, Kyle!" I screamed, pushing my hair back from my face. "The one you walked in here with."

Recognition slowly dawned in his eyes and he gaped. "Who – Ally? Fuck no! Are you crazy?"

"I *saw* you," I countered shakily, trembling. "You were –" I shook my head and pointed at him. "You had your arm around her shoulder."

"She's Linda's *niece*," he strangled out, looking horrified. "She's practically family." Shaking his head, he seemed to sober himself because this time, when he closed the space between us, he didn't stagger. "Lee, I know whose bed I slept in last night." I flinched and he cringed. "I wouldn't do that to you. I wouldn't do that to *us*."

"You always do that to us," I choked out, backing away. "It's your thing."

"That's not fair, Lee."

"*You're* not fair, Kyle!"

"Look, you're drunk," he growled, running a hand through his hair, clearly frustrated. "Come on; I'll take you up to bed." He tried to take my hand but I snatched it away.

"Why?" I demanded, shaking from head to toe. "So you can sneak out on me again?" I shook my head and backed up. "I don't think so."

"You can walk out of here or I can carry you out –" He closed the space between us and hooked an arm around my waist. "But either way, you're coming with me."

I could see his friends were watching us – along with the rest of the room, we were making a huge scene, but I was beyond caring. "Careful, Kyle," I choked out, my voice laced with emotion. "Keep this up and I'm going to start thinking you actually care."

I tried to step around him, but he moved so fast that I didn't have a chance to escape before he picked me up, tossed me over his shoulder, and carted me out of the kitchen.

"Let me go," I growled, thumping his back. "Put me down, dammit!"

Complying with my wishes, Kyle put me down in the hallway only to slam me against the door under the stairs a moment later. His body crashed against mine at the same time his lips came crashing down on mine and I completely freaking lost it. My hands moved of their own accord, reaching up to knot in his hair as I kissed him back with a hunger that bordered on pain. Our kiss was hot, ruthless, and overloaded with feelings as we attacked each other's lip viciously. I was overwhelmed, hurt, and angry with him and I showed him just that with every thrust of my tongue.

Meeting every thrust of his hips with my body, I pressed against him, loving the feel of having his big body dominate mine. His fingers dug into my hip as he continued to pin me to the door, grinding his body against mine. Reckless, I bit down hard on his lip, causing him to grunt in what seemed pained-pleasure. He responded by tightening his fist in my hair and yanking my head back.

We kissed like this for an age, both fighting one another for something we weren't entirely sure of until our bodies slowly relaxed. Finally, the kiss softened and Kyle pulled back to look at me. "You drive me fucking crazy." He stroked my nose with his. "Did you know that?"

"Right back atcha," I breathed, sagging against him.

"We have to talk." His voice was gruff, his eyes burning with heat. "You know that, right?"

I nodded slowly, struggling to get a handle on my erratic heartbeat. "Yeah."

Sighing heavily, he pressed his brow to mine. "Come upstairs with me?"

"Now?" I asked, uncertain.

"Now," he confirmed gruffly, blue eyes locked on mine.

Only two options occurred to me at that moment. The first was to run back to my room and avoid Kyle – go back to pretending that it was just friendship between us. The second was to give in to my fears and embrace my feelings.

"Please?" he whispered and I knew right there that there was only one choice.

Nodding slowly, I slipped my hand into his and let him lead me upstairs.

When he opened his bedroom door and gestured me inside, surprise shot through me. I'd never been in his room before. Trembling, I stepped inside and he followed, closing the door behind us.

Running high on a foreign concoction of vodka and hormones, I steadied my trembling hands at my sides and took in my surroundings. Even in my drunken haze, I could tell that Kyle's room was pretty clean for a man. All of his dirty clothes were piled on top of a laundry hamper instead of strewn across the floor. Several shirts hung on coat hangers on the back of his closet door. His bed – a huge king, was dressed. The blue comforter strewn over his mattress was creased, but I had to give him props for making it this morning.

He didn't need to make it this morning, Lee, because he slept in your bed last night.

My cheeks flamed at the memory.

"I didn't do what you think I did," Kyle said, dragging my attention back to him. He was leaning against his closed bedroom door, watching me carefully. "I didn't run out on you, Lee."

Unable to suppress the sigh building up in my chest, I let it out and slowly lowered myself down on the edge of his bed. "It doesn't even matter anymore."

"I *didn't* run out on you," he repeated. "There was an emergency at work."

I shrugged. "Okay."

"You don't believe me?"

No. "It's none of my business," I replied wearily. "I don't need an explanation."

"Well, I'm giving you one anyway," he shot back. "And it's the truth."

"You didn't come back all day."

Kyle stared hard at me for a long moment before sighing heavily. "Because I had to do something." Rolling his shoulders, he pushed off the wall and closed the space between us. Dragging a small, duck-egg colored box from his pocket, he dropped it on my lap and sank down beside me. "Happy birthday, Princess."

My mouth fell open. "You remembered?"

"You're my best friend, Lee." He shrugged and nudged my shoulder with his. "Of course I remembered."

Oh god.

My heart.

My poor, poor heart.

Stunned, I opened the *Tiffany's* box and looked inside. A white gold chain with a small, shimmering jewel stared back at me. "Kyle –" my breath escaped me in a rush. "You didn't have to do this."

"It's black fire opal," he explained. "Your birthstone."

"Whoa," I breathed. "This is too much."

"You're worth it," was all he replied. Withdrawing the necklace from its box, he placed it around my neck. "You deserve a helluva lot more," he mumbled, tying the clasp at the back.

Completely freaking reeling, I stared down at the expensive jewel around my neck and shivered. "Thank you," I whispered, blinking back the tears. "So much –" Words breaking off, I climbed onto his lap and threw my arms around his neck.

Kyle stiffened for a moment, body rigid, before slowly relaxing. His arms came around me; one hand on my lower back while he smoothed my hair back from my face with the other. "Are you *crying*?" Leaning back, he tipped my chin up, forcing me to look at him. "Shit, don't cry, Princess," he groaned, noticing the tears in my eyes. "Don't be sad on your birthday."

"I'm not," I sniffled, hiccupping. "I'm just…" I shrugged. "I'm drunk and emotional."

"Yeah." He brushed the pad of his thumb over my cheek, wiping a rogue teardrop. "I know the feeling."

We stared at each other for the longest moment, blue eyes on gray, and I held my breath, head spinning as I lost another piece of my heart to this man.

"Lee." His voice was torn. "I'm a bad bet, baby." Shuddering, he leaned in and pecked my lips with his. "I break things." His breath fanned my lips, sending shivers down my spine. "That's what I do."

When he tried to lean back I pulled his face back to mine. "Don't break *me*, Kyle," I whispered, touching my forehead to his. "If you need to break something, break my *fall*."

A pained growl tore from his chest and our lips crashed together, moving together in perfect synchrony, as we kissed the pain away. Because this hurt. Whatever was happening between us was *painful* and I knew he felt it, too. I could see it in his eyes tonight, feel it in the urgency of his kiss, in his almost frantic touch as he rolled me onto my back.

Falling heavily on top of me, Kyle continued to kiss me like he was dying of thirst and I was his last hope of water. Letting my legs fall open, I gripped his hips and pulled him down on me, rocking my softness against his hardness and then whimpering into his mouth when he hit all the right spots.

Raising himself up on one elbow, Kyle broke our kiss long enough to reach behind him and tug his shirt over his head. Tossing it on the floor, he lowered his mouth to mine once more, kissing me deeply, punishing my heart with his temporary affections. His skin was hot, his body hard and muscular, making me feel incredibly small as I moved beneath him, taking all that he was willing to give me. I wasn't sure if it was the alcohol flushing through his veins that was making him do this, or if he had felt the shift like I had, but he was touching me, *finally*, so I kept my mouth shut.

He'd remembered my birthday.

He bought me a gift.

That had to mean *something*.

Leaning back to kneel between my parted thighs, Kyle reached for my hand and pulled me into a sitting position. His eyes never left mine when he reached for the hem of my shirt and slowly lifted it up. Holding my hands up, I shivered when he gently tugged it over my head and tossed it away. My breasts were bare to him, nipples straining, as his mere presence set alight a fire deep in my belly. "You're beautiful," he whispered, smoothing my curls back off my shoulder. His fingers lingered on my cheek and he leaned in and pressed a kiss to my collarbone. "I could keep you."

I wish you would.

Shivering, I reached for the buckle of his belt, heart hammering violently in my chest. He watched me carefully as I fumbled with his belt before finally managing to get it open. Pulling myself up on my knees, I hooked my fingers into the waistband of my sweats, inhaled a steadying breath, and then pushed them, along with my panties, down my thighs.

"Yeah?" he asked, tongue darting out to wet his bottom lip.

Trembling, I nodded slowly and lay back down on the pillows. "Yeah."

Hovering above me, Kyle kissed a trail from my lips to my breasts, all the way down my stomach until stopping at my hip bone. Hooking his fingers into the waistband of my sweatpants, he slowly tugged them all the way off until I was naked and spread open beneath him.

"I love these." His hands clamped down on my hips as he tugged me further down the bed. "Your curves are insane, Princess." My body jerked and my back arched off the bed when I felt his mouth against my most intimate of places. "You're so fucking wet." He pulled my clit into his mouth and my eyes rolled back. "You like that, baby?" I felt him push a finger inside me. "You like when I fuck your tight pussy with my fingers?"

"Yeah," I moaned, arching myself into him. "Please don't stop."

"Don't worry," he growled, flicking his tongue over my clit. "I won't."

Clenching my eyes shut, I fisted the covers in my hands and rocked my hips as the newly familiar feeling of ecstasy started to build up inside of me – slowly at first, and then growing harder, hotter, faster, closer. My legs trembled, my body shook, my vision blurred until I knew I was on the crest of the most illicit wave of pleasure. Just before I could reach it, Kyle pulled away from me, leaving me a whimpering mess on his bed.

Never once taking his eyes off mine, he stood up and moved for the button of his jeans. Popping it open, he lowered his fly and pushed his jeans and boxers down his hips.

My breath hitched in my throat when I saw him – *all* of him – hard, long and thick. He reached for a condom on his nightstand, rolling it on with master precision, and a jolt of panic trickled through me when I contemplated how that was supposed to fit inside me, but then he was back with me – back *on* me – and my worries disappeared. Pressing my body deeper into the mattress with his, he kissed me deeply and I could taste myself on his tongue.

Too aroused to be embarrassed, I clung to him, my fingers digging into his broad shoulders as he hitched one of my thighs around his waist. I could feel his erection against me, hard and unyielding, and I forced myself to relax as he reached a hand between us and positioned his –

"What the hell are you doing!"

My heart just about jumped out of my chest when I heard the woman's furious snarl. The bedroom door banged against the wall, making a loud cracking sensation.

"Jesus fucking Christ, Rachel!" Jerking away from me, Kyle scrambled for his clothes while I dove under the covers. Pulling his boxers up his thighs, he tucked himself in only to reach back into his underwear and remove the just-about unused condom. I flamed in embarrassment and pulled the sheets up to my neck. "You have no goddamn right coming into my room like that," he continued to say, sounding furious. "You don't own me, dammit!"

"Maybe not, but you sure as hell owe me," Rachel hissed. Her cheeks were as red as her hair and I felt myself wilt under her furious glare. "You piece of shit," she growled. "You promised me! Your loyalties should lie with *me*." Stalking towards him, she reared back and struck his cheek with the palm of her hand. Kyle didn't even flinch. "You owe me, Kyle," she snarled. "After what you did –"

"Don't go there, Rachel.," he warned, rubbing his cheek as he glanced over at me. Guilt filled his eyes and he quickly looked away. "Not here."

"Her, Kyle?" Rachel's attention turned to me and her face contorted into an expression that was truly terrifying. "I've tolerated everyone else because you promised. But *her*? You're different with her. " She shook her head and sneered. "Why? You said it yourself; she's a fucking hillbilly hick, so why is she so goddamn precious to you? Why is she different from a hundred others?"

He called me a hillbilly hick?

Kyle's guilty eyes landed on mine and I flinched. Uh, no, I was *so* not staying here to listen to this. I was out of here. Scrambling off the bed with the sheet wrapped around me, I moved for the door but Kyle blocked my path. "Don't go," he pleaded, holding his hands up. "Please. I can explain."

I really couldn't see how.

"He's said worse about you, fatty," Rachel taunted. "Nice gold, by the way," she added, gaze locked on my neck. "*Tiffany's?*" She smirked cruelly. "Signature Kyle Carter move. Did you suck his cock for that, sweetie?"

"Step aside," I strangled out, breathing hard as I tried and failed to sidestep Kyle. "I want to leave."

"Please don't listen to her," he said almost desperately before turning to Rachel. "If you want to keep your shit to yourself then you better get the fuck out of here now," he roared, running his hand through his disheveled hair. "Because I'm just about ready to lay it all out there, Rachel."

Her eyes widened in disbelief. "You wouldn't dare."

"Try me," he roared back.

She stared hard at him for a long moment before letting out a high-pitched scream and stomping her foot. "Fine, but you better come –"

"Get the hell out," Kyle cut her off with a vicious snarl. "Now."

Rachel stormed away only to spin around in the doorway. "You think you're special now, hick, but don't get too comfortable in his bed. He has an incredible knack for making a girl feel like she's his whole world when she's just another hole for his cock." Her eyes narrowed on me. "I hope you enjoy being second best because he's always going to be mine, bitch. *Always.*" She slammed the door out behind her and Kyle threw his head back and roared.

Not wasting a split second, I grabbed my t-shirt – *his* damn t-shirt – off the floor and quickly pulled it on before snatching up my raggedy sweatpants.

"What are you doing?" he demanded when I moved for the door. Fear flickered in his eyes. "Lee–"

"What do you think I'm doing, Kyle?" I strangled out. "I'm leaving."

"Please don't," he replied, voice torn, as he moved to intercept me again. Cupping my face in his hands, he exhaled a ragged breath. "I can explain —"

"Don't touch me." I jerked away from him and ran out. I heard him calling my name, but I didn't stop running. I needed him to back off and give me space.

Thankfully, the party had cleared out, and the downstairs was void of people when I toppled off the bottom step of the stairs. *Thank god for small mercies.* Trembling, I burst into the kitchen and ran straight to the sink. Turning on the faucet, I gathered water between my hands and splashed it on my face, striving to find my composure.

"It's not what you think," I heard him say from behind me and my heart withered up in my chest.

"Go away, Kyle," I replied wearily. "I don't want to hear it."

"She's crazy," he urged, sounding frustrated. "I hope you know that."

"That's a terrible thing to say about your girlfriend," I shot back shakily, keeping my back to him.

"She's not my girlfriend, Lee," he was quick to deny.

"No?" I sighed, emotionally drained. "Then what is she, Kyle?"

"She's…it's complicated," he settled on.

"Complicated." I gripped the sink and nodded. "I see."

"No." He closed the space between us and placed his hand on my hip. "You don't, Lee. You don't *see* it. There's so much that you don't get, and I can't tell you. I want to – fuck, I want to, but if you knew, you'd never look at me the same way."

I clenched my eyes shut. "Try me."

"I…what?"

"Try me," I repeated, knuckles turning white from the force I was using to grip the sink. "Let me be the judge of how I'll react."

"I *can't*," he whispered. "I'm sorry."

"Then you should just go back to her." Tears flowed freely down my cheeks as I turned to face him. "And whoever else you're fucking."

"Don't say that," he said gruffly, reaching for my hand. "You have no idea how hard this is for me."

"Then tell me," I strangled out, chest heaving. Imploring him with my eyes to just open up and let me in, I whispered, "Just *tell* me."

"Lee, I…I…" He shook his head and I watched as the shutters came down – as the walls around him grew fifty feet tall. "There's nothing to tell."

A sob broke through me. "Liar."

His nostrils flared. "Princess –"

"Don't call me that," I sobbed, yanking my hand free from his. "Not when you turn right around to her and call me a fucking hillbilly hick!" Jerking away from him, I backed away, still spitting my pain like verbal bullets. "I bet you had a good laugh at my expense, didn't you? What else did you say about me behind my back? Huh? Because your girlfriend seemed to know an awful lot about me when she cornered me earlier tonight. Did you call me a whore, too? Did you laugh at how easy it was for you to get me on my back?" Tears fell freely down my cheeks as my heartbreak soared. "I guess you're right. I must be a whore to fall on my back for you. To spread my legs like a –"

"Don't!" He strode towards me and backed me up against the counter. "Stop it," he warned. "Don't say shit like that about yourself."

"That's what you see me as, though, isn't it?" I clenched my fists. "You *used* me, Kyle. You led me on!"

His eyes narrowed. "Well, if you didn't make it so fucking easy for me, we wouldn't be here, would we? I tried to keep this from going any further." His face reddened. "I warned you – I fucking told you that I wasn't good for you! But you kept coming back. Fucking throwing yourself at me," he spat. "You're a fucking tease, Lee!"

My blood ran cold and my hand swung out before he could finish what he was saying, connecting with his face. "You bastard," I screamed, tears flowing freely from my eyes.

Kyle's expression was one of pure rage when he grabbed my wrist. "Don't. Ever. Fucking. Hit. Me. Again."

My breath came in strained pants.

My heart was palpitating.

We stood frozen like that as Cam burst into the room with Derek following behind. "What the *hell* is going on?" Trembling, I tore my eyes off Kyle and turned to face her. "Lee," she continued, looking horrified. "Are you okay?"

"Kyle, man, let go of her arm," I heard Derek say and it was only then that I registered the pain shooting up my hand. Stunned, I looked down to find him still holding my wrist. My anxiety, along with the memory of my father's voice, spiraled me into a full-blown panic attack and a pained whimper tore through me.

"I should've drowned you in a barrel when I brought you home from the hospital."

"You're a little whore, Delia. That's all you'll ever be."

"You wanna defy me? Go out with boys like a little slut? Let see what boys look at you now –"

I could hear the sound of his belt.

I could smell leather mixed with blood.

I could taste the blood in my mouth

"You're a little cock tease, aren't you?"

"Kyle!" Derek clamped a hand down on his shoulder and shook him. "Let go."

Kyle, who seemed to be in a trance up until this moment, suddenly jerked to life. "Shit," he strangled out, releasing me quicker than lightning. "I didn't know I was – I'm sorry!"

Cradling my hand, I sank to the floor in a fit of tears. I couldn't breathe. I couldn't get a handle on myself. Rocking back and forth on the floor, I urged the painful memories of my past to leave, but his voice wouldn't go...

"I should've drowned you in a barrel when you were born." My father repeated the words I had heard every day of my life for the last eighteen years. *"You're a dirty little whore, Delia – just like your Mama was."* I didn't protest. I certainly felt dirty. Especially after last night.

The sound of Daddy's belt cutting through the air was as familiar to me as the sound of a kettle whistling. The pain that washed through my skin was as familiar as breathing. Pain engulfed me. The familiar taste of metal flavored my mouth, trickling down my throat, making it hard to breathe. Still, I didn't make a sound. I didn't dare. Daddy was furious and if I begged him, things could quickly get worse. And I knew in my heart and soul that I wouldn't survive worse...

Not anymore.

As the pain threatened to overwhelm me, I allowed myself to float away – to fall into my memories. And in that exact moment I promised myself that if I survived the night, I would fight. I would try and make a life for myself.

I would run.

"You ain't so damn special now, are you, girl?" Daddy demanded, continuing to whip me with the metal clasp of his belt. I could feel the blood trickling down my backside, seeping through my clothes, my underwear. My skin felt as if it was about to burst into flames. I closed my eyes and imagined. I invented a man. A beautiful, brave man would burst through the door right at this very moment and take me away from this life. Give me love and a life and a family so different to how I had been raised that I would never be afraid again. I gave myself up to that notion. I survived the night because of it.

I prayed for the future I feared I would never see. I longed to see Cam's face just one more time. Just once more and I would be content.

The fear was climbing in my throat and I couldn't stop the strangled screams coming from my mouth as I struggled to breathe. I shook my head, trying to rid the memories from my mind. I couldn't close my eyes. I wanted to, but I was too afraid of what would come next…

My head hit the back of the couch with a loud thud and, as per usual, I curled up in a ball and waited for the pain. His boot drove into my face with such force that it took the air clean out of my lungs. I couldn't call for help if I wanted to, not that it would make a difference.

Nobody was coming to save me.

They never did.

I didn't know what to do. Fear was spiraling out of control. I wanted to scream but the reality was I was terrified to breathe. Pain. I'd never experienced pain like I was feeling now. I was in agony. My back felt as if pieces of skin were being sliced from the bone. Tendons and muscles stretching and ripping apart. I knew in my heart that this wasn't repairable. I wasn't repairable. No one would ever love me. I was the monster that killed my own mother.

God, I missed my mama so bad. I just wanted a pair of safe arms to fall into. My mama should have taken me with her when she went to heaven. It would have been easier. To have never felt pain. To have never known fear.

My head was spinning, my vision was blurred. My heart was palpitating. I couldn't breathe past the pain this time.

It was too pungent.

It was too crippling.

He didn't apologize, he never does, he just continued beating me into a state of semi consciousness.

I could taste the blood in my mouth, it was pungent, overwhelming and dripping down the back of my throat along with a piece of my tooth.

I wondered if tonight would be the night he finally finished me off. Would tonight be the night my father finally made good on his threats?

I hoped so.

I couldn't take another night like this. If he didn't finish me off then I would do it myself. Surely death would be easier than this. I remembered a film I had once watched. Forrest Gump. I thought of the girl who prayed to turn into a bird. Well, I didn't pray to be a bird.

I prayed to be dead.

"Jesus Christ," Kyle roared, and his voice brought me back to the present. "What's happening to her?" Kneeling down on the kitchen floor, he cupped my face in his hands. "I'm sorry," he strangled out, eyes frantically flicking over me. "Lee, baby, I'm so –"

"Get back!" Cam shouted as she ran over to where we were both crouched and shoved Kyle away. "Are you hurt?" Dropping to her knees, she wrapped her arms around me and pulled me into her arms. "Did he hurt you?"

Shaking my head, I sobbed loudly. "My…my…my…" I couldn't say anything. I couldn't catch my breath. "C-Cam –"

"Shh, Lee. It's okay," she coaxed, tightening her arms around me. "You're not there. You're here with me and you're safe, okay? Nobody is going to hurt you here. Just breathe."

"I c-can't." I was too scared to breathe.

"You can," she corrected calmly. "Nice and slow." She smoothed soft circles over my back. "That's it. Good girl."

I panted, gasped, and clawed for air for several minutes until I wrangled my emotions into somewhat of an order.

"Okay?" Smoothing my hair off my face, Cam pressed her brow to mine, eyes locked on mine. "Better?"

Sniffling, I nodded and allowed her to help me to my feet. "Ugh, you stupid fuck!" Cam snarled when her eyes landed on my wrist. "Look at what you did," she screamed, glaring at a pale Kyle. "Look at her fucking hand, Kyle!"

I glanced down and, sure enough, there were purple finger-prints on my wrist.

"Lee, I'm so sorry," Kyle said, tone desperate. "I didn't –" He moved towards me as if to hold me and I stumbled away. He flinched. "I didn't realize…"

"Back the fuck up," Cam ordered, wrapping her arms around me protectively.

He shuddered. "Jesus, I'm so fucking sorry."

"Get him out of here," Cam growled as she held me tighter. When neither Kyle or Derek, who was flanking him, moved, Cam screamed. "Get him out of here, Derek. *Now*!"

"Come on, man," Derek coaxed, grabbing Kyle's shoulders and steering him towards the door.

"I didn't mean it," Kyle choked out. "I would never hurt her."

"I know," Derek replied. "It's okay. I've got your back."

"Go!" Cam screamed.

"We're going!" Derek roared back, wrapping his arm around Kyle's shoulder as he led him away.

THIRTY-TWO

REELING IN THE AFTERMATH

KYLE

"WHAT THE FUCK WAS THAT?" Derek demanded, but I couldn't answer him. I couldn't *breathe*. The sight of Lee huddled on the floor, terrified of *me*. *Her wrist?* Jesus Christ, I was the lowest of the low. There were no words to describe the kind of bastard I was.

"I didn't mean it," I continued to mumble as I paced the living room. "I didn't mean it, Der."

"I know," he replied, holding his hands up. "Just take a minute, man. It's *okay*."

"Did you see that?" I strangled out, panicking. "Did *I* do that?"

"No." Catching a hold of my shoulders, he steered me over to the couch and pushed me down. "You didn't. You couldn't have. So, just calm your shit and *breathe*."

The living room door opened and Cam stepped inside before quietly closing it behind her.

"Cam." I stood up as she strode towards me. "Is she –"

"Listen to me, dipshit," she hissed, knotting her fist in my shirt. "If you ever lay so much as a *finger* on that girl again, I will rip your fucking heart out." She shoved me hard for emphasis. "Are we clear?"

"Cam!" Derek snapped. "Back off. He didn't mean it –"

"I don't give a shit what he meant," she snarled, keeping her blue-eyed glare on me. "He never touches her again!"

"Cam, I didn't –" I stopped short, not knowing what to say. "I didn't realize I was holding her wrist." Pathetic, but true. "I've been drinking." Another disgusting, pitiful excuse. "I didn't know." I honest to god hadn't realized her wrist was in my hand. I'd been so caught up in what she was saying. *In my feelings.* "I'm *sorry.*"

"Yeah, well, she came here to get away from one abusive bastard, not to find another," Cam shot back, furious. "So, save your excuses."

My heart stopped dead in my chest, my brain sobering quickly. "What the fuck are you talking about? Abusive bastard?" When she didn't respond, I narrowed my eyes. "Cam, you better start talking."

"Don't go there, Carter," she warned. "I keep enough of your secrets. This is not my story to tell."

"What story?" I demanded. "What happened to her?"

"Maybe you should have asked Lee why she moved here before you went all *Rocky Balboa* on her and scared the shit out of her," she hissed. "I mean, are you that stupid, Kyle? Can't you see how different she is to everyone else? Can't you see *her*? I *told* you she was fragile. I *warned* you to stay away from her." Narrowing her eyes, she hissed, "You better fucking pray that she doesn't run again, because if she goes back to Louisiana, she's *finished.*"

Pain sucker punched me straight in the chest. "What does that mean?"

"It means that girl has lived through more horror than you could dream up," Cam snarled. "What Lee has suffered would make you, me, and everyone else *pray* for death." Shaking her head, she blew out a frustrated breath. "You know what? I wouldn't be surprised if she isn't here tomorrow – god knows, I'd be gone if I were her." With one final glower, Cam stalked out of the room.

"Shit." Derek, who had been standing quietly beside me, sighed heavily. "Dude, what the fuck is happening around here?"

I had no idea.

But I was going to find out.

LEE

I had often contemplated death.

Be it an accidental series of events, or accidentally on purpose. God knows my daddy had threatened me with murder enough times. He didn't love me much as a child. He loved me even less as an eighteen-year-old girl. I guess I'd always known I was his biggest regret, but I knew it just that little bit more on days like this... When I sported a swollen lip, two bloodshot eyes, and a pain in my back that made me want to keel over like the dog he thought I was and pine.

I couldn't live like this a second longer. He was going to kill me if I stayed here. And I hated myself for wanting to stay. I hated myself for still caring about the man who did these things to me.

This was rock bottom. I was scared to death of dying here, on the floor of my father's house, with no one noticing my absence. I had to get out of here. I had to run. I couldn't take this life any longer. Daddy had taken everything away from me as punishment for something Perry Franklin had caused. I knew I was to blame as well, though. I shouldn't have gone to prom. I disobeyed my father and now I was reaping the consequences of my actions.

I lay, curled up in a ball, on the floor until my father grew tired of beating me and retreated to the couch. And then I waited some more until the sound of his loud snoring filled the silence.

I knew this was my last shot. My only opportunity to escape this life. I didn't have a future in this town. I didn't have a life. I needed to claim that right back. I didn't want to live with this feeling of hopeless-

ness inside of me a second longer. It was killing me slowly from the inside out. I had to let go of this part of my life. I had to live.

Quietly, I went to my room and grabbed the two duffel bags I had packed and stashed in fear of a night just like this one. And then I slipped my hand into the torn side of my mattress; pulling out the small stack of bills I had spent years saving up. I could hardly walk through the pain, but I forced myself to do it anyway.

Wiping my brow, I inhaled a steadying breath, reveling in the air filling my lungs, cleansing me, assuring me that I was still alive. I waited until the darkness fell, and with it, came the cloak of invisibility. The opportunity to escape. He was passed out on the couch, drunk off whiskey and power.

I could see him from where I was cowering on the staircase.

I needed to be brave.

I needed to find the courage to leave.

To move my feet and get out of here.

I had to go.

Staying wasn't a viable possibility anymore.

Creeping downstairs, I held my hand against my racing heart and forced myself not to breathe too loudly. He could wake and I could die. I was more afraid of the first than the second. Death in this instance seemed like a glorious mercy.

There was a darkness deep inside of me. I knew it. I felt it. To leave him on his own, I was being selfish, but I couldn't stop myself.

My legs were moving me forward, out the front door and further away from our house, from the life I'd been living.

I didn't know what kind of a future existed for me outside of Montgomery but I knew I had to try. If I stayed, I would die. It was as simple as that. And call me selfish, but I wasn't ready to die. I wanted to experience living first. Even if it was only for a little while. Even if it was for just a day…

By the time I reached the bus station in the next town over, I couldn't feel my toes. Blisters were forming on the heels of my feet, but the scent of freedom was pungent and exhilarating. My heart was thumping with excitement. My stomach was twisting in knots. I felt like I was riding on a roller coaster.

I was so close.

I was almost there.

After walking six miles with two duffel bags in my arms and an army of angry welts on my back I was here.

I was almost free.

"Where are you heading to, miss?" the lady in the ticket booth asked.

I paused, red-faced, as I furiously tried to decide. "University Hill," I finally replied. "Boulder, Colorado."

"That's a long way from home, darlin'."

I smiled. "I know."

She handed over my ticket and as I walked towards my bus bay, I raised my face towards the sky, gazing up at the stars shining above me. Maybe this was my destiny. Maybe, I needed to be on this bus. Maybe I would have a life.

I had hope now.

This was my only hope.

Cam lay on my bed, facing me. I didn't remember climbing the stairs or getting into bed. She looked sad. I felt dead. "I'm sorry," I croaked out, shivering when she stroked my cheek with her warm hand. "For messing everything up for you."

"I love you, Lee." Sniffling, she wiped a tear from her eye. "You know that, don't you?"

"Yeah." I nodded. I knew Cam loved me. She was the only person in the world who did. "I know."

"So, I'm going to ask you some questions and if you can't say the answers out loud, then just shake or nod your head, okay?"

I nodded, smiling at the old game she was playing with me. This was how Cam had talked to me as a child, when I couldn't talk, when I'd been too afraid to.

"Did it stop?" she asked. "After I left? Did *he* stop?"

I quivered and shook my head.

Tears welled from both our eyes as Cam wrapped her fingers around mine. "Did it get worse? More violent?"

I nodded slowly.

Cam blanched as she sucked in a deep breath. I didn't attempt to lie. Not to her. Cam knew well what my father was capable of. She had seen the bruises. "Is that why you freaked out over the dress? Are you scarred? Worse than before?"

Tears were pouring from my eyes, but I couldn't make a sound. I nodded slowly, knowing what her next question would be before she asked it.

"Can I see?"

Trembling, I rolled onto my stomach and nodded into my pillow.

With gentle fingers, Cam lifted the back of my t-shirt.

And then she started to cry.

"I'm okay," I squeezed out, keeping my face buried in the pillow. "Don't be sad for me."

"You're not going back there," she choked out, pulling me into her arms. "I don't care what happens between you and Kyle, I'm gonna take care of you."

Sniffling, I slowly relaxed in her arms.

"Promise me, Lee," she begged. "Promise me that you'll *never* go back there."

"Yeah." My voice cracked. "I promise."

THIRTY-THREE

BLURTING SECRETS AND BREWING STORMS

LEE

WHEN I WOKE the following morning, it was to an empty room and another pounding headache. *This is becoming the norm,* I thought to myself as the wind and rain hammered against my bedroom window. *You deserve this headache,* my conscience sneered, *this is what a hangover feels like.*

Exhausted and feeling like hell, I stretched my arms above my head only to yelp when a sharp pain shot up my hand. As I stared at the purple fingerprints marked into my wrist, the memory of last night flooded me. Full of shame, I debated curling up in a ball and holding my breath. I had hoped that it was all a terrible dream, but no such luck.

Gingerly, I slowly rolled my wrist, biting down on my lip when pain seared me. *God,* I couldn't wait on tables one-handed. Morose, I rolled out of bed and trudged downstairs to use the landline. I didn't have a cell phone and I needed to contact Linda to let her know that I wouldn't be able to work today.

Please don't fire me, please don't fire me, I mentally chanted when I skulked into the thankfully empty kitchen and dialed her number.

Linda answered on the first ring and had already heard about my injured hand. *Mr. Carter* had signed me off work for the rest of the week.

"What?" I strangled out, frowning.

"Don't worry," she replied in that raspy voice. "You'll still be paid."

Stunned, I thanked her and rang off before moving straight for the coffee machine.

Coffee.

I definitely needed to make coffee.

I was surprised to find it already prepared. I was usually the first up in the morning. I frowned as the wondrous aroma filled my senses.

"Lee." Cam's voice came from behind me and I almost jumped out of my skin before swinging around to find her standing in the kitchen doorway, armed with two mugs of steaming coffee.

"Cam." I slapped my good hand to my chest. "You almost gave me a heart attack."

"My bad," she replied, walking over to the table. "I was bringing this up to you." Taking a seat at the table, she placed the mugs down and crooked her finger. "Come here."

Anxious, I joined her at the table. She pushed a mug towards me and I gratefully snatched it up, taking a huge gulp. "So." I looked at her. "The weather's bad, right?"

Cam arched her brow. "You want to talk about the weather?"

I shrugged. "I don't know."

"Yeah, Lee," she sighed. "The weather's crazy. There's a storm rolling in. It's supposed to hit us later tonight."

"Really?"

"Really." She nodded. "So, how are you feeling?"

"Um…okay. I think?"

"Do you want to talk about last night?" I could hear the sympathy rolling off her tongue and I cringed.

"No," I whispered, taking another sip. "I really don't."

"Well, that's too bad," she replied. "Because we're going to."

My heart sank. "Cam, I'm fine. Last night brought back some ugly memories for me, but I'm okay." I lifted my cup with my sore wrist and whimpered before quickly changing hands. "Honestly."

"See, that doesn't float with me," she replied. "Because I've been thinking all night, and I know there's more to this."

"M-more?"

"More," she confirmed. "What happened, Lee?"

"W-what do you mean?"

"With your father," she said. "What made you leave – and don't say because he whooped you, because that prick has been putting his hands on for as long as I've known you, and you've always covered for him." She stared hard at me. "There's more to this and I want to know. Something changed. What was it?"

"N-nothing," I mumbled, red-faced.

She nodded stiffly. "Fair enough. You'll talk when you're ready."

Now, I felt awful. Cam had taken me in with no explanation, and the girl was a good friend to me – my only friend. I hated keeping secrets from her, and she deserved to know why I had landed on her doorstep. I took a deep breath and let it out. "Two months before I came here, I was attacked."

Cam gasped. "You were robbed?"

I wished it had been so uncomplicated. I would have happily handed over my purse if it meant that my life stayed on course. "Uh, no," I whispered. "It was a different kind of attack."

"Oh, fuck no!" she hissed, awareness dawning on her, and I flinched.

"You don't believe me." Of course she didn't. No one had believed me when I went to the police. *Not even my father.*

"Believe you?" Cam gaped at me. "Of course I *believe* you, Lee." She grabbed my hand and squeezed. "When you say you were attacked," she paused, clearly struggling with how to sentence the next question.

"He didn't," I hurried to say. "I mean, he nearly did, but I got away." *Barely,* I wanted to add, but I didn't think Cam needed to hear the gory details.

"Oh, thank Jesus," she sighed, relieved. "Who was he? Did you see his face?" Her eyes narrowed. "He was charged, wasn't he? Lee, tell me you nailed the bastard to the wall."

I sucked in a shuddering breath, holding back the tears. "Yes, I knew him. His name is Perry Franklin. He was in my English class at school. It happened after prom. I wasn't supposed to go, but Perry asked me and I really wanted to go." I begged her with my eyes to understand. "Daddy was gone out of town on *work,* or at least that's what he said he was doing–" I paused to shrug before continuing, "and I had just wanted to be *normal* for one night – to experience one normal teenage moment, but prom was a complete disaster. He, ah, he didn't touch me until he dropped me home." I cringed thinking back.

"Keep going," was all Cam said.

"When I got out of the car, he walked me to my door, but when I tried to say goodnight, he wouldn't leave –" I couldn't say the words aloud. *I couldn't do it.*

"Tell me, Lee," Cam coaxed.

"He touched me," I confessed. "He tore my dress, held me down on the porch and he tried to..." I swallowed the lump in my throat. I could remember the feel of his rough fingers, ripping my panties away as he tried to shove his fingers inside me…

Run.

Get away fast.

Leave now.

The warning messages that my gut instinct was sending to my brain were in direct contrast with the dirty looks and hushed whispers of jealousy half the girls in my grade were shooting at me all night long.

They were jealous of who I had come to prom with.

I was terrified of who I had come to prom with.

All the way home in his car, I had the most unsettling feeling in the pit of my stomach. I shouldn't have gone out tonight, not to the school gym, and not dressed in one of Cam's cast-off dresses. Daddy was going to hit the roof when he found out.

What the hell had I been thinking when I said yes? I guess I hadn't thought much. I'd never been asked out, not once in eighteen years, so when Perry Franklin asked me to go to prom with him, I'd momentarily lost control of all rationality and made an impulsive decision. Chances were, I'd made my last.

"C'mon, baby girl," Perry crooned, tightening his hold on my hand so much I lost feeling in my fingertips when I moved to go inside my house. "Let's hang out here for a bit."

"No thank you," I strangled out, breathing hard and fast as he yanked me away from the door. He wasn't asking, I realized. He was ordering – something I'd realized very early on in the night that Perry liked to do.

Half leading me/half dragging me towards my porch swing, Perry sank down and dragged me down on his lap. *"Move your hips, Delia,"* he hissed in a threatening tone as his nostrils flared. The smell of alcohol wafting from him was strong and I was starting to panic. *"Make me good and hard."*

"No –" My pulse was roaring in my ears as I tried to free myself from Perry's death grip. My heart was palpitating for all the wrong reasons and I knew I was in trouble. *"I want to go inside,"* I strangled out, scrambling off his lap. *"I...don't...please let me go home, Perry."*

His eyes flashed with something dark and then I was on the flat of my back with the air knocked clean out of my lungs. My jaw ached so hard from his fist and I wanted to scream, but his weight on my body was suffocating.

"You know you want it, Delia," Perry grunted, as he tore at my dress like some crazed animal. *"Get on your back, darling."*

Perry groped me roughly as he lapped his tongue over my face and lips. I held my breath for as long as I could, held my body stiff and rigid, giving him nothing in return.

When I needed to breathe, I opened my mouth, inhaled a huge mouthful of air, before screaming at the top of my lungs, praying to god someone would hear me.

"Shut the fuck up, bitch," he snarled, clutching my throat with one hand, while he freed himself with the other. *"You're gonna take me, and you're gonna enjoy it, you little cock-tease."*

"I won't," I sobbed, pushing futilely at his chest. *"Please stop this. I don't want this."*

Panic gripped me when I felt his hands tearing at my panties. *"Stop!"* I screamed, scratching and tearing at his face. *"Get off me..."*

"Bruno attacked him before he could go any further," I whispered, blinking back to the present. "He bit him on the ankle and scared him off."

Cam's brows shot up. "Your dog?"

I nodded. "I reported what happened, but I wasn't taken seriously." I shrugged helplessly. "His uncle is the town Sheriff and my complaint was dismissed. I was so afraid it would happen again – that he would get me the next time." I shivered and tightened my grasp on my mug. "He told me that he would. He said that he was going to get me." I sniffled. "He called me a cocktease –" I burst into tears. "He said it was *my* fault, Cam – that I led him on and everyone believed him." I sniffed the tears back and continued. "Well, you know the way my father is. He was very upset with me."

"Hold the fuck up." Cam frowned. "Jimmy was upset with *you*?" She sounded appalled.

"Well, Daddy didn't exactly believe me," I explained wearily. "He said that I must have encouraged Perry – led him on in some way. He said I was…and he…" I stopped short. I couldn't say it. I couldn't tell her about my father's belt and the whooping he gave me for being a dirty whore. *For being easy.* "He called me some names and punished me," I finally said instead. "I think that's why I lost it with Kyle last night," I added quietly. "He called me those same names."

"Kyle's a prick," Cam growled. "Your dad's a bigger one."

"Daddy refused to take me to the hospital afterwards," I quickly continued. "He said that it was my punishment." *I now carried those scars on my back every day to teach me a lesson.* "Anyway, Daddy pulled me out of school because of the scandal so I didn't get to graduate, and he made me quit my job. Perry was extremely popular and the captain of the football team, so I was branded a liar all over town. I stayed for a while after it happened, I *tried* to get on with life, but I couldn't live like that anymore – not with everyone ignoring me and whispering about me behind my back."

"Jesus," Cam choked out. "What the hell is wrong with people?"

"It got worse at home," I told her. "More violent. More *severe*. And then one night, when I thought it was my *last night*, he passed out on the couch after beating me to a pulp, and I ran." I exhaled a ragged breath. "I gathered everything I owned and ran straight to you."

"What did he hit you with, Lee?" she asked. "I guess from the scars on your back that it wasn't his fist this time?"

I shook my head. "No. Not his fist."

"I can't believe this," she hissed brokenly. "You told me that it stopped, Lee –" Her voice cracked. "I never would've left you there if I knew." She was crying again. "I'm so fucking sorry for letting you down."

"This is not your fault, Cam," I replied, squeezing her hand. "You couldn't have stopped it any more than I could."

After what seemed an eternity, Cam seemed to find her voice again. "Shit," was all she said.

"Yeah," I agreed. "But you can't tell anyone else. Not Derek or...or not Kyle, okay?"

"Does Kyle know about any of this?"

"No, and he doesn't need to," I replied, panicking at the thought. "I'm serious, Cam. I don't want him to know anything about that part of my life."

"That will be kind of hard considering you live with him," she drawled. "Oh, and there's also the tiny matter of you being in love with him."

My breath hitched. "I'm not in love with him."

"Uh-huh."

"I'm not!"

"*Sure* you're not," she shot back sarcastically. "And I'm saving myself for marriage."

My cheeks flamed in embarrassment and I sagged in defeat. "Am I that obvious?"

She smiled sadly. "I tried to warn you." Yeah, I knew she did and I wished that I had listened to her. My heart was hurting so badly right now. "And I'm hoping you guys can move past last night," she added with a grimace. "Because if the shit hits the fan with you two, well, you're last in..."

First out, I added silently.

"It's his place," she added quietly.

"Yeah." I nodded, hearing everything she wasn't saying.

I was in some serious trouble.

"Yeah," she agreed with a sigh.

"What am I going to do?" I whispered. I needed this room. I had nowhere else to go. I'd burned my bridges back home.

"Just keep your head down and wait for this fight to blow over," she instructed gently. "If he wants you out, I don't have the power to stop him, but I'll be leaving with you." She narrowed her eyes. "And I'm telling you this now; if I ever see another bruise on your body, I will cut the bastard."

KYLE

"Are you listening to me, kiddo?" Linda looked at me with a worried expression from the other side of the table. We were having breakfast together at the hotel...well, she was. I couldn't eat. The combination of guilt and alcohol churning around inside of me rendered it impossible to eat.

No, I wanted to say. *I'm not okay,* but I kept it to myself. I didn't want her to look at me with the same disgusted expression Cam had.

I wasn't needed in the hotel today, but I couldn't stay at the house. I had to get away. After last night, I wasn't sure how I could face Lee again.

"Kyle?" Linda placed her hand on mine, dragging me from my thoughts. "Did you hear me?"

"Sorry," I muttered, shaking my head. "My head's not in this place today."

She smiled at me. "Where's your head at, kiddo?"

I wanted to tell her.

I wanted to offload all my shit on her right here and now and have her fix the mess I'd made of my life.

But I couldn't do it.

Linda didn't know all the things I'd done. She didn't know about the Rachel thing, and if she ever found out about it, along with what had happened last night with Lee, I would lose her, too.

"It's all so fucking messed up," was all I replied, *all I was willing to give*.

She stared back at me, eyes full of love.

I flinched and looked away.

I didn't deserve her to look at me like that.

"Women have a way of doing that, kiddo," she mused. "I'm guessing a woman is the reason you have that *lost puppy* look on your face."

Regrettably, I nodded.

If she only knew the half of it…

THIRTY-FOUR

DIRTY WORDS AND STOLEN INNOCENCE

LEE

BY 10PM THAT NIGHT, I was famished. I'd rushed upstairs after my talk with Cam and had stayed holed up in my room all day, too ashamed to be around the boys. Too fearful of facing one particular boy.

God, I needed this room. I need my job and the fresh start Boulder offered me. Therefore, I had decided that I was going to try my hardest to keep my head low like Cam said and not antagonize Kyle Carter. I would stay out of his way from here on out and not give him another reason to throw me out. Although, I was fairly certain that would happen regardless. I had well and truly burned my bridges by slapping him. The things I had said to him had been awful, too. Good god, what came over me? I was not an aggressive person by nature. Not in the slightest. I *hated physical* violence. I had acted completely out of character, but he called me those names…

Shuffling out of bed, I grabbed my torch, crept to my door, and listened to the howling of the wind. The storm Cam had predicted would hit us tonight had well and truly struck, taking with it the electricity. I didn't mind. I was used to the dark.

Besides, I had been exposed to some crazy weather back home. This was a piece of cake in comparison.

I knew Cam and Derek were at a friend's house because she had popped her head around the door hours ago to lend me her torch and tell me that she'd see me in the morning. Slipping out of my room, I tiptoed downstairs and into the dark kitchen. Lightning forked outside the window as I attempted to make a one-handed cheese sandwich. Not bothering to sit down, I ate my sandwich over the sink, watching in fascination as mother-nature transformed the night sky.

Grabbing a bottle of water from the fridge, I tucked it under my arm and snatched up my torch with my good hand before moving for the stairs. Four steps up and the torch light began to flicker rapidly before dimming out completely. Stifling a groan, I felt my way in the darkness, touching the walls and banister as I went. Tripping several times, my hand finally found the door handle for my bedroom and I hurried inside and closed the door behind me only to stumble over something on the floor.

Confused, I righted myself and looked around at the candles lighting up the room. I frowned. What the hell? My eyes landed on the man lying in my bed and my heart skyrocketed in my chest. That wasn't my bed. This wasn't my room.

Oh no.

"Lee?" Kyle sat up slowly and rubbed his eyes. He placed the battery-operated radio he had been holding on his nightstand and I registered the soft, melancholy sound of Guns 'N Roses' *Don't Cry* as it wafted from the little plastic radio speaker. "What are you doing here?"

"Oh my god, it's your room!" I strangled out, dropping both my water and my torch with fright. "I'm so sorry." Stumbling, I bent down to grab my goodies. "I didn't mean to come in here." Goddammit, they rolled under his bed. "Just give me a second." I dropped to my knees and stretched my good hand out, desperately trying to retrieve my stupid bottle. "And I'll be out of your hair, I promise."

When his mattress squeaked, I froze on all fours. A dozen different scenarios ran through my mind – all of which resulted in me being turfed out on the streets.

I jumped into action and leapt up from the floor. "You know

what; I wasn't thirsty anyway," I babbled, backing away blindly. "It was dark in the hallway. The storm confused me. Well, not the storm, but I just... I didn't mean to come in here...I meant the second door on the right." I swung around and grabbed the door handle. "The second door, dammit –"

"Wait."

Freezing, I remained completely still, my body obeying his command.

"Wait," he repeated, voice barely more than a broken whisper.

I sucked in a ragged breath, but didn't dare turn around. I could feel him right behind me and the hairs on the back of my neck rose.

"Wait," he said for the third time, this time a pained plea, and I felt his fingertips brush against my shoulder, touch featherlight. "*Wait.*"

Inhaling deeply, I slowly turned around to face him and immediately wished that I hadn't. He was naked everywhere with the exception of a pair of black boxer shorts. In the dim candlelight, I watched as Kyle took a safe step back, eyes locked on mine, expression wary.

"Are you okay?" he croaked out.

"Me?"

"You," he confirmed gruffly.

I swallowed deeply. "I'm okay."

Pain flickered in his eyes and he reached his hand out to gently trace his thumb over my injured wrist before quickly pulling away. He took another step back and pushed his hands through his disheveled hair.

He was *nervous.*

I placed my hands behind my back and whispered, "I'm fine." I was afraid to say anything else that may lead to another argument.

"Lee, I never meant to –" Groaning as if he was in physical pain, he bit down hard on his lip and began to pace, clearly agitated. Pacing was his jam, I decided. The man loved to pace. "I've never –" he paused and clenched his eyes shut. "Fuck." I watched his chest rise and fall quickly. "I have never laid a hand on a woman in my life," he finally declared in a torn voice, finally standing still. "I swear to god, Lee." He kept his eyes closed as he spoke. "I need you to know that. I need you to know that I would *never* intentionally hurt you. Not in a million years. I'm *not* that guy."

My heart broke at the sight of his distraught expression. I wanted to find the words to heal him – to soothe his pain. I wanted him to stop feeling so bad for something I started. "You didn't," I finally replied. "I mean, it's *okay*, Kyle. It was my fault. I know you're not that guy."

His eyes snapped open and it was obvious that I had said the wrong thing because he was glaring at me. "How was me fucking marking your skin *your* fault?" he demanded, voice torn. "*None* of what happened last night was *your* fault."

He moved towards me so fast that I backed against the door. A small cry tore from my throat and Kyle jerked away from me, horrified. "Jesus Christ, you're afraid of me," he strangled out, clamping his hands down on his head. "I fucking frighten you, Lee!" He dropped his head in shame, body trembling.

"It's okay," I choked out, breathing hard. "It's okay."

"No." He shook his head, shoulders slumping. "It's not."

I was afraid of him, but not for the reasons he thought. I was afraid of how he made me *feel*.

I could feel his regret.

I wanted to comfort him.

So, I did.

"I'm not afraid of you, Kyle," I whispered. Tentatively closing the space between us, I reached up and cupped his cheek with my good hand.

He stiffened, rejecting my affections just like he always did, before slowly leaning his cheek into my touch. He shuddered and I felt wetness on my fingers.

"Look at me," I demanded hoarsely. "Please."

With a pained groan, he looked at me, eyes glistening, eyelashes damp.

My heart cracked.

"I am *not* afraid of you." I wiped a lone tear away and stepped closer. "Don't torture yourself over something *I* caused."

"I shouldn't –"

"You did nothing," I cut him off. "I slapped your face and you reacted on instinct. It was an accident." I rubbed my thumb across his cheek, desperate to comfort him.

He straightened up then, standing tall and determined. Leaning close to me, he bent his head to my ear and whispered, "I promise you that I will never hurt you again." Stepping back, he pointed to my wrist. "*That*," he choked out. "Will *never* happen again. Not ever."

Never happen again?

"Do you want me to leave?" I blurted out, feeling panicked. I didn't mean to be so blunt, but I needed to know where I stood and if I had a place to stay.

Kyle blinked. "*What?*"

"Cam said that you might not want me anymore." I flushed bright red at my verbal blunder. "I mean, that you might not want me *to stay here* anymore."

Leaning down, he pressed his forehead against mine and sighed heavily. "You can't still want to stay here, Princess."

My heart sank.

Oh god.

He wanted me gone.

He was just too nice to say.

"Please, Kyle," I begged, cresting on a panic attack. "I have nowhere else to go. I can stay out of your way. I promise I won't cause trouble for you and Rach –" I couldn't say her name so I settled on saying, "I'll be invisible," instead. I knew he hated desperation in a woman – he had told me as much, and here I was, begging and desperate, but I had no other option.

"That's impossible," Kyle groaned and his minty breath hit my face like a drug.

"Okay." Tears fell from my eyes and I nodded in gloomy acceptance. He wanted me out of his life. "I understand."

The song playing ended and another started. This time, David Gray's *Say Hello, Wave Goodbye* floated from the plastic speaker on his nightstand.

Fitting lyrics, I thought dejectedly.

Kyle cupped my cheeks gently, forcing me to look up at him. "Because there's no fucking way you could *ever* be invisible to me, baby."

I blew out a ragged breath. "Really?"

He nodded slowly. "Really." Lifting my injured hand to his mouth, he pressed soft kisses on the inside of my wrist. I gasped from the sweet gesture. He stepped closer then, body pressing closer to mine, and I could only watch in sweet anticipation as he lowered his head to mine. "Tell me to stop."

"Don't stop," I breathed, my heart fluttering like crazy. "Not ever."

His lips found mine, soft and probing, and I sagged against him. He ran his tongue against my lower lip and I parted my lips, welcoming his tongue with hot swipes of my own. His arms came around me, holding me close with one hand, while he cradled the back of my head with the other, and my emotions sizzled inside me.

The room felt clouded with sexual tension as the lust building inside of me, the one only he seemed to ignite, roared to life. When I sucked on his tongue, Kyle growled into my mouth and our kiss changed from gentle and sweet to severe and hungry. My lips matched his with a desperation and hunger of my own as I pressed my body against his, urging him to never stop.

His hand was in my hair now, fisting my curls, as he pressed me to his bedroom door and kissed me deeply, hips rocking with every thrust of his tongue. With his other hand, he touched my hip, my cheek, my arm, my stomach…

Fireworks exploded inside me and I could barely contain my emotions as my body thrummed in excitement to his touch. Willing to give him all of me and more, I sagged against the doorframe and gave myself up to his touch, trusting him not to break me tonight.

Achingly slowly, he broke our kiss, breathing hard, and stepped back. Never taking his eyes off mine, he smoothed his hands from my shoulders to my hips before reaching for the hem of my shirt. Pausing, he watched me carefully.

Seeking my permission, I realized. I knew I shouldn't let him touch me. He was another woman's man – his was every other woman's man – but I was in love with him. Oh god, how I'd fallen for him and I would take any piece of him I could.

Releasing a shaky breath, I raised my hands above my head and nodded.

His eyes darkened as he slowly pulled my shirt over my head and tossed it on the floor next to us. Braless, my breasts felt heavy and tender, nipples straining. I was naked from the waist up, but my entire soul was bare to this man. My feelings for him were overwhelming and I trembled against the doorframe.

"We shouldn't be doing this," he whispered as his conflicted gaze roamed over me. "*I* shouldn't be doing this."

Breathless, I nodded. "Yes, you should."

Groaning, he lowered his head and pulled my nipple in his mouth, swirling his tongue around the tip. I felt my legs grow weak as he tugged my nipple between his teeth and looked up at me. "Yes...please," I begged, my body thrashing against the door. "Kyle, please..."

And that's when he lost it.

Releasing a hungered growl, he grabbed my thighs and hoisted me up. Instinctively, I wrapped my arms and legs around him as he slammed our bodies together, lips crashing down on mine. I couldn't feel the pain in my wrist now. My body was too consumed in raw pleasure. Our tongues licked, sucked and collided with a passion I had never felt in my whole life. I was his.

Jesus, this man *owned* me.

"I want you so fucking bad, Lee," he growled against my lips. "I can't think straight anymore."

Oh god. "I want you, too." I kissed him hard. "All of you."

"Yeah?" was his throaty response.

I nodded against his lips. "Yeah."

With my body wrapped around his, Kyle walked us over to his bed. Lowering me onto the mattress, he kissed me hard before climbing to his feet. "No," I strangled out, feeling devastated. "Don't stop!"

"Shh, baby," he whispered, leaning over me to hook his fingers into the waistband of my pajama bottoms and panties. "I've got you." He dragged them down my legs and then tossed them away before pushing my thighs apart, baring me to him. "You are so fucking beautiful," he said gruffly, pressing a kiss to my inner thigh as he settled between my legs. "It's too much."

In that moment, with the way Kyle was looking at me, I *felt* beautiful. He ran his tongue up my thigh and I bucked restlessly. "Relax," he coaxed, sliding a finger deep inside me. "Let me make this good for you." His thumb rolled over my clit. "Christ, princess, you're so fucking tight."

"I'm sorry," I moaned, arching into his touch. "Is that bad?"

"Jesus," he growled. "You're killing me."

He traced my clit with his tongue and I cried out. "I want

you!" My admission was embarrassingly honest. "Oh god, Kyle," I cried. "I want you so bad."

"I've gotta taste you first," he growled, suckling me. "I've gotta taste this tight pussy." Heat pooled between my legs and everything inside of me tightened. "Hmm, so fucking wet and sweet." His tongue speared me and I almost jackknifed off the bed. "I'm gonna eat this pussy, baby."

His dirty words were pushing me higher, harder. Whimpering, I clutched his bedsheets and rocked against his face. His tongue flicked over my clit. "Kyle!" I strangled out, reaching for his hair. "Jesus…" Trembling, I knotted my fingers in his hair as my body jerked uncontrollably.

"Yeah, baby, come for me," he ordered. "Come in my mouth." He plunged his tongue inside me, licking and sucking. "This pussy is mine!"

"Yours!" I screamed out as everything inside of me contracted. I felt so close, something so close. Desperate for *more*, I grabbed at his shoulders, pulling his body on top of me. "Make me come."

"Fuck yeah." Pressing me into the mattress with his big body, he plunged his tongue into my mouth while he wrestled to free himself from the confines of his boxers.

When he pushed his boxers down his hips and his erection sprang free, my breath caught in my throat. Clueless but willing to learn, I reached a hand between our bodies and fisted the surprisingly smooth shaft of his cock. He was hard and big, *scarily big*, and I didn't even care. He could break my body apart right here and now and I would gladly burn in the aftermath.

He kissed me deeply and I could taste myself on his tongue as he settled heavily between my legs. "I want you coming on my cock," he growled as he fisted my hair. His eyes were wild and fevered as he hitched my thigh around his waist. "Sucking me in tight with that sweet, little pussy." I felt his erection probe against my wet folds and I gave myself up to him. I wanted this. No man had ever made me feel the way Kyle did. I wanted him to have me.

"You're gonna feel so good," he continued, taunting me with his dirty words. Rearing back, he teased me with the head of his erection. "I'm gonna fuck your brains out, baby." He pressed a hard kiss to my lips. "Fair warning."

Afraid that he would stop again before he followed through on his promises, I wrapped my legs around his waist and pushed my heels against his butt.

"Lee, wait, I need a co–" he began to say, but his control faltered and he plunged deep into me, tearing through me hard, deep, and right to the hilt. "Fuck."

And the pain I felt in that moment as Kyle tore through my virginity was agonizing. A pained cry tore from my chest as I clung to his shoulders, body burning, eyes watering from the intensity.

"Jesus Christ," he strangled out, freezing inside of me. His entire body tensed and stilled. "Christ, Lee, baby, why did –"

I grabbed his face before he could say another word and crushed my lips to his. Kissing him hard, I forced my mind past the pain and gingerly bucked my hips upwards. Kyle groaned into my mouth as he sunk in deeper, taking both my virginity and my heart with a single thrust.

Drowning in emotion, I clung to Kyle as he held himself still inside of me. We were breathing hard, both looking at the other with wide, fearful eyes.

"I didn't know," he strangled out, pressing his brow to mine. "I'm sorry."

"Don't stop," I begged. Shuddering above me, he clenched his eyes shut. "Kyle, I'm begging you! Please don't stop."

"I *hurt* you," he strangled out. "You're *shaking*."

"It's okay." I shook my head and pressed a kiss to his lips. "You'll hurt me worse if you stop."

He stared hard at me for the longest moment and I honestly didn't know what he would do, but then he closed his eyes, buried his face in my neck, and began to move. Slow at first and then harder and faster until my back was arching off the bed and my body burned with a different kind of feeling. The dull ache between my legs was eclipsed by the throbbing deep inside of me, as my body learned the feel of his intrusive thrusts, and then greedily welcomed him.

Slamming himself inside me over and over with powerful, deep thrusts, he followed through on every one of his promises. Overwhelmed, I clung to him and rode the unfamiliar wave, knowing I was getting too attached to a man I couldn't be sure of, but resigning myself to just living in the moment. Tonight, right now in this very moment, he was *mine*. I clung to that small sliver of hope, blocking out all fear of what would come tomorrow, as I reveled in the feel of him making me a woman.

THIRTY-FIVE

I TRIED TO PROTECT YOU

KYLE

WHEN MY BEDROOM door flew open tonight, the very last person I expected to see was Lee standing in the doorway. We were in the middle of a power cut, my bedroom was littered with candles I had been stealing light from to get some much-needed paperwork done earlier, when she walked in, once again throwing my life on its axis.

Completely fucked from the get-go, I watched as she dropped whatever she was holding and began to ramble. I couldn't hear a word of what she was saying because I couldn't get my damn mind to focus on anything except how beautiful her tits looked as they spilled over the damn tank top she had on. I was torn between staring at her tits and the tiny pair of pajama shorts she had on that hung low on her curvy hips.

Jesus Christ.

She was painfully beautiful.

Instantly hard, I shot up into a sitting position to hide my growing dick, only to shove a fist in my mouth when she dropped down on all fours. She had the best ass, round and ripe, and it was hanging out of those damn shorts while she looked under my bed for whatever the hell it was that she had dropped.

My heart nearly leapt out of my chest when she went to leave and I must have begged her to "wait," a dozen times while I scrambled off my bed and tried to figure out how to save us. My throat was so raw that it was hard to speak. I knew that I didn't deserve to breathe the same air as her after last night, but Christ, I needed Lee to know I wasn't that guy. I would *never* hurt a woman. Whoever the fuck she was running from in Louisiana, I was *nothing* like him and I needed her to know that. "Are you okay?" I reached out to touch her, only to swiftly think twice about it and snatch my hand away. I was desperate to keep her here with me. Touching her was *not* the way to do that – or so I had thought.

Everything that happened after that passed by in hazed blur of emotions and feelings too fucking scary to contemplate, until I found myself, once again, pushing the limits with this girl. I had no fucking clue how we had gotten to the point where she was naked on my bed beneath me, but I couldn't stop. I didn't have an ounce of self-restraint left inside of me. I'd used it all up these past four months – trying to not do *exactly* this. My heart was going crazy in my chest at the sight of her. I'd caught feelings, I realized. Like the fucking idiot I was, I'd screwed up and caught feelings for the girl.

More than just feelings, asshole.

Jesus.

Shaking my head, I forced the terrifying notion from my mind and concentrated on eating her out. *I want to keep you,* the words were on the tip of my tongue, but I held them back and allowed my dick to take control of this precarious situation because my brain, the traitorous piece of shit, had deserted me entirely. And god knows, my heart was making trouble for me.

Slapping a firm censor on my rogue chest muscle, I told Lee everything I wanted to do to her body, keeping that dangerous four-letter word out of the equation. It had no business coming out of my mouth. Whether I felt it or not, it was pointless. I couldn't *keep* her.

Feeling frantic, I ate her pussy like a starved man at a feast. Every time I had my mouth on her, the same wave of desperation washed over me. It scared the hell out of me because I never knew if this time would be the last time. And the prospect of the last time made me feel like I couldn't *breathe.*

When she pulled on my shoulders, encouraging me to come to her, I shook like a fucking teenager. She wanted me. After all the shit I'd done and all the pain I'd caused her, she wanted me inside her. Humbled, I pushed my boxers down and thrust my tongue into her mouth, wanting nothing more than to fall inside this girl and never come back. She asked me to break her fall and I was secretly praying that she could break mine because I was falling through this life and I needed something. I needed *her*.

Hard and horny, I told her everything I wanted to do to her, all truths, while I wet the head of my cock with her pussy lips. I knew I needed to slow this down and get a handle on myself. At the rate I was going, I was going to come the minute I pushed inside her, but Lee pressed her feet against my ass, pushing me into her.

"Lee, wait!" I strangled out, trying and failing to hold back. "I need a –"

Condom, I mentally finished as I sank deep inside of her. Startled by the resistance I was met with, and then unintentionally plowed right through, I groaned. She was tight. She was too fucking tight. I heard her pained cry. Her small fingers dug into my shoulders and I froze.

Oh no.

Oh fuck no.

"Jesus Christ," I choked out, stilling inside of her, as awareness washed over me. I'd just taken her virginity. I'd just fucked it out of her. "Christ. Lee, baby. What did you –"

Lee grabbed my face and kissed me hard, cutting me off midsentence. When she bucked her hips upwards, I groaned into her mouth, hips rolling instinctively, and I slid deeper into her.

What was she *doing*?

I was *hurting* her.

Desperate to stop the aching I knew she must be feeling, I locked my limbs into position and remained rigidly still, eyes locked on hers. "I didn't know," I whispered, dropping my forehead to hers. "I'm sorry."

"Don't stop," she begged, looking up at me with wide, trusting eyes.

I clenched my eyes shut, knowing that I would never in a million years deserve this girl or her trust.

"Kyle, I'm begging you," she sobbed, cradling my face in her small hands. "Please don't stop."

"I *hurt* you," I bit out, willing her to take a damn minute and realize how bad of an idea I was for her. "You're shaking."

"It's okay." Shivering, Lee stretched up and pressed a kiss to my lips. "You'll hurt me worse if you stop."

It was at that exact moment that I realized just how badly I was fucked. Call it defrosted, thawed-out, or call it resurrected from the dead, but I swear to god, I'd never felt my once-frozen heart pump harder for another human being.

My eyes were glued to hers, a million unspoken words on the tip of my tongue, as I watched her watch me. The sound of her pleading was my undoing. She didn't need to beg me for a damn thing. I could hate myself later.

With a flushed shiver, I buried my face in her neck and started to move. Filled with self-loathing, I did what she asked to do; I fucked her, slow and soft, hard and fast. Shaking, I buried myself to the hilt inside of her over and over, feeling more exposed in this moment than I'd ever been. She cried and mewled and clawed at my chest, so I fucked her harder. I gave her exactly what she asked for, my own body working to maximum capacity as I filled her up with furious thrusts.

"Please, Kyle, I can't, " Lee cried out when her pussy tightened around me. "I'm so…oh god!"

Reaching a hand between us, I thumbed her clit, never once slowing the rhythm of my hips as I pounded into her tight, little virgin pussy. Desperate to save myself from this emotional avalanche I was suffocating under, I pinched her clit and sagged in relief as she came apart in my arms, her pussy clenching me so tightly it felt like she was swallowing my dick. Completely fucking reeling, I collapsed in a heap on top of Lee's sweat-soaked body and poured myself inside of me, filling her to the brim with seed I had no business sowing.

Burying my face in her neck, I continued to pump my hips, emptying myself into her, all the while I contemplated what the fuck I had just done.

LEE

Kyle stayed inside me for a long time afterwards. He was hot and sweaty and trembling from head to toe as he remained on top of me, face tucked into the crook of my neck. I wasn't sure what to do, so I just held him close and trailed my fingers through his hair.

Several more minutes passed by before he slowly eased himself out of me. I winced at the unfamiliar sensation of him pulling out. All of this felt so foreign to me and I was sore. My body was aching, my heart was vulnerable, and when Kyle rolled away from me and laid down on the far edge of the bed, I felt *hollow* inside. Like someone had taken a blunt object and carved a hole straight through me.

He didn't speak a single word to me as he lay on his back, staring up at the ceiling with a haunted expression etched on his face.

Horrified, I sat up and draped the bedsheet around my naked body. I didn't know if I should leave or not. I wanted him to look at me. To say something – anything to put me at ease. He did neither.

Instead, he flung his arm over his face and continued to ignore me.

The reality of what I'd done came crashing down on me and I jumped off his bed. Stifling a sob when I saw the blood on his bedsheets, the same blood that was smeared on my thighs and on *him*, I gathered up my clothes and dressed in tumultuous silence.

Still, Kyle said nothing.

Body aching and trembling from head to toe, I stumbled to the door and threw it open.

"I tried to stop this," he croaked out, face still covered. "I tried to protect you.".

Not bothering to respond, I slipped out, closed the door quietly behind me, and stumbled through the darkness to my room.

THIRTY-SIX

LEE

WHEN I WOKE the next morning, Cam was sitting on the end of my bed, casually flicking through a fashion magazine. "Jesus, Cam!" Startled, I pulled myself up on my elbows and blinked the sleep from my eyes. "What are you doing here?"

"Oh, good, you're not dead," she replied, nose still stuck in her magazine. "I thought you might have been considering it's midday and you've slept through work –hey, do you think I could pull this look off?" She turned the magazine to face me and pointed to what I could only describe as a nearly naked lady clad in neon strips of fabric. "Too much?" she asked with a shrug.

"Uh, maybe just a tad," I offered. "And I'm not due at work today," I added, shifting into a sitting position.

"Hmm." Flicking through the magazine, Cam reached for a packet of chips on my mattress and munched happily.

Propping my back against my pillows, I bit down on my lip when I felt the aching between my legs. "How long have you been in here waiting for me to wake up?" I asked, watching her with wry amusement.

"Since I got home. So... a little over an hour," she replied. "Like I said, I thought you were dead." Smirking, she closed the magazine and waggled her brows at me. "I thought the wicked witch of the dick had slipped some poison in your apple while I was away."

"The wicked witch?"

"Rachel," Cam filled in. "Who else?"

I groaned. "Oh god."

Cam laughed. "She's crazy. Sincerely, sometimes, I think she means it when she threatens war on me."

I blinked rapidly. "And that's funny how?"

"Because I can take her," Cam said with a grin. "Now. Get out of bed. Since you don't have work today, you can keep me company." She smiled again and examined her fingernails. "Damn, Der is a beast."

I gaped at her. "*What*?"

She grinned. "Well, last night, we decided to try –"

"Wait," I hurried to say, holding my hand up. "If whatever you decided to do last night with Derek is even *remotely* related to your sex life, then I promise you that I *don't* want to know."

She winked. "Your loss."

I shuddered. "I'll take your word for it."

"Oh, please." Her eyes sparkled with mischief as she grinned at me. "You just wait until you get yourself some high-quality dick on demand and then we'll talk. You'll see, Lee-Bee."

"Cam!" I choked out.

"Relax." She threw her head back and laughed. "There's nothing wrong with a woman enjoying sex."

"Yeah, but still…" I grimaced. "That's crude."

"Oh shit!" Her eyes widened and her smile fell. "Oh, Lee, I'm sorry. I didn't mean to be insensitive."

"Insensitive?" Oh my god, did she know what I did last night? Could she tell? I glanced down at myself. Was she some sort of missing virginity detector? "I didn't –"

"I shouldn't say crap like that to you after what happened at your prom. I'm just…I'm not sure how I should behave around you now and I'm not good at filtering my thoughts."

I mentally heaved a sigh of relief before registering her words. "You treat me the way you always have, Cam. I just want a fresh start. Just be *normal* with me."

Cam was quiet for a moment and then nodded. "Done deal, babe."

I let out another sigh of relief. "Thank you."

"I have a modeling shoot in an hour, so get out of that bed and into the shower," she ordered, rising gracefully to her feet. "Scrub that sexy ass up and you never know, you might get spread."

"On a magazine?"

"Or on your back."

"You're disgusting."

Cam laughed. "I say we go check out a movie after my shoot and grab some dinner. Make a girly day out of it. Have some *fun* for a change." I flopped back down on the bed and Cam threw a pillow at my head. "I mean it – get your hot ass out of bed and take a shower."

She swanned over to the door and I slowly dragged myself out of my bed. Standing up, I gingerly tested my legs on the floor, feeling sore and stretched.

"'Atta girl," Cam called over her shoulder. "Wear something sexy."

"Wait," I shouted back. "I don't own anything sexy – and don't suggest that dress."

"Just go have a shower," I heard her call back as she disappeared from sight. "I've already put an outfit in the bathroom for you."

Oh great.

Snatching up my toiletries bag, I crossed the hallway to the bathroom and swiftly locked myself inside. Switching on the water, I prayed to Jesus that there was some hot water left in the tank. Scorching hot water sprayed from the shower head.

Bingo.

I stripped down and stepped into the shower. Numb, I soaped myself with my favorite strawberry-scented shower cream. I wanted to wash away last night. I wanted to erase all memory of his reaction from my mind.

His reaction made me feel dirty.

It made me feel like a whore.

I blinked back the tears that threatened to spill, refusing point blank to shed another tear over him.

Shivering, I forced my mind to empty and scrubbed myself raw.

KYLE

When the sun came up the next day, I found myself in the same position, on the flat of my back, staring up at the ceiling, with the smell of her all around me. The power was back on, but I didn't care. Body rigid, I breathed through my mouth and tried to wrangle myself together. It wasn't coming easily to me, though.

Fucked.

I was thoroughly fucked.

Whatever hope I had of keeping her in my life was gone now. I'd quite literally fucked it all away. I had no clue how to approach Lee after what happened between us. I had no goddamn clue how to explain myself, my past, or my actions. I knew she was awake. I heard her shuffling around in her room over an hour ago, and then heard the shower running from across the hall. She'd been in the bathroom for half an hour and I was still lying in my bed, contemplating how I was going to face her.

Jesus, I was such a pussy.

With a pained groan, I rolled out of bed, threw on a pair of sweatpants, and shrugged on a t-shirt. I knew what I had to do and the thought made me sick to my stomach. Furious with the world, I reached for my phone off my nightstand only to flinch when my gaze landed on my bed. My heart sank and accelerated all at once as I took in the sight of my blood-stained sheets.

Asshole!

With a stomach full of shame, I stripped my bed and balled

my sheets up. I was never going to be good enough for that girl, but now…fuck, now I was starting to think that I needed to be. Jesus Christ, I had never been so conflicted about anything in my life.

So torn up.

So fucking trapped.

No, pulling off the Band-Aid was the best approach.

I had to stop this before I broke the girl beyond repair because I wasn't ever going to be free. Regardless of how much I wanted things to be different, I knew there was only one way this could go. With a weary sigh, I gathered up my bedsheets and went downstairs to face her.

THIRTY-SEVEN

HICKEYS AND HEARTACHE

LEE

I WAS NOT in a sexy mood. I was in a shitty one. Still, I did as I was told and dressed in the white gypsy dress with the off the shoulder straps that Cam set out for me. To be fair, it wasn't as revealing as I had expected it to be. It flattered my curves by cinching at the waist before flaring loosely to just above my knees. Slipping a pair of flat white pumps, I smoothed my dress down and checked my reflection in the mirror.

The skirt covered the scars on my upper thighs, and the full back of the dress covered the ones on my lower back. I was grateful Kyle hadn't noticed them last night. It was bad enough that Cam knew.

Blow-drying my dark brown curly hair until it fell in loose curls down my back, I applied some makeup, painting my lips a glossy red. I gave my gray eyes the smoky effect that Cam had taught me to do and then I brushed some blush to my cheeks, hand stilling when my eyes landed on the huge, purplish bruise on my neck.

Oh my god.

Kyle had *branded* me.

Heart leaping, I touched my fingers to the hickey and shivered.

Don't think about it, Lee.

You'll break.

Shaking my head, I grabbed the tube of foundation and covered it as best I could and took one final glance at myself in the mirror. Besides the faint, icky love bite on my neck, I actually looked okay. My waist looked very narrow, but damn, my hips were huge. I looked like a heifer. Cam's mother had once referred to them as *childbearing hips*.

Shuddering at the thought, I slipped out of the bathroom and made my way downstairs. When I walked into the kitchen, Cam wolf-whistled from her perch on the counter, where she was sucking on an ice-lolly. A choking noise from behind me made me realize that we were not alone. Spinning around, my eyes landed on Kyle and Derek, who were sitting at the kitchen table. Kyle had his coffee cup held up to his mouth and seemed to be frozen in his seat. Our eyes locked and I felt a blast of heat crawl up my neck. Quickly turning my back on him, I walked over to the coffee pot and grabbed a mug. I couldn't deal with him right now – not with Derek smirking at me and Cam grinning like the cat that got the cream.

"Now that's what I've been talking about for years," Cam said, pointing at me with her popsicle. "You are smoking hot, girl."

"Please don't," I muttered, concentrating on filling my cup. I could feel Kyle's steel blue eyes boring into my back and my body flamed in heat.

"I'm simply stating the obvious," Cam continued, clearly not registering the hidden plea in my words, as she turned to the guys. Jumping down from the counter, she sauntered over to the table and pulled out a chair next to Derek. "Babe, doesn't Lee look sexy?"

I trembled as I turned around to face my three roommates sitting at the table, staring back at me. I felt like a damn show pony.

"Oh, *hell* no, babe," Derek laughed, holding his hands up. "I'm not falling down that snake pit. Ask Kyle – he's impartial."

Don't ask Kyle.

Don't ask Kyle.

Don't ask Kyle.

"Kyle, doesn't Lee look sexy?"

Don't answer.

Don't answer.

Please god, don't answer.

"She always looks beautiful," Kyle replied, eyes locked on mine for a long beat before he dropped his attention to the newspaper open in front of him.

"Duh." Cam rolled her eyes and threw her legs over her boyfriend's lap. "I said sexy."

"She's always that, too," Kyle shot back gruffly, not missing a beat, as he flicked through his paper.

Derek bit down on his fist to stop himself from laughing.

"Come and sit, Lee," Cam said before delving into conversation with Derek. I instantly knew what she was trying to do. She was trying to break the ice between Kyle and me because she thought we were still in a fight since the party. *If only she knew.* She clearly thought we could patch things up. I wanted to tell her that the ship had sailed. After last night there was no slipping back into any kind of friendship with him.

Resigned, I shuffled awkwardly to the table, taking the last remaining seat – which, of course, was the one next to Kyle. *Dear god, this was a slow form of torture.* I eased myself down, careful not to brush against any part of him. Despite my best efforts, my knee brushed against his thigh and I squirmed in discomfort, hands clasped tightly in my lap. Kyle roughly cleared his throat and looked up from his paper.

Our eyes locked.

Blue on gray.

Pain on regret.

Sorrow on guilt.

My breath hitched and I quickly trained my attention on Cam, who was giving Derek an animated run-down of her botched bikini wax, to which he dutifully replied with what I presumed were supposed to be supportive compliments on how he enjoyed said botched wax job. Honestly, I couldn't even think of repeating their conversation in my *mind.*

Kyle caught my attention again. "Are you okay?" he mouthed, and when his fingers touched mine under the table, I literally jumped out of my chair.

"Christ, Ice, you're jumpy today," Derek remarked, glancing

from me to Kyle and then back again. A huge grin of recognition spread across his face and he waggled his brows. "Why could that be?"

"I'm just tired." Blushing, I grabbed my mug and moved for the sink to wash up. "I didn't get much sleep."

"No sleep, huh? I wonder why that could be." He tapped his chin, sarcasm dripping from his tone. "Hmm, I wonder. Any ideas, Cam? *Kyle*?"

"She's probably not used to sleeping in strange beds," Cam replied with a shrug. I gasped, coffee spluttered from Kyle's mouth, and Derek burst out laughing. "What?" Cam asked huffily. "She hasn't been here long enough to break it in." Kyle choked harder and Cam's eyes narrowed. "What's going on?"

"Nothing," Kyle replied.

"Lee –"

"Nothing!" I agreed, tone hard, as I turned my back to them and rinsed my mug under the faucet.

"Oh shoot, I've lost my keys." Derek announced in an overly enthusiastic tone of voice, clearly lying through his teeth. "Cam, can you help me look for them?"

"But they –"

"*Now*, Cam," he cut her off. "I really need my *keys*."

"Oh yes, your keys," she finally replied, playing along now. "I think I saw them in my room."

"Wonderful," he replied. "Let's check together."

I glanced over my shoulder just in time to see Derek hurry out of the kitchen, with Cam making cut-throat gestures to Kyle as she reluctantly followed after him.

"Lee," Kyle said when the kitchen door closed behind them.

My breath hitched and I spun back around, giving him my back.

"Lee, talk to me."

I gripped the sink and breathed slowly.

"Please, just say something."

"There's nothing *to* say, Kyle," I squeezed out, trembling. "Your actions told me everything I needed to know last night."

"I'm sorry."

"Yeah." Nodding, I grabbed the dirty dishes off the draining board and tossed them in the sudsy water, scrubbing furiously. "Me, too."

I heard a chair scraping against the tiles moments before his hand touched my shoulder. "I'm sorry." His fingers grazed my bare skin. "Are you sore?"

Clenching my eyes shut, I resisted the urge to lean into him. Instead, I did what was safe for my heart and I shrugged his hand off. Of course I was sore, I ached in ways I never knew I could, but it was my heart that was hurting hardest.

"I didn't know, Lee." He sounded torn. "You should have told me it was your first time."

"Don't worry about it," was all I replied.

"Can you just look at me for a minute?"

No, I couldn't. It wasn't safe for me to do that.

"Look at me, Lee." His arm came around my waist, forcing me to turn and look at him. "Come on, baby, just *look at* me."

"It's *okay*, Kyle." I pulled away from him and turned back to look out the window. "I don't need to hear the speech and you don't need to feel guilty. You didn't do anything I didn't want you to do. End of."

"Dammit, Lee, would you just stop turning away from me!"

Reluctantly, I looked up at him. His eyes held the world of regret, and I cringed.

"Last night..." he began and then shook his head. "Lee, it was the b –"

"Biggest mistake of your life," I filled in before he could say the words and ruin me. "Let me guess; it shouldn't have happened, it can't happen again – oh, and you're sorry for leading me on?" The dam broke and tears poured from my eyes. "I've got it, okay?" I sniffled. "Loud and clear."

"That is *not* what I was going to say." He glared hard at me before releasing a pained sigh. "But I'd be lying if I said I wasn't sorry."

I flinched. "Okay, you're sorry. You don't want me. You regret what happened. You're with Rachel. I get it, Kyle, I do." Blinking back my tears, I stepped around him and put some space between us. "So please, *please*, just *stop* talking about it."

Running a hand through his hair, he shrugged helplessly. "Lee, I don't know what to do here." He opened his mouth to say something else but swiftly snapped it shut. Jaw clenched, he looked around aimlessly. "I don't know what to tell you other than I'm so fucking sorry."

"Okay," I strangled out, crying hard now, furious with myself for my weakness.

"Don't cry, baby," he croaked out, closing the space between us to pull me into his arms. "It shreds me when you cry."

"Then stop making me cry," I whispered.

———

"So, are you going to tell me what all that was about in the kitchen?" Cam asked when we climbed into her car after her shoot later that day.

"What?" I decided to play dumb as I fastened my seatbelt. I had deftly avoided the interrogation until now, hoping that she wouldn't bring it up.

"I'm blonde, Lee, not stupid," she shot back, pulling out into traffic. "I know something's up with you and Kyle. You two were acting all kinds of fucked up this morning, and you've barely been able to string two sentences together since you saw him."

"I'm fine," I whispered, clasping my hands together on my lap. "And nothing happened."

"Bullshit," she tossed back. "But I get it. You're not ready to talk."

"Sorry," I mumbled.

"It's cool," she replied. "But you should know that I can see your poor attempt at covering your *love bite*."

My eyes widened and I slapped a hand over my neck.

Cam chuckled. "I can't believe you let that fucker brand you."

KYLE

"So, you finally gave in and nailed the ice queen? Was she worth the wait? Did she have the pussy of all pussies? Are you sunk? Planning round two yet?" Derek's smart-ass remarks, once the girls had left, were the reason he was currently pinned against the wall with my hand around his throat.

"Say that again," I snarled, beyond furious. "I fucking dare you."

He grinned, unfazed. "I'll take that as a big, fat *yes*."

"*Der.*"

"Alright." He held his hands up. "I'll be good."

Agitated, I yanked my hand away from and stepped back. "Don't talk about her like that again," I warned. "Ever."

Derek straightened himself up and let out a whistle. "Well, shit," he mused. "You're in love, aren't you? You got attached. Caught yourself some big ole feelings." He grinned. "Terrifying, isn't it? To have your heart walking around outside of your body."

"No," I spat, horrified. "Jesus!"

"Dude, she totally sunk you," he laughed. "Don't even deny it."

"Stop it," I warned, panicking at the thought. "I'm not sunk, Derek. Girls don't *sink* me."

"Not girls," he corrected. "Girl. As in one particular southern girl."

"No," I denied, bristling, as I paced the room. "She didn't *sink* me. I don't fucking *love* her. I'm not feeling shit. You got that?"

Lies.

All lies.

"Okay," he replied with a smirk. "If that's how we're playing this, then fine. But fair warning; Cam is going to flip the fuck out."

I narrowed my eyes. "Cam can kiss my ass."

"Cam will *kill* your ass," he corrected. "In case it passed your attention, she's a little over protective of Ice – Lee." Stepping around me, he strolled over to the counter and poured us two mugs of coffee. "And just because you don't wanna talk to me about the wild and reckless storm sex that didn't happen last night – but totally fucking happened – doesn't mean that Lee will feel the same way." He took a sip of his coffee and handed me the other mug. "She'll tell Cam, dude. That's what girls do. They tell each other all kinds of crazy shit."

"Shit," I muttered, shoulders sagging.

"Yep," he agreed, taking another sip. "So, do you wanna talk about it?" He smirked. "Get your side across to me before my woman comes home on the rampage, demanding I take her side – which I absolutely fucking will because I know what's safe for me."

Hell fucking no I didn't want to talk about it. This was *Lee*. I'd ruined enough of her. I couldn't go back to that night, or change the way I behaved after. I was rough with her. *I was way too rough.* I wasn't going to soil her reputation as well. "I screwed up, Der," I growled, agitated. "Like the biggest fucking screw up of screw ups. Just leave it at that."

"I'll say," he agreed with a knowing sigh. "If those sheets are anything to go by." He grimaced. "Didn't know she was a virgin, huh?"

"The fuck?" I gaped at him.

Derek had the decency to blush. "No, I'm not a creepy bastard," he explained, taking another sip of his coffee. "I had a laundry to do and I, uh, saw the sheets in the machine. " He shrugged. "It was a rough guess, but judging by the look on your guilty assed face, and considering that fact you don't hang out with many virgins, I'd say I'm dead on the money."

Oh, this was fucking fantastic.

Depressed, I walked over to the table and collapsed onto a chair. "I didn't know." Setting my mug down, I dropped my head in my hands and groaned. "She didn't *disclose* that piece of information."

"Shit." He sat down beside me and patted my shoulder. "On the bright side, at least you know that you're the only one."

"Yeah." I knew that and the thought *thrilled* me. I wanted to kick myself in the balls for that. I should *not* be thrilled that I took Lee's virginity. I shouldn't feel *proud* about it. Jesus, I hated myself.

"Fuck knows how many Cam had before me," he added quietly.

"True." We both knew how openly Cam had given out her *favors* before she and Derek hooked up, which explained a lot of why Derek was so fucking paranoid. It didn't bother me. Not one of the three of us were whiter than white, but it drove my buddy batshit with jealousy. They were together now, though, something Lee and I weren't – something that Lee and I could never be. She had no future with me.

"Fuck." Frustrated, I released a growl and pulled on my hair. "How do I get myself into this kind of shit, Der?"

"Simple; you let your dick do the thinking," he replied breezily.

"Hmm." It wasn't my dick thinking last night. It was something else entirely and that scared the hell out of me.

"Dude, what are you gonna do about Rachel?" he asked then. "That bitch will go nuclear on Lee if she gets wind of you two hooking up."

I already knew that.

God, why did he keep speaking my fucking thoughts aloud? It was bad enough they were in my head. I didn't need to hear them come out of his mouth, too.

Fuck my life.

"There is no me and Lee," I groaned. "*You* know why I can't, Derek."

"Kyle, man," he sighed, squeezing my shoulder. "You know that I love you like you were my own retarded brother, right?"

"Wow." Sitting back, I glared at Derek. "Thanks, *friend*."

"Just hear me out," he said and I tensed. I knew what he was going to say and I also knew that it would not make a blind bit of difference. "You've got to stop punishing yourself for what happened nearly *two* years ago. It *wasn't* your fault, Kyle. It was a fucking accident that shouldn't determine the rest of your life."

"You don't get it," I muttered, cringing.

"I get it," he shot back, tone serious. "But Rachel is a big girl." Shaking his head, he released a frustrated growl. "You *don't* have to go through with it, Kyle."

"Yeah, man," I whispered in defeat. "I do."

THIRTY-EIGHT

REGRETS AND WHISKEY

LEE

SEVERAL WEEKS PASSED by before Kyle finally attempted to speak to me again. Twenty-six miserable days, to be exact. Days I'd spent pretending that I wasn't hurting, and Kyle spent pretending that I didn't exist. He ignored me at home, avoided me at the hotel, and I walked home every night from work alone.

On Friday evening, after almost four weeks of a standoff, the frigid silence was finally breached. I had just finished my shift and was leaving the hotel through the back exit when Kyle chased after me. "Lee!" Catching a hold of my arm, he pulled me back to face him. "Lee." Backing me up against the wall of the building, he exhaled a shaky breath. "I need to talk to you." He leaned into me, his face inches from mine. "It's important." The smell of whiskey on his breath, blowing into my face, was like a wrecking ball to my nerves. "I need to ask you something."

"No." If he thought he could click his fingers and I would come running then he had another thing coming. I was done with being his plaything. "You're drunk," I added, pushing at his chest with both of my hands and stepping around him. "I'm not doing this here – and not while you're in this condition. If you want to talk to me, you can do it when you're sober." What the hell was he doing, drinking at work? It wasn't like him. He was usually fiercely controlled when he was at the hotel. "And not when I'm just after finishing a twelve-hour shift on my feet."

"I wanted to talk to you sooner," he slurred, falling into step beside me as I marched down the sidewalk. "I just –"

"It doesn't matter," I snapped, folding my arms across my chest. "Just go away."

"Where are you going?"

"Away," I bit out.

"Are you running from me?"

"No, Kyle, I'm not running. I'm *leaving*," I shot back. "There's a difference." Bristling, I added, "I'm *walking* home."

"Fine," he mumbled. "I'll walk with you."

"Don't put yourself out on my account," I muttered, teeth chattering from the cold. "I'm sure you have plans." Unable to stop myself from spilling my pain, I hissed, "I'm sure Rachel or one of your *friends* would be more than thrilled to have your *company*."

Stumbling slightly, he stepped in front of me, causing us both to halt in our tracks. "You're my friend, Lee," he said with a hurt expression etched on his face. "My best friend."

"No," I choked out, emotions threatening to get the better of me. "We are *not* friends anymore. I don't need a friend like you!"

"Did you bleed?"

My mouth fell open. "*Excuse* me?"

"Your period," he slurred, frowning. "Did you get it?"

In all my life, I had never felt more shame than I did at this moment. "I can't believe you just said those words to me."

"I'm sorry, but I have to ask," he muttered, eyes bloodshot, breath stinking of whiskey. "I need to."

"Yes," I replied, face flaming in embarrassment. "I did."

He sagged in relief. "Really?"

"Really," I confirmed grimly. "I'm on it as we speak, so don't worry because you're in the clear. Now, *goodnight*." I sidestepped him and strode off down the sidewalk, but he grabbed my elbow and dragged me back to him. "Let go," I bit out, shaking now. "Now."

"Don't run off," he tried to coax. "We should talk."

"You could have spoken to me anytime in the last month, but you didn't," I strangled out. "You *ignored* me."

"I wasn't ignoring you," he spat, narrowing his eyes. "I was dealing with shit."

"You're always dealing with shit," I tossed back, voice cracking. *While I'm always waiting for you.* "Now, I've told you to leave me alone, so please do it." I knew I sounded like a bitch, but I was so damn broken. This boy had ripped me apart, piece by piece, smile by smile, kiss by kiss, and I was just trying to protect what was left of my heart. Furious with myself for feeling guilty for being mean to him, I hissed, "Leave me *alone*."

"You're fucking impossible, do you know that?" he snarled, losing his cool now. "I don't know why I even bother."

Ouch. "Oh yeah? Well, I ask myself the same question about you, Kyle," I tossed back, hurt. "God!" I pressed my fingers to my temples. "I can't deal with this."

"Well, neither the fuck can I!" he roared, kicking the ground. "Dammit, Lee –"

"Are you all right there, Lee?" Mike's voice broke through the tension and I swung around to see him approaching warily. "You all good?"

"She's fine, asshole," Kyle snarled, stepping in front of me. "We're having a private conversation, so keep fucking walking."

"It doesn't sound all that private to me, *boss*," Mike shot back hotly, stepping closer to us. Tension was emanating from both men and I felt myself wither from the sudden change in atmosphere. "Maybe you should keep walking, Carter," Mike added, brown eyes locked on Kyle's. "All the way back to the *home* you crawled out of."

"Do you have something you wanna say to me?" Kyle growled, bristling. "If you wanna say it, then fucking say it!"

"They should've left you where they found you," Mike sneered, glaring at Kyle. "Where you belonged."

Kyle smirked. "Still holding grudges, *bro*?"

Mike glowered. "Never stopped, *bro*."

"Good." Kyle narrowed his eyes. "Neither did I."

Whoa, what the heck was happening here?

"I need to go," I announced, feeling anxious. "Can you give me a ride home, Mike?" I didn't want to leave them both here to tear strips off one another. "Please?"

Mike smiled and Kyle blanched.

"Lee!" He grabbed my hand and pulled me towards him. "Do not go *anywhere* with him."

"Kyle, you *promised*," I whispered, yanking my hand free from his grasp.

Kyle released me as if I had burned him, eyes locked on my hand in horror. "Yeah," he mumbled, backing up. "I did."

"You ready, Lee?" Mike asked, holding a hand out to me.

Kyle flinched and looked away. "Do whatever the fuck you want, Lee," he sneered, turning his back on me. "I'm done."

"Yeah." Exhaling heavily, I turned around and walked towards Mike. "Me, too."

First thing tomorrow, I was going apartment hunting. No room was worth this continuous heartache.

———

"Do you want to talk about it?" were the first words Mike had spoken all evening when he pulled his car up in front of my house – Kyle's house. I had to wait at the hotel for a couple of hours while Mike finished his shift and, to be honest, I was grateful for the delay. I did *not* want to go home tonight. Several cars filled the driveway and the sidewalk, causing that familiar sinking feeling of dread to kickstart in my stomach.

Another party.

With a resigned sigh, I unfastened my seatbelt and turned to face Mike. He really had a lot going for him. He was an attractive man, and he had *normal* seat belts in his car. It wasn't fair of me to cause trouble for him. "I'm sorry about Kyle. I'm sorry that you were dragged you into my personal life."

"I don't mind being dragged in, Lee," he replied. "I'm worried about you." He gave me a sympathetic smile, his brown eyes warm. It made a change for a man to look at me with kindness, rather than disgust and anger. "I wish you would have told me about him earlier," he mumbled. "That you were involved…" He shook his head. "I could have warned you."

"I'm not involved," I mumbled. "Nothing's happening."

He arched a disbelieving brow.

I turned away.

"Fair enough," he conceded. "Just tell me that you're okay."

"I'm fine, Mike," I muttered, fighting back to tears that threatened to fall.

Do not cry.

Do not cry.

"You're not fine." Mike placed his hand on mine. I flinched from the contact, but forced myself not to panic. "I know Kyle Carter better than you do," he continued. "And I get that he's your roommate, but, Lee, the guy is bad news. He *ruins* women and doesn't give a shit while he's doing it. If you knew the half of what he's done —" he stopped and sighed. "Look, they're clearly having another party. Do you want to stay at my place tonight? Get a little distance from him?" Seeing my horrified expression, he quickly added, "On the couch, of course."

"No." I wished I had somewhere else to go. I didn't want to go inside and face Kyle, Cam, or that bitch Rachel — because I just *knew* she would be inside. I couldn't stay with Mike, though. I didn't want to blur any lines and I wouldn't feel safe. "Thank you, but I'll be fine, I swear," I added, opening my door and stepping out.

"Alright." He was at my door in a flash. "At least let me walk you up to your room. Otherwise my conscience won't let me sleep tonight."

Wary, I studied his face. He seemed genuinely concerned about me. "Okay," I whispered, nodding. "Thank you, Mike."

KYLE

She brought him back with her.

Lee brought that piece of shit back to my goddamn house –
with her!

I honestly couldn't believe my own eyes when I watched her
walk up the staircase with him trailing after her.

Blind rage, more potent than ever I'd experienced, boiled my
blood and I had to lock my limbs into position to stop myself
from chasing after her – something I seemed to be making a bad
habit of. Furious, I tore my eyes away and shivered as a cold rush
of god only fucking knew what rolled down my spine. "Fuck!" I
snarled, driving my fist into the fridge in sheer, hopeless frustration. My knuckles throbbed and I welcomed the pain – anything
to distract me from the godawful hemorrhaging ache in my
chest.

The people in my house were staring. I was too drunk and
confused to care. Let them look. If they didn't like it, they could
get the fuck out. There was only one person whose opinion I
cared about, and right now, she was upstairs with that backstab-
bing little shit.

God, I'd made a total mess of everything. Rubbing my hands
down my face, I exhaled a pained groan and rested my forehead
against the fridge. I knew it was a dick move, blindsiding Lee at
work, but Jesus, I had to talk to her. The half bottle of Jack I'd
drained had given me the Dutch courage I needed to ask the

question that had kept me up all night, every night for the last month.

She had her period.

My first, last, and *only* time not wearing a condom and I was off the hook.

I could breathe again.

Except I *couldn't.*

Because...I didn't know why. I only knew that the walls were closing in around me and I was suffocating.

Christ, I should have spoken to her sooner, explained why I couldn't give her more. Told her the fucking truth about Rachel. No. Rachel had me by the balls, and Lee? Well, she had me by another organ I didn't know worked until she walked into my life. I shuddered at the thought of her rejection. I couldn't tell her shit. But dammit, I should have said *something*, and not let this silence go for so long.

I saw it in her eyes tonight. Drunk or not, I could see the disgust in those gray eyes when she looked at me. Lee hated me and I had no one to blame but myself. Dammit, I bet that rat bastard Mike was enjoying this. He was probably filling her up with more lies about me.

"What did the fridge ever do to you?" Derek asked, coming to stand beside me. His tone was light, but his eyes were narrowed in concern. "You okay?"

Was I okay? Fuck no, I was *ruined*. I couldn't talk to him, though. No, I needed to talk to Lee. Shaking my head, I pushed past him and made for the staircase.

"Don't." A hand clamped down on my shoulder. "Leave her be, man. She's been through enough already," he added with a sigh. "Cam's right. She's not like us. She can't handle your shit."

"What the fuck do you know about her?" I demanded, spinning around to glare at him. I was shaking with anger. I knew my beef wasn't with Derek, but right about now anyone would do as a punching bag. "Well?"

"A lot more than you do by the sounds of it, asshole," he replied calmly, hand still firmly clamped down on my shoulder. "Now, calm your tits before you make this a million times worse for yourself."

"*How*?" I was right in his face, leaning down, with my brow pressed to his. "How can this get any worse?"

"Kyle, man, breathe," he coaxed, undeterred by my melt-down. "Just *breathe*."

I *couldn't*. My chest felt like it was going to explode. The thought of her upstairs with that prick was literally suffocating me. "Fuck it," I choked out, pushing past Derek.

"No, you don't −" He dragged me back again. "Dude, I'm on *your* side."

Grappling to restrain me, he grabbed my shoulders and forced me to look at him. I had a few inches on him and right now, with my current state of whiskey brain, I knew I was being impossible, bucking and trying to break free of his bear hug, but I couldn't help it. "It hurts," I strangled out, chest heaving.

"I know," Derek agreed, green eyes laced with sympathy. "And I know you hate him − I hate him, too. I hate the whole fucking lot of them right along with you, buddy, but now is *not* the time to air your dirty laundry." He squeezed my shoulders. "You need to sober up."

I stopped struggling and slumped against him. "But she's up there with *him*, Der." My voice cracked. "She's fucking up in her room with *him*!"

"Actually, she's not." Derek turned me around and my gaze landed on Mike climbing off the bottom step of my staircase. "See, man? It's not happening again. History isn't repeating itself."

Sagging in relief, I felt like the weight of the world had been lifted from my shoulders. "She sent him away," I strangled out. "Thank Christ."

Stopping at the front door, Mike turned around and smirked at me. "Feeling okay there, brother bastard? Got a problem?"

I barreled towards him. "Oh, you're gonna find out all about my problems, *brother*."

"Keep walking, asshole," Derek said, stepping between us before I had a chance to follow through on my promises. "Prefer-ably into busy traffic."

"Tell Lee that I said goodnight." He smirked. "She should sleep well after −"

"You're a dead man walking!" I snarled, lunging forward.

"Kyle, he's not worth it," Derek hissed, shoving me back and then holding me off long enough for Mike to slip out. "Come on, man, he's just trying to fuck with your head. *Don't* let him win again."

"That mother fucker better not step one foot inside my goddamn house again," I warned. "I mean it, Derek. If he or any one of his scumbag family comes inside my house again, I'll finish what he started two years ago."

LEE

"Are you sure you're gonna be okay here, Lee?" Mike asked, lingering in my doorway. "My offer still stands."

"I'll be fine, Mike," I said, holding my door, ready to close it – if he would just get out of the way. I was dropping major hints here. At first, I thought it was sweet that he walked me to my room, but now I was beginning to get worried. "But thank you so much," I hastily added. "You're a good friend to me." *Now go home.*

Mike's smile faltered for the briefest moment before swiftly slipping back into place. "I want to be more than a good friend to you, Lee," he said, tone a little deeper than before. "I like you a lot." He leaned down and kissed my cheek. "I think we could be more than good together."

I froze on the mortal spot.

"I just want you to know that you have other options," he continued. "The world doesn't start and end with Carter."

He left after that, leaving me standing in my bedroom doorway, completely freaking reeling.

THIRTY-NINE

DON'T GIVE UP ON ME

LEE

I SLEPT BADLY LAST NIGHT, tossing and turning and worrying myself half to death. I'd been worried that Kyle would come to my room. I'd been even more worried that I wouldn't send him away if I did.

I needn't have bothered.

He never came.

For some ridiculous reason, that made me feel even *worse*. After our fight yesterday, I was in turmoil. I felt like crap and everything hurt. My head. My heart. My stomach. Deep down inside the logical part of my brain, I knew that us not talking last night could only be a good thing. Kyle was wasted and usually when there was alcohol involved, our discussions went one of two ways. We either tore strips off each other, or we tore each other's clothes off.

Not good.

Not good at all.

By eight-thirty the following morning, I was up, showered, dressed, pleased to have finished my horrendously painful period, and ready to start my day – a day that was void of plans since I didn't have to work this weekend. Two whole days to myself with nothing to do and nowhere to go. Deciding on giving the downstairs a deep clean, I kicked on my old tennis shoes and pulled my curls back into a loose ponytail before quietly slipping out of my room and tiptoeing down the staircase.

"Lee –wait up."

Stiffening, I clutched the bannister and debated my options. I thought about running, I really freaking considered it, but there was no place to run *to*. Reluctantly, I released my death grip on the bannister railing and turned to face him. "Yeah?"

He was closing out his bedroom door, looking a little disheveled and a lot beautiful, and my heart leaped in my chest. I tried not to stare at his bare stomach, or the line of dark hair that disappeared under the waistband of the low-slung jeans he had on. "I thought we could do something today?" he said as he snapped the buttons on his red and black plaid shirt into place.

I blinked in confusion. "What?"

"Do something," he repeated, having the good grace to look embarrassed. His eyes were bloodshot, with dark circles under them. I guessed that's what he got for getting so trashed last night. "If you'd like to?"

"Kyle, you haven't spoken to me in a month." I frowned. "Why do you want to do something together now?"

"You have the day off work. I have the day off." He shrugged. "Why not?"

Well, that was the most disappointing reason that could have come out of his mouth. I shook my head and continued down the rest of the stairs. I needed to get out of here – go for a walk and clear my head. I supposed I could go apartment hunting today, but honestly, I didn't have enough to rent a room, let alone a whole apartment, so that notion was a bust.

"No, wait – *wait*." Kyle rushed after me, stepping in front of me and blocking the front door. "That was a stupid thing to ask." He scrunched his brow. "*I* was stupid."

I sighed wearily. "What do you mean?"

"I just want to talk to you, Lee," he said, tone gruff and oddly sincere. "Just…"

"Just what?" I pressed, about done with his games.

"I just –" He ran a hand through his hair and sighed heavily. "I miss you."

"I've been here," I muttered. "I didn't go anywhere. You're the one who –"

"I know, Lee," he replied, eyes locked on mine. "I *know*."

He certainly looked like he did. Shoulders sagging, I nodded, feeling some of my anger drain out of me. It was tiring holding onto grudges, and it made me feel just a tiny bit better that he was owning his behavior.

"I want to spend time with you," he continued. "Where it's just and me."

"I don't know," I whispered, feeling my heart thud dangerously close to enemy territory. "I don't think that's a –"

"I can fix this," he said in a passionate tone. "I can. I swear. If you just give me another shot, I'll fix this, Lee."

Another shot at what, I wanted to ask, but my pride refused to let me. "What did you have in mind?" I finally replied. My brain was screaming at me *not* to do this, but my stupid heart was compelling me to give him that shot. "To do today," I added, hating myself for being so weak. "With me."

Relief flashed in his eyes and he smiled down at me. "I'll do whatever you want me to do," he said. "We can do anything you want."

"I'll let you decide," I whispered, tearing my eyes away from him before I fell right back into his trap.

Too late, my brain hissed.

KYLE

Lee was in my truck. This was good. This meant that I had time to figure out how the hell I was going to turn this around. It meant I had time to explain myself. Problem was, instead of explaining myself, the only words that had come out of my mouth were "*you're welcome,*" when she thanked me for helping her with her seatbelt, followed by, "*Are you warm enough?*" when she shivered in her seat.

Not knowing what to do or where the hell to take her, I decided on heading for the mountains. There was an abandoned quarry about thirty minutes from here where, if all else failed, she could throw me to the outlaws and gang members that had made the quarry – or, the *Ring of Fire* as it was known on the streets – their lair.

I tried to focus on the narrow, winding road ahead of me, but my eyes kept drifting over her body. Goddammit, she looked adorable today, wrapped up in her khaki coat. She had the hood pulled up and the furry bit framed her face. She looked like a tiny Eskimo. *The sexiest fucking Eskimo I'd ever seen.* "Are you warm enough?" I asked again, and then mentally kicked the shit out of myself for transforming into a goddamn parrot. "You look cold, Princess."

"I guess I'm not used to the Coloradan weather," she replied, giving me a tight smile.

"This is mild, Lee," I chuckled, taking note of her little red nose. "Wait until the snow comes. Could be any day now." She shuddered and I couldn't help laughing. She looked so fucking cute. "So," I added, clearing my throat. "Do you have any plans next weekend? Halloween?" What a stupid fucking thing to ask. "Trick or treating?" *God, I was a douche.* My plan was to keep her talking long enough so that she would feel comfortable and open up to me again, not scare her off with my bullshit rambling.

"I'm not a big fan of Halloween," she replied quietly. "And I've never been trick or treating."

"What?" I looked at her again. "Never?"

Lee shook her head. "Never."

My brows shot up. "Well, shit." Even I, the kid who'd been passed from pillar to post, had been trick or treating. Fair enough, most years my costume consisted of a black trash bag over my shoulders and a dollar store mask, but still…

"Have you?" she asked, curious now.

"Yeah, when I was small," I told her. "Why haven't you?"

"Um…" She shifted, clasping and then unclasping her hands. "I was never allowed."

"Why?"

"You would have to ask my father."

"I'm asking you."

She shrugged, offering me a sad smile. "It doesn't matter."

I wanted to reach out and hold her hand, but I was too scared of guaranteed rejection. "Did you like school when you were growing up?" I asked then, desperate to keep her talking. "What was your favorite class?"

"I enjoyed the learning aspect of school." She was being implicit. "I liked Math and English."

"What about the rest of it?" I asked, taking a sharp corner. "You know; going to field parties with your friends, school dances, homecoming, dating?" I was prying. I knew I was, but I had this itch inside of me to know her inside out. "Were you a little queen bee?"

"I didn't have any friends and I wasn't allowed to date," she came right out and said, eyes locked on the windshield. "The first party I ever attended was when I moved here. The night you and I –" She blushed and swallowed deeply. "I've had all my firsts here."

Well shit.

Feeling like the worst piece of shit on the planet, I rubbed my hand over my chest, feeling the well-deserved burn. "Yeah," was all I managed to reply.

"What about you?" she surprised me by asking. "Were you popular in high school?"

"I was an *asshole* in high school," I offered with a grimace. "I moved around a lot during elementary and middle school, but I guess you could say I did alright for myself in high school."

"I can believe that." Lee's lips twitched. "So, were you one of the popular football jocks?"

"Hardly." I snorted. "I had a few issues with my temper. Contact sports weren't a recommended hobby for me." Another grimace. "I did some dumb shit when I was younger. A lot of parties, a lot of drinking and smoking –" I cut myself short, deciding she didn't need any more reasons to dislike me. "I used to swim," I offered up the one decent piece of information I could gather from my memory. Still did most days in the hotel pool. "Played guitar, too."

"Really?" She turned to look at me, eyes bright. "Were you good?"

"I don't know." I scratched my jaw, thinking about it for a moment. "I didn't do it to be good. I did it to escape."

"From what?" she asked, gray eyes glistening with understanding.

"Life?" I offered, turning my attention back on the road. "Being in my own head for too long?"

"Hmm."

"So, you said that you weren't allowed to date in high school, but you had to have snuck out at least once," I tossed out, desperate to steer the conversation away from my less than stellar past. "You're amazing, Lee Bennett. You can't honestly expect me to believe that you've never been on at least one date." Now I was being nosy. I peeked over at her and frowned. Her face was deathly pale, her body rigid. "What about your prom?" I added, clutching at straws. "You had a date for that, didn't you?"

A sob tore from her throat and I gaped in horror. Shit, she looked completely devastated. What the hell did I say?

"Wait, Lee," I began, trying to fix whatever it was I had done wrong this time. "I didn't mean to make you –"

"What did Cam tell you?" she asked brokenly.

Cam? My brows furrowed. "Enough," I lied through my teeth, smelling secrets. "But I'd rather hear it from you." Cam hadn't told me shit. I didn't have a clue what she was talking about, but judging by her reaction, I guessed I was on to something. "Tell me."

"It was a mistake." Her voice was low and pained. "I shouldn't have gone." She pressed her fingers against her temples and clenched her eyes shut. "It was my own fault."

"I don't see how," I offered, hoping that she would fill in the gaping gaps.

"Kyle, if I'd have stayed at home like I was *supposed* to then none of what happened afterwards would have happened," Lee whisper-hissed, eyes filling with tears. "I'd have my high school diploma and, who knows, maybe I'd be in college by now."

What the fuck did she do? Where did she go that stopped her from graduating high school? I racked my brain for the most ambiguous response I could muster. "What do you think would have changed if you hadn't gone?" Yeah, I was kind of proud of myself for that one. "Hmm?"

"You mean aside from the fact that I wouldn't be a high school dropout?" she tossed out, tone laced with self-loathing. "God."

"Yeah," I replied, tone even, as I treaded carefully. "Aside from that?"

"I wouldn't be here, for one."

Ouch.

That stung like a bitch.

Lee sighed heavily and I could hear the pain in her voice. "I'd still have nightmares, but at least I would only have one monster to run from." Yeah, I knew about the nightmares. They were fucking scary. But one monster? How many monsters did she have? "And I wouldn't be so paranoid."

"Paranoid?" I asked. "About what?"

Sniffling, she nodded. "That every time a man came too close, he might try to rape me."

I couldn't see straight.

I couldn't fucking breathe.

My mind couldn't focus on anything other than that one word.

Rape.

Someone had tried to *rape* her?
Lee.
My Lee?
Mother Fucker!

FORTY

LEE

I HATED Cam for telling him. I hated Kyle for making me tell him *again*. Cam, I would forgive, but not Kyle. Not now that he was ignoring me again, driving in absolute silence, with his jaw ticking and his thigh bopping restlessly. He'd asked me and I'd told him. It wasn't the worst secret I had, but it was a close second.

"You can let me off anywhere here," I whispered, not knowing where in god's name we were. I didn't care. I'd rather walk than be treated like this. Because I was so done with the silent treatment. I didn't deserve this, dammit. "Kyle," I snapped, when he didn't slow down. "Please let me out." I was done. I was so completely done with all the bullshit. I should have never climbed into his truck. I should have never climbed into his *bed*. I was a *glutton* for his punishment.

"No." He was gripping the steering wheel so tightly that I thought the skin around his knuckles might crack. "I, uh –" His jaw ticked and he swallowed hard. "Just...give me a minute."

"No." Close to tears, I shook my head. "Please just let me out now."

"Lee, baby, I'm having a hard time trying to stay calm right now, a real fucking hard time." He rolled his neck and inhaled deeply through his nose. "If you get out of this truck, I'm going to lose it."

"Oh my god, you didn't know." My mouth fell open as awareness smacked me straight in the face. "Cam didn't tell you anything, did she? You *tricked* me."

"Who was it?" His gaze snapped to mine and I could see the guilt written all over his face. I could also see crazed fury in his eyes. "Who did this to you?"

"It doesn't matter." My shoulders sagged in defeat. "It's in the past."

"It *matters*," he corrected, jaw clenched. "It matters to me."

"It's just a boy from back home," I mumbled, feeling my face burn hotter than a furnace.

"A name!" he snapped and then swallowed deeply, Adam's apple bobbing in his throat. "I need details."

"Why should I tell you anything?" I heard myself say. "When you so clearly don't trust *me* to confide in."

"I *do* trust you," he was quick to correct and then frowned at his admission. "Shit." His brows shot up. "I *trust* you, Lee."

"Wow, don't sound too happy about it," I muttered, looking away.

"I'm just learning a lot of new shit today," he replied gruffly. "I'm trying to deal here."

Throwing my hands up in resignation, I looked at him. "Okay, Kyle. You go ahead and deal."

"I need to know," he declared, hands gripping the wheel. "Please. I need to – you have to tell me."

"Why should I –"

"Lee, *please*." He clenched his jaw. "Just tell me, and I'll answer your questions."

I contemplated his gruff words and shivered. I could tell he was trying to control his temper and a part of me wanted to put him at ease. "Perry Franklin," I whispered.

"Okay." He nodded almost frantically. "Thank you." I could tell he was filing the name away in his head somewhere. "When?"

I look up in confusion. "When?"

"Yes, *when*, Lee." Kyle slammed his palm on the steering wheel. "When did this happen? When did this guy attack you?"

His voice rose into a furious snarl. "And when the fuck were you going to tell me?"

He didn't give me a chance to answer before the truck swerved to a stop and then he was pulling me into his arms, telling me everything would be all right. I was so completely taken aback by his response that I found myself spilling my guts in raw, vivid, horrifying detail. I bared my soul to him, letting all the pain and suffering I felt from that night just weep out. I revealed much more to him than I had to Cam, the police, or even myself. I told him all about how I'd been tricked into going to the prom with Perry. I told him all about the bet he'd made with his teammates to take my virginity. About how it felt when he held me down. How powerless I had felt. How a part of me had wanted to die. I wasn't sure why, but I held nothing back from him. Because in some messed-up, confusing way, I felt like he could *heal* me. At this moment, I felt like Kyle Carter could break my fall. That he could give me back that piece of me Perry had stolen.

I let him hold me.

I let him kiss my hair and rub my back.

I let myself cry in his arms and be comforted by his words.

Because he believed me.

Not once did he question my validity.

He didn't just listen to me.

He *heard* me.

I felt like a weight had lifted off my shoulders, and imagined this us what it would have felt like if someone had believed me when it mattered. Kyle might not love me, or want me the way that I wanted him, but a part of him *did* care. He cared, and for now I was safe.

I didn't tell him about my father, though.

Not even Kyle could fix that piece of me.

KYLE

Hours later, Lee and I were sitting side by side on the back step of the house. The sun was going down, we were drinking coffee, and I could feel her slowly withdrawing back into her shell. *Again*. Jesus, I wanted to smash that fucking shell. I wanted to keep this girl in the present with me. Not that I deserved it. But right now, after what I'd learned, I needed her to just stay with me in the moment. For a long time after our talk, after her fucking revelation, we'd almost seemed to be in sync with one another, but now that we were back on The Hill and out of the confines of my truck, I could feel her putting distance between us. That didn't work for me. I couldn't cope with the distance. I knew I was playing a dangerous game and being a selfish prick, but now that I had my friend back, I couldn't bear the thought of letting it go again. *Letting* her *go again*.

"You good, Lee?" I asked for the fiftieth time as I blew into my mug and racked my brain to find the words I knew she needed to hear me say. She was overthinking things. Doubting herself. Doubting *me*. I wanted to make her feel better. She needed to know that I didn't judge her or blame her for that asshole's actions.

"All good, Kyle," she whispered, keeping her gaze trained on her tiny sneaker clad feet stretched out in front of her.

I arched my brow. "You sure?"

She shrugged and offered me a pained smile.

Fuck.

Do something, Kyle.
Make this better for her.
Fix her, dammit!

"I grew up in care." The minute the words fell out of my mouth, my brows shot up. Well shit. I rubbed my jaw and took a swig of coffee. That wasn't something I had *ever* anticipated telling her, but there it was. "And I have ADHD." Another something I didn't anticipate telling her. "I'm hyper as fuck, baby."

Lee turned to face me, eyes wide with surprise. "But...but... but you're *rich*." Her gray eyes widened even further and she slapped a hand over her mouth. "Um..." She grimaced. "Ugh." Shaking her head, she tried to register what I had told her. "Okay," she finally said, composing her thoughts. "So, I'm not entirely surprised to hear you say that – that you have ADHD, I mean," she quickly clarified. "You're a little..." She smiled before whispering, "Twitchy."

I smirked. "You noticed?"

She grinned. "You are the king of pacing, Kyle Carter. It's like your thing."

"Yeah." Chuckling, I nodded. "I guess it is."

"You manage it okay?" she asked then, nudging my shoulder with hers. "With medication?"

"Yeah," I replied with a sigh. "I've got it together."

"It's because you're full of brains," she offered.

I cocked a brow. "Is that so?"

Smiling, she nodded. "Smart boys pace."

"You're fucking adorable." Smirking, I leaned close and nudged her shoulder with mine. "And I wasn't always rich."

"No?"

"No, Princess," I chuckled, though it was a hollow sound. "Far from it."

"Oh."

She didn't say anything after that, and it both comforted and confused me. Was she afraid to ask? Did she not care? "What are you thinking?" I asked her, needed to know.

Lee nibbled on her lip. "Honestly?"

"From you?" I nodded. "Always."

"I want to ask you a million and one questions," she admitted, setting her mug down on the step beside her. "But I'm not sure if you want me to." Twisting around to face me, she blew out a shaky breath. "I don't want to push."

Push me, Lee. Just keep pushing me, something inside my chest urged, *I know I'm a fuck up, but please don't give up on me.*

"Why don't you ask me one question at a time," I said gruffly. "And we'll see how it goes?"

"Yeah?"

Repressing a shiver, I nodded. "Yeah."

"Okay." She eyed me warily before saying, "How does a man go from being in foster care to owning a string of hotels?"

"Start smaller," I replied thickly. "Smaller questions, baby."

She blushed. "I'm sorry."

"Don't be sorry," I told her. "It's just…" I shook my head and sighed. "It's a really long fucking story and I don't want to bore you."

"You won't," she assured me in a small, reassuring tone of voice. "You couldn't."

"My mom was only sixteen when she had me," I came right out and said, deciding Sarah Carter was as good a place to start as any. Besides, she was the starting point of my tale of trauma. She was the beginning of my end. Or I was the beginning of *her* end. I shuddered at the thought.

"Sixteen is young," Lee whispered, giving me a warm smile. "My mama was young having me, too."

"She was too fucking young," I agreed gruffly. "She was…" I grimaced, trying to find the right words. Deciding there wasn't any, I said, "She was all fucked up in the head." My shoulders sagged. "Drugs."

I felt Lee's hand on mine, small, warm, and offering me the world of silent comfort.

"I didn't know my father," I quickly continued and then frowned. "Shit, I don't even think *she* knew my father. Not well, at least." I watched Lee's face for a reaction. She didn't look horrified or disgusted. She looked at me with accepting eyes. "I don't remember her clearly," I added hoarsely. "Just that she was blonde and beautiful."

"I bet she was," Lee said softly, stroking her thumb over my knuckles.

"She died when I was three – from an overdose." I sighed heavily and rubbed my face. "Kind of."

Her brows furrowed. "Kind of?"

"Yeah," I replied, tone clipped, unwilling to delve any further into that particular shit storm. "Since she didn't have any family, and my father was a John Doe, I was turned over to the state." Lee grimaced and I shrugged. "Spent the best part of the next decade swapping one shithole home for another."

"Kyle." Lee rested her cheek on my arm and sighed. "I'm sorry."

"Yeah." I nodded. "Me too."

"So…what happened?" Hooking her arm through mine, she shifted closer. "How did it all change?"

"That's the fucked-up bit," I mused, scratching my chin with my free hand – the one Lee wasn't clinging to. "When I was twelve, my bio dad's dad found out about me." I shrugged. "Fuck only knows how he found out I existed, but he landed on the doorstep of one of the place's I'd been staying at, demanding to see me."

"Really?"

I nodded. "Crazy old fucker filed for custody shortly after." I scrunched my nose up at the memory. "All of a sudden, I went from being a glorified orphan to having this millionaire grandfather with a shit ton of property, who wanted to *claim* me."

"And what did you want?" she asked softly.

"Out," I replied. "I wanted out, Lee."

"Oh." She swallowed deeply. "I see."

"He was approved guardianship of me – or custody, or whatever the fuck you want to call it, and I moved to Boulder to live with him."

"Where have you been?" she asked. "Before that?"

"Around," I offered with a shrug. "Everywhere."

"Whoa," she breathed. "That must have been kind of crazy."

"Understatement of the century," I chuckled. Grandpa and Linda had found me at a time when I was starting to lose hope and find trouble. "It was… a different world to me."

"He died?" she asked then. "Your grandpa?"

"Yeah." I nodded and swallowed hard. "Two years ago." I shrugged again. "Left me everything."

"Do you miss him?" she asked, nuzzling her cheek against my arm. I welcomed the touch. I welcomed *her*.

Fuck.

"Huh?"

"Your grandpa," she repeated. "Do you miss him?"

"I…" Well shit, I didn't expect that question. I'd never been asked that before. "Frank was a hard man," I settled on saying. "He, uh, wasn't the soft and fuzzy type of grandfather you see in the movies." I turned to look at her, finding those big gray eyes staring back at me. "He saved me, Lee. From a life of being passed around like a fucking parcel. I'm more grateful than anything."

"So, you miss him," she whispered knowingly.

"Yeah." I blew out a heavy breath and wrapped an arm around her. "I really fucking do."

"What about him?" she asked, voice uncertain. "Do you see *him* now?"

I stiffened, knowing exactly who she meant.

My dad.

Lee noticed and snuggled closer into my side, nuzzling my arm with her cheek until my body slowly relaxed. "It's okay," she coaxed soothingly in that sweet southern drawl. "It's all okay."

"He has his own wife and family," I told her, tone clipped to keep the emotion from spilling over. "I see him occasionally, but I don't acknowledge him as anything more than a sperm donor." Lies. I didn't see him as anything more than the grown-ass man who knocked up a sixteen-year-old child and ruined her life before walking the fuck away. "He's not my father," I continued, tone hardening. "I've never had one of those."

"No," she replied in a voice so small it was barely audible, clearly deep in thought. Turning to look at me, she stretched up and pressed a lingering kiss to my cheek.

My brows shot up, heart hammering. "What was that for?"

"For being Kyle Carter." Smiling, she stroked my cheek with her small hand. "For enduring what you have." She kissed my cheek again and pulled back to look at me, gray eyes burning holes straight through my fucking *soul*. "And for becoming the best man I know."

Well shit.

Clearing my throat, I quickly looked away.

I couldn't answer her.

She'd taken the air clean out of my lungs.

Weirdly enough, Johnny's Cash's *Hurt* burst into my mind,

playing on a loop pedal in my brain, the lyrics burning holes in both my chest and my conscience.

She was my sweetest friend.

This girl right here.

The lyrics of the song were a stark warning of what I represented to her.

Of the damage I could cause to her.

Fuck.

LEE

I wanted to ask Kyle a million more questions, but I held my tongue. I could tell that this offering of information had come at a great cost to him. The man did not trust easily, but he'd given me that today. He'd given a tiny piece of him and trusted me not to break it. I was overwhelmed by both my emotions and my feelings for him as we sat together in companionable silence.

It was getting dark out now and the chill of the night air was seeping into my bones. Instead of retreating to my room like I knew I should, I wanted to pull his face down to mine and cradle his cheek to my chest. I wanted to nurture this broken man and heal all of what no one else seemed to realize was broken inside of him. Because I could see it now. I could see his fractured heart mirroring every fractured piece of mine.

More pieces of the Kyle Carter jigsaw slid into place in my mind. He was brave and he was a proud man. He didn't like to show weakness. I don't think he liked to *feel* weakness. But he offered it up anyway. *To me*. He exposed himself to ease *my* pain.

Oh boy, I was in some deep trouble with my heart.

"I don't want to hurt you again," he said then, turning his blue-eyed gaze on me. "I *never* wanted to hurt you."

He had – in a million different, aching ways– but right now, I honestly didn't care. "It's okay." Breath hitching in my throat when he pressed his forehead to mine, I reached up and stroked his cheek. "You're okay." I felt a shudder roll through him and my heart squeezed tightly. Call me a pushover, but I knew that I could forgive all of his outbursts and misgivings. I could get over the way he'd left things. Because I could see something. Something inside of *him* that connected with *me*. "I forgive you," I whispered, shivering when he stroked my nose with his.

"I don't deserve it," he whispered back, hands moving to my hips.

"I know," I agreed, climbing onto his lap to straddle him. "But I'm forgiving you anyway."

"I don't deserve *this*, Lee." He exhaled a shaky breath and dropped his face to my shoulder. "Christ, my heart's going fucking wild in my chest." He groaned against my shoulder. "Why do you have to be so good?" His voice was torn. "Why do you have to be so…*you*?"

"Kyle?" I breathed, my wild heart mirroring his in this moment.

"Lee."

I swallowed deeply. "Don't do it again, okay?"

"I don't want to do it again." He raised his head to look at me, eyes laced with pain and regret. "But I'm not good at not breaking things."

"Try," I begged, wrapping my arms around his neck. "Just *try*."

"I, uh –" With lonesome, vulnerable blue eyes, Kyle nodded slowly. "I'll try." Reaching a hand between us, he cupped my cheek. I didn't bother resisting the pull. Instead, I wholeheartedly leaned into his touch. "You make me feel wild, Lee Bennett," he confessed with a small shake of his head. "I'm so fucked in the head for you."

"Yeah?" Closing my eyes, I leaned into his hand, loving the feel of him. *Maybe just loving him*. His lips brushed the cheek he wasn't cradling and a delicious shiver rolled through me. "I think I know the feeling."

"I'm gonna figure this out, Lee," he whispered, lips trailing to the curve of my jaw. "I'll make this right." He inhaled deeply and tightened his hold on me. "Somehow." He kissed my chin and then the tip of my nose. "I promise."

I was foolish.

I was playing a reckless game of tennis with my heart, serving my heart back to him like it was some disposable yellow ball that wasn't of vital importance to my being, but I *couldn't* stop.

Because I believed him.

Because I loved him.

The good, the bad, and the broken.

Releasing a ragged breath, I opened my eyes and looked straight into his, feeling more connected to this man than anyone else in my life. Lovingly – recklessly – I leaned in close and pressed my lips to his. His lips melded against mine so perfectly that there was no room for doubt. Everything just *fit*.

Kyle kissed me back without hesitation, lips soft, touch gentle. It was a slow-burning kiss that ignited a glowing warmth in my chest. Shifting my legs so that I was no longer straddling him, but rather, resting sideways in his lap, he held me to his chest with one arm, keeping the other on my cheek. Neither of us seemed to be in a rush as we sat on his back doorstep, with me in his arms, and our lips moving almost exploringly against the others. It was a lover's kiss. A kiss a man gave to the woman he loved. At least, that's what it felt like.

"Kyle, do you wanna go shoot some pool down at the – oh shit, my bad."

Derek's voice broke through my lust-filled thoughts and I tore my lips from Kyle's, eyes wide, breathing hard and ragged. "God."

"No," was all Kyle replied before pulling my face back to his and reclaiming my mouth. "No pool," he said against my lips. "Don't run." His voice was thick and gruff, his eyes dark, cheeks flushed. "Stay."

Body tingling, I fell back into his kiss, uncaring that we were on full display for our roommate. I was pulsing with need. I could feel him hardening against my bottom. I was going straight to hell. I might be a lot of things, but I was *not* running away tonight.

I love you.

Don't break me.

Don't let me down.

I love you so much.

In one swift movement, we were standing. Well, Kyle was standing. *I* was wrapped around him like ivy. Keeping a protective hand around my back, he walked us into the kitchen and straight past Derek, lips never leaving mine. He took the staircase two steps at a time, carrying me effortlessly as if I didn't weigh an ounce. That was a lie. I had curves and a serious pair of heavy-boned hips on me. I was no skinny Minnie. It didn't seem to matter to Kyle, though. He walked us up the staircase and into his bedroom without breaking a sweat – or our kiss.

"Leave it off," I said against his lips when he reached for the light switch. "Please," I added as a nervous tremor rolled down my spine at the thought of the explanation I would have to come up with if he saw my ugly scars – or the fear that he would run in absolute disgust and horror in the opposite direction. For the millionth time in a matter of months, I thanked Jesus that the bathroom had been clouded with steam that day. "I prefer the dark."

Without a word, Kyle retracted his hand from the switch, leaving us in a cocoon of comforting darkness breached only by the streetlamp outside the window, and walked us over to his bed. Tonight was different. I could see it in his eyes when he gently set me down on his bed. I could feel it in his touch when he slowly grazed my cheek with his thumb before stepping back, kicking off his boots, and unbuttoning his shirt.

This wasn't a reckless act, I realized. This was a premeditated decision that we were both making with no alcohol to blur the lines – or blame. He was standing in front of me with his shirt hanging open and his eyes on me almost hopefully.

He's letting you choose, my brain registered. *Decide, Lee.*

Exhaling shakily, I pulled myself onto my knees and dragged my t-shirt over my head. Never taking my eyes off his, I reached behind me and unsnapped the clasp of my bra, letting it slip from my shoulders.

His breath hitched, gaze moving straight to my bare breasts. Tongue snaking out to wet his full bottom lip, he reached for the waistband of his jeans. I watched, with my heart in my mouth, as Kyle pushed both his jeans and his boxer shorts down his legs and stepped out of them. Standing naked in front of me, he continued to watch me, eyes blazing with something more than just heat.

Trembling, and knowing that it was my turn, I clumsily climbed off his bed. Breathing hard, I stood before him and reached for my jeans. Kicking off my sneakers, I flicked the button of my jeans and pushed them down my hips, along with my panties, to pool on the floor with his discarded clothes.

And there we were, chest to chest, skin to naked skin, secrets exposed, hearts on the line, each silently begging the other to be gentle as we navigated this terrifyingly new and unfamiliar territory.

Towering above me, Kyle moved first, closing the space between us and causing a shiver to roll through me when I felt his hard erection graze my belly. "Delia Lee Bennett —" with a resigned sigh, he reached out and tucked my curls behind my ear, fingers lingering on my cheek, "I knew you were trouble," he told me, voice gruff, eyes burning with something deeper than I dared depict. "The minute I laid eyes on you."

"You kissed me first," I breathed, shaking now as the pressure in my chest threatened to overtake me.

He smiled almost sadly. "Yeah, I kinda did, didn't I?"

"Yep." Unable to stop myself, I reached up and placed my palm on his chest. "Which makes you the troublemaker."

Kyle didn't smile. Instead, he stared so hard at me, I felt like he was trying to mentally climb into my mind. "You're kind of important now." The words sounded both torn from his chest and reluctantly spoken. "To me." Snaking a hand between us, he covered the hand I had resting on his chest with his. "Fucking inconvenient, huh?"

"Yeah," I breathed, nodding up at him. "Very."

"So, I might need you to stick around," he added, voice wary, eyes vulnerable. "Even though I'm prone to fucking up." He swallowed deeply and moved closer. "A lot."

"Stick around," I breathed, pressing my body flush to his. "Well, I just got here, so..."

"And, uh —" he swallowed hard again. "And maybe just have a little patience while I figure this all out."

"Patience." I exhaled a shaky breath. "I've been known to be a patient person."

"I might push it," he confessed, lowering his face to mine. "I might push *you*." He stroked my cheek. "Away."

"I might not leave," I whispered back, groaning when his lips brushed over mine. Light. Too freaking light. I needed *more*.

"You might not mean that," he argued, lips brushing against mine again. "You might run."

"I, uh, hmm —" His tongue trailed up my neck and I sagged against him. "I might not need to."

"I hope you're right," he said, hooking arm around my back and lifting me onto his bed.

"Yeah," Nodding, I cupped his face in my hands and pulled his body down on mine. "Me, too."

Digging my heels into his plush mattress, I dragged myself onto the middle of the bed, encouraging him with my fingers and tongue to come with me. I needed him close. Without hesitation, Kyle obliged and I moaned into his mouth. God, I loved the feel of having his entire weight on top of me, pinning me down. It was a strange thing to turn me on, but having this 6'2, finely cut, muscularly built, beautiful man – who I trusted –weighing heavily down on me was *thrilling*.

Letting my legs fall open, I welcomed him between them, holding him close as I kissed him deeply. Grinding his body against mine, Kyle only broke our kiss to reach into his night-stand and withdraw a condom, and then he was back to me, back on me, lips on mine, skin on skin.

Pulling up on his knees, he continued to kiss me while he tore open the foil wrapper and sheathed himself. "I want in you," he whispered against my lips. "So fucking bad."

"I know," I strangled out, desperate to feel him again. "Me, too."

"Your period," he continued, tugging and sucking on my bottom lip. "I don't care, not with you, I'll have you any way I can get you, but if you're too sore –"

"I'm finished," I hurried to tell him, heart racing, body pulsing with need. "It's all good."

Exhaling a ragged breath, he nodded and pressed his brow to mine. "I need in now, Lee." He rubbed himself against me. "I just…" Shaking his head, he leaned in and pressed a drugging kiss to my lips. "I really fucking need in, baby."

"It's okay." Opening myself up to him, I blew out a trembling breath and nodded. "You can have me."

Keeping his eyes locked on mine, Kyle rested his weight on one arm and slowly pushed inside me, watching my every move as he sank deeper inside me, inch by achingly delicious inch. "Christ, you're so tight." A vein bulged in his neck. "Are you okay?" His voice was raspy and breathless. "Does it hurt?"

"Not this time." Arching my back, I moaned when I felt him

push all the way inside me, filling me up. "I just feel so stretched," I breathed, clinging to his neck. "Don't stop."

"Fuck," he growled, dropping a kiss to my lips as he slowly withdrew and then pushed back into me. Melding his lips to mine, he kissed me to the same rhythm he fucked me; slow, soft and sweet at first, and then gradually getting faster, harder, wilder, deeper until we were both breathing hard and groaning against the other's lips.

"That's it," he continued to hiss against my lips, giving me that dirty talk I knew I should hate but secretly loved, as he pounded himself into me. "Fuck me back, Princess. Give me that pussy. Squeeze my dick. Fuck!" Thrusting hard into me, he hooked an arm around my back and dragged me onto his lap, bodies still joined in the most primal way. "Tell me what you want," he growled, kissing me hard. "Come on, Princess." Another teasing flick of his tongue. "Talk to me."

"Oh my god." Wetter than I'd ever been, I bucked my hips against his and flopped back on the mattress, head smacking against the pillows in quick jolts from the sheer vibrations rushing through me as he moved faster inside me. "Fuck me," I cried out, reveling in the blissful sensations rushing through me. "I want you to fuck me hard."

"Like this?" he purred, catching a hold of my hips as he upped the ante and hammered into me. "Or harder?"

"Yes," I practically screamed, hands flailing out to grasp blindly at the sheets, as the pressure in my body grew to the point I felt I was going to explode. "Jesus!"

Breathing hard, Kyle stopped mid-thrust and squeezed my hips.

"No!" I practically cried out in devastation when the feeling growing inside of me slowly dulled. "Why'd you do that to me?"

"Come here," he said, pulling me into a sitting position, still pulsing inside me. Confused and aroused, I let him pull me onto his lap. "You're so beautiful," he told me, pressing a kiss to my lips before slowly lifting me off his erection. "I forgot to tell you that." He heaved a loud shaky breath. "I got caught up in you."

"Where are you going?" I croaked out, distraught, as I watched him roll onto his back. "I thought you wanted me –"

"I *want* you," he confirmed gruffly, crooking a finger. "Come here."

My heart jumped in my chest as a bolt of desire ricocheted through me. "Huh?"

"Ride me," he ordered softly, settling down on his back. He patted his muscular thighs. "You can have me, too, baby."

Oh my god…

Clumsily, I crawled up his big body and threw a leg over his hips, eyes locked on his sheathed erection, and wondering how the *hell* that fit in my body. He was big and thick and long and… Shaking my head, I worried my lip, uncertain. "I've never done this before."

Smiling, Kyle clamped his hands on my hips and lifted me onto his body so that I was hovering above his cock. "I want you to have the power," he told me, reaching a hand between us to stroke himself. "I want you to know that you *always* have power when you're with me." He grinned wolfishly. "Even when I get carried away."

"Kyle –" my voice cracked and I shook my head, stunned by how many wonderful layers this man had. "I'm not afraid when I'm with you."

"Good," he growled, pulling my face down to his. "Now –" Pressing a hard kiss to my lips, he flopped back on the pillows and arched a brow, "Ride my cock."

Jesus.

Feeling flustered, aroused, and oddly bold, I reached between our bodies and gripped his erection. Keeping my eyes locked on his, encouraged by the blazing heat in his blue eyes, I slowly lowered myself down on him, biting down on lip to stifle a moan that seemed to escape me anyway when I felt him stretching me out.

"So fucking sexy," Kyle purred, looking up at me through hooded eyes as his hands moved to my smooth down my hips. "Jesus, I could just eat you up."

Feeling shy, I placed my hands on his hard, ripped stomach tentatively rolled my hips, testing out the sensations.

"Aw, fuck, baby," he groaned in approval, hips thrusting upwards. "You're a grinder."

"Hmm?"

"Grind those hips, Lee, baby," he encouraged, shifting beneath me. "Fuck me good and hard." Tightening his hands on my hips, he thrust up at the same time he pulled me down on him. "Take whatever the fuck you want from me."

I want your heart; the words were on the tip of my tongue as I started to move above him – as I started to *ride* him.

Trouble, Lee.

You're in big trouble.

I didn't care anymore.

I welcomed the dark side of life because it didn't just have cookies.

It had Kyle Carter.

"Yeah, Lee," Kyle continued to coax a little while later, hissing out a sharp breath, as I slammed myself down on him, my movements wild, free, and completely unlike me. Our bodies were slick with sweat and my heart was racing so hard I thought it might burst. Something had to burst, I thought. I needed something. "Fuck, baby, I need to come so bad."

"God!" I cried out, frustrated that the feeling I was chasing seemed to be linger just out of my reach, no matter how hard I fucked him or how quickly I rolled my hips. Tears of absolute frustration filled my eyes as I worked myself over him, trying and failing to find my orgasm. "It won't work for me!"

Rolling me onto my back in one swift movement, Kyle settled above me and hitched one of my legs around his waist. "Shh, baby," he purred, pressing a soft kiss to my lips. "I've got you."

And god, he most certainly did.

Now, I was very new at this, had no prior experience to compare this to, but I swear this man had miracle hips. Rocking into me, he angled himself at the perfect point of pleasure and I felt myself shiver and clench. "Better?" he coaxed, pressing another soothing kiss to my swollen lips. Nodding, I hooked an arm around his neck and just *relaxed*. "I'll make you feel good," he continued to tell me as he hit that perfect spot over and over again.

"Kyle!" I blurted out, panicked. "I'm gonna come."

"Yeah, you are." He growled against my lips. "Ride it out, baby."

"I'm...oh...god!" Clenching my eyes shut, I clung to him as shock after rippling shock of absolute ecstasy rolled through me.

"Jesus," he strangled out, burying his face in my neck as he started to shake above me, hips jerking violently.

He's coming.
In you.
Because of you.
You make him come hard.

The notion started the process of ecstasy all over again and another wave of heat and pleasure shocked my body. He continued to move inside of me as I came hard around him for the second time. "Lee." Exhaling a ragged breath, hips still jerking, he pressed a kiss to my neck and sighed. "Shit, Lee."

Here we go, I thought to myself, *watch him run.*

Body tense beneath his, I waited for Kyle to, well, do a Kyle on it and freak out and throw me out. "You okay?" he asked instead, surprising me with his tender, gruff words.

Nodding shyly, I whispered, "I'm okay.

"Good." He slowly pulled out of me, pressed a quick kiss to my lips, and then climbed off the bed. Looking like he didn't have a care in the world, he padded to the door, completely naked and still sporting an impressive erection.

Stunned, I sprang up in the bed and watched as he slipped out of his room.

Oh my god.
Oh my freaking god.
He's gone!

Blinking back the familiar tears of rejection, I scrambled off the bed and lunged for my clothes, desperate to get back to my room now.

"Lee?" Kyle asked less than a minute later when he sauntered back into his room, condom-free, and with a wad of tissues in his hand. "Where are you going, baby?"

"Huh?" Springing into a standing position, I draped my jeans of all things in front of my body and squirmed. "I mean…huh?"

"You're leaving?" he asked, closing his bedroom door behind him, brows furrowed. "You're not staying?"

"I didn't…I wasn't… I thought you were –" Breaking off, I shrugged helplessly. "I thought you left."

"I went to the bathroom," he explained, watching me with that same confused expression. "To *clean up.*"

"Oh." Nodding, I continued to hold my jeans in front of me like a shield. "I didn't know that."

"Are you still planning on leaving?" he asked, eyeing me warily. "Because you don't have to go."

My brows shot up. "I don't?"

"Jesus." Guilt flickered in his eyes and he blew out a frustrated breath. "I'm an asshole."

I blinked rapidly. "Um…"

Closing the space between us, Kyle tipped my chin up with his fingers. "Stay with me." Leaning in, he pressed a kiss to my lips. "Sleep with me."

I exhaled shakily. "Really?"

"Really." He nodded and gently pried my jeans out of my fingers. "Pick your side, Princess."

"My side?"

He smirked. "Of the bed."

Oh god…

FORTY-ONE

GREEN TIGHTS AND GRAY EYED MOTIVES

KYLE

"DUDE, what the *fuck* are you wearing?" Derek demanded from my bedroom doorway on Halloween night, interrupting me from stalking my room like a madman.

"She's late," I snapped, bristling with nerves. "And I'm –" I looked down and gestured to myself. "I don't know what the hell I am," I snapped, pacing resumed. "Goddammit, Der!"

"I can't –" clutching a hand to his chest, he doubled over from the sheer height of laughing at me. "You've lost your fucking mind, Carter!"

I swung my furious – and blushing like a goddamn teenage girl – glare on him. Holding up a finger, I hissed, "If you even think about telling anyone what you saw in this room tonight, I will kick your ass. I will feed your balls to your precious blender and then I'll serve you to your girlfriend." Bristling, I rolled my neck from side to side and readjusted my junk. "This is the most degrading moment of my life," I added in a warning tone. "So, just…just stem the usual Derek-sarcasm bullshit and say *nothing*."

"Couldn't you have gone for someone manlier?" he snickered. "Like Batman or Arrow?"

"Eat shit." Self-conscious, I glanced down at the green tights I had on and swallowed a whimper. "Lee's favorite book as a kid was Peter Pan."

"So?" Derek staggered over to my bed, holding his stomach, laughing his ass off. "Cam's favorite book was Winnie the Pooh, but you don't see me walking around like Tigger, do you?"

"Get out," I ordered, pointing to the door. "Go now."

"You are so pussy whipped, dude," he laughed, completely unfazed. "And you're not even gonna get your dick sucked for this." He wiped his eyes. "This is a whole lot of effort you're making for a girl who's just a *friend*."

Shows how little you know about it, I thought to myself with a smirk.

"You *are* fucking her," he accused then. "You fucked her last week, didn't you? You said it was just a kiss!" His mouth fell open. "You *lied* to me."

"It's not your business, Der," I shot back. "*She's* not your business."

"Jesus," he muttered, shaking his head. "You're with her."

I wasn't sure what I was doing with Lee, but we hadn't slept apart in over a week. I couldn't explain it, and was terrified of overthinking it, but I was definitely *something* with her. "We're friends," I finally settled on. "Good friends."

"Fuck buddies, more like," he corrected. "Dude, you're so screwed."

Yeah, I was well aware. Narrowing my eyes, I hissed, "Tell anyone about this – " I gestured to my outfit, "Or tell anyone about Lee, and I'll *bury* you, Der."

"I'm *shaking*," he snickered.

"You will be when I tell Cam about the sex tape you made with your buddy's sister in high school."

Derek's mouth fell open. "You lie."

I arched my brow. "Try me."

Derek's face paled and I knew I had the douche's silence. "You're a cunning bastard."

I smirked. "I do what I have to."

"Fine, I'm going." Derek rose from my bed and walked to the door. "Keep your tights and secret girlfriend–"

"She's *not* my girlfriend," I snapped, bristling. "She's my friend!"

"Yeah, dude, sure thing." Stopping in the hallway just outside my bedroom door, Derek turned around and grinned at me. "Good luck tonight with your hot *friend* and your fairytale book outfits," he said with a shit-eating grin on his face before he jumped into the air and clicked his heels together. "*I wish I was a boy,*" he squealed in a high-pitched voice. "*I wish I was a real live boy.*"

"That line's from *Pinocchio*, you asshole!" I snarled, lunging after him.

"Dude, I didn't realize you were such a fan of Disney," Derek laughed over his shoulder.

"I didn't realize you were such a fan of my fist," I called back, closing in on him on the staircase. Spearing him on the bottom step, we collided on the floor just as the front door swung inwards.

"*Oh. My. God.*" Cam laughed as she stood in the doorway. "Kyle, what the fuck are you wearing?"

"He's Pinocchio," Derek snickered from beneath me.

"Pan," I bit out, reluctantly lowering my fist and climbing off the douche. "I'm *Pan*."

"The original lost boy," Cam mused, clicking her tongue as she looked me over. "Suits you."

Shuffling uncomfortably to my feet, I shifted my attention to the motive for this madness. The motive for *all* my fucking madness. "Uh, surprise?"

"Kyle?" Lee asked as she stepped around Cam, eyes wide. "What are you doing?" Thank fuck she wasn't laughing at me. I didn't think my pride could take it. Reaching up on her tiptoes, she flicked the feather on my hat and frowned. "Why are you dressed as Peter Pan?"

"You said you've never been trick or treating." I shrugged, ignoring the snickers coming from Derek and Cam. "I thought we could go?"

"Really?" Lee gazed up at me with glassy eyes and a huge smile. "You want to go with me?"

"Dude, you are twenty-two years old," Derek chimed in with a stunned expression. "You cannot be fucking serious."

Lee's smile fell and I wanted to kick Derek in the junk. "I fucking am," I told him, bristling. "If Lee wants to go trick or treating, then we are *going* trick or treating."

Folding his arms across his chest, Derek shook his head. "No,

I'm sorry, but I'm gonna have to step in. It's one thing to run around the house in a pair of tights, but the streets?" He gaped at me. "Where's your clarity, Kyle?"

She's my clarity, I mentally hissed back. *Now shut the fuck up and let me ruin my life in peace!*

Ignoring him and his solid dose of common sense, I turned to Lee and asked, "Do you want to go trick or treating with me, Princess?"

Derek groaned loudly. "Ice, I'm begging you not to do this to him —"

"Shut up," I warned, holding a hand up to him. "Well?" I offered her my very own tailored Lee Bennett smile – the one only she seemed to draw from me. "It's just me and you. Ignore the douche. What do you want to do, Lee?"

"I, uh…" Her gaze flicked from Cam, to Derek, and then finally back to me. "I want to go with you."

I grinned, Cam cheered, and Derek groaned like he was in physical pain. "You're a lost cause," he announced. "Say goodbye to your balls, Geppetto. It's over for you."

"Pan," I corrected, still smiling like a fucking dope down at her. "Okay." I nodded. "Let's do this."

"But I don't have a costume," Lee said, pulling that gorgeous bottom lip into her mouth.

"Yeah, you do. It's on your bed," I replied, taking her shoulders and steering her towards the staircase. "So, go and get your ass ready, Tinker-bell," I said, playfully slapping her peachy ass. "Before all the good candy's gone."

"Okay!" Squealing with excitement, Lee hurried up the staircase with Cam hot on her heels. I remained exactly where I was, watching her every move until she disappeared from my view. Only then did I release the pressure of air that had built up in my chest.

"Dude." Derek slapped a hand on my shoulder. "You're in deep trouble."

Didn't I know it?

LEE

I didn't think it was possible to love Kyle any more than I already did.

I was wrong.

When Cam opened the front door tonight, and I saw Kyle dressed in that Peter Pan outfit, I honestly thought that my heart was going to burst clean out of my chest. For the last week or so, Kyle and I had been twisted up in this cloudy and confusing arrangement that consisted of spending every waking hour together. I didn't understand what was happening between us. I was confused without a label to explain it, and even more terrified of asking for one and being rejected. Either way, he did this for me. He dressed up as Peter Pan and made a complete idiot out of himself just to make me *happy*. In turn, I donned the Tinker-bell costume he bought me and went trick or treating with Kyle. We looked ridiculous, knocking on doors looking for candy, but he didn't seem to care, so I forced myself not to either. He seemed to have this knack of putting me at ease, and I knew at this moment, as we stood outside a creepily decorated house waiting for candy, that I would always be in love with Kyle Carter.

And it was entirely his fault.

Kyle had a way of turning my world inside out and upside down, blowing it to pieces, and then putting it back together. It was a dangerous thing to love a man who had the ability to destroy me. I knew that he had ruined me for every other man and worse, I didn't care. Something inside of me warned that I would never want anyone else.

"I think we have enough candy to see us through until Thanksgiving," Kyle announced, waving a bag of candy in front of us when we finally made it back to Thirteenth Street. He was smiling and holding my hand as we walked towards our house, looking about as relaxed and carefree as I'd ever seen him – well, except for when we were alone in his room at night.

"You're just a big kid at heart, aren't you?" I mused, grinning up at him as he one-handedly opened a piece of candy and popped it into his mouth.

"Oh, I'm big all right," he purred, waggling his brows. "As you well know."

I blushed. "You're impossible."

"And strong, too," he continued with a devilish wink. "Wanna see?"

"What?" My eyes widened and Kyle threw his head back and laughed. "How?"

"Come on, my little fairy, I'll give you a ride home," he chuckled, hunching down in front of me. "Hop on; your chariot awaits you."

"*What*?" I laughed.

"Just get on my back, Princess."

"Kyle, no."

"Lee, *yes*."

"I can't."

"You can."

"But –"

"Get your sexy ass on my back or I'm gonna get you on yours right here."

Failing miserably to stifle a laugh, I climbed onto his back. "I'm too heavy."

"You're like air," he corrected, standing up and hoisting me into the standard piggy-back position. "Now, watch me get you home before the clock strikes midnight."

"First Pan, and now Cinderella lines?" Rolling my eyes, I wrapped my arms around his neck and locked my ankles together. "Wow, you're on a roll tonight."

"Come on, Spider-Monkey," he teased as he took off running down the street.

"That one is definitely from *Twilight*," I squealed, clinging to him for dear life. "You have no originality, Kyle Carter."

"Sounded good though," he laughed.

"Yeah." I bit down on my lip and grinned. "It did."

———

We were still laughing when Kyle pushed the front door open and stumbled inside. However, my laughter quickly died in my throat when my eyes landed on the crowded hallway. Music was blasting from the stereo, the smell of alcohol and cigarettes was pungent, letting me know that one of Cam's parties was in full swing.

"Shit." Kyle tensed. "Shit!" His hands fell from my thighs. "Goddammit."

I took that as my queue to get down. Withering a little on the inside, I wiggled down his back. "Are you okay?"

"Let's go upstairs," he said, catching a hold of my hand. "Let's just…" He broke off and muttered a string of curses before shaking his head. "Let's just go now."

"Uh, okay?" I agreed, allowing him to pull me towards the staircase.

"We'll just hide out in your room or something," he added, pushing me up the steps in front of him. "Wait for the place to clear out."

"Okay – wait!" I paused mid-step and turned to frown at him. "*What*?"

"Please just keep walking." Looking agitated and a *lot* panicked, Kyle tried to usher me up the stairs. "*Walk*, Lee."

I didn't move. "Hide out?" I frowned. "Because of your tights?"

"Lee." Kyle shook his head, looking flustered. "Please just move. We can talk upstairs."

"Well, isn't this sweet? The leader of the lost boys and his little fairy whore."

Stiffening at the sound of her voice, I looked around Kyle to see Rachel standing at the bottom of the staircase, dressed as a slutty devil, with horns on her head and not a lot else on her body. The costume suited her. *Evil bitch.*

"It's Halloween," I shot back, narrowing my eyes right back at her. "You could have dressed up as something other than your usual evil self." I'd had more than enough of Rachel Grayson and her nasty comments. I wasn't about to let her ruin my perfect night with Kyle.

"Lee." Body rigid, Kyle shook his head as if to say don't.

I gaped at him for a brief moment before my heart plummeted in my chest.

Oh no.

No, no, no, no.

"Lee, go upstairs now," he said quietly, not meeting my eyes.

"*What*?"

"Yeah, Lee, run along," Rachel mocked cruelly. "This is a big girl's party."

"Come with me," I heard myself say, snatching his hand back up. "Just ignore her."

"I can't." Ripping his hand free from mine, he exhaled a pained sigh. He ran a hand through his hair, knocking his feathered cap to the floor. "So just...*please* get out of here." With another shake of his head, he whispered, "I can't be near you right now," before turning around and walking down the staircase to her. *Her!*

"Why are you doing this?" I strangled out, tears welling in my eyes as I bent down and picked up his cap.

"Because I have to," was all he replied and I quickly turned away, unable to bear watching him walk away from me.

Again.

When I opened my eyes again, they were gone.

FORTY-TWO

LEE

THE FOLLOWING MONTH WAS COLD. It was freezing on The Hill and even more arctic on Thirteenth Street – *our* house, to be exact. By late November, the snow was sticking to the ground and turning my internal body temperature on its butt. I was used to sunshine and *heat* in the South. These erratic snowstorms, cold fronts, and plummeting temperatures were like nothing I'd ever experienced before.

Plummeting temperatures and plummeting hearts.

Kyle and I didn't speak after Halloween night. Not one word was uttered in several weeks. The atmosphere between us was thick and strained now and *everyone* noticed – especially since Kyle walked around the house with a black cloud hanging over his head. He snapped at Cam, argued with Derek, and blanked me completely.

To say I felt devastated was a serious understatement. To be fair, he had tried to talk to me after the Rachel incident, but I'd swiftly shut him down and walked away. Because I couldn't do it. I couldn't *take* any more of his games or rug pulling. Back to our role as strangers, we passed one another like ghosts in the night. No eye contact. No smiles. I had been sick over Thanksgiving last week with a stomach bug – something I was weirdly thankful for – because it meant that I didn't have to sit at the table and break bread with the man who'd broken my heart.

I was still recovering from my illness when Cam asked me to go for a walk in Chautauqua Park this morning. Even though I still felt weak, I agreed to go with her because it was better than being stuck inside the house and walking on eggshells around Kyle and his perpetual mood swings.

"You okay there, Lee?" Cam called over her shoulder from a good ten feet ahead of me.

"No." The cold air was cutting into my face and my eyes were burning. I had the worst stabbing pain shooting down my side and desperately needed to sit down. "I need to take a rest." Not waiting for her response, I sank down on the snowy path, panting, and clutched my side as another dart of pain shot through me. Lord, I was so unfit. It was embarrassing.

"You are so unfit," Cam voiced my thoughts aloud when she reached me.

"It's not funny," I strangled out, resisting the urge to curl up in a ball on the snow and stay there. "Could we head back, Cam?" I bit out, hand still clamped on my side. "I don't think I can walk much further."

"Yeah, sure." She extended a hand and dragged me to my feet. "You should have said you weren't feeling one hundred percent," she added, eyeing me warily. "Jesus, Lee, you look like death warmed up."

"I know." Shivering, I brushed the wet sludge and gunk from my jeans and forced a smile. "I'll be okay."

"That bug really took it out of you, didn't it?" Cam said, slinging an arm around my shoulders as she led us back to the car. "Come on, Lee-Bee. I'll make us some hot chocolates."

"Sounds good."

———

The house phone was ringing when we finally arrived home after our walk, bone cold and soaked right through. Exhausted, I plopped into one of the chairs at the table while Cam went over to answer it. "Hello, you're through to the house of all things kinky," Cam said in a playful tone. "This is the resident sexpert speaking."

My mouth fell open and I shook my head at her. God, I didn't know why she *always* had to answer the phone like that.

She's probably as sick of veering off calls from Kyle's women as you are.

I grimaced at the notion.

"Are you serious?" Cam demanded, drawing my attention back to her. Paling, she clutched the phone to her ear for several moments before holding it out to me.

Stunned, I stared at the receiver, wondering who the hell would be calling me. Trembling, I stood up, walked over to my friend, and took the phone from her.

"Hello," I strangled out, panicked now. "This is Lee?" My heart dropped into my stomach at the sound of the voice on the other line. "*Daddy?*"

KYLE

I would like to say that Derek and I had our own lives outside of our female roommate counterparts, and that we didn't mope about all day waiting for the girls to return, but if I said that then I'd be a liar.

Where the fuck were they?

I hadn't seen either one since yesterday.

Lee still wouldn't look at me, and hell, I didn't blame the girl, but I needed to talk to her. I needed to apologize for everything and make things right. Somehow. Time was slipping by, too fucking quickly, and as more weeks passed by without a thaw, the harder it became to breach the silence. Today, I had decided when I woke up this morning. Today would be the day I hounded her until I broke her down enough to have her hear me out for five goddamn minutes. Because I couldn't take this silent treatment another day. I couldn't take not having *her,* period.

Shaking my head to rid my mind of Lee, I concentrated on my surroundings and stifled a frustrated growl. My eyes were glazing over from the sheer amount of time we'd been playing Xbox. I wasn't into the game. I didn't even fucking like computer games. Never had. Sitting still was something I had a hard time doing and this blasé bullshit wasn't helping the restless streak of panic inside of me.

Derek sighed loudly for the *fiftieth* time in the past hour and I lost it. "If you do that again, I'm gonna stick my foot up your ass and give you a fucking reason to sigh," I snapped, twisting on the couch to glower at him. Christ, he was getting on my last nerve. Here I was, desperately *trying* to keep my mind off Lee and how fucked up the situation between us had become, and he was moping over a girl who actually gave him the time of day.

"Dude, we are so pathetic, sitting here like a pair of pussies," he grumbled, sighing *again*. "Fuck the girls," he added. "We should be out on the tiles, munching some bush."

"Munching some *bush*?" I shook my head in disgust. "You're fucked in the head, Der." How was this freak my best friend? "Dude, you have a girlfriend," I added. "You remember Cam, right?"

"Yeah, I remember Cam." Derek dropped his controller down on the coffee table. *Thank Jesus*. I tossed mine down quickly before he changed his mind. I couldn't take another minute of that game. "And I also remember where she and Lee are right now."

"Wait – what?" I glared at his sulky face. "Where are they right now?"

"Fucking Montgomery," Derek growled and my blood boiled.

"As in, *Louisiana*?"

"Yep."

"What the fuck?" I gaped. "Why? How did I not know this?"

"Lee went home," he explained, still sulking. "Cam took her. They left last night."

"Are you fucking *serious*?" I was on my feet and moving before my brain caught up. "Dude, you waste half my day – not to mention a million brain cells I'll never get back – playing that shit when you knew the girls were gone to Louisiana?"

"Fuck them, Kyle," he huffed. "Cam's probably honky-tonking her little ass around some bar by now and not giving two shits about me."

"You dipshit." Could he hear himself? "Don't you care that there's probably fifty guys right now trying to get in your girl's panties?" *And my girl's.* "Goddammit." With a shake of my head, I grabbed my keys and headed for the door, not waiting for Derek's response.

"Aw, shit," I heard him shout a few moments later.

"Yep," I agreed, throwing the front door open and heading for my truck.

LEE

"What are you going to say to him when we get there?" Cam asked, and I honestly didn't have an answer for her. We had been driving all night and we still had another couple of hours to go before we reached our hometown. I planned on using those to plot how I was going to approach my father.

I didn't know what I was going to say. I didn't know whether I would be able to *breathe* when I saw him, let alone speak. What do you say to the man who raised you, tortured you your whole life, and was now lying in a hospital bed?

I had no freaking clue.

I only knew that I had to do this.

A heart attack, he said. I was *not* surprised. Daddy smoked cigarettes like he breathed air.

Constantly.

"I'm more worried about what he'll say to me," I finally replied, voice small, like my confidence in this moment.

"You know, you don't have to do this, Lee," she said, casting a nervous glance in my direction. "I can turn this car around and we can be back to The Hill by nightfall." She reached across the console and squeezed my hand. "You can walk away from this. You owe that man *nothing*."

I knew that, but I also knew that my mother wouldn't want him to be alone.

For Mama, I mentally whispered. *For closure.*

FORTY-THREE

PEDAL TO THE METAL

KYLE

"DUDE, I swear if she's with another guy when we get there, then I'm totally done," Derek continued to ramble from the passenger seat of my truck. "I mean it this time, Kyle. I'm not taking her shit anymore." His rants didn't even render an answer. He was talking out of his ass. Still, I nodded or shook my head whenever he looked at me to mollify him.

To be honest, my mind was nowhere near Cam and Derek's fucked up relationship. It was fixed on mine and Lee's.

Why did she need to go home?

Was she sick?

Was she running again?

Was she leaving me?

For good?

Jesus, I was fucking pathetic.

I wasn't hers to leave.

I wasn't anything.

"Dude, did Cam mention anything about why Lee needed to go home?" This was the fourth time I had asked Derek that question since we hit the road. Every time I asked, he distracted me with some sob story about Cam. It was getting to the point where

I wanted to puke. Dammit, I should have caught a flight, but I didn't fucking think any of this through. When Derek told me that Lee was gone, I just climbed into my truck and started driving.

His phone rang just then and my heart flipped. "Who is it?" I demanded, casting a sideways glance in his direction. "Is it Cam?" *Is it Lee?*

"It's Camryn," Derek grumbled as he glared at the screen. "Finally."

"Well, answer it, dumbass!" I barked, agitated.

"Alright, alright." Huffing out a breath, Derek pressed a button and put the phone up to his ear. "Hey, baby, are you okay? Did you get there safely?"

What. A. Pussy.

So much for his ranting.

I rolled my eyes and gripped the wheel.

"Oh, that's good, I guess," he continued, tone soft and coaxing. "How's Lee holding up?" I strained to hear Cam's voice on the other line, but it was too muffled. "No, I didn't say anything," he added, whispering now. "Yeah, I know."

Didn't say what?

I narrowed my eyes, instantly suspicious.

"Cam, baby, relax. I didn't tell him." Derek glanced at me and shifted uncomfortably. "Can I call you back later? I can't talk right now." *Oh, this was getting interesting.* "Yeah, he's with me."

I waited until he put the phone back in his pocket before speaking. "You've been holding out on me, buddy," I hissed. "Start talking. Now."

FORTY-FOUR

LEE

"DO you want me to go in with you?"

"No." My body shook with every step I took closer to that hospital room. "I have to do this myself."

"I'll be right out here, okay?"

Nodding, I swallowed deeply and pushed the door inwards before stepping inside.

"Delia?"

Panic seized my lungs, making it hard to breathe; the sound of his voice was the catalyst for my terror. With a great deal of effort, I approached the weathered looking man in the bed in front of me. Tubes and machines were attached to his chest, face and body. I swallowed the vomit that threatened to spill and whispered, "Hello, Daddy."

His face looked much older than when I had last seen him and I felt like crying. I knew he had done some terrible things to me, but this was my father. The only family I had in the world. God, I felt so conflicted as I stared down at his sunken face. "H-how are you f-feeling?" I couldn't get my words out properly. They wouldn't form in my throat. I was too frightened. Of the past. Of the present. Of the unknown future. Of potential retaliation. "I'm, uh –" I stopped, unsure of what to say and finally realizing that there wasn't anything *to* say.

You owe him nothing, Cam's words floated through my mind. *You don't have to do this.*

Run, another part of my mind insisted. *He's a bad man.*

"I'm glad you came, Delia," he said hoarsely. "Didn't think you would." Swallowing deeply, he added, "Wouldn't have blamed you if you hadn't."

"Yeah." Sighing heavily, I slumped down in the chair beside his bed. "I almost turned back twice."

"Well, I'm glad you changed your mind," he replied, reaching for my hand. "It's good to see you."

Panic stricken, I flinched and jerked out of the chair, unwilling to accept any kind of touch from him. "I uh…" Shaking my head, I pushed my hair behind my ears and took a safe step back. "How bad is it, Daddy?"

"Don't you worry about me, Darlin'." He tried to pull himself up, but winced in pain and flopped back down. "Daddy will be just fine."

More's the pity, an evil part of me hissed and I shuddered in shame. "Okay," I said instead, watching him warily. "That's good."

"Is it?"

Swallowing deeply, I forced a small nod and squeezed out, "Of course."

"Aw, Darlin', you don't know how happy it makes me to hear you say that."

I didn't respond.

What could I say?

I didn't have a single thing to say to this man.

"I've stopped drinking," he offered then. "I've been going to my meetings again – every day."

"That's good." I nodded again. "Really good, Daddy."

"I'm sorry," he added, watching me with those terrifying, cold eyes. "For what I did."

"Which time, daddy?"

His brows furrowed and I found myself backing up for the door.

"Every time," he said quietly. "When I woke up and found your room empty, I realized that I had to change."

I couldn't believe what I was hearing. I couldn't trust *him*. This was a trick. My father didn't show remorse because he didn't *feel* remorse. He was up to something. "I'm not coming home, Daddy," I strangled out, keeping a hand on the door. "If that's why you're saying these things –" I shook my head and opened the door. "I won't come home."

"Will you at least come back to see me?" He rubbed his stubbly jaw with his huge hand. "Before you get up and leave again."

"Okay," I forced myself to say, shivering. "Tomorrow."

Nodding stiffly, he balled his hands into fists at his sides and scanned me up and down. "Where are you staying while you're in town?"

"I don't know." I swallowed deeply. "Probably in a motel or something."

"You can stay at the house."

"No." I shook my head, not wanting to go anywhere near that house. "Camryn is with me. She drove me here."

"Cam Frey?" Daddy pondered this for a moment. "You can both stay at the house."

"I don't think that's a –"

"Stay at the house and feed that mutt of yours," he cut me off by saying. "If the bastard hasn't starved to death since I've been here."

"Oh god." My heart plummeted. "Bruno."

"Come back, Delia," he called out when I turned to leave. "Don't forget to come back to your old man."

"I'll see you tomorrow," I whispered before rushing from the room, skin crawling.

KYLE

I listened impatiently as Derek muttered and mumbled his way through his explanation. *"Lee's father had a heart attack,"* was one of the only things that made sense, followed by, *"That's why she went home,"* and *"He's fine, though, as far as Cam knows."*

"That's it?" I demanded as relief flooded me. She wasn't running from me. "That's the big secret?"

"Well –" He shifted in obvious discomfort. "Not exactly."

"Dude, you better start talking fast, or I'm gonna toss your ass out of this truck quicker than you can say Okla-fucking-homa," I warned, just about done with being on the outside of this fucked up inner circle of secrets that seemed to revolve around Lee.

"Fine," he grumbled, holding his hands up in defeat. "But you have to promise that you won't flip out and lose your shit."

"Don't give me a reason to flip out and lose my shit and we'll be peachy."

"I'm serious, *Kyle*."

"So am I, *Derek*."

"Okay, okay," he said with a sigh. "I found out some stuff about Lee and why she might be staying with us."

"Stuff?" I tensed. "What kind of *stuff*?"

"You're not gonna like this, dude," he warned and then let the words rush from his mouth. "Cam said Lee's father is an abusive drunk who used to knock her around. Apparently, the last time he beat her, it was so bad that she had to run in the middle of the night to get away. *Apparently*, he's been doing this since she was in diapers – beating her, locking her up in the house, and keeping her tucked away from the real world. Which, if you think about it, kind of explains why she's so jumpy and…*off.* "

"What?" Furious, I slammed on the brakes. "Seriously – *what*?"

"Jesus fucking Christ, Kyle," he strangled out, gripping the dashboard. "Are you trying to get us both *killed*?"

"Are you serious?" Horns were blaring around us as I reluctantly pulled into the hard shoulder. I turned to face him. "Tell me that you're not serious!"

"I wish I wasn't." Derek fidgeted nervously. "Shit, Kyle, *I'm* not even supposed to know this," he added with a grimace. "Cam let it slip the night you and Lee had that fight in the kitchen."

"What the actual fuck, Derek?" I snapped, bristling. "That was nearly two months ago!"

"I know, Kyle. But Cam was drunk," Derek shot back defensively. "I wasn't sure if she was talking out of her ass or what the hell was going on." With a pained sigh, he rubbed his forehead. "She was crying in her sleep, rambling all kinds of crazy and sobbing her heart out about scars."

"Scars?" I blanched. "On Lee?"

"Yeah, dude," he confirmed. "On her back."

"She doesn't have scars," I argued, frowning. "I would have seen them."

"Well, Cam seems to think that she has," was all he replied.

"I would know," I continued. "I would've –" I stopped short, thinking to the no-lights rule Lee was so adamant on following every time we were in bed. "Shit," I muttered. "Shit, Der!" I couldn't deal with this. My mind reverted back to the night before Halloween, when I'd thought I felt something on her back, something rough, but I was too fucking horny at the time to stop and check. Were those grooves in her back that I had felt *scars*?

Jesus Christ, I wanted to hit something.

"And she's what; gone back to Louisiana to hold his fucking hand?" I demanded, feeling at a loss.

"Kyle, he's still her old man." Derek shrugged. "Her mom's dead. She has no brothers or sisters. I guess her father is all she's got."

Not anymore.

She had me.

FORTY-FIVE

LEE

AFTER LEAVING THE HOSPITAL, Cam insisted on us staying at my father's house. She wanted me to get some of my things and knew this was probably my only chance of getting any of my possessions. Even though I knew she was right, there was only one reason for me returning.

Bruno.

When we pulled up outside the old battered farmhouse, and the sound of a dog barking filled my ears, I leapt clean out of her car in my rush to get to him.

"Bruno," I squealed, bawling like a freaking baby at the sight of my old chocolate lab bounding towards me. "Hey boy," I cried, dropping to my knees. "I've missed you – yes I did. I've missed you so much." Holding my arms out for him, I half-laughed/half-cried as he bounded towards me. "Did you miss me – ooof!" Bruno barreled into my arms, knocking me onto my back, and attacking my face with slobbery kisses. "Oh, you did miss me, didn't you, boy?" I laughed, wrapping my arms around his neck. "You look fed," I told him as relief flooded me. "He took care of you, didn't he?"

"That old guy is still alive?" Cam mused, standing above me. "Well, shit."

"Of course he is, aren't you, Bruno?" I cooed, my voice taking on the universal dog tone. "Because you're the best boy in the whole entire world."

———

Several hours later, we sat on the porch swing in our pajamas, sipping cocoa, with Bruno passed out at our feet. The night air was calm and mild and it smelled like *home*. I loved the mildness of Louisiana winters. Compared to Colorado, this was *heaven*.

"Wow," Cam mused as she blew into her mug. "I can't believe he apologized."

Neither could I. "I'm still trying to get my head around the conversation," I admitted, taking a sip from my mug. "He was so *different*, Cam – nothing like the way he used to be."

"It's an act," Cam shot back without missing a beat. "To get you to move back home."

"Yeah." Shivering, I rested my cheek on her shoulder. "Probably."

"Well, you're not moving back home," she added, resting her cheek on my head. "Because you, my dear little Lee-Bee, belong in Boulder with moi."

I smiled at her words. "God, I love you."

"Love you, too," she replied in an oddly serious tone. "You're like a baby sister to me, Lee. I'm always going to protect you."

"I know," I replied softly.

"Always," she vowed.

Bruno jerked to his feet then, growling and barking, before setting off down the porch steps like a bat out of hell in the direction of the headlights traveling down my father's narrow laneway.

"Looks like we have company," Cam muttered as she stood up and walked over to the steps of the porch, attention riveted to the large vehicle pulling up outside my childhood home.

The passenger door of the truck opened first. "Miss me much?" Derek asked, jumping out with a huge grin on his face.

My mouth fell open at the sight of him.

"No freaking way!" Cam squealed before bounding down the

steps of the porch and throwing herself into his arms. "You *asshole!*" she scolded as she wrapped her arms and legs around his big body and squeezed. "You never told me that you were coming."

"I'm a spontaneous guy," he chuckled. "Love you, Bam-Bam."

"Love you back, jerk face," she groaned before slamming her mouth to his.

And off they went on yet another x-rated make out session.

The driver's door swung open then and my heart skyrocketed. Clenching my eyes shut, I remained exactly where I was, sitting on the porch swing and clasping my mug so tightly I was surprised it didn't shatter. My body locked up in anticipation because I knew *he* was walking over to me. I could hear his footsteps on the gravel and then the porch steps. I just didn't know which version of Kyle I was going to get.

"Princess."

One word from his lips had me – albeit, regrettably – whipping my head up, eyes wide and locked on his.

"Lee," he said gruffly as he stood in front of me with his hands shoved in his jeans pockets and the hood of his navy hoodie pulled up.

"So, you're here." I blurted out, not knowing what else to say at this moment. It had been a long time since we were face to face. A trickle of anxiety rolled through me. *Don't get attached,* my brain commanded, *don't get your hopes up. You know he'll let you down again.*

"I'm here," Kyle confirmed thickly.

"You came an awfully long way just to drop Derek off," I replied, suppressing a shiver from the weight of his blue-eyed stare, as I placed my mug on the floor. "That's kind of dumb."

"What if I came for you?" Closing the space between us, he reached for my hand and pulled me up. "What would you say?"

"I would say that you've had a wasted journey." Trembling, I stepped out of his arms and put some much-needed space between us. "Because I'm not your friend anymore."

"I know that I fucked up that night, Lee," he said. "Colossally."

"You *think?*"

"I know," he growled. "I get it. I do. And I'm sorry."

"Do you have any idea how you make me *feel?*" Shaking my head, I threw my hands up, beyond frustrated with this man.

"You just keep fucking up, Kyle. Over and over again. It's like you're on a loop of destruction." Exhaling a choked breath, I looked up at him and whispered, "I can't risk going another round with you." My shoulders sagged. "Because I always *lose*."

"Lee, I get it," he replied, pushing his hood down to run a hand through his thick hair. "I get that I've made you feel like that, but I swear to god, you're not losing anything –"

"How can you stand there and say that?" I choked out. "You walked away from me. Again, Kyle. I thought we were – I thought you – and I…" I shook my head and turned away. "Forget it."

"I can't," he strangled out, reclaiming the space I'd put between us. "I can't forget about it," he whispered, standing so close to me that I could feel his chest rising and falling against my back. "I *can't* let us go."

"There is no us," I replied weakly. He dropped his face to my neck, lips brushing my bare skin and god forgive me, but my resolve started to weaken. "Don't," I begged, too worn out to fight my feelings. "Don't play me."

"I'm not." His arms came around my middle and I felt myself sag against him. "And if I am playing, it's for keeps."

God…

KYLE

When I stepped out of my truck, I was terrified that Lee would send me away. She certainly looked like she wanted to kick my ass, and I sure as hell didn't blame her. Of course, being Lee, she threw my world out of kilter and killed me with kindness and quiet, graceful disappointment instead. When she caved in and let me hold her, I visibly sagged in relief, because I honest to god felt like I needed to hold her like I needed to breathe. It wasn't a requirement anymore. It was a necessity.

I'd been fucking up so fantastically these days that I was humbled by her grace when she opened her door and welcomed me inside. Within minutes of arriving, Cam and Der had slipped upstairs, clearly back on the love-train, which left me alone with Lee. Well, Lee and her huge motherfucking dog. A dog that had the good sense to guard his girl against the imminent threat. Even the fucking dog could tell that I was a bad bet for her. Still, I attempted to win him around, keeping a safe distance from his human. We were sitting on an old frayed couch in the open plan kitchen/living area and Bruno had planted himself firmly between us. *Clever bastard.*

"Would you like some more cocoa?" Lee asked, breaking the uncomfortable silence that had enveloped us.

Offering me a weak smile, she held her mug up to me and I swallowed down a groan. No. God no! That stuff was like drinking lead, but the hopeful look on her face had me nodding like a dog. I wanted to keep her smiling, and if that meant drinking shit stain cocoa for the night, then, dammit, I'd man up and do just that. God knows, I owed her more. "Sure." I smiled. *You are so fucked.* "I'd love some more." *Please don't poison me.*

With a small nod, Lee climbed to her feet and hurried over to the kitchen section of the shithole room. I turned my attention to Bruno, narrowing my eyes when I found him eyeing me up with those all-seeing/all-knowing dog eyes. "Dude, you're killing me here," I mumbled, low enough so that Lee couldn't hear me. "Isn't there a nice bitch or a bone you could go play with?" I added, shooing him from the couch. The cranky bastard growled again and I jerked away. Yep, I was definitely going to get my ass ripped up before I left this dive.

While Lee prepped another batch of homemade poison, I took the time to take in my surroundings and felt a pang in my chest. It hurt my heart to think that she lived here for eighteen years. It was a glorified shithole, and that wasn't me being a snob. I'd lived in some questionable accommodation myself down through the years. This place really *was* a shithole. The room we were in was tidy enough but it was run down and bordering on uninhabitable. The unpainted walls were damp, which was fucked up considering the location, with crumbling plaster. The roof, from what I'd seen when I showed up, was missing more than a few ridge tiles. The wooden staircase in the left corner of the kitchen was neither carpeted, nor varnished, and looked worryingly weak. The unfinished concrete floor here was sunken and uneven. The furniture was old-fashioned and weathered, some pieces were trashed, and I assumed from the look of the makeshift chairs at the ancient table, many pieces were handmade.

"Sorry, we're fresh out of cocoa," Lee apologized as she handed me a steaming mug. "Coffee will have to do."

Thank you, Jesus.

"Coffee's great," I replied, taking the mug, and reveling in the aroma. "Thanks."

"That's okay," she replied quietly. "Come on, Bruno." Clicking her fingers, she walked over to the shabby, dilapidated door. "Go and do your business." Obediently, the old dog climbed off the couch and trotted outside. "Good boy," she cooed, tone approving, as she closed the door behind him.

I threw another massive *thank you* to the man upstairs.

"So," she mused, lowering herself back down beside me. "You're here." Blowing into her mug, she took a small sip, eyes locked on the floor. "Care to tell me why? The real reason, Kyle. I don't want to hear that you drove through multiple states because Derek had a booty-call to attend."

"Sure, Princess," I replied, setting my mug on the coffee table in front of me, and mentally blocking out the image of Derek's 'booty-call' taking place upstairs. "When you tell me why you're really here."

"You know why." Lee frowned, eyeing me warily. "My daddy —"

"I know your father had a heart attack," I cut her off and took her mug, setting it down beside mine. Twisting sideways to face her, I reached for her hand. "I want to know what *you* are doing back here. *You*, baby."

"Who have you been talking to?" Lee whispered, paling.

Lie or tell the truth?

Truth or bullshit?

Fuck it.

"Derek told me that you have a rocky relationship with your father." *Smooth, asshole.* Grimacing, I carried on like a fucking idiot. "He told me a few things that make me question your sanity for coming back here," I added, watching her carefully, smoothing my thumb over her trembling hand. I could feel her pulse fluttering in her wrist and it was taking every ounce of self-control inside me *not* to put her wrist to my lips. "What are you doing here, baby? You don't owe this creep a damn thing."

"This is none of your business – or Derek's," Lee choked out, gray eyes filling with tears. "You have no clue –"

"Lee, don't pretend with me." Reaching up, I cupped her face in my hands, forcing her to look at me. "I care about you for Christ's sake. I *want* to help you." Exhaling heavily, I pressed my brow to hers. "Let me back in, baby."

LEE

"You don't care about me, Kyle," I choked out, feeling cornered and vulnerable. "Don't lie to my face." Shaking my head, I shifted away from him, needing to put space between this man and my heart. "Oh god," I sobbed, dropping my head in my hands. He *knew*. He knew about my father. *Fucking Cam!* "You weren't supposed to know," I squeezed out hoarsely. "No one was."

"That's bullshit." Standing up, Kyle ran a hand through his dark hair, clearly frustrated. "I *care*, Lee. I wouldn't be here if I didn't." Bristling with tension, he began to pace the room like someone jacked up on too much caffeine. "I know that I fuck up, okay?" he added, tone exasperated. "I get it. But I care – I care a fucking lot about you – so, I need you to let me in." Closing the space between us, he crouched down in front of me and cupped my cheek. "I *care*," he repeated slowly, blue eyes laced with sincerity. "Talk to me."

"No." I shook my head and moved to pull away, but he held me there.

"Let me in," he whispered, tucking my curls behind my ears. "I *won't* let you down again."

"I don't trust you," I strangled out, heart hammering violently. "You always let me down and it always hurts worse than the last time."

"I know." Pain flickered in his eyes and he visibly shuddered. "But I'm done with that," he urged. "I'm done fucking us over."

Exhaling another pained breath, he said, "Talk to me. Let me in. I can help you."

"What do you want to know, Kyle?" I heard myself say, the floodgates of my heart well and truly bursting open. "About how my father used to beat the shit out of me? Or how he locked me away from everything normal and kept me stuck in this goddamn house for eighteen years?" He flinched and I choked out a sob. "Or maybe you'd like to hear about how he pulled me out of school in my senior year and killed all my hopes and dreams?" I was on a roll now, unable to stop my pain from spilling. "Will that somehow help you? Huh? That's what you want me to tell you? You want me to let you into my inner circle of pain?"

"Lee –"

"Do you get a kick off hearing about my fucked-up life?" I demanded brokenly. "Well, there it is." Sniffling, I hissed, "Turns out that I'm just as messed up as you – probably more."

"Jesus, Lee, I don't –"

"Do you want to see?" I hissed then, taking leave of my senses, as I jerked to my feet and reached for my shirt. "What he did to my body." I whipped my shirt off. "Would it make you feel better to see how badly he beat me for being a whore and easy – but hey, it looks like you *both* thought that about me "

Glowering, Kyle rose to his feet, but I held my ground. "He hurt you?"

"You both did," I strangled out, placing a hand over my heart. "But the scars you left on me are inside here."

"Lee, don't," he choked out, looking wounded. "I didn't –"

"Here, you might as well take a good look –" I jerked my pajama bottoms down, stepped out of them, and turned around, giving him my back. "This is me, Kyle," I sniffled. "Scarred and imperfect and nothing like your *precious*Rachel." Exhaling raggedly, I added, "I'm broken."

"Jesus Christ." He sucked in a sharp breath. "What did that fucking monster do to you?" I felt his fingers on my spine and I flinched. "Lee –"

"*Don't* touch me," I warned, stiffening. He reached a hand around me and pulled me into his chest. "I said, don't touch me, Kyle!"

"Don't fight me," he whispered when I tried to push him away. "I'm not running, baby." He wrapped his arms around my body and nuzzled my neck. "I'm staying right *here*."

And just like that, all of the fight went out of my body.

Succumbing to the pain, I let Kyle hold me.

FORTY-SIX

FEELING STABBY

LEE

"HE KNOWS?" Cam asked when I climbed into the passenger seat of her car the following morning.

I fastened my seatbelt and nodded.

"Everything?" she asked, turning the key in the ignition.

I thought for a moment. Kyle knew about Perry and now he knew the worst part of me; the dirtiest corner of my secret life. "Yes."

"Well, shit." She let out a shaky breath and pulled away from the house. "I think I might've been wrong about you staying away from him." She cast a meaningful glance in my direction before turning her attention back to the road. "He's different with you, Lee." Her brows furrowed. "He's *changing*."

"In what way?" I asked, studying her thoughtful expression. Could it be possible that Kyle really *was* changing? We hadn't spoken in a month before last night, and I had missed him, desperately, but I couldn't keep riding this rollercoaster of passion and pain without a safety belt to protect me.

"I'm not sure how to explain it, but he *is* different with you, Lee-Bee," she mumbled. "It's like you've woken up a part of him that's been missing for years."

I pondered her words. Whether I had changed Kyle or not was irrelevant to the fact that he had perpetually changed me. "I'm in love with him, Cam," I whispered, clasping my hands together on my lap. "A lot."

She glanced sideways at me, blue eyes full of warmth. "I know, babe."

KYLE

When I woke up the following morning, I was still reeling and *drowning* in my outrage. As for my anger? It was so potent that I could *taste* it. I held Lee all night, wrapping her up in my arms in her small twin bed, while she broke my fucking heart with her truth. The things he did to her? I couldn't comprehend it. I didn't dare let my mind wander into that cesspool of memories because I couldn't handle it. I couldn't fucking cope with knowing that she had been so neglected and abused. It made me want to kill him.

My stomach rolled thinking about the welts and scars across her back, ass, and thighs. What kind of a monster did that to his kid? I had a fucked-up family but they *paled* in comparison to Lee's father. I wanted to kill him, more than I had ever wanted to harm another human being in my life. It was a conflicting feeling because I sure as hell wanted to kill the wannabe rapist, too. Perry Franklin. Yeah, I'd put a few feelers out and knew all about the prick. Money had its benefits when a man was chasing down scum, but, then again, it was also good to have blonde best friends with similar, vengeful motives and crucial contacts. I'd find him. His card was marked. Shit, the only thing that had stopped me from combing the streets for Perry-boy, or taking a detour to the hospital to see daddy-dearest, was Lee. She had been so small and fragile in my arms... so fucking broken.

I was in way over my head with this girl, but I couldn't back out now. It was like someone had hooked me up to an IV and I was slowly consuming her pain. Worse, I didn't want the connection to be severed. I wanted to be all wrapped up in this girl, regardless of how much it hurt. Walking away was not an option anymore. I got that now. I needed a new plan because I couldn't give her up again. Pacts, guilt, and promises to Rachel aside, I was all in with Lee. I wanted to protect her from all the cruel, torturous bullshit blows she had been dealt. I wanted to pack her up in my truck and take her far away from here and *keep* her with me. I just wanted to keep her, *period*.

Fuck.

Lee had cried herself to sleep in my arms last night and was gone when I woke up in the morning. She had left a note to say she was going to visit her father at the hospital. How she could show that bastard a sliver of compassion was beyond me. Her actions just proved another point; the girl was an angel. *The best person I knew.*

After reading her note, I made her bed, and went downstairs, anxiously awaiting a phone call to give me the location of Perry. Thrumming with energy and fresh out of Adderall, I made myself a cup of coffee and paced the downstairs, unable and unwilling to settle the fuck own. Someone had to pay for this. *Someone would.* I would make damn sure of that.

After pacing around Lee's shitty childhood home for the hundredth time, I slipped outside, investigating the yard and surrounding area, all while my brain went batshit on me. I couldn't rein myself in today. I couldn't *breathe*. I needed water. I need a big-ass swimming pool to drown my energy in. Laps. They helped. I didn't have a pool here, though. Desperate to wear myself out before I blew a circuit, I walked for hours, and when that didn't help, I whipped my shirt and hoodie off and ran.

LEE

This time, when we arrived at the hospital, Cam insisted on coming in with me. Too emotionally weary to put up a fight, I accepted my fate and trailed after her.

"Camryn Frey," Daddy acknowledged when she marched into the room ahead of me, back straight, nose cocked in the air. "You're still knocking around with my baby, I see."

"Jimmy Bennett," she responded coolly, flicking her long blonde ponytail over her shoulder. "You're still breathing – unfortunately."

"Hello, Delia," my father said, turning his attention to me. "I'm really happy you came back, darlin'."

"Hello," I muttered, keeping my distance from his bed. He looked far more alert this morning and old habits die hard.

"So, how have you been, Camryn?" Daddy asked, turning his attention back to my best friend. "What have you been doing with yourself since leaving Montgomery?"

"Oh, you know, a little of this, a little of that," she said airily. "Mostly, I've been taking care of the shell of a girl behind me."

I cringed.

"I gotta tell you, Jim, it was real fun seeing the horror scene of scars you left on her body," Cam continued, tone laced with venom. "How'd you do it this time? Huh? Your fists? Hmm, no –" She shook her head. "You're more creative than that, aren't you?"

"Cam," I breathed, panicking.

"Maybe it was your belt, or the fire poker?" Cam hissed,

ignoring me. "No, no, wait –" She narrowed her eyes. "I forgot the tire iron was always a firm favorite of yours, *wasn't it*?"

"Please, Cam –"

"No, Lee. He needs to hear this," Cam snapped, glaring at my father. "You could have *killed* her," she spat, shaking now. "Did you ever think about that?" She balled her small hands into fists at her sides. "But I guess that never worried you considering you killed her spirit years ago."

My father turned to look at me. "Delia, you know I –"

"Cut the Delia shit," Cam snarled. "You know she hates that damn name."

"That's her name," my father bit out, and I shivered.

"No, that's your dead wife's name," Cam corrected hotly. "Your *daughter's* name is *Lee*. I know you find it hard to separate the two in your fucked-up head. But this –" She gestured to me. "Is *Lee*."

"Cam," I strangled out, panicked. "It's okay."

"No, it's not," Cam shot back, narrowing her eyes at my father. "She's not your wife, and it's *not* her fault that her mother died. She was an innocent baby, Jimmy. Your wife died in childbirth and it was a fucking cruel twist of fate, but you laid all that blame on a motherless child. You beat the living shit out of her for something she had no control over!"

I felt like fainting. "God."

"So, go ahead and apologize, Jimmy," Cam demanded. "And call your daughter by her fucking name when you do it."

"I'm sorry, Lee," he bit out, eyes hardening.

"Good." Cam nodded in approval. "Now, I've spoken to your nurse and she tells me that you'll be just fine in a few days. So, first thing tomorrow morning, I'm taking your daughter back to Colorado with me. If she chooses to visit with you again before we leave, well, that's her choice –" Pausing, Cam looked back at me briefly before facing my father once more. "Personally, I think she should leave you here to rot, but she has a good heart and I won't argue with her if she wants to visit, but rest assured that she won't be staying." Flicking her ponytail once more, she gave me a tight smile and moved for the door. "Oh –" Pausing in the doorway, she turned to glare at my father. "And if you so much as look at her side-ways again, I will personally rip your heart out and give you a better reason than you already have to be lying in that bed.

With that, Cam sauntered out of the room, leaving me alone with my father.

"I'm going to go, too –"

"That girl has a mouth on her," my father grumbled, eyes narrowed on the door Cam closed behind her. "Just like her piece of shit daddy." Turning back to face me, he said, "Do you see him, too?"

"Who?" I squeaked out, heart hammering in my chest.

"Fuckin' Ted Frey," Daddy snapped. "And his whore wife."

Cam's parents. My father had always loathed Cam *and* her parents. "N-no, Daddy," I whispered. "Not since they moved away. I only live with Cam."

He grunted out a breath. "Are you planning on coming back to see me? This evening?"

I shook my head. "I don't think so."

"So, you're just gonna leave me here to rot?" His eyes hardened to steel. "After all I've done for you. You're gonna listen to that blonde tramp and let her lead you astray? You know I love you, Delia. Everything I've done is because I love you."

"I'm, ah, I'm leaving," I strangled out, edging closer to the door. "My life is in Boulder now."

"I think you should stay here," he said, voice menacingly soft. "With your daddy – where you belong."

"I, uh –" I shook my head and reached for the door, hands trembling. "Goodbye, Daddy," I whispered. "Take care of yourself." Hurrying out of the room before I heard his response, I slumped outside in the corridor, breathing hard. "God."

"You did it," Cam praised, pushing off the wall to join me. "You fucking did it, babe. You walked away from him."

"I think I'm having a panic attack," I admitted, clutching my chest.

"No, Lee-bee, you're having your first taste of freedom," Cam corrected with a chuckle as she slung an arm over my shoulder and walked us away from my father's hospital room. "Tastes good, huh?"

"Um…" I nodded. "I think so?"

"You know what else is gonna taste good?" she asked with a mischievous glint in her eyes. "Celebratory shooters." She grinned. "We are going to go drinking, dancing, and breaking boys' hearts."

"I don't know, Cam," I mumbled, worrying my lip. "I'm a lightweight, and I don't want to break anyone's heart. Besides, I'm not dressed for bars," I added. I had put a jean skirt, blue camisole, and cowboy boots on this morning – hardly going out clothes. Cam was her usual gorgeous-self in a tight-fitting, lace, off-the-shoulder white blouse and leather mini, while I looked out-and-out country. "And I'm only nineteen."

"It's happening, *princess*," she replied teasingly. "So, just get with the program and let me do the thinking for us."

Oh lord.

KYLE

Hours later, when I had finally managed to simmer the fuck down, I made my way back to the house, slick with sweat and with my shit somewhat together.

Derek was sitting on the porch swing with the fleabag himself when I reached the house. "Evening," he mused when I collapsed in a heap beside him and narrowly avoided Bruno's snap attack.

"Yeah." Breathless, I tossed my shirt and hoodie on the floor and pressed my hands to my head. "Girls back yet?"

"Nope. They're still out. Cam said she'll text me in a bit." Patting the beast on his meaty head, Derek smiled wryly. "Are you off your meds now, or something?"

I narrowed my eyes. "Don't start."

"Fair enough." Stretching his arms above his head, he yawned loudly. "So, did you and Lee straighten everything out last night?"

"Fuck if I know, Der." I shrugged and dropped my hand to rest on my stomach. "Everything is still all screwed up."

"Yeah." He tickled Bruno behind his ear and I gaped. How was it that the damn dog let Derek pet him, but when I went to touch him, he all but ate my fucking arm off? "Was it true?" he asked then, tone quiet. "About her father?"

"All of it and more."

"Shit." He let out a whistle and turned to face me. "You're gonna break her if you don't choose." His green eyes were full of concern. "It's going to end badly, Kyle, and you're not the only one invested anymore."

"Yeah." I could hear the warning in his words and I knew what I had to do. "I know, man."

I had to phone Rachel.

FORTY-SEVEN

HONKY-TONKIN'

LEE

SEVERAL HOURS, not to mention several bars, later, Cam and I were well on our way to being wasted. We were squashed into a booth in an over-crowded honky-tonk bar, with country music blasting around us, and cowboy hats galore.

"To closure," Cam slurred as she clinked her shot glass against mine. The Stetson she'd coaxed from a handsome redneck at the bar earlier was perched on her blonde head as she bounced around on her seat, just itching to join in on the line dancing.

"Right back atcha," I giggled, tipping what had to be my tenth shot back my throat. Not once had I been carded, which probably wasn't something to be proud about considering I could no longer feel my fingers or toes. Either way, I didn't mind. I was feeling too liberated to be worried.

"Where the hell is my man?" Cam growled, impatient, as she slapped her shot glass down on the table and reached for her beer bottle. "I texted him hours ago." Taking a swig of bud, she winked devilishly at me, lips pursed around the rim of the bottle. "Mama needs some loving."

"Oh my god," I choked out, laughing. "You did not just say that."

"Whiskey makes me fucking horny," she laughed and then jumped to her feet. "Come on –" Reaching for my hand, she dragged me out of the booth. "Dancing – we're dancing now." Hollering and cheering like a banshee, Cam led me to the packed dance floor, shaking her booty to the music. "Move your ass, Lee."

I tried! I really freaking tried to follow the set moves, but I didn't have a clue. Hovering back from the flash mob shaking their asses to Luke Bryan's *Country Girl*, I watched Cam fall effortlessly into sync with their patterns, laughing and joking as she moved.

Giving up, I bobbed and swayed like an idiot at the edge of the dancefloor, feet shuffling awkwardly until the song ended, people broke off into partners – *thank the lord* – and Cam swaggered back to me. "Come on," she laughed, taking my hands and pulling me onto the dance floor just as Gretchen Wilson's *Redneck Woman* started to play.

The girls around us started screaming and cheering, clearly delighted with the live band's choice of song, as they dragged their men onto the dancefloor, suggestively grinding their bodies against them. In the throes of my drunken haze, I hoped these girls had a church to attend in the morning because holy lord, this was not an appropriate way to be dancing in public.

Knowing that I was never going to look as good as Cam did dancing, and deciding that I was too buzzed to care, I gave myself up to the music, moving my body to my own rhythm. I could feel the hot sweat trickling down my chest as I moved my body in time with the music, laughing as Cam danced like a crazy woman, screaming the words of the song back to the band. I grinned when I heard her southern drawl creep back into her voice as she let loose.

"Yee-haw, bitches," a familiar voice hollered moments before a huge, shaved-headed man bounced his way onto the dancefloor, calling out, "Come on, dude. It's like a scene from the fucking movies in here," as he swaggered towards us.

"You," Cam purred, crooking her finger at Derek as he prowled towards her, brows waggling, shoulders bopping. "You're late, cowboy."

"My apologies, pretty lady," he crooned, closing the space

between them. Hooking an arm around her waist, he dragged her flush against his chest. Leaning down, he whispered something in her ear, something that made her eyes light up, before twirling her out. "Saddle me up, Miss Cammy," he purred, dragging her back to his chest. Reaching up, he snagged her Stetson and placed it on his head and grinned. "I'm your stallion tonight."

"Damn straight you are," she laughed, hooking an arm around his neck as he hoisted her into his arms and danced her around the floor, uncaring of who was watching them.

"Lee!" Cam half-laughed/half-squealed as she wrapped her legs around her boyfriend's waist, holding on for dear life as he jumped and bucked around like a young buck. "Five minutes!" she laughed, keeping a hand on his head to keep his hat in place. "I prom – ah, Der, you dick! Don't drop me!"

Laughing, I nodded and held my thumbs up, giving her the go-ahead. Swaying from side to side, I watched the band on stage as the lead female singer finished her song and stepped aside. The male singer stepped up to the microphone and started to play a very sexy version of Josh Turner's *Your Man*.

I freaking *loved* this song.

A pair of strong arms came around me then and I froze, body rigid, breath escaping my lips in an audible gasp. "Shh, baby," he whispered into my ear, gently tugging me back to rest against his chest. "I've got you."

"Kyle." Relieved, I slumped against his big body. His grip tightened around my stomach protectively. I sighed in contentment, shivering when his scent filled my senses. He might be a jackass, but he was my jackass. Maybe that was the drink talking. Wait – did I say that out loud?

"I'm your jackass?" he chuckled, lips brushing my ear. *Yep, I said it out loud.* "Come on." Taking my hand, he led me onto the dance floor. "You shouldn't be standing on the side-lines, Princess."

"What are you doing?" I asked, following him blindly onto the floor, passing countless slow-dancing couples as we moved.

"I'm taking you for a dance," he replied, tone amused, as he twirled me out and then quickly pulled me back to his chest. With one hand pressed to my lower back, he held my other hand to his chest. Other couples swayed around us. I just stared at his chest, concentrating on the way his dark shirt moved when he moved us around the floor.

"You can dance," I accused, surprised.

"I know." He smirked and pulled me closer, holding my body tightly to his. It was everything in this moment. "I'm full of surprises," he added, dropping a kiss to the top of my head. "Just relax, Princess. I've got you."

Shivering, I closed my eyes, absorbing every second of this dance, safely tucking the memory in a special box in the back of my mind labeled *Kyle*. "I missed you," I confessed, chewing on my lip, as I pressed my cheek to his chest.

"Even though I'm a jackass?" he teased, thumb smoothing over my wrist. "Hmm?"

"You're my jackass." Wrapping my small arm around his waist, I pressed closer to him, narrowing my eyes at the group of women hovering nearby who were blatantly staring at him. *Back off.*

"Yeah," he said gruffly, tipping my chin up. "I am."

My breath hitched in my throat when Kyle leaned in and pressed a soft kiss to my lips.

"I'm sorry." Stroking my nose with his, Kyle nuzzled my cheek. "For all of it." Pressing another featherlight kiss to the curve of my jaw, he pulled back to look at me. "I'll do better." Leaning back in, he pressed another soft kiss to my lips and I couldn't take it. He moved to pull back and my hand shot free of his, cupping his jaw and holding him to me.

"I'm trying to be good here, Lee," he groaned, still moving us to the rhythm of Josh Turner's *Your Man.* "I'm trying to treat you like a –"

"Stop talking." My breath was coming hard and fast, nerves and lust threatening to overtake me, as I pulled his face down to mine. "And don't be good."

"Ah, fuck –" I silenced him with my lips, and when he groaned into my mouth, lips parting, I took the opportunity to slide my tongue inside. Feeling bold, I reached up and trailed my fingers through his hair, kissing him deeply.

"Keep it up, Princess," Kyle growled against my lips when I slipped a hand into the waistband of his jeans and squeezed his butt. "See where it gets you."

"Back in your bed?" I teased, trailing my lips down his neck. "Because right now, that sounds pretty good to me."

"My bed is the *only* bed you're gonna be in," he warned and then hissed out a deep, guttural growl when I suckled on his neck. "From here on out. You got that, baby?"

"Yeah." Nodding, I trailed my tongue back up his neck and found his lips again. "I've got it," I breathed, crushing my lips to his.

"You're ruining me, Lee," he said against my lips. "You know that, right?" Cupping my cheek, he stared down at me, forcing me to meet his gaze. His blue eyes were like black pools of desire as he stared at me, cheeks flushed. I knew what he wanted. I could *feel* his want pressing against my belly, and I wanted it just as badly. It should have unsettled me – how I could give myself so wholly and completely to a man who, just a few short months ago was a total stranger, but it didn't. I felt an invisible pull towards this man and time didn't come into the equation. "You've fucking *ruined* me," he bit out, brow pressed to mine. "I'm so fucking sunk, Lee."

I wasn't sure what he meant, but when his lips landed on mine, his kisses hungry and frantic, I decided that it couldn't be a bad thing.

"Take me home, Kyle," I breathed, tearing my lips from his chest rising and falling quickly. "I want you inside me."

His fingers dug into my waist and he smiled that adorable dimpled grin. "You feeling needy, Princess?"

"Don't make fun of me." Releasing a frustrated growl, I hooked my fingers in the waistband of his jeans with one hand, and with the other I did something I had never done before. I cupped his freaking penis.

Jesus, I was losing my freaking mind.

I had no clue what to do with it once it was in my hand, but I was drunk and horny, so I went with my basic, female instincts and gave it a squeeze, thrilled when it thickened even more, straining against its denim confines.

"Fuck," Kyle hissed, biting down on his bottom lip, hips thrusting into my touch, all traces of humor gone now. He looked at me with lust and raw, primal desire.

Hooking an arm around his neck, I leaned up on my tip-toes, pressed my cheek to his and whispered, "Don't make me beg."

Those words seemed to be Kyle's undoing because he pressed a hard kiss to my lips before grabbing my hand and dragging me off the dancefloor.

Struggling to keep up with his long strides as he strode towards the emergency exit at the back of the bar, I clung to his hand, legs breaking into a drunken half-run.

Pushing through the emergency door, Kyle looked around before dragging me out of the bar and into a back alley. The door of the bar slammed shut behind us and he was on me, pushing me up against the wall.

"You wanna get fucked?" he purred, dragging my skirt up to pool at my waist. "Hmm?" Hooking his fingers into the waistband of my panties, he pushed them down my legs and then dropped to his knees to help me step out of them. "Is that it, baby? Your pussy's hungry for me?" Burying his face between my legs, he trailed his tongue over my slit before standing back up. "If you wanna get fucked, Princess, then you're gonna get fucked."

Breathless and panting, I sagged against the wall at my back, completely turned on by his naughty words. "I wanna get fucked," I breathed, watching as he slipped my panties into his back pocket and flicked his belt open. "I want you inside me."

"*Fuck*," Kyle growled, grabbing a condom from his wallet. His black shirt was molded to his chest, emphasizing his powerful frame, as he freed his erection and quickly rolled a condom on. "You are so goddamn *sexy*," he purred, closing the space between us and pressed a hard kiss to my lips. Reaching down, he grabbed my thigh and hoisted me up. "Wrap your legs around me," he ordered, lips moving against mine, as reached a hand between us and guided the head of his cock inside me. "Hold on tight."

Trembling, I locked my ankles together, thighs hugging his hips, as he pushed deep inside me. "God," I whimpered, scrambling to wrap my arms around his neck as he fucked me hard, punishing me with thrust after delicious thrust of his hips. The familiar ripples of pleasure darted through me, igniting a deep heat in my body, as my body sucked him in.

"Christ, you're so fucking tight," Kyle snarled against my lips, and then, in a much softer tone, pulled back, and whispered, "Are you okay?"

"Don't stop," I cried out, dragging his lips back to mine, as my body raced for release. "God!"

Groaning into my mouth, he upped his pace, moving faster, deeper, harder, until I was moaning loudly. "Your pussy was made for me, baby," he purred, thrusting harder.

"Oh god…" My eyes rolled and my head fell back. I was so close. "Jesus…"

"Only me," he hissed, fucking me hard and fast. "Your pussy is mine." He thrust harder. "You got it?"

Trembling, I nodded frantically. "Yes."

He stilled inside me and I cried out in frustration. "What are you –"

"Say it, Lee." He pressed his forehead to mine, breathing hard and fast. "Say it and I'll let you come."

"What the hell?"

Grinning, he thrust hard, making my eyes roll back, before stilling once more. "Tell me," he teased. "Tell me you're mine." He kissed me hard. "Tell me who owns this tight pussy and I'll let you come."

"Jesus Christ, Kyle, it's yours!" I screamed in frustration. "I'm all yours! My pussy. Me. You freaking own me, okay!"

"Damn fucking straight you're mine," he snarled, kissing me fiercely, hips thrusting at a delicious pace.

"Oh god." My head fell back, smacking hard against the concrete at my back. "I'm gonna, I'm gonna –"

"Come?" he filled in, thrusting deeper. "Go for it." Rolling his hips, he thrust into me so hard I fell over the edge, crying out his name as he continued to pump me relentlessly. "Ride it out, baby."

Crying out, I came hard around him, taking him with me. "Fuck, Lee –" Groaning, he buried his face in my neck and shuddered hard, milking his orgasm out with deep, jolting bucks of his hips. "Shit," he chuckled, sounding a little breathless, lips moving against my neck. "I didn't expect this when I showed up."

Breathless, I laughed and pulled his face to mine. His cheeks were flushed, his lips swollen, and his hair disheveled. "Hey."

"Hey." Smirking, he pressed a gentle kiss to my lips, still hard inside me. "You good?"

Nodding, I shivered into his touch and cupped his cheek. "All good."

"Listen, I'm going to fix –" His words broke off when his phone rang out loudly. Muttering several profanities under his breath, he pulled out, lowered me to my feet, and pulled my skirt back into place. Disposing of the condom, he quickly tucked himself away before putting the phone to his ear.

And answering the freaking call!

"Yeah," he said, giving me his back while he spoke down the line. "Where are you?" His brows shot up. "You're sure?" He released a furious growl. "I *know*, and I *will* – yeah, I get that. I'm not stupid. You're positive? Good, keep your eye on him. Don't let him leave."

Chest heaving, I watched as he nodded and spoke in a much quieter tone into the phone, his attention completely riveted to the person on the other side of that call. I couldn't hear the conversation and I didn't want to. This was wounding. He took a freaking phone call while we were being intimate. Granted, our intimacy had taken place in an alleyway, but still. It stung. It felt like every other time he'd rejected me and my pride was wounded.

"I have to go," Kyle said then, addressing me, as he ended the call and slid his cell back into his jeans pocket. Running a hand through his hair, he looked me up and down and then released a frustrated sigh. "Do you want me to take you home first?"

It was obvious from his sudden change in mood that he wanted to do *anything* but take me home, but I stiffened my spine and said, "yes," anyway. He was not going to fuck me in an alleyway and leave me here. Giving me a ride home was the least the jerk could do.

"Lee, I'm not –" Shaking his head, he blew out another breath and scrubbed a hand down his face. "We'll talk later. I just really need to do – fuck." He moved to close the space between us only to stop and run his hand through his most definitely just-fucked hair again. "Look, I'm –" Exhaling heavily, he muttered, "my truck is up here," before striding off.

Struggling to maintain control over my tattered emotions, and blinking back my tears, I trailed after him, keeping my own pace, knowing full well that he didn't want me to catch up with him.

When I finally reached his truck, Kyle was leaning against it with the passenger door open. Ignoring his outstretched hand, I attempted to climb up by myself. It wasn't easy to get into his truck on a normal day, but with slippery cowboy boots and a belly full of alcohol it was damn impossible. My legs were too short, my skirt was too tight, and my limbs were too poorly coordinated to gain any friction. Muttering a curse, I tried to jump up instead, grabbing onto the leather seat with my hands, but I couldn't hoist myself up.

The sound of Kyle laughing only infuriated me further and I lost my grip, falling backwards. "Come on," he chuckled, breaking my fall before I landed on the sidewalk. "Let me help you, baby," he added, one hand clamped on my waist as he pushed my skirt down with the other. "Before half of Louisiana sees that sexy ass." With that, Kyle literally picked me up and deposited me into the passenger seat. "Watch your fingers," he said with a wink before closing the door. He climbed in beside me and slid the key into the ignition.

Watch my fingers like I was a freaking toddler.

He was cracking jokes now?

I couldn't keep up with the man's mood swings.

Huffing out a breath, I folded my arms across my chest and seethed in silence, just about done with this whole damn night. When he didn't pull away, I turned to glare at him. "Problem?"

He smirked and that damn dimple made an appearance. I wanted to *lick* it. "Buckle up, Princess."

Bastard. He knew I couldn't work the damn thing. Grumbling, I attempted to fasten my seatbelt, knowing it was useless. I couldn't figure out this damn three-point harness. "Come on, come on," I muttered, pulling and tugging on the belt, willing it to fasten, while he chuckled quietly beside me. "Oh, I bet you think this is hilarious, don't you?" I snapped, dropping my hands to my sides in defeat. "Fine. Help me. I'm a lost cause."

Grinning, Kyle leaned across me and fastened my belt with ease. His hand brushed my breast as he worked and I sucked in a sharp breath, nerves still frazzled. His heated eyes landed on mine and I held my breath, too affected by this man than was safe for me. Leaning close, he pressed a lingering kiss to my jaw, inhaling deeply before whispering, "All set," and pulling away.

The drive back to my house was too long and too short all at once. Not one word was spoken between us and I spent the entire drive reeling in my drunken thoughts. When he pulled his truck up outside my father's house, he kept the engine running.

"You're not coming inside," I deadpanned. It was a statement, not a question, and it stung something fierce.

"I told you that I have something I need to do," was all he replied, tone gruff, as he leaned over and unfastened my seatbelt. "I'll be back."

"Yeah," I muttered, anger boiling inside me. "Sure."

When he swung his door open and moved to climb out, I wanted to lunge across the console and scratch his eyes out. "Don't bother," I warned, shoving my door open. "You know, I have no clue what I've ever done to make you want to torture me like this, but I can't take it anymore."

"Lee, I'm not trying to hurt you."

"And yet you do it so effortlessly," I bit out, lip wobbling.

"Fuck." He threw his head back against the headrest and sighed. "You don't understand what's happening here –"

"You're right, Kyle, I *don't* understand," I snapped, trembling now. "I thought we were friends – that's what you said you wanted. You drove all the way down here to be my friend. To make things up to me. But friends don't treat each other the way you treat me. Friends don't blow hot and cold on each other." I narrowed my eyes, hating the sensation of my tears as they trickled down my cheeks. "And friends don't *fuck*, Kyle."

He clenched his eyes shut and I lost it. "That's it, Kyle," I hiccupped, choking out a sob. "Close your eyes and pretend I don't exist." Sniffling, I scrambled out of the truck, landing awkwardly on my hands and knee before quickly righting myself. "You're getting really good at it," I added before slamming the door shut and storming away. I heard his truck rev up and tear away, but I didn't dare look back, unwilling to give him the satisfaction of seeing my meltdown. Crying hard, I sank down on the porch steps in the darkness and buried my head in my hands as my body racked with tremors.

I felt broken.

Well and truly broken.

FORTY-EIGHT

KYLE

LEAVING her there almost killed me. It took everything I had inside of me not to turn back. My emotions were raging a war inside of me, with my fucking heart demanding that I go back to Lee and do whatever I had to do to fix this, because I swear to god, when I saw her slump down on the porch steps, so tiny and fragile, a part of me worried that I had wrecked this forever for us.

However, the other rage burning inside of me was more forceful than my shame or remorse. It was the same rage that had been building inside of me since Lee's admission and it was the one that had compelled me to keep driving until I reached the bar we'd been in less than an hour ago. He was there – had shown up when I was outside with Lee. The phone call I'd gotten from Cam back in the alley had confirmed that.

Storming through the double doors at the entrance, I scoped out my surroundings, eyes peeled for a red- checkered shirt, leather waistcoat, and a baseball cap. *Tacky as fuck.*

"Perry Franklin?" I called over the band's eardrum-bursting rendition of *The Devil Went Down to Georgia*, as I approached a group of three guys propped at the bar. *His fucking henchmen, no doubt.*

I *knew* it was him.

He was the guy in the picture Cam had sent to my phone.

This was him.

Perry the wannabe rapist.

"What's it to ya, city boy?" the broad one drawled, eyeing me warily.

"Come outside with me and I'll tell you all about it," I hissed, striving to keep my head.

"Ain't he preppy?" his buddy in the wife-beater snickered. I had on dark jeans and a black button up, but I guessed that I did look out of place next to these pricks. "Where'd you stray in from, pretty boy?" he taunted, folding his meaty arms across his chest. "Looks to me like you're a long way from home and all by your lonesome."

"I agree," the other friend sneered. "I think you're in the wrong bar, boy."

"Enjoy molesting teenage girls, do you?" I asked, keeping my eyes on the prick with the baseball cap slung on backwards. "Yeah, of course you do – a big, ugly, piece of shit inbred like yourself." I smirked, daring him with my eyes to react. "You've got all those rapist instincts in you, don't you? You just *love* victimizing women."

"Who the fuck do you think you are, city boy?" Perry snarled, shoving past his head friends and stepping up to me, pressing his beefy chest to mine. He was the tallest of the three and I had a good three inches on him. He outweighed me by at least thirty pounds, but I was far from a preppy, trust fund baby. "Coming in my town and throwing 'round accusations. I didn't rape nobody!"

"But you tried, didn't you, shithead?" I seethed, needing him to throw the first punch so I could rip his fucking head off. "Uncle Sheriff might have given your rapist ass a get of jail card, but you won't get that from me."

Out of the corner of my eye, I spotted Derek moving through the crowd towards me, but I shook my head, warning him off.

This bastard was all mine.

"I could buy your little uncle cop with the flick of my wrist," I continued to taunt. "This whole fucking backwards town if I felt inclined." Pressing my forehead to his, I hissed, "In fact, I think I'll do just that." Smirking, I continued, "That sleazy garage you spend your pathetic days slogging away at? I own it now. This bar? It's mine. The rundown trailer you lay your head at? Consider it repossessed. The dealership you lease your mediocre second-hand Chevy from? It's mine." I stepped closer. "I'm gonna own you, *boy*."

"You ain't goddamn right in the head," he growled, shoving me hard in the chest. "City boy's fuckin' crazy."

Yeah, screw waiting for him to strike first. Fuck self-defense. I was going to kill this creep.

Laughing, I reared back and threw a punch, socking him in the face. There was a satisfying crunch and blood sprayed from Perry's nose. He staggered backwards and I wasted no time in lunging for him, taking him to the floor. "That's for touching my girl, you sorry-ass piece of shit," I snarled, crushing my fist into his face over and over. "You fucking rapist bastard!"

One of his buddies lunged for me then, dragging me back long enough for Perry to scramble to his feet and get a punch in on me. Snarling, I reared my head back and connected with his buddy's nose before ripping free from his hold. The other friend took my distraction as the perfect opportunity to sucker punch me in the jaw. Furious, I spat the blood that was pooling around in my mouth out before diving for Perry, spearing him into the frame of the bar.

"I didn't touch your girl," Perry roared, shoving at me. "You're a goddamn lunatic! I ain't never seen you a day in my damn life, fool!"

Breaking free from another one of his friend's holds, I lunged for his throat.

"Lee Bennett?" I hissed, clutching his throat only to be dragged back by both of his friends. "Ring any bells, you fucking serpent?"

His face paled, eyes widening for an instant before his expression twisted into a cruel sneer. "Her? Ah, man, that bitch is frigid," he laughed, blood staining his teeth. "You're welcome to test her out – she'll make you work for it, though." Sneering, he hissed, "But she sure tastes good when you get her on her back."

"You're a fucking dead man!" I snarled, trying and failing to break free from his buddies' holds as they dragged me to the floor, letting me know with their fists and boots that it was my turn to take an ass kicking, with Perry joining in. I struggled to break free, but the bastards had me pinned face down, with my arms behind my back.

"Oh hell, fucking no!" I heard Derek roar above the screams of the crowd. Moments later, he threw himself into the mix, fists flying like he was Kung Fu fucking panda with a Stetson. Ripping one of Perry's goons off me, I managed to scramble out from beneath the other and grapple Perry to the floor, taking plenty of side-swipes from his buddy in the process.

All hell broke loose then, and there was a whole lot of screaming, kicking, punching, and glass shattering.

"Not his face, you prick!" Cam screamed as she leveled one of Perry's friends – the one punching Derek – over the head with a whiskey bottle. He dropped to the floor like a sack of potatoes and she kicked him in the nuts before scrambling onto the bar. "Back off, assholes!" she screamed, reaching for the beer tap. Seconds later, a steady stream of beer rained down on all of us. Reaching into her bra, she pulled out a lighter. Holding it in one hand, flame ignited, she continued to spray beer on us with the other. "Put another finger on my boys and I'll smoke you fuckers out." Chest heaving, she turned to glare at me. "Let's go. He's not worth going to jail for."

Exhaling a furious snarl, I glared down at Perry, who was on his back beneath me. His eye was swollen shut and blood was trickling from his mouth, but he was conscious, which was a lot more than he deserved. "I'm gonna take you down for this," I hissed in his ear, unable to resist hitting him one more time, before staggering to my feet. "This isn't over."

The bartender rushed towards me with a bat and I held my hands up. "We're leaving."

"God, baby, you are *badass*," Derek chuckled, helping Cam down from the bar. "I'm so fucking hard for you right now." A steady stream of blood was trickling from his eyebrow, but he didn't seem to care as Cam yanked him towards the door.

"Let's go," she barked, catching a hold of my hand and dragging me along with them.

"You know, you really should be more selective about who you serve here," I called out, keeping my eyes locked on Perry as Cam dragged me through the exit. "Rapists are bad for business."

———

"Fix this," Cam hissed when I pulled up outside Lee's father's house a little over an hour later and saw her still slumped on the porch steps with her head in her hands.

"Dude," Derek muttered, rubbing his jaw. "You fucked up."

"No shit," I bit out, feeling like I had been knifed in the chest.

"I don't care what you have to do to make this right," Cam growled. "Or who you have to let down in order to do that –"

"Rachel," Derek not-so-subtly coughed from the backseat.

"Smooth, Der. Real smooth, baby," she told him before turning her attention back to me. "You need to fix this," Cam bit out, reaching across me to push my door open. "That girl deserves the best. Unfortunately for her, she's got her heart set on you. So, stop fucking breaking it!" With another huff, she slapped my shoulder and said, "Now, get over there and make it right. You have ten minutes. If you don't fix it by then, I'm getting out of this truck, and I'm taking that girl far away from you. This is your last chance, Carter – wait!" Grabbing my face, she squeezed my cheeks between her long-nailed fingers. "You're all messed up." Pulling a tissue out of the glove box, she wiped a streak of blood off my cheek and gave me a stiff nod. "Better. Now, go be a man – and maybe flash that dimple." Releasing my cheeks, she gave me a thumbs up. "Make mama proud."

Fuck me.

Climbing out of the truck, I closed the door behind me and made my way towards her, breathing hard and uneven. What the hell had I done to this girl? *The fuck was wrong with me?*

"Lee," I strangled out, heart breaking in my chest when I heard her quiet sobs. She stiffened but didn't look up. "Baby." Darting forward, I closed the space between us. "Shh." Crouching down in front of her, I placed my hands on her knees. Jesus, she was freezing. "Hey – shh, shh, shh, don't cry."

Sniffling, she cried harder.

"Come on," I coaxed, hands trembling as I reached up and tucked her curls behind her ears. "Look at me." Tipping her chin up, I cupped her cheek. "Don't be sad. I'm an asshole. Don't cry over me," I begged, knowing that I would give a kidney to stop her feeling like this. "I'm sorry for doing this to you." It shredded me to know that I was the cause. I was destroying this amazing girl piece by piece. "I'm done fucking up."

"You s-said that the l-last t-time," she hiccupped, leaning her cheek into my hand. "I'm in so much p-pain."

"Lee –" Swallowing deeply, I leaned forward and pressed my brow to hers. "I'm sorry."

Choking out a pained sob, she threw her arms around my neck, clinging to me like a child and I swear this was a new low point in my life. "You k-keep hurting m-me," she strangled out, clutching me so tightly I could feel her heart hammering in her chest. "So b-bad, Kyle, and I c-can't t-take it anymore."

"I'm so fucking sorry, baby," I strangled out, feeling my throat squeeze up. Christ, I could hardly breathe. "I'm a bastard."

"I *love* you," she sobbed, knotting her fingers in the front of my shirt. Sniffling, she pulled back and looked me dead in the eyes. "I'm so in l-love with y-you."

"Really?" My heart flatlined in my chest before bursting back to life, hammering violently. "You love me?"

"Y-yep." Sniffling, she nodded, tears trickling down her puffy cheeks. "Too much."

"You probably shouldn't do that," I replied, tone hoarse, heart racing. She meant it. Jesus Christ, she *meant* it. She loved *me*. I was drowning in an overwhelming cocktail of emotions. "I don't deserve it." My heart was bouncing between utter possessiveness and sheer adoration for the girl. "You shouldn't love me, Lee." Exhaling heavily, I cradled her cheek in my hand. "I'm not good for you."

"Because you're a bad b-bet," she choked out, sniffling. "Too late."

"Fuck." I couldn't do this anymore. I wanted so badly not to let her down again. I just wanted to deserve her love. "I'm in." Exhaling a ragged breath, I pressed my lips to her forehead and pulled back, eyes locked on hers. "I'm in, okay?" Wiping a tear from her cheek, I kissed her lips. "I'm *in*, Lee."

"Really?"

"Really." Nodding slowly, I stood up with my newfound resolve in place and pulled her to her feet. "Really, really," I whispered, lifting her into my arms. "I'm not leaving again."

I wasn't.

I *couldn't.*

With my lips melted to hers, I carried Lee upstairs to her childhood bedroom. There was no fucking way I was leaving her tonight.

Setting her down on her bed, I took my time undressing us both, needing to be inside this girl more than I needed my next breath, but forcing myself to go slow. It wasn't about sex. That wasn't what I was craving. It was the *connection* I was desperate to feel. I *needed* it. To just be *with* her.

Pulling back the covers on her old twin-sized bed, I climbed in beside her, shivering when she wrapped her body around mine, lips fused together.

And then I did something with Lee Bennett that I had never done with another woman before.

I made love.

FORTY-NINE

LEE

I KNEW I was on the cusp of waking up. Sunlight poured through my bedroom window and I tried to lull myself back to sleep, but it wouldn't come. The wonderful dream I was having pulled further away from my reach as I was dragged into consciousness.

Groaning awake, I tried to roll onto my stomach to block out the sunlight, but found myself trapped beneath six feet two inches of man, muscle, and morning wood. Kyle's face was buried in the crook of my neck and both his left arm and thigh were thrown over my body, rendering me helpless.

He was also naked.

And…so was I.

His big hand was cupping my breast like it was his personal comforter as he pinned me to the mattress, breathing deep and even, his hot breath fanning my neck.

Overheating from the furnace of a man on top of me, I wiggled out from beneath him and rolled onto my side, giving him my back. Grumbling in his sleep, Kyle snaked a hand out and pulled me back to his chest, nuzzling my neck again. Mumbling something incoherent in his sleep, he curled his big body around mine, rock hard erection digging into my butt.

Biting down on my lip, I tried to smother my smile as I thought about last night.

He came back.

I had truly thought it was over, but Kyle had come back. More than just coming back, he made promises, told he was *in* – whatever the heck that meant – before taking me up to my room. My body broke out in goose pimples when I thought about how it felt when he was inside me last night. *Different.* That's how it felt. Everything was slow and gentle; his kisses, his touch, how he moved inside of me… *all of it.*

He was with me last night; really and truly *with* me. He didn't fuck me. Last night, it was more. It meant something deeper to him. The smell of sex was all around me and I knew that if I looked in the trashcan in my room, I would find countless condoms, but I didn't care.

Because everything had changed.

Heart skipping and bucking restlessly against my ribcage, I snuggled closer into his embrace, wanting to feel as close to him as my own skin.

Don't get your hopes up, a niggling voice in the back of my mind persisted. *He's made these promises before.*

I tried to block that voice out, but I couldn't.

What if he was back to the old Kyle today?

What if he ignored me again?

What if last night was just another one-night stand and it didn't mean as much to him as it did to me?

What if, what if, what if…

And just like that, my good mood morphed into crippling anxiety. No longer overheated, I pulled free from his embrace, with ice in my veins now.

"Where'd you think you're going?" Kyle's voice was thick and gruff. "Hmm?" Clamping a hand on my hip, he tugged me back to his furnace chest. "Come back to me."

"Sorry," I whispered, pulse quickening when his lips grazed my bare shoulder, trailing a path of kisses up my neck, limbs still locked tight with tension.

Releasing a heavy sigh, Kyle rolled me onto my back and pulled himself up on an elbow to hover over me. "Are you?" he whispered, stroking my cheek. "Sorry about last night, I mean." His eyes searched mine. "Do you regret it?"

"Jesus!" Gasping in horror, I gaped at his bloodied and bruised face. His eyebrow was busted – his lip, too – and he was sporting one hell of a shiner under his left eye. "What happened to your face?"

Smirking, he winked. "I told you that I had something to do last night."

"Something that involved you getting beaten up?" I demanded, pulling myself up on my elbows to inspect the damage. "God, Kyle." Reaching up, I trailed my fingertips over his battle wounds. "What happened?"

"Trust me, I'm fine." He grinned wolfishly, a dimple popping in his cheek. "Besides, if you think I look like shit, you should see the other guy," he added with a chuckle, skimming his thumb across my cheek.

"Hmm." Lord, even all battered up, I'd never seen anything so perfect or beautiful in my life. Trailing my thumb over his bottom lip, I whispered, "Well, don't make a habit out of wrecking this." Smirking, I teased, "This face is my favorite part of you."

Grinning, he arched a brow. "Oh yeah?"

"No." Chuckling, I shook my head. "I like all your parts."

"Back to my earlier question," he said, and this time there was a nervous tone to his voice and a raw vulnerability in his eyes. "Do you regret last night?"

Heart racing, I smoothed my fingers over his worried brow and whispered, "Do you?"

"Not even close." He leaned down and pressed his lips to mine, busted lips and all. "I meant what I said last night."

I felt my body relax as the tension in my limbs oozed away. "Really?"

Nodding against my lips, he pulled back to look at me. "I wish you could see yourself through my eyes." Smiling, he trailed his thumb over my cheek, palm cradling my face. "You'd never doubt yourself again." Sighing contently, he added, "Never seen anything like you before, Lee Bennett, that's for damn sure."

"Please don't ignore me again, Kyle." Clenching my eyes shut, I exhaled a slow, steadying breath, desperately trying to get a handle on my feelings. "That's all I'm ever going to ask from you." Opening my eyes, I forced myself to look at him. "Just…just don't ignore me again."

"I won't," he promised, eyes laced with sincerity and guilt. "I'm done doing fucked up things, Lee." Shaking his head, he leaned in and kissed me. "I won't mess it up again."

———

"Do you want to see him before we leave?" Cam asked. Piling our bags into the trunk of her car, she furrowed her brows. "I think it's a terrible idea, but I won't stop you."

"No, I don't want to see him again," I replied, helping her with our bags. Wiping a trickle of sweat from my brow, I pressed a hand to my stomach and inhaled several shallow breaths. I felt rough. Like, pass out on the floor and spew my guts up rough. Whiskey was the drink of the devil and I was a child of Jesus. "I'm not doing this again," I told her, groaning when a wave of nausea swept through me. "From here on out, consider me a pioneer." A darting pain shot through my pelvis and I groaned. "God."

"You'll get used to it," Cam laughed. "Now, back to your dad."

"I mean, I'm glad that he's going to be okay, but that's all I can feel for him." Shrugging, I tossed an old stuffed-animal on top of the heap and sighed. "I'm done, Cam." I sighed. "I'm just… I'm done living like that."

"Good." Closing the trunk, she walked over to me. "I'm proud of you, babe." She gave me a one-armed hug and tucked me into her side. "Uh oh," she chuckled, pointing towards the front porch to where Kyle was holding a hand up to Bruno as he gingerly tried to attach a leash to his collar. "Five bucks on the dog taking a chunk out of lover boy's ass before the day's over."

"Are you going to tell me what they did last night?" I asked, arching a brow at her. I'd told Cam about last night, not every detail, but the important parts. She knew that Kyle and I had made up. Now it was *her* turn to explain the cuts and bruises on both Kyle and Derek. "Hmm? Were they brawling or something?"

Cam shrugged, feigning nonchalance. "I have no idea what you're talking about."

"Are we really bringing the flea bag with us?" Kyle asked,

coming to join us with a less-than-impressed looking Bruno on a leash.

"Yes," Cam and I said together.

He eyed my dog warily and then jumped back when Bruno growled at him. "Yeah, fuck this," he muttered, thrusting the leash at Cam. "He can ride with you and Derek." Shuddering, he took a safe step back from Bruno. "He keeps giving me this evil dog stare," he complained, narrowing his eyes at my dog. "It's freaking me out."

"He can smell your fear." Laughing, Cam swung her car door open and Bruno bounded inside, tongue lolling to one-side. "Good boy," she cooed, patting his head before closing the door. "He's just sizing you up, Carter," she cackled. "To see if you're good enough for his girl."

"Oh, yeah?" Kyle grabbed me and tossed me over his shoulder. "Well, do you see this, dog?" he laughed, slapping my ass. "She's my girl now."

"Oh, god –" My stomach rolled and I slapped a hand over my mouth, tasting the burn of alcohol as it clawed its way from my stomach to my throat.

"Ooh, you're so brave when he's locked inside the car," Cam choked out through fits of laughter as Bruno scratched and tore at the window, yodeling loudly. "Let's see how brave you are when I let him out." She motioned towards the door handle and Kyle quickly set me back down.

"Let's not do anything hasty," he laughed, hands up, edging closer to his truck. "You coming, Princess?" he called, opening the passenger door for me.

Keeping my hand securely over my mouth, I held up two fingers and darted for the house, barely making it to the bathroom before the alcohol last night made a glorious reappearance.

Dear lord, I was never drinking again.

FIFTY

LEE

THE NEXT FEW weeks were like my own little slice of heaven, where I ate, drank, and breathed Kyle Carter. Something had changed for him in Louisiana, something significant, because he was a different person since returning to Boulder. He was *present* and forthcoming, and he treated us like we were in an actual relationship now. Of course, we didn't have a title, and I had no clue whether this meant as much to him as it did to me, but the other women had stopped, Rachel was gone, and he spent every minute of his free time with me, including night-time sleepovers. That had to mean something, right?

Aside from when we were at home with Derek and Cam, Kyle kept his hands to himself around other people. I knew he was keeping whatever we were on the down-low, but I had a feeling that had more to do with the fact that I was his employee. It stung, but I understood, and he *never* ignored me.

When Kyle came into the restaurant now, he came alone or with Linda. There weren't any more *lunch dates* with beautiful willowy girls and he always sat in my section, distracting me for an ornate amount of time with suggestive comments and stolen touches whenever we handed over menus and food orders. He was friendly, sweet, and kind to me, and I found myself eating lunch with him most days since Mike never seemed to be on the same shift as me anymore. And talking? Lord, we did a whole heap of talking. It was ridiculous how we could spend so much of our day together and still have something to talk about. *But we did.*

Even Bruno was slowly warming to Kyle, and had given up trying to snap his ankles off when we took him out for his walk – something we did together every morning before work and just before bed. I knew Kyle wasn't keen on my dog so it meant a lot to me when he bought Bruno his very own doggy bed, which was pride of place in front of the fireplace in the living room.

"There you are," his familiar voice purred in my ear, distracting me from my reverie. Moments later, two strong arms came around my middle, pulling me into a chest of hard muscle. "Fuck, I've missed you." His lips grazed my neck, tongue sweeping out to tease the flesh covering my fluttering pulse. "You smell like me."

"Hey." A delicious shiver rolled through me and I dropped the cleaning rag and polish I'd been cleaning his desk with before turning to face him. "Why aren't you at college?" I asked, eyeing his wine-colored hoodie and jeans. "I thought you had classes this afternoon?"

"I just told you." Shrugging, Kyle dropped his book bag on the floor and pushed his hood down, still grinning. "I missed you," he purred, hands moving to my hips. "Couldn't concentrate on a damn thing knowing you were here." He tightened his hold on me. "Needed to see you first."

"Kyle," I admonished gently when he leaned in and peppered my neck with kisses. "I'm trying to…hmm…work."

"You don't have to," he coaxed, turning me in his arms to face his desk once more. "You can just be with me. Let me take care of you."

"Yeah, that's not happening," I breathed as his hands trailed from my hips to my breasts. "I need to…work."

"You could quit," he purred, teasing my nipple. "Enroll at CU with me." Hands moving to the hem of my pinafore, he gently nudged the fabric up to pool at my hips. "My treat."

"Yeah right," I scoffed and then moaned loudly when he cupped my ass cheek and squeezed. "Don't play with me."

"Princess, you are so fucking distracting that I feel like we need to rethink your job description," he growled, rocking himself against me. "If you're not gonna take me up on my offer, we're gonna need a plan B."

"Plan B?" I breathed, resting my head against his chest. "Like what?"

"Would you be opposed to being tied up naked in my bed all day?" Tilting my face up to his, he claimed my mouth with a heart-searing kiss. "Hmm?"

"I'm pretty sure that goes against company policy," I argued weakly, rocking against him. "There are rules about that kind of thing," I whispered, running my fingers through his silky hair. "Rules *you* made."

"Yeah?" he replied gruffly. "I'm pretty sure that what I'm about to do to you blows those rules out the window." Pressing another hot kiss to my lips, he placed his hand on my back and smirked. "Bend over, baby."

Trembling, I obliged. Leaning over the desk, I gripped the edge and placed my cheek on the freshly polished wood. I felt his fingers slide into the waistband of my panties and I pulsed, shivering when he slowly dragged them down my legs. The sound of a zipper came next, followed by the familiar crackling of a condom wrapper tearing.

"This pussy was made for me," Kyle growled in approval, stroking the head of his cock against my pussy lips. "Do you want this, baby?" He pushed inside of me, just a teasing inch before pulling back and rubbing the wetness of his cock over my slit. "You want me inside this tight pussy?"

"Yeah, I want this," I breathed, pushing against him. "I want you inside me."

"Fuck," he growled before thrusting deep inside of my body. We both moaned loudly as he settled on a rhythm of furious fucking.

"You feel so good," I cried out, pushing into each thrust, reveling in the way he stretched me out. "I love you so much."

His pace faltered for the briefest of moments before switching to a slow, drugging rhythm. "You're mine, Lee," he said, leaning close to my ear. "Okay?" Pressing a kiss to my jaw, he continued to move in and out of me. "I am always going to want you."

Catching my chin with his hand, he angled my face to his. "That's never gonna change, baby."

Breathing hard, I nodded and pressed my lips to his, accepting everything he was willing to give me. He didn't tell me that he loved me, but telling me that he would always want me was a decent consolation prize. I focused on those words as the swell of pleasure building inside me boiled over.

KYLE

"Mr. Carter," Mr. Peterson, my econ professor, acknowledged when I rolled into class ten minutes before the end of the lecture. "How *generous* of you to grace us with your presence today."

"My bad," I muttered, finding a seat in the front row. *I'm not even sorry*, I thought to myself, unable to keep the just-fucked smirk from my face. I guess it matched my hair. Jesus, I couldn't get enough of that girl. I had Lee on the brain and the smell of her in my nose. *Block her out*, I mentally instructed myself. *Just get through this class and you can go home and fuck her.*

"This is your last class with me before winter break," he pointed out, waiting for me to take my seat before continuing. "And your final year." Coming to stand in front of me, he kept his voice low as he spoke. "Poor punctuality and absenteeism aren't like you."

Yeah, he was referring to when I dropped off the face of the earth to chase Lee around Louisiana. And the three extra days after we'd come back that I'd locked us away in my room. "Sorry, Larry," I muttered, tossing my book bag on my desk. "I've had a lot going on lately." *Like my sexy roommate who I can't keep my hands off – or my dick out of.*

As fond as Larry Peterson was of me, I didn't think he would take too kindly to me skiving off class to make out with my girl. Then again, if he saw Lee I had a feeling he might understand.

"I understand that you're under a lot more pressure than the average student," he replied in a kinder voice, brown eyes full of concern "But you graduate in the summer, Kyle. In six months. Your business can have all your focus then, but for now, I need you to *stick* with the program. You've worked too hard for too long to lose your focus on the final hurdle." He stared hard at me when he whispered, "Don't blow it."

Nodding curtly, I stewed in my bad mood and indignation until class was over. Storming out of the business building, I stalked across the quad, feeling hard done by. I had straight A's in his class—in *all* of my classes. I had a 4.5 GPA, dammit! It was fucking petty to badger me about missing a couple of classes. My grades hadn't even slipped.

I was still scowling when I stalked into the jam-packed student café to meet my friends for our daily post-class catch-up. Cam, who was already sitting at a window seat, waved me over.

"Hey," I acknowledged glumly, dumping my bag on the floor and slumping down on the chair opposite her.

"Hello to you, too, sunshine," she quipped, arching a brow. "Dare I ask who put you in such fine form this evening?"

"Fucking Peterson." Resting my elbows on the table, I dropped my head in my hands. "Thinks he knows everything about my life – as usual."

"Really?" Cam raised her brow as she swallowed a sip of her latte. "I thought he liked you?" she added, wiping foamy milk from her top lip. "Aren't you that particular teacher's pet?" She waggled her brows. "His little bitch boy, kissing ass for extra credit?"

"Oh, shut the hell up," I grumbled. "And he *does* like me – that's the damn problem." Frustrated, I leaned back in my chair and sighed. "He's all up in my business because I missed a few of his classes."

"When we were in Louisiana?"

I nodded.

"Awh, he probably just missed your fat, overachieving brain in the front row," she snickered. "All lonesome without his best boy."

"You suck, dude," I deadpanned, narrowing my eyes at her.

"Here you go, honey." A familiar brunette waitress, the one with the huge rack, placed a steaming cup of black coffee in front of me and smiled. "Thought I'd save you from having to join the queue."

"Uh, yeah, thanks a lot… Lauren," I replied, eyeing her name tag. Pulling a twenty out of my wallet, I handed it to her and smiled. "I appreciate it."

"No problem." She beamed back at me. "I remember just how you like it." She twirled her hair around her finger and giggled.

I stared blankly. "Uh, okay?"

"Sure thing, honey."

"And…keep the change?" I offered, feeling a little uncomfortable.

"Oh, thanks," she giggled, placing her hand on my shoulder. "You were always such a *generous* guy."

Trying and failing to shake her hand off, I turned to Cam for help.

Rolling her eyes, Cam snorted and gave me one of her *'you've made your bed, now lie in it'* looks.

"So," Lauren continued, her voice a breathy purr. "My shift finishes in like five minutes and my place is just off campus." She winked. "You remember where I live, right?"

Oh, for Christ's sake. So that was what the sexual innuendos were about. I looked back to Cam, who gave me a *'yeah, you put your dick in that, dumbass'*.

"I'm seeing someone," I blurted out, surprising all three of us. "It's serious." Whoa, what the fuck was coming out of my mouth? "I'm not interested in any hook-ups." I shifted, uncomfortable. "Sorry."

Dammit, I wished Lee was here with me so this girl and all the others would back the fuck off, but the need to protect her from Rachel and all my other bullshit kept me from making us public. The all-expenses-paid trip to Paris I'd doled out to Rachel and her buddies had bought me some extra time, but I knew that I had to figure this shit out soon. Preferably before she rolled back into town and ruined my life with the kind of painful precision only she could execute.

"I'm sure I can get you interested," Lauren purred, planting her hands on her hips. "If it's Rachel you're talking about then you were seeing her last time, too. I mean, everyone knows you guys have an open relationship."

"Um, sweetie?" Cam cleared her throat, and leaned forward, chin resting on her perfectly manicured fingers. "Maybe you could go and bury your nose in a book – preferably one that explains body language, so the next time you can read the signs when a man *isn't* interested." Smiling, she added, "Better yet, listen to the fucking words coming out of his mouth."

"Bitch," Lauren hissed, glaring at Cam.

"Be gone, demon," Cam shot back with a dismissive wave.

"That was brilliant," I chuckled, watching Lauren storm away. "You are awesome."

"And *you* are a slut," Cam countered, checking her cuticles. "A re-formed one, if you know what's good for you."

The café door swung inwards then and Derek strolled in, looking as chipper as always. "Family," he acknowledged, clapping my shoulder before making a beeline for his girlfriend. Twisting his baseball cap backwards, he plastered a loud, overly dramatic kiss on Cam before sinking onto the chair beside her and repositioning his cap. "Thank Jesus we're finishing for the holidays on Friday." Holding an arm up, he beckoned a waitress to our table "I need a reprieve." Thankfully, a different one came to take his coffee order. "Because if I have to sit through another one of Professor Garethy's lectures on maternal fucking monkeys, I swear to god I will stab myself in the eyes with this spork." He gestured to the plastic spork on the table.

"Kind of defeats the purpose, dude," I quipped. "Considering you'd be blind and *not* deaf."

"You obviously haven't met Garethy," Derek huffed as he shrugged off his coat. "Trust me, Kyle, I'd be doing my eyes a kind mercy."

"Oh, my poor baby," Cam cooed, leaning in for a kiss. "Let's go home and I'll give you a show that will make you reconsider going blind."

"Jesus," I muttered, shuddering. "You two are sick."

FIFTY-ONE

DECK THE HALLS

LEE

CHRISTMAS WAS my favorite time of year. Even when I was a little girl and Santa didn't bring me presents, or I didn't get any turkey, I still *adored* the holiday. I used to love listening to the Christmas songs on the radio, and eavesdropping on the other children in my class as they conversed about what toys they were getting, or how their mamas would bake apple pies and cinnamon rolls.

My favorite Christmas was when I was seven. My father's appendix had burst on Christmas Eve and he was rushed to the hospital. He'd left me with Cam's parents – much to my delight. I *loved* their house. It was always so clean and smelled so nice. I got my very first Christmas present that year. A Malibu Barbie. I remembered Mrs. Frey telling me that Santa knew I was sleeping at their house and had left my present there. I also remembered the sad look on her face when I had asked her if Santa knew how to find my daddy's house because I had never gotten a present from him before. She had cried and I'd thought I was in big trouble for making her cry, but instead of hitting me, Mrs. Frey had hugged me. *It was the best Christmas.*

"Since you're the baby of the house, you should do the

honors," Kyle teased, bringing me back to the present when he placed a glass angel tree topper in my hands.

It was the week before Christmas, and he was standing in front of me, wearing only a pair of unbuttoned black slacks. His jacket and tie were slung over the arm of the couch and his white shirt was draped around me like an oversized dress. Cam and Derek were out at a party and we had made the most of an empty house. "The floor is yours, Princess."

"Uh, I don't know if you've noticed or not," I said, pointing to the tree that we had spent the past three hours decorating. "But that's a seven-foot Christmas tree, Kyle Carter, and I'm about two feet too short, ahhhhh –" I squealed in surprise as Kyle lifted me up.

"Make sure it's on straight, baby," he instructed, tone amused.

I slid the Angel on top and then checked twice before nodding. "Okay, it's straight."

"Good job." Kyle set me down and we both stepped back to admire our work. The tree looked quite tragic. Mismatched baubles were scattered on the branches, with every different color of tinsel to boot. The lights were a hideous blue.

"Oh god." I laughed, nudging his shoulder with mine. "I guess we won't be winning any awards for decorating."

"I don't care," he replied, slinging an arm over my shoulder. "It's the first Christmas I've wanted to celebrate in years – ever, actually." He winked down at me. "I'm proud of our shitty tree."

Our tree. "This is my first Christmas having a tree to decorate," I replied, turning my attention back to the tree. "Daddy never got one for the house."

"That's so fucked up," Kyle growled, tensing beside me, and I instantly regretted saying anything.

"I'm sorry," I mumbled before hurrying to clear away the empty boxes and containers.

"Why are you sorry?" he asked, trailing after me.

Opening the door under the stairs, I stacked the boxes inside before turning to face him. "For bringing him up." I closed the door and leaned against it. "For making you angry."

"I'm not angry with you, Lee." Closing the space between us, he kissed my forehead. "I'm fucking furious with him. When you tell me you've never been trick-or-treating or that you didn't have a Christmas tree, it makes me want to get in my truck, drive back to Montgomery, and kick his ass."

"Well, you've fixed those things for me," I whispered, leaning in and pressing a kiss to his chest. "You've given me a whole lot of firsts."

"Yeah?" He rubbed my cheek with his thumb.

Shivering, I nodded. "Yeah."

"It's not enough." Leaning down, he studied my face with a serious expression. "I want to give you all your firsts." The door-bell rang, but Kyle made no move to answer it. "I want to fix everything for you, Lee." He kissed me softly. "I want to give you everything you've never had – anything you want."

I smiled up at him. "Then you've already given me everything –" Patting his chest, I slipped around him and moved to answer the door, "Because all I want is you."

"That will be twenty-two dollars even," the delivery guy said, eyes widening when he took in my attire. I blushed, mentally cursing myself for answering the door in a man's shirt. "Hey, doll, you visiting?" he asked, voice taking on a deeper tone. "I get a lot of calls to this house and I know I would remember a pretty face like yours."

"Um, no, I live here." Reaching for my purse off the desk table, I fumbled with the clasp, trying to get my cash out.

"Really?" he purred, leaning closer.

"Uh, yeah, really."

"Not from around here?" he questioned, watching me with overly keen eyes. "Where's that sexy drawl from?"

"Um..." I shifted awkwardly from foot to foot and tightened the lapels of Kyle's shirt around my body. "I'm from Louisiana."

"Nice." The delivery guy grinned. "I'm Jessie. And you are?"

"Taken." A firm hand clamped around my waist. "She's taken," Kyle said coolly, pulling my back flush to his chest. "By me," he added, holding out a fifty-dollar bill. "Keep the change."

The delivery guy's eyes widened as he pocketed the cash. "Oh, uh, hey, Carter." Red-faced, he mumbled something about being in a rush before thrusting the pizza box into my arms and hurrying off.

Giggling, I closed the front door and moved for the living room, only to stop when I noticed Kyle's expectant expression.

"What?" I laughed, stepping around him and making a beeline for my usual perch on the couch. "What's that look for?"

"*What*?" Kyle repeated, trailing after me. "Baby, you can't go answering the door looking like *that*."

"Relax." Flopping down on the couch, I tore open the pizza box and devoured a mouth-watering bite. "It's just a –" Pausing, I lifted my legs for Kyle to sit down and then lowered them onto his lap, "It's just a shirt, Kyle."

"Exactly," he countered, smoothing a hand over my calf. "It's just a shirt. Just a very white – very *see-through*– shirt."

"I forgot I was wearing it, okay?" I shot back between bites. "I was rushing to beat you to the door because I wanted to pay this time and forgot what I was wearing."

"Two things." Kyle grabbed the pizza box from my lap and tossed it on the coffee table. Slipping his hands around my waist, he pulled me onto his lap so that I was straddling him. "First, as sweet as I think it is that you want to pay, you're my woman, so you won't be paying for our food." I opened my mouth to protest, but he silenced me with a kiss. "Second, the only person who's going to see these gorgeous tits and that perfect pussy is *me*." He lowered his head, nipping my breast through my shirt. I panted, instantly wet. "Third –"

"I thought you said there were only two things," I moaned, writhing against his hard-on.

"I thought of a third," he explained, popping the buttons on my shirt.

"Okay," I breathed, rocking my hips.

"Third –" Sliding my shirt down my shoulders, Kyle fell onto his back, taking me with him. "Sit on my face."

Oh god.

FIFTY-TWO

KYLE

I COULDN'T FACE GOING HOME this evening. Knowing that Rachel was due back tomorrow had my head in a goddamn spin. Slumped at my desk, I mulled over every possible scenario until I was blue in the goddamn face. How could I go home and face Lee? She never once asked me about Rachel since returning from Louisiana and I hadn't dared bring it up, either. Because I didn't know what to do. I wanted Lee. I wanted to be with the girl. Fuck that, I *was* with her. I just... I needed to get myself away from Rachel.

She *would* be back in the morning. I had no doubt about it. Tomorrow would mark the two-year anniversary of the day I lost control of my future and that bitch never missed a chance to haul it over my head.

When I called her back in Louisiana and offered to foot the bill for that damn trip to Paris that she had been nagging me for, it seemed like the perfect temporary solution. Except now she was coming back and my perfect plan didn't seem so fucking perfect anymore.

The way I saw it, I had two choices.

One; tell Lee everything and risk her hating me forever.

Two; make another deal with the devil herself.

The thought of losing Lee was too fucking painful to even contemplate. I couldn't do it. I *couldn't* give her up. Bargaining with Rachel was my only option. Money. She could have it all. I was done. I was so fucking exhausted riding this rollercoaster of deception. I wanted off, dammit. I needed out of this power-struggle because I sure as hell couldn't live my life like this anymore. Not now that I had something worth living for. A future with a good woman who, despite my misgivings, had decided to love me.

"What's troubling you, kiddo?" Linda's soft voice filled my ears and I jerked up to find her sitting at my desk, brown eyes warm and locked on mine. "I can hear you thinking from all the way down in my office."

"I can't tell you," I squeezed out, knees bopping restlessly as I dropped my head in my hands once more. "You'll think I'm a piece of shit." Pulling on my hair, I muttered, "You'll hate me."

"Doubtful," she mused, reaching over and taking my hand in hers. "You're my favorite boy in the world." Smiling kindly, she gave my hand a squeeze. "There's nothing you could say that would make me stop loving you."

I didn't deserve this woman.

I didn't deserve Lee.

I didn't deserve Rachel's wrath!

"I fucked up," I confessed, hardly able to meet her gaze. "The night Frank died?" Exhaling raggedly, I felt my shoulders slump in defeat. "I took a life away."

I expected Linda to scream, or hit me, shout at me, or hell, even flinch. I did not expect her to laugh. "Oh, kiddo."

"I'm serious, Linda," I bit out, body rigid. "I took a life away – I took someone's future. It was a complete fucking accident, but it doesn't change the fact that it happened. I got behind the wheel. I was driving. The blood is on *my* goddamn hands."

"Okay," Linda said, sobering quickly. "Why don't you start at the beginning and we'll take it from there."

"Are you sure you want to hear it?" I croaked out.

"Positive," she confirmed. "Start talking."

Inhaling a deep, steadying breath, I opened my mouth and told Linda everything. I bared my fucking soul to the woman, warts and all.

"So, that's the reason you put up with her abusing you like she does?" Linda asked when I finished. "That's why you tolerate her using you like her own personal cash-cow?" Her eyes narrowed. "Her own goddamn pillow-pal?"

Dejected, I nodded. "What else can I do? I was the one driving the car that night. I caused her injuries. It's my fault and I've got a responsibility to the girl. I *promised*." Exhaling another pained breath, I squeezed out, "You know what happened to my mom." Clenching my eyes shut, I repressed a shudder. "You know how she died." My shoulders slumped in defeat. "I did it again. I broke another girl."

"You didn't break your mom," Linda snapped, tone heated. "She broke herself, Kyle Carter, and she failed you along the way."

"And Rachel?" I strangled out.

"I don't know, kiddo." Standing up, Linda walked over to the mini bar and poured two tumblers of whiskey. "Something doesn't add up," she mused, setting a glass down in front of me. "This doesn't feel right to me."

"I know," I groaned, dragging my hand through my hair. Nothing about the situation felt right to me, either, but I'd been over it obsessively with a fine-toothed come for two damn years. "If I had a way out, I would have found it by now," I told her and then tossed my drink back. Climbing to my feet, I went to the mini bar and poured another. "It feels *wrong* to me, too."

"Bring that bottle over here, kiddo," Linda instructed, slumping down on her chair. "I'm gonna need it."

Wordlessly, I passed Linda the bottle and sat back down.

"Go through it once more," she said and I could see the wheels turning in her head as she silently assessed the situation.

"Really?" I deadpanned.

"Just humor me, Kyle."

"Fine," I groaned. "Fine. I was coming back from the reading of Frank's will and I'd just found out that he left me everything –"

"And your daddy had a meltdown," Linda mused. "Vowing to make you pay for stealing his inheritance."

"And my sperm donor had a meltdown," I corrected. My so-called father had gone berserk; threatening me with lawsuits, vengeance, and god knows what else, but I hadn't given two shits about his feelings. Because I was the one who held Frank's hand as the life slowly seeped out of him. I was by his side. Not my father, or his wife, and certainly not my goddamn brother. *No, because he was too busy…* "David Henderson is a spoiled prick." I looked Linda dead in the eyes. "You know that I never wanted a dime of that money."

"Keep going," was all she replied.

"When I got back to Frank's house after the reading, I was drunk. Too fucking drunk. You remember," I added, shoulders sagging. "You put me in a cab that night and sent me home. I was a mess. I was grieving and all fucked up. I just…" I threw my hands up. "I missed the old man."

"Go on," she urged.

"Rachel was there," I bit out, jaw clenched. "When I walked inside. She was in my grandfather's house with *him*. Fucking like rabbits on his kitchen table when the man was barely cold in the ground."

It still hurt to think about it. Not the fact that Rachel cheated on me, but that Mike – my own goddamn brother –screwed me over. We were friends until then. He'd been the one person in the family that I actually enjoyed spending time with. And then he fucked me over. Just like his father. Just like they all did.

"We had a fight," I explained, remembering my reaction to finding them. "He sprouted a bunch of bullshit about how I had screwed his family over with Frank's inheritance, and how Rachel was with him first." I shook my head, still feeling the pang of betrayal. "I had to get out of there, Linda. It was either leave or kill him." Reaching for the bottle of Jack, I poured myself another glass and tossed it back. "So, I grabbed my keys and I got in the car."

"Keep going, kiddo," she coaxed, snatching my hand up and giving it a reassuring squeeze.

"She followed me," I strangled out, chest heaving. "Climbed into the passenger seat." Guilt seeped through me as my panic rose. "I told her to get out – I swear, I told her to go, but she just… she wouldn't fucking go!" Exhaling a pained growl, I forced the words out. "I was pissed, so I drove off with her in the car with me. She didn't have a seatbelt on. I was off my face –" Breaking off, I dragged in a steadying breath before finishing, "I wasn't concentrating – couldn't see straight. I ran a red light, flipped the car, and killed her baby."

FIFTY-THREE

NEW PLANS AND OLD HABITS

LEE

"SO, I was thinking we could throw a party tomorrow night?" Cam asked as we all sat at the table having dinner – minus Kyle. He had to work late for the third night in a row. "What do you guys think?" Her eyes lit up as she spoke. "Think festive vibes. Green and red jello shots. Loads of mistletoe hanging from the ceiling. Mariah Carey belting out the good stuff. It will be fabulous."

"Tomorrow's Christmas Eve," I reminded her.

"I know," she replied, her smile still firmly in place. "What better way to celebrate than with our old friend *Tequila*."

I shuddered at the notion; my stomach twisting up in protest, not liking the thought of tequila one bit – or the memory.

"Cool, babe," Derek replied between mouthfuls of lasagna. "Think you can swing it before tomorrow night?"

"Oh, my sweet, innocent baby." Cam smiled sweetly at him and patted his head. "I am the queen of planning." She turned to me, expression expectant. "What do you think, Lee?" she asked before taking a swig of beer from her bottle. "Are you down?"

No. I was so far up from down that I couldn't see the freaking down. I still wasn't comfortable with the crowds and parties, but

I didn't want to be a buzz kill. "Sure." I smiled weakly and then jolted in my chair when a stabbing sensation tore through my body. Jesus, I felt like I was dying today. "I don't mind," I offered before swallowing a mouthful of lasagna. It tasted gorgeous, like all of Derek's cooking usually did, but I had no mind for it. I'd woken up to the heaviest period known to mankind and all I felt like doing was curling up in a ball and dying.

"Well, I mind," Kyle slurred as he staggered into the kitchen with a face like thunder.

Lord, what was wrong now?

"You okay, dude?" Derek asked, eyeing Kyle with concern.

"Never better, Der," Kyle sneered, moving straight for the liquor cabinet. "Never fucking *better*."

Without a word, I stood up and took my plate to the sink; the appearance of whiskey making what little was left of my appetite disappear.

"Isn't it a little early for Jack to make an appearance, man?" Derek asked calmly, clearing his plate from the table and joining me at the sink. "You good?" he mouthed, nudging my shoulder with his.

Nodding weakly, I turned my attention to the dishes. I was contemplating jumping into the sink to see if the drain would suck me down. I didn't know how to handle Kyle when he was in this kind of mood.

"Mind your business," Kyle spat. "Don't need a goddamn babysitter, Der."

"You've got it, buddy. You go right ahead and suit yourself," was all Derek replied before stalking out of the room, tossing a dish rag at Kyle as he went.

"Jesus, are you having a tantrum because I want to throw a party?" Cam demanded huffily, folding her arms across her chest. "We throw parties here all the damn time, Kyle. What's the problem?"

"The *problem*, Camryn, is that I don't want to come home to another goddamn party in my house –" Cracking the lid off, he poured a huge glass of whiskey and tossed it back before continuing, "Not tonight. Not tomorrow night. And the not the fucking night after." He refilled his glass and quickly tossed that back, too. "Is that clear enough for you?" He poured himself another glass and pointed it at her. "Or would you like me to repeat myself?"

"You're an asshole," Cam spat, shoving her chair back. "I hope you know that." With that, she stormed out of the kitchen, hissing, "Fuck you, Carter. I pay my rent. If I want a damn party, I'll have one!"

"I don't want a party," Kyle slurred, clearly speaking to me now. "I don't want you at any damn party!"

If he was looking for an argument, he wasn't going to get one from me. I was too weary and in too much pain to care about stupid parties or argue with drunk douchebags. "Okay." Picking up the dish towel, I began to dry the plates. "No problem."

"Okay?" he asked, sounding a little taken aback. "That's it?" Confusion laced his tone. "You're not going to fight with me on this?"

Was there any point? He didn't want me around his friends. A blind man could see that his little tantrum was about that. "No, Kyle, I'm not going to argue," I replied flatly. "You don't want me there. You obviously have your reasons." Wiping a bead of sweat from my brow, I clutched the draining board as another monster-cramp rocked through me. "It's whatever."

"Lee." Sighing heavily, he closed the space between us and wrapped his arms around me. "Don't be pissed," he slurred, burying his face in my neck and the smell of whiskey on his breath almost knocked me for six. "*None* of this is what you think."

I didn't *care* about any of this. I honestly felt like I was two seconds away from passing out on the floor. Right now, his issues were the last thing on my mind.

"I'm gonna make this all right," he continued to slur. "I've got a plan." He kissed my neck. "I'll be free soon, baby."

What the heck was he talking about?

Scratch that, I didn't care.

Swallowing down a whimper, I continued tidying the kitchen in numb, calculated moves. I was trying so damn hard not to vomit. "You want some help, Princess?" When his fingers splayed across my stomach, I jerked away, grunting out a pained sigh.

"What's wrong?" he hurried to ask, glazed eyes finding focus on mine.

"It's my period." Flinching, I sagged against the counter. "I'm cramping so bad."

"Shit, babe," he slurred, hands on my hips. "What can I do?"

Get me a tranquilizer? "Nothing," I whispered, chewing on my lip. "I'll be fine."

"Do you want a bath?" he offered, brows furrowed deeply. "I can do that for you."

He could hardly walk a straight line. "I'm okay," I replied, setting the dish towel down on the draining board. "I might go to bed, though."

"Can I come?"

I tensed.

"Just to hold you," he mumbled, expression pained. "Just to be close."

"Yeah, Kyle," I sighed wearily. "You can come."

FIFTY-FOUR

THE CHRISTMAS EVE BASH

KYLE

IT WAS Christmas Eve and festive music was pumping through the house. Countless bodies were crammed into my downstairs, all drinking and partying it up. Twelve beers in, and I was well on my way to being wasted. I figured I deserved to get shit faced. I had a bad feeling about tonight. I could feel it in my gut. Shit was going to go down tonight. The date was enough to make my skin crawl.

December twenty-fourth.

Two years to the day since the accident.

The difference tonight, though, was that I had a plan. Thanks to Linda, I could see a tiny flicker of light at the end of the tunnel. All I had to do was keep my head and follow through.

Lee was upstairs and I knew that I should be up there with her. She'd been sick all day with period cramps, and I felt like a piece of shit for leaving her alone, but I had to do this. I had to talk to Rachel first. I couldn't risk her intercepting Lee before I had a chance to straighten this whole goddamn mess up and tell her myself.

My stomach churned when I thought about how I'd left her curled up in her bed, though. She was deathly pale and didn't want me to leave. She fucking begged me to stay upstairs with her. I planned on getting my ass back up there as soon as I could.

Grabbing a bottle of whiskey from the cabinet, I chugged it straight from the bottle, body bristling with tension, as I watched her swagger towards me, all red hair and black heart.

Showtime.

LEE

I was dying.

I knew it.

All day, I'd writhed in agony, burning from a fever, and barely managing to cope with the pain. Now, though, it was even worse. My body was in spasm, my limbs jolting violently, as the pain in my pelvis, stomach and back threatened to swallow me up.

The urge to use the toilet was potent, and I dragged myself out of bed on my hands and knees. Crying hard and ugly, I grappled to drag myself to my feet, only to stagger backwards when a swell of dizziness engulfed me.

"Cam?" I cried out, terrified now, as I clung to the wall and forced my legs to move. "Cam?" I knew she couldn't hear me. I couldn't hear myself over the music blasting from downstairs. Body racking with tremors, I tried to make it to my bedroom door, but the pain was too severe, causing me to collapse on my hands and knees again.

I had this sick wave of Déjá vu, remembering how sick my father had been when his appendix burst all those years ago. Was that what was happening to me? Oh god, I needed a doctor. I needed it to stop.

On my hands and knees, I crawled at a snail's pace across the deserted hall and into the bathroom, breathing labored. By the time I reached the toilet bowl, I was dry-heaving, but the only thing coming up now was green bile.

"Kyle!" I whimpered when another sharp pain darted through my pelvis. "Oh god, Kyle!" I tried to scream but my voice came out more like a strangled whisper. "Kyle," I screamed, louder now as my panic built. "Please! Someone help me."

Pushing my panties down my legs, I screamed in terror when a thick, gushing flow of bright red blood oozed down my thighs.

The blood on my legs was the last thing I saw before everything grew light and pain free.

Sinking to the floor, I closed my eyes, body jerking violently, and let the darkness take me.

FIFTY-FIVE

BITCHES AND BLOOD LOSS

KYLE

"RACHEL," I acknowledged coolly as she approached me, wishing I could be anywhere but near this devil woman.

"Kyle." She smiled up at me with that look I knew well. *Not tonight, Satan. Never a-fucking-gain.* "So where's your little roomie?" Arching a menacing brow, she glanced around us. "I haven't seen her around tonight." She smirked. "Don't tell me that you got sick of her already?"

Nope. Got no plans on it either. My body was racked with tension, but I managed to keep my face void of emotion. I had a plan and I needed to stick to it. The dirt Linda had dug up was like a winning lottery ticket. I just needed to hit my jackpot. "We need to talk."

"Talk?" She stepped closer, pressing her body against mine, and I flinched.

"Talk," I confirmed, taking a step back.

"Really?" She closed the space between, pinning me against the wall. "What if I don't wanna talk, Kyle?" She trailed a long nail from my throat to my stomach, hooking her fingers into the waistband of my jeans. "What if I wanna fuck?"

"Stop it," I snapped, removing her hand. "That's not happening."

"Oh yeah?" Smiling darkly, she hooked her fingers in the waistband of my jeans once more and tugged hard. "You remember the date, don't you?"

How the fuck could I forget?

"Kyle?" I heard some guy call my name from the hallway. "There's some chick in the upstairs bathroom calling out for you. She sounds upset, dude – crying and shit."

My heart sank into my stomach.

Aw, shit!

Lee…

I went to move for the stairs, but Rachel yanked me back. "Why don't I come upstairs with you and have a little chat with Lee?" she sneered, fingers digging into my arm. "I'm sure she would *love* to hear what I have to say."

I stiffened. This was *exactly* what I was trying to avoid. Rachel also knew this because she smirked in triumph.

Derek, who was standing nearby, glared at Rachel and then looked at me with the most disappointed expression I had ever seen. Shaking his head, he shoved through the crowd and hurried up the staircase.

Well, fuck him. This was hard enough without being judged. I knew what I had to do and if I didn't go with Rachel now and get it over with, I'd never be free of the woman.

I had to do this, dammit.

"You ready to get out of here?" Rachel asked, squeezing my hand. "My place?"

Nodding stiffly, I moved for the door. "Let's just do this before I change my mind."

LEE

In the thick fog of darkness, I could hear banging and then Derek's terrified voice was in my ears.

"Ice!"

Something hard shook my shoulders.

"Lee! Jesus Christ, *Lee*."

"Oh my god!"

"Is she dead?"

"Someone call a fucking ambulance!"

I could feel someone lifting me off the floor, but I could not move a muscle.

I couldn't open my eyes.

"Kyle," I mumbled drowsily. Kyle. Where was Kyle?

"Yeah, I need an ambulance – I don't know what's wrong with her!"

Cam?

That was Cam.

"She's covered in blood and vomit!"

"Jesus Christ, tell them to hurry up."

That was Derek.

"You're gonna be fine, Ice," his voice was back in my ear, tone soothing and coaxing. "I've got you." Strong arms tightened around me. "You're gonna be just fine, sweetheart."

"Oh my god, is she breathing!"

"Keep breathing," Derek coaxed. "There's an ambulance on

the way for you." A huge tremor racked through him. "Just hold on for me, Lee. Just hang in there, sweetheart."

FIFTY-SIX

KYLE

"I'M OUT, RACHEL," I announced as I stood in the middle of her penthouse suite – a suite I paid for. "I'm done. This is over." As I spoke the words, I felt the manacles around my wrists loosening. Unable to stand still, I paced around her kitchen, too fucking excited with the prospect of freedom.

"What do you mean you're *out*?" She narrowed her eyes. "Out of what, Kyle? Out of your *responsibilities*?"

I anticipated the wine glass that sailed from her hand and ducked out of the way in time, watching as it sailed past my head and shattered against the expensive ivory wallpaper. "You know what happened," I said calmly. "It was a goddamn accident. If I could take back what happened that night, I would."

"But you can't!" she hissed.

"No," I agreed. "I can't."

"And you can't walk away from your promises," she added, glowering at me. "You ruined my life and now you're gonna be a man and suffer the consequences of your actions."

For the first time in two years, I didn't flinch at her words. For the first time in two years, I felt like fighting *back*– because I had something to fight for now. My phone was vibrating in my pocket and I knew it was either Derek or Cam, but I didn't let it distract me from the task at hand. They'd been calling me constantly since I left the party and I knew they were pissed with me, but I'd deal with them later. Right now, I had a much bigger fish to fry.

"You can blame me for crashing the car, Rachel," I continued, keeping my tone even. "That part was *my* fault, but the reason I crashed was *yours*."

"You crashed!"

"You pulled the wheel!" I snapped, finally allowing myself to shift some of the blame that had been weighing on me like a crane.

"You were drunk!" she screamed.

"You knew that and climbed in with me anyway."

"You killed our baby!"

"Liar," I roared back at her, losing my cool. "Don't fucking lie to me!"

She blanched and strode towards me. I didn't bother moving. I knew what she was going to do. Her hand struck my face. "You bastard," she screamed. "How can you call me a liar? You crashed the car. You caused me to lose *our* baby. *You* killed it, Kyle, and it's your fault I can't get pregnant again." She was shaking with anger. Good, I needed her shaken up.

"You fucked my brother," I countered hotly. "Repeatedly. For *months*. Behind *my* back – or were you fucking me behind *his* back?"

Her eyes widened. "I don't know what you're talking about!" she snarled. "I've already explained that what happened with Mike was a one-time thing."

"Yeah," I sneered. "Sure it was, and I'm the King of England." I shook my head in disgust. "You wouldn't know the truth if it smacked you in the face."

"Don't you dare –"

"You're a liar, Rachel," I pressed. "A cold, vindictive, money-hungry whore. You were with him first, weren't you?" I demanded. "Mike? You were his girl? You only decided to shift your game plan onto me because you realized that I was the bigger meal ticket. He was a well-padded trust fund baby, but I was heir to the fucking *empire*!"

She paled and I knew I was dead on the money. Thank Jesus I

had confided in Linda. There was a reason people said two heads were better than one. If I hadn't opened up, I would have never known the truth. The phone call I received from Rachel's mother earlier tonight – a phone call orchestrated by Linda – had confirmed that everything I believed for the last two years was a lie. "You fucked my relationship with my brother," I snarled. "It's gone. Broken. Fractured. Never coming back. All thanks to you. Not that you have a heart to care."

"Where is all this coming from?" she demanded, eyes wild with panic.

"The night I caught you fucking Mike?" I explained. "It was the very same night you told me that you were pregnant with my baby – something you decided to announce on the very same day I had inherited a windfall from my grandfather. Weird, huh?"

"Coincidence," she huffed, folding her arms across her chest. "What are you getting at?"

"Well, it got me thinking."

Her eyes narrowed. "Thinking about what?"

"About why a woman pregnant with a man's baby would go and fuck his brother."

"I've already told you that Mike was a one off," she hissed, cheeks reddening.

"You told me a pack of lies," I shot back, tone hard. "The jig's up. I've been putting dates together and realized that the *baby* couldn't have been mine."

"Wh-what?"

"The dates," I replied, keeping my tone purposefully soft. "They don't add up."

"Of course they add up!" she spat, trembling now. "Because it's the truth."

"No," I corrected. "They don't. I was with my grandfather day and night for six solid weeks running up to his death – and your so-called conception. And I've never *not* worn a condom with you. I never came inside you, sweetheart, not even with a rubber on my dick. I *always* pulled out." Sneering, I added, "Can't be too careful with clingers."

Rachel stared at me, silent for a change.

"So then, when the dates didn't add up, I started to think that Mike must have been the one that knocked you up. Well –" Pausing, I sneered at her. "Mike or some other poor bastard, but you blamed the baby on me."

"You're wrong," she hissed.

"I'm not done," I mused. "So, that makes me wonder even more; why lie about the baby being mine if it was his? Mike's a good-looking guy, wealthy, good *teeth* – a nice little coup for a gold-digging whore such as yourself."

"You don't –"

"And why is it that I never even heard about you being pregnant until *after* the crash?" I demanded, cutting her off. "Was it because you told Mike that it was his?"

Her eyes widened.

"That's it, isn't it?" I laughed humorlessly. "He thought you were having his kid – right up until the reading of the will. You clearly didn't expect Frank to leave everything to me, did you? No, you thought Mikey-boy was onto a winner. I was just the bastard son and Mike was the golden boy – the true heir to the Henderson Hotels."

"You're wrong," she spat, shaking.

"I'm not wrong," I countered. "I'm dead on the money." I pulled my phone out of my pocket and dangled it in front of her. "I had a little chat with your mother today, who, needless to say, was shell-shocked with what I had to say."

"You spoke to my mother?"

"Mmm-hmm." I nodded. "You can imagine my surprise when she confirmed, no –*assured* me that you weren't pregnant when you were brought in to the hospital that night because you had to be tested before getting x-rayed, and the test had come back as a big, fat, negative."

"Wh-what?"

"Your mother seemed to be under the impression that you had surgery on your *spleen* that night and not a *hysterectomy* like you told me."

LEE

I could hear the paramedics talking above me as they worked on my body. I could *feel* their hands on my body, luring me back to consciousness. Inside, I was screaming out Kyle's name at the top of my lungs and it wasn't until my eyes sprang open that I realized I was screaming for real.

"Shh, shh, sweetheart," Derek coaxed, clutching my hand with both of his. "I'm right here with you, Ice. You've got this."

Got what? "Got what?" What the hell was happening to me? "Derek," I gasped when my eyes landed on his face. It was fuzzy and blurred, but I could hear him. "Where's Kyle?"

"Shh," he coaxed, giving my hand a squeeze. "You're gonna be fine, okay?"

A loud sob came from close by. "Lee-Bee," Cam's voice floated through my ears. "It's okay, babe. Try to stay calm."

"Cam," I strangled out, panicking now. I tried to move my hand towards her, but an agonizing pain shot through my body and I screamed at the top of my lungs. "Help me!"

"We are," Derek coaxed, stroking my forehead. "You're in an ambulance. Lee. You're on the way to the hospital." He squeezed my hand again. "We're right here with you."

I shook my head in confusion. "Kyle?" I twisted my head from side to side. I couldn't see him. "Kyle?" I cried out hoarsely. "Kyle?"

Cam and Derek looked away.

What was happening?

"Are you the father?" one of the paramedics asked Derek as he held my wrist in his hand, timing my pulse. He looked furious when he asked, "Did you leave her in this condition?"

"No." Derek shook his head and then whispered something to Cam.

Her whole face caved as she burst into tears. "Oh god!"

The father? "What are you talking about?" I cried out. "The father of *what*?"

The female paramedic offered me a reassuring smile. "Delia, please try to stay calm."

"But I don't know what's happening to me," I sobbed, writhing in agony. "Help me!"

"We are concerned that you may be having a miscarriage," she said, blowing my freaking mind. "The best thing you can do now is to breathe slowly and try to stay relaxed for the baby's sake. We'll know more when we get to the hospital and run some tests."

"The baby?" I shook my head. "What baby? I'm *not* pregnant!" I screamed.

"Lee, honey –"

"No, I'm not!" I choked out. "I'm on my period."

The paramedic frowned. "Have you skipped a period?"

"Never!" I shook my head, terrified. "I swear to Jesus, I'm not late and I'm not pregnant!"

"We need to hurry it up," the male paramedic said. "Patient with intra-abdominal hemorrhaging, and suspected ectopic pregnancy," were the last words I heard before the darkness swallowed me up once more.

FIFTY-SEVEN

CLOSURE

KYLE

"YOU WERE NEVER PREGNANT, WERE YOU?"

"You don't know what you're talking about," Rachel screamed, lunging for my phone. I let her take it, more than happy to let her see what I'd seen. She scrolled through my phone frantically, her fingers a blur of movement, deleting messages as she went. It didn't matter. She couldn't delete my memory. I was finally *free* from her hold.

"You really are a sick little girl," I taunted. "You know, I'm not even angry with you. I just *pity* you more than anything."

"Fuck you!" she screamed, throwing my phone at me. "You have no clue what you're doing. You're overthinking things. Messing with something that is bigger than you –"

"I know that it takes a sick woman to fake a pregnancy," I sneered, cutting her off. "I know that much! But it takes a bitter, twisted, conniving *whore* to allow a man to walk around for two fucking years thinking he made her infertile – thinking he killed her baby and her chances her having another one!" I shook my head in disgust. "Game's up, Rachel. I win and you lose. Now, go find yourself some other fool to leech off because I'm cutting you off."

"It took you long enough to figure it out," she finally replied, voice breaking off in a twisted laugh. "And you're supposed to be a bright, college boy."

"They don't teach a class on lying whores," I spat, bristling.

"What about innocent whores?" she countered, on the attack now. "Do they teach you how to deal with those?"

I tensed and Rachel grinned. "She's not a whore."

"She's been on her back with the biggest manwhore in Boulder between her legs," Rachel sneered. "That not only makes her a whore, but a fucking idiot, too." Narrowing her eyes, she hissed, "Do you think your little princess will understand all of this? Do you think she'll understand you and your baby brother sharing a girl? Do you think she'll be able to forgive you for all the lies?" Laughing, she gestured a hand between us. "Do you think she'll forgive you for coming to my place tonight?"

"We didn't do anything," I bit out, tensing. "I haven't laid a finger on you in *months*."

"It's your word against mine, lover boy," she laughed cruelly. "And you don't have the greatest rap sheet for being honest."

"She loves me," I growled.

"Which only makes your betrayal worse!" Rachel laughed. "You've been lying to her for months, Kyle. Playing with her like she was your personal plaything, and then tossing her back into your toy-box when I told you to. She was sick tonight," she continued, twisting the knife. "She needed you. She was crying. We both heard that. And you came to *me*."

"Because I didn't have a choice!" I roared, shaking now.

"You had a choice," Rachel countered. "And you chose me. There is no way she'll forgive you for it."

"She loves me," I repeated, feeling at a loss. "She fucking *loves* me – and unlike you, that girl is a goddamn saint!"

"Saintly enough to put up with your bullshit?" Rachel sneered. "Doubtful."

"You don't know *anything* about her," I said through clenched teeth.

"I know enough to know that little miss southern belle won't look twice at you once she finds out about the double life you've been leading." Rachel stepped up to my chest. "Wake up, Kyle. You've lied to her, cheated on her, and left her alone to be with *me*." She threw her head back and laughed. "I bet you haven't even told her that you love her back, have you?" I froze and Rachel's eyes gleamed. "Oh my god, I'm right, aren't I?" She threw her head back and laughed. "You love the girl, she's probably the first person you've ever loved besides that old hag Linda, and you can't even express it. Do you know why? Hmm? I do. It's because you are *broken*. You don't work right – just like me. You're not capable of loving someone without destroying them, Kyle Carter, so if you care about that girl, like I think you do, then walk away before you destroy her. Walk away before she ends up killing herself to get away from you– just like your mother did."

FIFTY-EIGHT

RUDE AWAKENINGS

LEE

THE SOUND of beeping filled my ears and I remained motionless, fighting consciousness, desperate to stay in the warm cocoon of darkness around me. I didn't want to wake up. Being awake meant pain. I couldn't take any more pain. I felt like I had been asleep for days and it wasn't enough.

"Lee-Bee?" a familiar voice filled my ears. "You coming around, babe?"

With a pained groan, I blinked my eyes open, wincing when bright lights burned my eyes. "Turn it off," I strangled out groggily, clenching my eyes shut. Too bright."

"I'm on it," Cam replied. Moments later, her hand covered mine. "All fixed."

Gingerly, I opened my eyes again, blinking rapidly to find focus before scanning the now-dimly lit room for her face. There were machines everywhere and I could feel the panic rising up inside of me. "Cam?"

"Right here, sleepy head," she replied, leaning over my bed. "Hey, pretty girl," she whispered, smiling down at me when she caught my eye. "Aren't you a Christmas miracle?" Pressing a kiss to my brow, she lowered herself back down on the chair next to my bed and held my I.V clad hand in both of hers. "Merry Christmas, babe."

"What happened?" I croaked out, clinging to her hand. "The blood?"

"You're okay," she hurried to soothe. "But you had us scared for a while, Lee." Her voice was thick with emotion. "You've been out for hours."

"I have?" Confused, I pulled myself up on elbows, only to wince in discomfort. "What's happening to me?"

"I promise that you're okay, but –" Cam dropped her gaze to our hands. "But maybe I should get a nurse to explain?"

"No." Shaking my head, I tightened my hold on her hand. "I want to hear it from you."

"Yeah." Nodding slowly, she leaned forward, resting her elbows on the edge of my bed while she cradled my hand in hers. "Do you remember the ride to the hospital, Lee? You were awake for parts."

Mind reeling, I leaned back against my pillows and tried to make sense of everything that had happened to me. "I remember the blood," I whispered, shivering. "And you and Derek." Swallowing deeply, I blew out a shaky breath. "I remember the man thinking Der was a father or something?" I frowned, confused. "What were they even talking about –" My words broke off and I froze as one word jumped out at me. "Cam, they said I was having a miscarriage?" I choked out. "But that wasn't true, right?" I looked to Cam, panicked and seeking reassurance. "I've had all my periods, and we're safe. Kyle is *always* safe!" *Except for the first time.* "I'm not pregnant, right?" I croaked out. "I didn't lose a baby?"

Cam winced and I knew.

I just *knew.*

"I am?" I breathed, heart racing violently in my chest. "Or I was?"

"Kind of both?" she replied, grimacing.

"Wh-what?" Tears filled my eyes. "I was pregnant? I lost my baby?" Oh god, I wanted to keel over. "I didn't know, Cam," I choked out, pressing a hand to my chest. "I swear I didn't –I never even skipped a period!" Sniffling, I blinked away the tears in my eyes, feeling them fall from my eyelashes to my cheeks. "This is my *fault.*"

"*What?*"

"I was drinking," I choked out. "I wasn't taking c-care of m-myself?"

"Because you didn't know," she replied fiercely, squeezing my hand. "And this was *not* your fault! The doctors said that you had what they call a concurrent ectopic and intrauterine pregnancy."

"A what?" I shook my head, confused and broken. "I don't understand those kinds of words."

"It means that you were pregnant with twins, Lee," Cam explained gently. "And one of the babies was in your fallopian tube instead of your womb." Smiling sadly, she reached forward and wiped a tear from my cheek. "That's what caused you to get so sick, sweetie." Shivering, she whispered, "It's really serious and you almost died, Lee. The surgeons? They had to remove one of your fallopian tubes, and I'm so sorry, sweetie, but the baby inside it was already dead."

Tears flowed down my cheeks as her words sunk in. "It died?" Clenching my eyes shut, I shivered violently, desperately trying to hold it together. "My baby?" Pain far more severe than what I'd endured speared me through the chest, making it hard to breathe. I had a baby and it was dead. It died inside my body and I hadn't even known. Devastation ripped through me.

Just because I hadn't known I was pregnant didn't mean that I didn't *want* my baby. And It wasn't just my baby to lose. I'd lost Kyle's baby, too. It had been dead inside me and I never knew. If I had listened to my body and gotten checked out sooner, I could have prevented this. I could have kept him or her alive. I curled my hands around my stomach, feeling empty and dead.

"You're still pregnant, Lee," Cam said then.

I froze, eyes flicking to hers. "Wh-what?"

"The baby in your womb?" She grinned. "It *survived* the surgery. The little fighter is healthy and strong, and the perfect size for thirteen weeks."

Survived?

Wait – thirteen weeks?

"But, how…how is that even possible?" I asked, stunned. "All the blood?" I shook my head. "How could a baby survive that?"

"They never operated on your womb," she explained, suppressing a shudder. "They just removed the tube." Exhaling heavily, she added, "The doctors say that it's extremely rare to have a surviving twin in these circumstances, but this little one's a fighter, just like her mama."

"*Her*?"

"Oh, it's too early to know yet." Cam patted my belly, eyes dancing with excitement. "But my money's on a curly-haired, blue-eyed, dimple-cheeked baby girl."

"Whoa," I breathed, reeling. "You've thought this out, haven't you?"

"Yep." She nodded eagerly. "While you've been sleeping, I've been planning."

"So, I'm due in June?"

"Late May," she corrected. "Dibs on godmother."

Stunned, I covered my stomach with my hand, amazed at what was still inside there.

A baby.

My baby.

Kyle's baby.

Our little miracle.

"Hey, Cam, where's K–"

"Hey – you're awake," Derek said, eyes twinkling with relief, as he strolled into the room with the biggest teddy-bear I'd ever seen in his arms, and a stream of pink and blue balloons floating after him.

"Don't you ever do that to me again," he warned, leaning down to kiss the top of my head. "I nearly had a fucking heart-attack." Propping the bear at the foot of my bed, he tied the balloons to the bear's monster-sized arm before moving for Cam. Brushing a tender kiss to her lips, he pulled her to her feet, claimed her chair and then dragged her down on his lap. "Now, how's our resident incubator?"

"Der," Cam groaned, elbowing him in the ribs. "A little tact."

"Oh, shit, yeah," he muttered, grimacing. "Are you okay, Lee?"

"Yeah, and I'm sorry, guys." I winced as I pulled myself up. "I just… I want to thank you both." My voice was thick and strained. "You saved our lives." I patted my stomach, already desperately in love with the little miracle growing inside of me.

I was devastated that I had lost one of my babies and I guessed those emotions would floor me later, but for now, all I could think was; I could have lost both and that put things into perspective for me.

"I remember hearing your voice in my head," I told Derek. "You were telling me to hold on." I shivered. "I did, Der. I held on to your voice. I think that's how I pulled myself back."

"Uh, yeah, sure, no, uh, problem." Derek's cheeks turned bright red and he shifted uncomfortably in his chair. "Just don't go telling any of the guys that," he added. "I don't wanna be nick-named *the baby whisperer* or some dumb shit like that.'"

Cam and I both chuckled at that.

"So, where's Kyle?" I asked quietly. "Is he outside?"

"Uh, yeah…" Cam jumped to her feet and moved for the door. "You can deliver *that* news, baby whisperer."

KYLE

When I finally turned my key in the door of my house on The Hill after the night from hell, I was bone weary and had the mother of all headaches. Last night had gone to hell in a hand-basket, but I didn't care. Because I was free. Fucking finally.

Slipping inside, I closed the door behind me and trailed through the house, stepping over trash and empty beer bottles. It was eerily quiet and that had my back up.

"Derek?" I called out, as this weird, nervous feeling trickled through me. "Cam?" I didn't dare call Lee's name out, knowing that she was probably still sleeping off her cramps. It was only 05:30. Dammit, I couldn't wait for her to wake up so I could talk to her– so I could finally let her all the way in. I had messed up by leaving her last night, but I could fix everything now.

I was free.

"Hey, bud," I said when I found Bruno passed out on the couch. "Where'd everyone go?"

Keeping my distance from my second-greatest torturer, I walked into the kitchen and sighed heavily. The place was a dump. Goddamn Cam. She knew the rules; throw a party and clean your shit up after.

Screw it, I needed a shower. I would deal with the mess later. I had a long fucking night with the she-devil and all I wanted was to shower and crawl into bed with my girlfriend.

Girlfriend.

Shit.

Padding lightly up the staircase, I passed Lee's bedroom door on my way to the bathroom, only to halt in my tracks when my eyes landed on her bedroom door. This was definitely weird. Lee *never* left her door unlocked, let alone wide-open.

I glanced inside and my pulse sped up.

Her bed was empty.

What the fuck was happening?

"Lee?" I called out, panicking now. "Where are you at, baby?"

I checked my room.

Nothing.

Fuck!

Had they all bailed out on me?

Slamming my hand on the bathroom door, I stalked inside only to slide across the tiles and almost break my fucking neck. Slipping on something wet, I managed to right myself on the towel rack before hitting the floor. "Jesus Christ," I strangled out when my eyes landed on the blood. It was *everywhere*. The toilet bowl. The sink. The floor. The fucking walls. Blood soaked towels were scattered everywhere. I was standing in a pool of goddamn blood. Chest heaving, I staggered out of the room, reaching for my phone. "Lee? Lee?" I roared, frantic now as I slammed my fingers over the keypad of my cell.

The battery was dead.

Jesus Christ, how long had it been dead?

Running for my room, I plugged it into the charger and paced the floor, waiting impatiently for it to start up.

What the fuck had happened here and where were they? I had only been away one goddamn night. Did someone die at the party? If so, wouldn't there be forensics combing the place, and yellow tape keeping me out? *What the actual fuck?*

Finally, my phone booted up and I was inundated with missed calls and text messages. Frantic, I scrolled through them. Fifteen missed calls from Derek. Twelve from Cam.

Dread filled my gut, and suddenly, I was afraid to read the texts. Steeling myself, I forced myself to click into each one.

Derek: *Dude, where the fuck are you?*

Derek: *Get your ass back here stat!*

Cam: *Come home, Kyle, there's something really wrong with Lee.*

Cam: *There's blood everywhere.*

Cam: *I'm scared.*

Derek: *Where the hell are you, shithead? We are in a goddamn ambulance.*

Cam: *Taking Lee to the hospital. Call me.*

Derek: *I'm gonna kill you.*

Derek: *Answer your phone, you stupid sack of shit. This is your girl I'm tryna save. Pull your dick outta Rachel, get in your fucking car, and follow us to the hospital.*

Cam: *You're a piece of shit.*

Derek: *Are you dead somewhere? I hope you're dead. Otherwise, I'm gonna have to kill you.*

Cam: *ANSWER YOUR PHONE!!!!!!!*

Derek: *Fucker.*

Derek: *Call me.*

Ice ran through my veins and I couldn't read any more. Running down the staircase, I threw the front door open and ran for my truck, dialing Derek as I moved.

He answered his phone on the third ring. "Dude, about fucking time –"

"Is she okay?" I demanded, turning the key in the ignition and tearing out of the driveway. "Where is she? What the fuck happened?"

I heard Derek snort. "In the fucking hospital, douchebag. She's lucky to be alive – no thanks to you."

"No thanks to me?" *Jesus Christ.* "Which hospital?"

"I don't think you should go anywhere near –"

"Which goddamn hospital, Derek?" I roared, losing my shit. "You know I'll find her either way."

He sighed heavily "St. Luke's."

I nodded, taking a left on tenth street. "I'll be there in twenty."

"Kyle, you might want to brace yourself," he said after a beat. "There's something you need to know –"

"Spit it the fuck out," I snarled. I needed to get to Lee, not listen to Derek and his bullshit. I should have never left her last night. I was fucking stupid.

He paused for a moment and then I heard him speak the words that tore through my heart with the force of a hurricane. "Kyle, she was pregnant."

FIFTY-NINE

LEE

I WOKE from an unsettled sleep to raised voices outside my room.

"Get out of my way, Derek."

"You need to calm your ass down."

"I need to see her!"

"Not like this, you don't."

Oh god.

Cam, who was asleep in the chair beside me, jerked awake and darted out of the room.

"All I'm saying is come back later – at a decent hour," I heard Derek say. "Let the girl sleep. She's fucking fragile right now, dude."

There was a long stretch of silence and then my hospital door burst open, with Kyle striding in.

Panicking, I clenched my eyes shut and feigned sleep, unwilling and unable to face him right now.

"If you wake her up, I will kill you," Cam warned. "I mean it," she hissed. "We're gonna go grab a coffee and you better not be here when we get back."

I heard the sound of a door closing and then the legs of a chair scraping along the tiled floor. "Lee, baby?" His warm hand covered mine. "Wake up…*please*." His lips were on my hand. "I'm sorry," he whispered. "I'm so fucking sorry."

Words.

All words.

Meaningless.

When I felt his hand touch my stomach, I snapped my eyes open and twisted away. "Don't," I warned, yanking my hand free from his. "*Ever* touch me again."

"Lee." His blue eyes were laced with pain and locked on mine. "Fuck, baby –"

"Why are you here?" I asked coldly.

"What?" His brows shot up. "I had to come." He shook his head. "I had to see you – make sure you were okay. My battery on my phone died," he hurried to explain. "I didn't know you were in here until I got home."

"Home," I deadpanned. "From being at Rachel's."

He shook his head. "It's not what you think, baby."

I stared blankly back at him and whispered, "I want you to leave."

He flinched. "Lee."

I didn't care. "Now."

"Don't do this," he begged, reaching for my hand again. "You're pregnant?" He swallowed deeply. "We're having a baby?"

"I want you to leave, Kyle," I whispered, snatching my hand away. "I'm not ready to talk about my baby."

"Your baby?"

I nodded stiffly.

"Our baby, Lee."

Tears filled my eyes and I shook my head. "No."

"Lee –"

"No!"

"Please don't block me out of this," he said, voice torn. "I've been going out of my mind –"

"*You've* been going out of *your* mind?" I choked out, anger and tears pouring out of my soul. "Have you any idea how afraid I've been?"

"I'm sorry –" He grabbed my hand again. "Lee, I'm so –"

"Stop it," I hissed, crying hard now. "Don't you dare tell me that you're sorry again." Trembling from head to toe, I glared at his face, hardly able to see him through my tears. "I nearly died last night, Kyle," I cried, furious. "While you were with *Rachel*, I nearly bled to death on the bathroom floor!"

"Baby –"

"I called you," I strangled out, chest heaving. "I begged you to *help me*."

"I don't…" His shoulders slumped and he dropped his head in his hands. "I'm so fucking sorry."

"No matter what happens, she always c-comes first for you, doesn't s-she?" I asked, sniffling. "She's your w-weakness, Kyle."

He lifted his face to look at me and I watched as a lone tear trickled down his cheek, followed by another and then another after that. Good, I wanted him to *suffer*. I wanted him to feel *my* pain. "She's not my weakness, Lee. She's my fucking punishment. You, baby… you are my biggest weakness."

"Then tell me why," I cried, tremors racking through me. "Tell me why you left with her last night? Why did you leave me? Why did you do that, huh?"

"I shouldn't have left you," he choked out, pushing his hands through his hair. "I needed to talk to her – to finish things."

"Finish things?" I cried, voice rising. "Things were already supposed to be finished, Kyle!"

"I know, Lee, I know," he hurried to say. "I haven't touched her, I swear." Dropping his head in his hands, he pulled on his hair. "Fuck, there's so much that you don't know, baby. I can explain everything if you just –"

"You're too late," I hiccupped. "You should have finished things with Rachel months ago, but you kept me your dirty little secret instead."

"No," he denied, shaking his head. "You were never that to me."

"I'm not stupid, Kyle," I cried out hoarsely. "I *watched* you keep our relationship hidden."

"I was trying to protect you," he ground out. "I wasn't ashamed of you. Fuck!"

"Well, there's no apology in the world that can make up for the fact that you knowingly left me sick and alone."

"Jesus Christ," he strangled out, twisting around in what looked like physical pain. "Lee, I swear, I didn't realize –"

"I am pregnant," I sobbed. "And it's yours – in case you might think otherwise."

"I don't think that," he bit out hoarsely.

"I didn't mean for it to happen," I added. "Just in case you think I tried to trap you."

"Lee, stop," he strangled out. "I would never think that about you."

"I know how low your opinion is of me."

He flinched and his shoulders sagged. "You're killing me."

"Good," I sniffled/sobbed. "Because you've already killed me. And I might be carrying one of your babies inside of me, but don't for one moment forget that I lost another."

"Jesus, baby." Slumping forward, he placed his arms on the edge of my bed and dropped his head down, shoulders shaking as his big body racked with sobs. "I'm sorry." His words were muffed and I knew he was crying. "I don't know how to fix this."

I reached a hand out, fingers itching to comfort him, but I snatched my hand away.

I *couldn't* comfort him.

Not now.

"Is it...is the baby okay?" he finally asked, lifting his face to look at me. "Are you?"

I looked away, unable to stand the sight of his agonized expression or his tear-filled eyes. I had never seen someone look so guilty. *So devastated.* "I need to rest now," I replied wearily. "Getting upset isn't good for the baby."

"Shit, yeah, of course." Standing up, he quickly wiped his cheeks with the back of his hand. "Can I come back later?"

"I don't think that's a good idea," I whispered, breathing hard and fast.

"Please?"

"I need some space, Kyle – some time to get my head around everything."

Flinching, he nodded slowly. "Okay." Inhaling a shaky breath, he bent down and kissed my forehead. I clenched my eyes shut, unable to watch him leave. "You'll never know how sorry I am," he whispered in my ear.

And then he was gone.

The minute the hospital door swung shut behind him, I let out a scream I had been holding in, allowing the sadness to envelope me, as I cried for my lost baby, and for a man who would never love me.

SIXTY

ROCK BOTTOM

KYLE

I MANAGED to make it to the truck before collapsing on my knees, mind reeling, heart cracking open in my chest. My life was a rail-roading before my eyes and I couldn't do a fucking thing to stop it.

I had finally done it.

I'd broken Lee in more ways than I had ever imagined humanly possible.

That frightened girl in the hospital bed? I did that. The dead baby? Mine. The blood? I left her lying in it. I had ruined her, and this time, I couldn't fix it. I couldn't make things better for her. She didn't want my words and wanted my actions even less.

Dropping my head in my hands, I cried hard and ugly, not giving two shits who heard me.

My world was broken.

It was fucking over.

I felt an arm come around my shoulders. "Come on, dude," Derek said, crouching down beside me. "Let's get out of here." Holding onto him for support, I staggered to my feet. "It's gonna be okay, man," he coaxed, opening the passenger door of my truck and shoving me inside. "You've got this," he added before closing me inside, rounding the truck, and climbing into the driver's seat beside me.

"No, I don't." Numb, I leaned my cheek against the car window and shivered. "I've destroyed her, Der."

"No, you haven't," he replied, turning his spare key in the ignition. "She's not broken, Kyle." The engine roared to life. "She's grieving." Reaching over, he squeezed my shoulder. "And so are you, man."

"Don't," I sniffled, shuddering. I didn't deserve his sympathy. "How can I be grieving for something I didn't even know I had?"

Derek sighed heavily. "Just because you didn't know you had it, doesn't mean you didn't want it, and don't miss it now that it's been taken away from you."

I didn't feel shit in comparison to Lee. She should have Derek's sympathy, not me. "I don't deserve to feel sad." Sniffing, I batted a tear away. "If I had been there –"

"No, dude, there was no hope," he quickly cut me off. "This would've always been the outcome. The baby couldn't survive in the tube." Pulling out of the parking lot, he maneuvered into the early morning traffic. "Lee is lucky to be alive. It's a fucking miracle it didn't kill her."

"Stop." I shuddered, blocking the thought from my mind. "I can't cope."

"But the one positive thing about this whole damn mess is that she's *still* pregnant." Stopping at a red light, he turned to look at me, expression serious. "This could be it for her, man."

"What do you mean?"

"Babies," he explained. "They removed her tube." He sighed heavily. "Docs said it'll be hard for her to conceive again."

"Jesus Christ." I hadn't even thought about that. "Fuck, Der," I choked out. "Shit…Fuck…Goddammit to hell!"

"Are you finished displaying your fine variation of the English vocabulary?" he quipped, smirking. "Because I wanna know the plan."

Plan? "What plan?"

"The plan where you find a way to fix this dinosaur-sized pile of shit you've buried yourself under," he shot back.

"I don't know." I couldn't think straight. My mind focused on the fact that Lee was *still* pregnant. She was alive and carrying a baby.

My baby inside her.

"Got any ideas?" I asked, turning to face him.

"Nope," he replied. "Sorry, dude, but when it comes to uteruses, I'm beyond out of my comfort zone." Offering me a smile, he added, "I'm down to help, though."

"Thanks, man," I muttered. "Appreciate it."

I didn't care what I'd have to do.

I was going to win Lee Bennett back.

And when I did, I was never going to let her slip away from me again.

I *wasn't* losing her.

I *couldn't*.

No goddamn way.

THANK YOU SO MUCH FOR READING!

Kyle and Lee's story continues in
Fall to Pieces, Broken #2,
available now.

Please consider leaving a review on the platform you purchased
this book from.

Broken series in order:
Break my Fall
Fall to Pieces
Fall on Me
Forever we Fall

OTHER BOOKS BY CHLOE WALSH

Thorn – Carter Kids #2
Tame – Carter Kids #3
Torment – Carter Kids #4
Inevitable – Carter Kids #5
Altered – Carter Kids #6

The DiMarco Dynasty:
DiMarco's Secret Love Child: Part One
DiMarco's Secret Love Child: Part Two

The Blurred Lines Duet:
Blurring Lines – Book #1
Never Let me Go – Book #2

-
Boys of Tommen:
Binding 13 – Book #1
Keeping 13 – Book #2
Saving 6 – Book #3
Redeeming 6 – Book #4

Crellids:
The Bastard Prince

Other titles:
Seven Sleepless Nights

PLAYLIST FOR LEE

Carrie Underwood – Blown Away
Taylor Swift – Wildest Dreams
Beyoncé – I was here
A Great Big World – Say Something
Enya – Only Time
Maria McKee – Show Me Heaven
Adele – One and Only
The Civil Wars – Poison and Wine
Sia – Breathe Me
Leona Lewis – Bleeding Love
Robyn – Dancing on my own
Martina McBride – Concrete Angel
The Fray – You Found Me
Marie Miller – 6'2
Shakira – Don't Bother
Kate Nash – Nicest Thing
Haley Reinhart – Can't Help Falling In Love
Anne-Marie – Alarm
Anna Nalick – Breathe (2am)

PLAYLIST FOR KYLE

Kings of Leon – Closer
Josh Turn – Your Man
Kodaline – Latch
Lovelytheband – Broken
Cage The Elephant – Ain't No Rest For The Wicked
Bressie – Break My Fall
Foster The People – Pumped Up Kicks
Gavin James – Always
Mick Flannery – Wish You Well
Ron Pope – A Drop In The Ocean
John Legend – All of Me
Lewis Capaldi – Bruises
Ed Sheeran – Give me Love
Nelly & Tim McGraw – Over and Over Again
Jamie Lawson – Don't Let me Let you Go
Jamie Lawson – I'm Gonna Love You
David Gray – This Year's Love
Nelly Furtado – Try (Douglas George cover)
Justin Timberlake – Mirrors

ABOUT THE AUTHOR

Chloe Walsh is the bestselling author of The Boys of Tommen series, which exploded in popularity. She has been writing and publishing New Adult and Adult contemporary romance for a decade. Her books have been translated into multiple languages. Animal lover, music addict, TV junkie, Chloe loves spending time with her family and is a passionate advocate for mental health awareness. Chloe lives in Cork, Ireland with her family.

Join Chloe's mailing list for exclusive content and release updates.
http://eepurl.com/dPzXM1